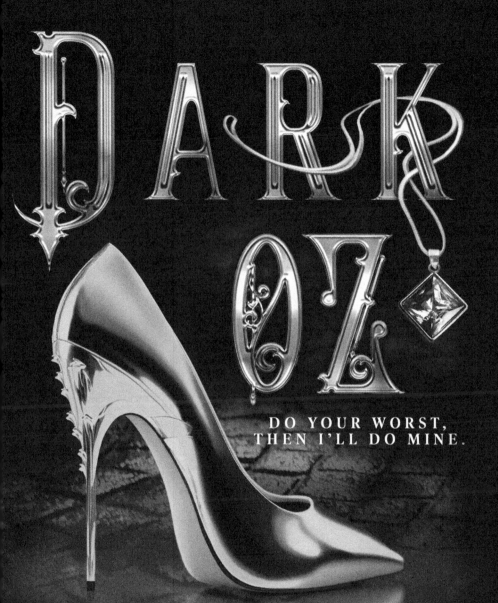

DARK OZ

DO YOUR WORST,
THEN I'LL DO MINE.

AUTHOR OF THE SUN SERPENT SAGA

GENEVA MONROE

Dark Oz

Geneva Monroe

Purple Phoenix Press

Dark Oz by Geneva Monroe

Copyright © 2023 by Geneva Monroe

Paperback ISBN: 978-1-960352-11-8

Published by Purple Phoenix Press LLC

Book Cover by Geneva Monroe

Illustrations and Photography by Geneva Monroe, Dean Zangirolami, Christopher Brewer, Lightfield Studios, Katsiaryna,

Content Warning

Dark Oz is an adult, why choose retelling, with darker elements, where the main character has multiple partners. **It is not intended for minors.**

Triggers include: human trafficking, abuse, discussion of off-page rape, sexual assault, child abuse and neglect, torture, murder, graphic violence, drug overdose, grief, loss of a parent and sibling, dubious consent, explicit and graphic sexual content, explicit and graphic language, graphic gore, bondage, mature language, and bullying.

Reader discretion is advised.

Your mental health matters.

Hotline Numbers

The main character of this novel has a history with human trafficking. There are several characters in the book who have been trafficked. While it is a major component of this story, and Dark Oz is a work of fiction, human trafficking is not.

If you or someone you know is a victim of human trafficking please call the number below. Every call is confidential and they are available 24/7.

<u>National Human Trafficking Hotline</u>
1-888-373-7888

No one should ever struggle alone. Your mental health matters. You matter.

<u>National Sexual Abuse Hotline</u>
800.656.HOPE (4673)

<u>National Domestic Violence Hotline</u>
800.799.SAFE

<u>National Center for Missing and Exploited Children</u>
800.THE.LOST (843-5678)

<u>Suicide and Crisis Lifeline</u>
988

PLAYLIST

MEAN!- MADELINE THE PERSON

NATURAL BORN KILLER- HIGHLY SUSPECT

CINDERELLA'S DEAD- EMELINE

HUSH- THE MARIAS

NUH UH - JADES GOUDERAULT

I FEEL LIKE I'M DROWNING

YOU SAY - LAUREN DAIGLE

DRAMATIC - CAT & CALMELL

RAPUNZEL - EMLYN

GIVE EM HELL - EVERYBODY LOVES AN OUTLAW

WHISPER - ABLE HEART

LIKE THAT - BEA MILLER

I DON'T BELONG TO YOU - MILCK

TRUST ISSUES - EMEI

MIDDLE OF THE NIGHT - LOVELESS

AFRAID OF THE DARK - EZI

CORALINE - MANESKIN

DEVIL IN A DRESS - TEDDY SWIMS

KILLER - VALERIE BROUSSARD

ODDS ARE - THE FIFTHGUYS, THATSIMO, RIELL

PRETTY IN THE DARK - ASHLEY SIENNA, ELLISE

This book is dedicated to
anyone who has ever needed to hear,
"You are more than the sum of what has been done to you."

-1-
THEA

"It was only a matter of time before I found myself leashed to the inside of one of these shipping containers."

"But you're her niece?" The girl tethered next to me made a pitiful look of remorse.

The dim light from the crack in the door did little to illuminate the interior, allowing the shadows to easily swallow her slight form. The truck hit a bump, sending everyone in the back jostling into the air. Until the chain linking us all together yanked us back to the wall. Pain spiked in my side on impact, streaking a blinding flash of light across my vision.

"Ow," I cried, adding to the chorus of moans. Before the doors had been sealed, I'd counted nearly a dozen women in this shipment. Small, compared to some of The Farm's deliveries. When they hauled me onto the truck, I was gaped at with a mix of confusion, desperation, and from some—vindication.

These unlucky souls didn't know; they never did. To the girls behind the bars, I walked the halls like a princess. To the men behind the guns, they saw only a ghost. But to my Aunt Em, I was nothing more than a burden. Reminding me I would fetch her far more than I was actually worth was her favorite pastime.

"It's true," I continued, not caring that this girl didn't ask to hear my story. I'd never been good with silence, and it wasn't like she was sharing. I didn't even know her name. She was just another number on a roster.

It had stung being told by my only family that I had a price tag, but not as much as the day she decided to start cashing in on her investment. What more could you expect from someone who ran a shipping company that also dabbled a bit in the transportation and sale of human beings? Definitely not love. Even asking for safety was asking for too much.

"I learned early in my childhood not to rely on anything but my wits. Of course, it was probably those same wits that landed my ass next to yours."

The only dependable thing in my world was disappointment, and that my willpower was stronger than any punishment Em could levy. I might be victimized, but I was never going to be a victim.

"I'm sorry," she whispered.

"Are you always this meek, or is it an act that you put on to try and discourage attention?"

She didn't answer me. That was probably how she'd survived as long in this hell as she had. I, however, hadn't been born with the *keep your mouth shut* gene. The only thing that had kept me alive was being the niece and heir to The Farm, but that fuse had run out and blown up spectacularly in my face.

"Like I said, don't worry about it. If it wasn't you, I'd have been caught trying to free some other girl." Flexing my fingers, I tried to force some blood back into them. The chafing at my wrists had long since passed raw. Dried blood crusted the edges of the plastic ties. The ache in my arms and my spine made it feel like we'd been here for days, though I knew it couldn't have been more than one.

The passage of time in the dark interior was impossible to track. I'd tried for the first hour to count, but the stifling air and the pain in my side made it too hard to focus. The temperature of the metal wall was considerably colder than it had been when I was first shackled to it, so chances were good that night had fallen. I needed air, something fresh to breathe. I was beginning to feel lightheaded, and it was making the dark, enclosed space of this truck feel infinitely smaller.

"Keep talking, Dorothy. It helps with the anxiety." This girl would know, and despite her tears, she seemed to be very calm about being shipped out to a new owner.

I swallowed back the debilitating fear, or maybe that was bile.

"It's not Dorothy, call me Thea." If I could scrub that name from the world, I would. But, if Em was disowning me, then she could keep the name Dorothy with her. "Em didn't take my betrayal well."

That was an understatement. Five days ago, Aunt Em tossed over a table, screaming about how the world *"never gave her a goddamn thing."* Of course, a woman who stuffed her mouth with the spoils of selling other women would consider herself the victim.

"Help me with this." I poked at her fingers until they found the same nut I'd been trying to wiggle free. I needed some fresh air, even if it was an infinitesimal amount. Together we slowly worked at the rusted metal.

"For months I did everything I could to undermine her."

The nut finally spun, and I was able to push the bolt free. Cool air and a tiny stream of light poured in from outside, allowing me to take my first real breath in hours. Fuck, I hated the dark.

"Like what?"

"It started as small acts of rebellion, but eventually, I got quite good at passing messages from the women trapped on The Farm to the outside world." Not women, girls—since that's what most of them were.

They were *stolen,* robbed of all free will, or at the very least tricked out of it. I couldn't sit there and watch as each was processed. Their value was calculated in exactly the same way Em calculated my own worth. Then, they were sold to the highest, morally corrupt bidder.

Well, fuck that.

I had less than nothing. But, I did get open access to most areas of The Farm. It wasn't enough to make real changes. But, one girl at a time, I tried.

"I got away with it the first few times. Anonymous tips had been made, and a few trucks had been stopped." Stopped, but never searched thanks to Em's high-placed contacts. Once the trucks passed over the border into Oz there was very little that could be done. In Ozmandria, so long as the people at the top got their cut, nobody cared about the morally right, gray or otherwise.

My aunt was good at greasing the right wheels. The stacks of money she moved were fat. It was enough to make the Quadrants stop asking where the money came from or what she was moving over the border.

"Yeah, I bet fuck all came from those stops." Ah, so 07151237 did have a personality.

"Less than fuck all. Em started looking for a leak. So I had to change tactics entirely." The girl huffed a sympathetic sigh. "What's your name? I can't keep thinking of you as some long string of numbers, and now that it's dark, calling you Freckles feels oddly wrong."

"It's changed over the years. But, mostly, I go by Toto."

"Toto is...unusual?"

"It is, but the nickname is all I have left of my family—" She sighed, the breath cooling the sweat that clung to my cheeks. "—but that was another life. Tell me more about your quest to undermine The Farm. I always loved a good tragedy."

"Not me. Give me a romance any day, the filthy kind where the smart-mouthed heroine gets railed by three guys at once."

"Ooo, and make one of them covered in tattoos with a tragic backstory."

I snorted a laugh. There was something wrong about laughing when there were others around us openly weeping, but I couldn't help it. I really liked her. I hated that I'd failed in freeing someone who still had so much life despite being in this system longer than anyone else I'd ever met.

I lowered my voice. Not that I cared who overheard us, but more because I didn't need Em knowing just how deep I'd gotten into The Farms archives. "There's one day a week when my aunt's focus was guaranteed to be away from the compound."

"Inspection day?"

"Inspection day." Em made the rounds to different processing facilities to assess the newly acquired assets, giving me the opportunity to have access to her office without the risk of being interrupted. None of The Farm staff would ever dare enter her office without her. Nobody was ballsy enough to incur her wrath, nobody but me.

"Luckily, the guard who watched her corridor was fond of me, or rather, he was fond of the things I could do for him."

"I know the type. Acts like he's your friend, so long as he's getting his dick sucked at the end of the night."

If only it was that simple. "After a bit of cajoling, he showed me how to look up records and where to find police reports." And the cost of his *friendship* wasn't anything Em hadn't already stripped from me. Every bruise, cut, and missing bit of my dignity was worth it to see Em's face turn scarlet when one of her sales fell through. One time, not only had the girl's father killed all of Em's men, but he'd freed a half dozen others, too.

"I managed it three times. On my fourth attempt, I didn't."

"You mean me."

"Yeah." I bit down on the inside of my cheek, the pain bringing my focus back. I couldn't tell Toto just how close I'd come to freeing her. It felt cruel now that everything had spun out of control.

I found a pattern in the missing persons cases. The same three anonymous files were reported weekly, every year, for eleven years. The descriptions of the missing girls were similar, and it didn't take much to realize that they must have been sisters. There wasn't much information on the person making the report, only a name, Daniel Kalidah, and an anonymous email. There was something romantic about the idea that he hadn't given up on finding his family after all these years. Knowing what I did about The Farm and how their stock was treated, there was a very slim chance any of these women were still alive.

Or so I thought, until Toto was brought in. She was beautiful, with long, flowing red hair and piercing green eyes above a sea of freckles, but it was the daffodil-shaped birthmark on her arm that caught my attention.

The first chance that presented itself, I checked her file. This girl had come through processing three separate times over *eleven* years. Three times in itself was unusual, but the dates matched perfectly.

Exhilarated by solving the case of the missing girl, I immediately opened the untraceable mailer program. According to her file, she was slated to be transferred in less than a week. I'd already been in the office longer than I should have, but I wouldn't get a second chance before Freckles was gone. I typed up a full description, as well as the date and time that a particular internet mogul would be making the exchange.

It felt like the hand of fate placing Toto in my path. After all of this time, I was going to be able to bring the mystery man a little bit of peace. I was just about to hit send when the sound of gunfire made me jump.

"There were two quick pops outside the door and nowhere in the small office to hide. It didn't matter because a heartbeat later, Em's second in command stepped over my guard's body and into the office."

Toto's pinky wound around mine. It was as much as our bindings would allow. But in the darkness, when I looked at Toto, all I saw was the light fading from my only ally's eyes. I knew then, as sure as I did now, there would be no mercy coming.

"So there you go. That was how I ended up bound next to the very girl I was trying to help." Em always found cruel twists of fate hilarious. She laughed for a solid minute after she realized who I was sitting next to.

I shouldn't have told Toto I could find her a way out. My past success had made me bold. Henry, Em's blood-stained right hand, had been waiting for an excuse to haul me to my aunt. I still don't know how he knew I was in there that morning, but I'd basically gift-wrapped my demise for him.

Toto placed more faith in me than I deserved. I'd been her last hope, but that was where she went wrong. Nothing about me was hopeful. Hope looked at me and rolled her eyes. If anything good ever came to me, it was because I made it happen, not because I hoped for it.

I wasn't exactly sure where I was headed. Before the doors of the container were sealed closed, Em folded a photograph of whatever John I'd been sold to. She slipped it into my breast pocket, knowing full well that I'd never be able to retrieve it with my hands bound above me. Then she had Henry beat me hard enough to turn my side purple, most likely cracking a rib. Once she was satisfied I'd gotten the message, she'd thrown me into the truck and walked away. Em never even bothered to say anything to me. Not so much as a goodbye for her little sister's only child.

"You're headed East, to an Oz distribution center." Chances were good I was headed there, too. "When the doors open again, they will untie us and move us into processing." Em had forced me to visit enough of these places to know there would be a window of opportunity. I knew what was expected of me and exactly what to expect from them. "We just have to be patient."

What I wasn't expecting was the photograph in my pocket to be of Eastin Witcher and for everything I thought I knew to be wrong.

-2-
CROWE

Where in the fuck was Gigi? I swear, if that girl wasn't so Oz damn useful, I would have cut her loose years ago—permanently. But she was annoyingly good at making friends with the right people, and those friends usually ended up lining my pockets. Albeit unknowingly.

I stared at the office building across the street, waving on a man who approached my cab. We picked Yellow Brick Cabs as our front for the anonymity that came with driving a cab around and the free pass to travel without a visa across the quadrant borders, but it also came with the annoying side of people trying to get a lift. It wouldn't be a problem if Gigi hadn't left me sitting on the road waiting for her late ass.

The only female member of the Northern Syndicate hired us to do a pick-up later today in the loading dock of Witcher Enterprises. Off the books, of course, the Syndicate had no clue about half the clandestine shit she was involved in. Not that I had any clue either; she hadn't even told me what to do after I retrieved the mystery package.

Gigi was being unusually vague on this job. Which normally Danny would never allow. But her tips always paid off and were usually *big*. She said the contents of the package were sensitive and details being leaked were too high risk, even using encrypted lines, burner phones, and my own personally crafted anti-hacking software. So, it looked like vague was what we were doing now.

To make me even more twitchy, earlier today, while casing the building, I saw Kinland Branch's supreme bitch in charge walk right through the front doors.

There were two people in the world I never wanted to see again. One of them was Eastin Witcher, and the other was her backstabbing cunt of a cousin,

Westin. The unlikely event of Eastin being here on the same day I was robbing the Kinland branch was too much of a coincidence. I didn't believe in those, and knowing Eastin was upstairs right now was enough to make my palms itch.

I sent Danny a text, informing him that she was now ten minutes late to the rendezvous.

I couldn't shake the feeling. Gigi was fucking us, and not in a way that was going to be fun. We weren't picking up something stolen from just any office building. I was smuggling something from Eastin herself. Whatever happened next would come back to bite us in the ass. I could feel it in my bones.

So why was I still sitting here? I should turn around and tell Gigi to shove her plans right up her perfectly round ass. I tapped a nervous rhythm against the steering wheel of my cab, glancing at my watch and then staring up at the penthouse windows. Truth was, I wanted nothing more than to fuck over the Witcher Empire.

Gigi had been clear, infuriatingly vague, but clear. Our cab was to be waiting outside the south doors of the office building. She would meet me there with more precise instructions at ten to midnight.

The building had been quiet for hours, but Eastin's army of asskissers were all still upstairs. To make matters worse, a Cyclone Shipping truck had pulled into the garage an hour ago. Cyclone Shipping meant fucking with Emily Rosen and The Farm, another entity I had no desire to entangle my business with.

I looked at my watch again, the crystal face glinting in the light of the dash. 11:53. No Gigi. Fuck me sideways. This was a setup, and my dumb ass was just waiting here like a good little puppy.

I shifted the car into gear and flicked on my turn signal to pull out when the back door swung open. Before it had opened more than an inch, I had my gun trained to the dead center of her perfectly styled blonde head.

"If you're going to be flashing a piece around, at least make it the one that doesn't say Desert Eagle down the side. It's more fun that way."

A salaciously curvy body slid into the seat behind me, wearing a black leather jacket over a light pink blouse and tight leather pants. Gigi gave her hair a flick with a light laugh that sounded deceptively innocent. She'd be sexy as hell if I didn't know she was a black widow in designer labels.

"Fucking hell, woman. You should be grateful all I did was pull it on you." I still hadn't lowered the muzzle, though. Gigi needed to start talking, and quick.

She pressed her full lips to the barrel, leaving a pink kiss mark over the word "Eagle." I growled in frustration. Today was not the day to try and play off bad planning as flirtation.

"Now, be a good boy and put away your toys. We have work to do."

I rolled my eyes and lowered the gun slightly.

All business now, her entire expression changed. The lines of those painted lips pressed flat. The edge of her jaw hardened as she raised her chin to me. "I just got confirmation that the package is intact. It will be arriving shortly. Details about delivery will be with the package."

"Why can't you just tell me now? You know, I do my job better when I can prepare for it."

Ignoring my comment entirely, she continued, "I need you to bring the cab down to the loading dock. The gate is already up. Security is mostly upstairs; nothing you can't handle. But be ready for anything. Delivery will be quick, possibly heated."

I nodded, thinking through the scouting I'd done earlier. From what I had seen, the loading docks were two levels down in the garage, connecting to the north side of the building. There was only one exit, and that was lousy fucking planning. I was already wishing the rest of our team was here to help with surveillance, especially if delivery might come with a side helping of bullet spray.

"You couldn't make it easy for a guy, could you Gi?"

"Once the package is secure, get the fuck out of here. I'll be in touch."

I winked at her, giving her the easy smile I always wore.

She shook her head. "And Crowe, watch your back."

-3-
THEA

The ding of the elevator echoed off of the stainless steel walls as we rose floor after floor. Each ear-splitting sound made the windowless confines feel like they were closing in on us. Henry's grip on my arm was hard enough to radiate all the way to my raw wrists.

From the moment the truck stopped, everything went upside down. It felt like my entire sense of reality was being spun around in a tornado. Instead of the truck being emptied at a distribution center, Henry climbed into the back of the container and dragged me into what looked like a parking garage.

Just me, the other girls were locked back up tight. That was the first unnerving thing, but the real headfuck was that Henry shouldn't even be here. He *never* did drop offs and shipments. The fact that his brutish hand was currently bruising my bicep was triggering every fear I'd ever had, because deep down I knew the kind of evil Em was capable of.

He sneered at me, which I swear showed a hint of amusement beneath his ire. "Almost there, brat. I've been waiting years to see your ass put in its place."

I mockingly smiled up at him, then slammed my heel down on the bridge of his foot. If everything was topsy turvy, then I might as well take my hits where I could get them.

"Motherfucker," he howled, immediately releasing my arm. The relief of the release was instantaneous. There was nowhere to go in the tight metal box, but that had really been about seeing the blood rush to his face and the momentary joy I got watching him hop in place. Plus, it distracted me from wanting to scream, so there was that.

It was short lived though. The back of his oversized hand cracked hard against the side of my face, his signet ring connecting solidly with my cheek bone. "Em might have tried to keep you pretty looking, but I really don't give a flying fuck what you look like. We aren't in Em's territory anymore. Try something like that again, and I'll ensure the first hole they stuff can't be your mouth."

I cradled my bound hands against my throbbing cheek, blinking away the tears and white spots still flitting across my vision. Henry Hickory was the worst sort of man, the kind who felt big by breaking those smaller than him. He'd been beating on me my entire life. If one good thing came from this day, it would be never having to look at his ugly face again. Not for the first time today, I pictured his death. Each time was more brutal and unique than the last. What I wouldn't give to make just one of them come true, although where I'd get honey and fire ants at this time of night was beyond me.

The elevator slowed, shifting with a gentle stop. The doors slid silently open revealing a sleek black hallway. Offices with glass walls lined either side of the corridor, distorted beyond them were the twinkling lights of a city.

"Where are we?" Em never dropped in cities, there were too many security cameras and people. It was always in the outskirts of Oz that she made her trades.

Henry gave me a push. "If you value your life, then don't fucking try anything."

"Was that *concern?*" I pressed my cuffed hands to my heart in shock. "Be careful, Henry, your humanity is showing. Are you going to answer my question? Where—the *fuck*— are we?"

He huffed, making his beer gut jiggle. I got my answer as we passed the painting at the end of the hall. It was of two women, tall, standing in neat pant suits, trademark glittering emeralds hung at their necks, and the confidence on their faces made it impossible to miss that they owned the world. By all rights they did, or at least half of it.

Eastin and Westin Witcher were media darlings on the surface. Upstart entrepreneurs and philanthropists, but beneath it they were two of the four tyrants that had carved up Oz. Or rather three ruling tyrants. A couple of years ago the North was seized by more of a syndicate. Together the Witcher cousins controlled the entire criminal world of the eastern and western quadrants.

The question was, why the hell was I here?

We turned a corner, fear halting me dead in my tracks. The silhouette behind the glass door shifted.

"No...no. No. No. No. No." I scrambled several steps backward.

Henry chuckled a deep rumbling laugh that never fully left his chest. "You haven't looked at that photograph in your pocket yet have you?"

Honestly, I'd forgotten about it. It was too dark to look at it in the truck, not that I could reach it with my hands bound to the side of the container. Henry had pulled me straight into the elevator. Even if I had remembered, there hadn't been a chance to look.

He slipped his hand into my pocket, gripping a handful of my breast in the process. I grimaced and looked away, not wanting him to see how much his hands on my body disgusted me. Looking at the opened photo held before my face, goosebumps pebbled over my skin and chills ran down my spine.

"As of 9am yesterday, you are now the property of Eastin Witcher."

"Why?" It was all I could think to say, staring dumbly at the stock publicity photo.

"Who fucking cares?" With a grin that looked like whatever was about to happen next was a treat for him, Henry pulled the door to the office open and shoved me inside.

The woman standing at the window turned to us. The cut of her angular face was interrupted by her long nose, which had a slight bend to it that said it had been broken at least once. She studied us for several long minutes, taking a slow stroll around me—marking my dirty clothes, matted hair, the cut at my bindings, and lastly the blooming bruise against my cheek. Normally cargo were cleaned up, and made to suit the tastes of the buyer, but bypassing distribution skipped that step of the game.

Eastin pressed a long fingernail into the sore spot on my cheek, forcing those white spots to streak across my vision once more. When I flinched, the slightest hint at a smile lifted the corner of her lips.

"She was to be delivered untouched." Eastin grabbed the hem of my shirt, lifting it over my head until it sat gathered at my still bound wrists. More fingers prodded against the dark purple marks along my ribs, and I hissed in pain.

"That's rather tender," I tried to say with a laugh.

Eastin increased the pressure along my rib, forcing me to bite my lip to keep from crying out. She leaned down low, hissing in my ear, "You are not to speak until you have earned the right to do so."

She snapped at Henry. "Remove her pants. I need to see that the rest of her is untouched, since apparently I can't trust the delivery service to make their shipments intact anymore."

"Yes, Ma'am. Err, Sir. Ma'am."

I couldn't help but laugh at Henry's ignorance. Bruised pride on full display, he made his handling rougher than necessary. I tried not to meet his eyes as he slid my jeans down my legs, and ignored the hand passing between my thighs to grab hold of where the fabric had folded.

With a quick step, I pulled my feet free of the cuffs. Henry's hands brushed along my thighs when he stood. I swallowed down the crawling sensation that made me want to scour every place he'd touched me.

"Well at least her legs are unmarked. Small blessings. Of course I expect remuneration for the damage done during transportation." Eastin circled the desk and picked up what looked alarmingly like a whip. Except where normal whips were long, this one was shorter and had nearly a dozen finely braided tails of red leather. The tassels glittered in the light from the small faceted gems lining each one. Shiny metal points adorned the ends of each strap. They flashed ominously at me as she ran it slowly through her fingers.

"I have a gift for you, Dorothy."

God, I hated that name. Eastin's scary sweetness wasn't doing any favors. It was eerily quiet. Guards stood silently in the corners of the room like gargoyles.

It made the gentle shhhing of the whip passing through Eastin's fingers sound like thunder.

Her eyes almost glittered with delight. What was she waiting for? Was I supposed to say thank you for what I was fairly certain was a torture device?

"The only marks she was supposed to have are the ones I place."

Beside me Henry made an audible gulping sound, and I laughed again. I should be more worried. A normal person would be pissing themselves right now. Perhaps I was already so damaged that I couldn't bring myself to worry, not when Henry's discomfort was so damn amusing.

"Of course, Ms. Witcher. I'm sure Em will pay whatever you demand," he mumbled out.

Eastin made a slight nod to a guard. In a flash of light the man wrapped a garrote around Henry's meaty throat. He made a pathetic strangled sound, his feet scrabbling beneath him, and his fingers straining uselessly at the wire. The guard muscled him to an outer terrace and with a heave tipped him over the railing. It was almost comical. Like a cartoon character walking off a cliff and hanging suspended in the air before plummeting, Henry's choked scream faded as he fell the fifty floors to the ground.

I will cherish the look of panic in his eyes for the rest of my life. "Fly, monkey, fly."

A slicing pain lanced the back of my thighs. Eastin swung the whip by her side, the smile on her face could only be described as feral.

"Do you like it? I had it made just for you."

"What?" I said, more in shock from the unexpected pain than anything. I ran my fingers over the welts striping my thighs, their tips coming back stained red.

In a blur of leather, the tailed whip flew again. This time I saw them crack, then white blanketed my vision. It was then I realized two things. Eastin had been gentle with that first hit, and I needed to be very careful if I was going to survive long enough to escape.

"You have still not earned the privilege of words."

I opened my mouth to protest, but the throbbing pain in my back made me close it again.

"Good. At least it learns quickly." She pointed at her desk with the hilt of the whip. "Kneel." Eastin turned to the guard, waving vaguely out the window. "Take a team and clean that up."

"Yes, sir." He said walking out of the room, leaving us alone. For some reason, knowing we were alone was what it took to make panic finally rise in my chest. Still, I'd had enough practice with Em to hide my fear. I walked calmly over to the desk, and lowered myself to my knees. I just had to play the good girl long enough to find a way out.

"Did Em tell you the truth about how your parents died, Dorothy?"

My parents? What the hell did my parents have to do with anything?

"No," I said quietly before adding a tentative, "sir." See, I could be—

Crack.

I arched against the pain in my back. Fuck, it burned. Trickles of blood slid in dozens of tiny trails along my spine. I shook, taking several deep breaths through my nose, trying to block out the impulse to scream.

"No?"

I blinked the tears from my eyes, using all of my free will to look at Eastin without flinching.

Crack.

I brought my hands up to muffle the agonized sob that I couldn't keep down. Nothing felt like this. Nothing. I couldn't breathe, couldn't think through the pain. It hazed over everything making the world look like it'd lost its color.

"I suppose that makes sense. Emily always was gutless."

She took the hilt of the whip, driving it under my chin to be sure I was looking at her. She pulled up on it, forcing me to stretch until I nearly toppled from my knees.

"I, sweet girl, killed them. Or rather, we killed them."

I sucked in a breath. We? As in, my Aunt Em and Eastin? My aunt was terrible to me, but she always made it seem like she'd loved my mother. I could barely remember my parents, but I knew for certain that their death had changed everything.

"We tried to kill you, too." She yanked the whip free, letting my body slump back down. "Unfortunately, you weren't in the car the day I ran it into the lake."

My heart was beating out of control. If it weren't for the reminder of the fresh pain at my back, I would probably be falling into a full blown panic attack. If I was supposed to die with them, then why bother keeping me alive all these years?

Eastin picked up a snow globe from the corner of her desk. She turned it upside down. Flakes of glitter swirled around a tiny replica of an office building with a peaked roof, the iconic terrace at the top making it clear it was this building. Eastin sat on the edge of the desk before me, placing the snow globe beside her.

"Your knack for survival turned out to be fortunate, when at the reading of the will we learned the controlling stake in your family's holdings wouldn't have passed to Emily as we previously thought. But they would pass to you, and your guardian. Otherwise, your foolish parents were giving everything to the *people of Oz*. What a fucking waste that would have been." Eastin rolled her eyes, like she wasn't personally responsible for a quarter of Ozmandria's population.

"Em got the money, with it she gave me the assets to seize control of all of this." Her long nails clicked against the top of the globe as she lovingly stroked down its side. "Now that you're 21, however, things have changed. Financial holdings passed to you on your birthday."

I had no idea. My parents had enough money to kickstart an empire? Em of course never mentioned any of this. All she ever did was talk about how much I cost her.

"Conveniently *your* will states that upon your demise all assets transfer to your closest living relative. Something I'm only too happy to help Emily with." My heart rate sped up, aching at its ferocity. Eastin tenderly stroked the leather whip over my bruised cheek. The faceted edges, still wet from my blood, scraped the raw surface. "I'm owed your blood, baby girl. I earned the right to take my vengeance on your flesh."

Vengeance? What had I ever done to her? I licked my dry lips.

23

"I think Emily thought holding onto you gave her some kind of power over me. I offered her money. She turned me down, at first. But you must have done something to make her really angry. Em sold you for not even half of what I offered the first time. She didn't even haggle."

I thought of the fury on my aunt's face when Henry threw me at her feet, the angry phone call she made immediately afterwards. *"She's yours. I don't care what you do with her. No, whatever you want."*

"Why?" The word slipped out before I'd realized what I'd done, and I instantly regretted it.

Eastin grabbed my chin, her thumb pressing hard against my damaged cheek. I cried out, a pained muffled sound forcing its way past my squished lips. Eastin pulled me towards her hard enough that I fell forward and had to brace against the desk. My wrists pulled at their bindings as I tried to find purchase.

"You want to know why I savor your pain? Why I *will* delight in your death?"

I tried to nod, despite the fierce grip Eastin held on me.

"Because your parents took everything I ever loved, leaving only wickedness behind."

My fingers bumped against something hard and cold. The snow globe. I acted on instinct. With both hands I latched onto the base. I pushed to my feet, swinging the full weight of the globe with all of the power I could muster.

The hard glass ball slammed into her temple. I felt the bone give way beneath me. Eastin fell to the ground with a withering sound. Before she could move again, I lowered the globe once more, smashing the bridge of her nose. A wide splatter of blood peppered the air. The glass broke and I rammed the pointed end of the building at her. I did it again and again, until she stopped fighting. The sounds she made went from pain, to something wet, and then she went completely still.

Standing, I dropped the building on her one last time. It slammed home in the wet pile of meat that had once been her face.

I stared at my shaking hands. My near naked body was coated in wet glitter and a speckling of blood that looked more like macabre freckles than the carnage at my feet.

I killed her.

Fuck.

I just killed Eastin Witcher.

That panic was rising again, along with a deep tremor. I couldn't breathe, couldn't swallow.

What the fuck was I going to do?

I was dead. Deader than dead. *And naked.*

-4-
THEA

I slid my shirt back up my arms, and over my head, wincing at the pain in my wrists, my side, and the way the thin fabric clung to the raw flesh of my back.

First thing I needed to do was cut these bindings, and fast, before the guards returned. I scrambled around the desk, fumbling at the drawers as I went. Eastin had to have scissors in here somewhere. All I could find was a silver letter opener. It wasn't even sharp.

I tried anyway, and gave a silent scream of pain and frustration when all I did was succeed in cutting up my wrists more. Maybe if my hands weren't shaking so damn much.

"You're going to need to be quicker if you want to get out of here before they return."

I screamed, jumping high enough I was certain my soul left my body. On nervous impulse, I flung the letter opener into the air. It cut across the room embedding itself in the painting of Eastin, silver handle wobbling from the center of her boob.

A woman stood in the doorway. She was clad entirely in black leather, a bit of a pink blouse poking out of the top, and long blonde hair hanging over one shoulder.

With a girly laugh, she said, "It wasn't enough to kill her once, you had to murder the bitch for a second time?"

I scanned the room for a weapon, seeing nothing of use in the minimalistic office.

"Come here and I'll cut the zipties for you." A streak of silver flashed in the darkness, followed by the snick of a knife opening.

"Why should I trust you?" Not that I ever trusted anyone, especially a stranger who materialized out of nothing and was brandishing a knife like it was some kind of magic wand.

"Because, girl, you're standing in your underwear and have no other option than to wait here to die. And nobody wants to die in day old, dirty underwear. Now get over here. You have approximately thirty seconds to leave this office and you're wasting all of them."

Fair enough. Carefully avoiding the growing pool of blood, I walked over to her. On my way, I detoured to give the red whip a kick across the room.

The cold blade slid against my wrist, before effortlessly cutting through the plastic ropes.

"That must be very sharp." I sounded dumb. It had to be the adrenaline making me dumb. Flexing my wrists, I tried to ignore the tingling sensation winding its way across the palm of my hands and down into my fingertips.

"Mmm. They usually are." She tucked the knife between her breasts. "Next you're going to need to take the emerald hanging from Eastin's neck. It's not just a pretty necklace, the stone is coded. That emerald will get you through any door and gate in the building. You have about three minutes before this whole place turns into a veritable fortress. When that happens, the only thing getting you out of the building is that stone."

I nodded, running over and yanking it from the vile woman's corpse.

"Go to the end of the hallway, put the emerald to the panel on the right. It's Eastin's private elevator. Take it all the way down to Sub Level B. I have a man down there doing a pick up for me. He's in a Yellow Brick Road Taxicab. Tell him *you're the package.*"

I blinked at her. Trying to take everything she said in.

She gave me a hard tug, pulling me down the hallway. "Say it, Dorothea."

Dorothea? I hadn't heard that name in a *very* long time. "I'm the package. Why do you know my name? My real name."

She pressed my hand with the stone to the call button.

28

"Wait, what about my pants?"

"There's no time." The doors swung immediately open. "Now this is very important. Dorothea Rosen doesn't exist anymore." I pressed the SB2 button.

"Ok."

"When Westin hears of what you've done, Dorothea will be as good as dead. You need to disappear. You need the Wizard. He can give you everything you need. Tell the cab driver to take you to the Wizard. Say it."

"The Wizard, he needs to take me to The Wizard."

"Good luck."

I held my hand over the door so it couldn't close.

"You aren't coming with me."

"I have to sort things here, seems someone killed Eastin Witcher tonight."

"I don't even know your name?"

"It's Gigi. Find The Wizard."

She pushed my hand back, and the doors closed with a tiny swoosh.

-5-
CROWE

The door slammed, smacking the head of the man I was dragging behind me. I hauled him on top of the growing pile of bound guards. Eastin really needed to improve her security requirements. It was laughable how easy it was to incapacitate these men. Maybe I didn't need my boys on this job after all.

My eyes locked on the security feed running across the monitors on the wall. Eastin had some poor woman on her knees and was whipping her with a flail. I always knew she was a kinky bitch. The girl didn't really seem to be into it, not if the way she shook and flinched after each hit was any indication. Eastin's brutality was a shame, too, because it was ruining what looked like perfectly flawless skin. Now, her back was little more than a map of criss-crossing lacerations and blood.

The woman reared up. I blinked in disbelief, watching her smash the witch right in the temple with that dumb snow globe she always kept on her desk. Eastin went down, hard. I clicked on the feed, enlarging the image. The vicious girl hit her over and over again. Her body stretched high, coming down with the full force of her muscle on each hit. I was right. She was most definitely not into it.

"Well, fuck me." I double clicked, zooming in further. She stepped back, looming over the now very dead body of Eastin Witcher. Her dark hair streaked across her cheeks, clinging to the spray of blood that peppered her face. Shock slowly settled into her expression. The girl's bound hands began trembling, then, just as quickly, the shock transformed into panic.

Why wasn't she moving? At most, there were minutes before Eastin's guards returned.

As if she could hear my thoughts, she jumped into action, searching for a way to free herself. I couldn't help the twitch of my lips. This woman was a fighter. She took her licks and came back kicking. There was something truly arousing about that. I sat back, reveling in the moment, then, reality came reeling back.

Holy fuck! Eastin Witcher was dead, and this entire building was about to become a war zone.

Fucking Gigi. Somehow she knew this was going to happen, and that bitch probably sent me here to take the fall. No wonder this was a one-man job. She only needed one man. I scanned the cameras for any sight of the blonde-haired vixen. But, of course, she was too good to be caught on camera. It didn't look like any of Eastin's security were on the penthouse floor. That was a small mercy, or else the building would already be in lockdown. I clicked on another camera. Her small army of trained monkeys were all dealing with a pile of blood and bones that might have been a man at one time. Out of curiosity, more than need, I flipped back to the feed in Eastin's office. The girl was gone.

A second later, I found her again, standing in the elevator, holding the door open and talking to someone just off camera. Gigi. I would bet my stuffing that was who she was talking to.

Gigi could deal with this mess on her own. I wasn't about to be some patsy for killing one of the world's most horrible cunts. She sure as fuck wasn't worth the inevitably painful death sentence that Westin would call down. Especially since I didn't even get the joy of being able to do it myself.

I ran across the loading dock, clicking a security fob. The cab roared to life with more horsepower than any cab should rightfully possess. With another click, a beep echoed in the garage to indicate that the security features were disengaged.

I slipped quickly into the front seat, throwing it into reverse and backing up before my door had even fully closed. I cranked the wheel, spinning the car a full 180, and angled straight for the ramp out of here when movement in my mirror caught my attention.

Behind me, the elevator doors slid open. Leaning against the wall, ready to spring out and attack anyone waiting for her, was the girl. Fuck. She looked in even worse condition than she had on the cameras. Welts and bruises coated far too much of her pale pink skin. And so much of that skin was on full display. Gigi had sent her down here in what amounted to nothing more than a stretched-out, old t-shirt. She didn't even have shoes on.

I don't know why I hesitated. This girl was not my responsibility. But there was something about the desperate intensity behind her movements that I couldn't ignore, couldn't fucking look away from.

Her eyes locked onto my car, and she ran straight for me. Relief washed over her features, like she had been expecting to see me.

Fuck. Fuck. Fuck. Danny was going to kill me. This was why we didn't do jobs without a plan.

When she reached the passenger side door, I lowered the window but kept my gun trained straight on her pouting lips. She pulled at the handle, making an exasperated whimper when she realized it was locked.

"Let me in," she demanded breathlessly. Of course the wildcat who had just pummeled the Witch of the East to death would demand her rescue.

"Start talking, gorgeous. Who are you? Why did you just kill Eastin Witcher?"

"Gigi sent me to you. She said something about a package."

I groaned, but I wasn't surprised. "That doesn't answer my question. You have five seconds to say something of value, and then I'm driving away. Whether you are in this car or not is up to you."

"Please. She said you would take me to The Wizard."

I barked out an incredulous breath. "Sorry, sweet lips. But you don't just go to The Wizard."

"Please. You're my only chance. She said you would help me."

Alarms on each pillar of the deck blared to life. Deafening shrieks bounced off the concrete walls. Lights flashed. Overhead flood lights illuminated every shadow on the floor, followed by the sound of metal slamming all around. I swiveled my head to the ramp. Heavy pillars rose up from the ground, blocking off the exit.

"*Fuck!*" I slammed the steering wheel, unintentionally hitting the horn. "*Fucking fuck!*" Furious, I looked back at the girl who had just doomed us both. She stood irreverently beside the car, looking for all the world like I was inconveniencing *her*.

"You really say that a lot, ya know—Fuck. You might want to consider introducing a little variety into your vocabulary." She chewed on her lower lip, like she was trying not to laugh.

Was she seriously teasing me right now? Any other time I'd show her exactly how far teasing me would get her, but these were not normal times.

"You just sealed our death sentence, pretty girl."

"Doesn't have to be." She reached under her filthy shirt and pulled out Eastin's glimmering emerald necklace. It swung between her fingers, catching the fluorescent light with each pass. "Gigi said it will get us out of any exit, even in lockdown. Take me to the Wizard and I'll get you out of this building."

My mouth hung open. I was transfixed by this impossible girl, like the swinging of the emerald had just stolen all of my common sense and there wasn't a brain cell left in my body.

"Options are in short supply and we are running out of time, *pretty boy*." Lengthening her spine to stand tall, she grinned down at me with smug triumph.

I was going to regret this.

"I'm not taking you to the Wizard, but if you get us out of this building, I'll do my best to keep you alive until we can figure out what happens next." I flipped the locks. "Get in."

"Wait. I have to do something first."

"Sorry, what?" She had to be out of her mind. "This isn't a leisure cruise. Get the fuck in the car."

"No."

I stared her down. For probably the tenth time in as many minutes, I couldn't believe what I was seeing. She held out her hand in a gimme motion.

34

"Give me your gun."

"Now, I know you're joking. I'm not giving you my gun."

"We don't have time for this. Do you want out of this garage or not? I'm not leaving until I do this. The longer you hold out, the longer this will take."

I climbed out of the car. "Lead the way but make it quick."

She strode straight for the Cyclone Shipping truck parked at the loading dock. From the plates, it was the same truck I'd seen arrive earlier. Suddenly, all the pieces fell into place: her general state of distress, her clearly abused body, the desperation in the way she drove that snow globe into Eastin's face. Without a doubt, I knew exactly what cargo that truck was hauling.

Without waiting to be asked, I leveled my gun and shot off the padlock keeping the back hatch shut. The girl didn't even flinch from the loud bang that was still echoing in my ears. Just how desensitized was she? Putting her whole body weight into it, she swung the doors open.

Inside, nearly a dozen women shrank from the sudden influx of light. A few scrambled away from the door as far as their bound arms would allow. Others cried with hope to their saviors.

Heh. Imagine it, me, a savior. There was a twist for the ages. The girl pulled a release on a chain, and the restraints holding the women in place dropped to their laps.

"Now we can go," she said with finality. The sounds of voices and screeching tires echoed around us.

"Not a second too soon."

We hurried back to the still-running cab. She hopped in beside me, bare legs sliding over the leather interior. "Things are about to get a little bit hot around here. You're going to want to buckle up." I reached over her lap, clicking her seat belt in place. She hissed in pain when my elbow brushed her side.

The dinging sound announcing the elevator chimed behind us. Leaning out of my window, my gun bucked as I fired off three shots in quick succession. I floored the gas pedal before I could see if any of them got back up. Unlikely, but hey, even I miss sometimes.

Tall steel pylons gleamed in the floodlights, blocking the exit. I was betting on the system recognizing the emerald and Eastin's self-centered need to never wait. It was a dangerous bet because if it didn't pay off, we were about to slam headfirst into an unmovable barrier.

As we approached the pillars, they lowered swiftly. With a yelp of excitement, I dropped the car into a lower gear and blazed up the spiraling ramp, drifting on each curve. Barrier after barrier parted for us.

Flashing my eyes on the rearview mirror, I said, "That didn't take long."

"What didn't take long?" The girl twisted, her long hair catching in the wind from the still-open window and slapping me in the face.

Two cars advanced, nearly clipping my rear fender. A spray-painted sign on the wall indicated we were approaching the exit, along with several armed gunmen on either side of the gate. Bullets caught in the windshield, spraying the concrete wall behind us.

"Don't worry. It's bulletproof glass."

I rolled down my window.

"Bulletproof glass doesn't work when you roll the windows down!"

"Lean back for me, sweetness."

"What?"

I reached over her lap, pulling the spare gun from the glove compartment. Then I pressed on her chest. "Lean back."

I clicked the car into auto-drive, then released the wheel and aimed out both windows. With a few well-placed shots, the gunmen on either side of the exit fell. The auto-drive spun the wheel sharply to the side, and we barreled onto the street in a sharp ninety-degree turn.

Taking only a second, I leaned over my passenger and aimed straight for the driver of the car tailing us. I braced my elbow against her breast, ignoring the softness beneath my arm and her breath along my neck.

"Seriously? Is that really necessary?"

"Always." One shot was all it took. The man fell on his wheel, turning the car and locking it at the top of the ramp, preventing anyone from following us out of the garage. Her hand rubbed at her chest where my elbow had kicked back into it. "I'll make it up to you later, I promise."

She groaned a low sound of annoyance, despite the fact that she was also smiling. We sped down the road, taking precautionary measures to lose any tails that we might have picked up on our exit. When we made it to the highway, I slowed back to the speed limit and flipped on my light, indicating to the world that we were just another cab with a fare.

I turned to look at *the package*. Even with all she'd been through, she didn't look flustered. No, she looked exhilarated, like she was tasting freedom for the first time.

How very foolish.

–6–
THEA

"I think now might be a good time for you to answer that question from earlier. What's your name, beautiful?"

Ignoring his question, I twisted in my seat to scope out the car interior.

"So, do all cabs have bulletproof windows?"

On a quick inspection, this was any taxicab you'd find lining city streets across Oz—until you really started looking. Beneath the surface, you could see panels built into the doors. I thumbed at the one next to me, feeling it shift beneath my touch.

"Don't touch that," my mystery driver snapped at me, but it didn't feel like there was any sincerity behind it. In fact, it almost felt like he was daring me to keep going. A row of buttons and switches lined the side of the steering column. Doubling down on the challenge, I leaned forward. There was a larger blue button behind the steering wheel demanding to be pushed. The tip of my finger barely brushed its glossy surface when he snatched my hand up in his.

"And you really, *really* don't want to touch that one."

A shiver of anticipation ran down my spine. I struggled to pull free, all the more determined to see what would happen when I did. His fingers wound into mine, and he lowered our hands, pinning them to the armrest. The callused pad of his thumb ran in soothing strokes over the back of my hand.

I laughed at the absurdity of it. For all the world, we would look just like any couple going for a ride. Well, except for the fact that I still wasn't wearing any pants, and I was beat to hell.

Not bothering to try and extricate myself from his grip, I used my free hand to flip open the visor mirror. Wincing, I got my first real look at myself since

Henry threw me into that truck. The thing staring back at me resembled a car crash more than a woman. I hoped Henry and his massive shiny ring were enjoying the lobby right now. Behind the veil of my limp, auburn hair, I was finally seeing the devastation that metal monstrosity had wrought on my face.

The bruise along my cheek had spread, looking almost like a bruised plum. Tiny blown blood vessels veined out from the point of impact. If I wasn't mistaken, there was also the faint white outline of Em's crest right in the middle of it all. I poked gingerly at it. Motherfucker, that hurt.

"It really isn't that bad."

Was he kidding? I shifted in my seat, noticing for the first time how very blue his eyes were, even in the dim light. This mark, coupled with the rings around my eyes from lack of sleep, made me look like some kind of clown school reject.

My *hero,* if you could even call him that, gave a tiny laugh at the incredulous face I must have been giving him. "When I was seventeen, I was hit upside the head with an iron spatula. Which, unfortunately, had just been used to move hot stones from an oven."

"A spatula?"

"Yeah. Never make a Nonna angry." He pointed to his temple, not bothering to release my hand. A crow was tattooed into the shaved side of his head, just behind his ear. The beak stretched to his temple, and the tail circled behind his nape, with one long feather draping down his neck. The long hair tied at the top of his head was the color of straw. Even in the dark light of the cab, it looked like it glowed golden with sunlight.

Biting back the pain, I twisted so that I could run my free hand along the image and through the downy softness of his hair. Hidden among the wings, was a lattice-work of scars, though they had been cleverly covered by the feathers.

"For two years, I had a fucking tic-tac-toe board burned on the side of my head. Not to mention half my damn hair had been burned off. The point is—" He pushed our joined hands back, running his thumb down my jaw. "—it's not that bad. That little love tap on your cheek will fade in a week, maybe two."

"I assure you, nothing about any of my marks were made out of love."

The car slowed, not much, but enough that I felt the change in inertia. When his leg shifted, I realized it was because his foot had slipped on the pedal.

"Why was Eastin Witcher whipping you?" There was a deadly chill in his voice, like deep shadows were hiding beneath all that sunlight. "Or better yet, why were you kneeling at her feet taking it?"

I shook at the memory but didn't say anything, choosing instead to watch the reflective mile marker signs zoom by one at a time.

"Okay. Given that you beat her face in with a snow globe, it's probably an overstatement to say you were taking it. Let's try this: why don't we start with your name? Because right now, I'm running out of things to call you, and I'm just gonna settle on Sugar Tits for lack of anything more fitting."

"Sugar Tits?"

He flashed me a devilish smile. "Absolutely. I'm positive you'd taste as sweet as cherry pie. You're avoiding my question."

I fidgeted with the hem of my shirt. It was so dirty that you could barely make out its soft blue color. When I shifted my weight the leather of the seats pulled at the tender skin of my bare legs, making his whipping comment that much more poignant.

"You saw all of that?"

The relief knowing that I didn't need to bear the load of that experience alone warred with my embarrassment. Eastin stripped me to my underwear and then made me kneel at her feet. Beatings aside, it was so degrading. By now, being degraded shouldn't faze me, but having your dignity stripped from you hurt every time, no matter how many times you'd been exposed to the harsh reality of this world.

"How? There was no one there."

"The security booth. I was scanning the feed to try and find Gigi on the cameras. Naturally, a woman kneeling before the Wicked Witcher herself gave me reason to pause."

"Well, the witch is dead, so it doesn't matter why I was kneeling."

I groaned and flopped back in my seat, sliding down like it could somehow hide me from all that had transpired in that room. I regretted it instantly. My back flared to life, eclipsed only by the pain in my side from what I was certain was a broken rib.

"How about, instead, you start by telling me why you were in that garage? Gigi said you were picking something up for her. Or, hey, how about you tell me *your* name?"

He seemed to consider it. The thumb resting against the wheel drumming in contemplation.

"My name is Vincent, but people call me Crowe."

"Because of the tattoo?"

"No."

I waited for him to explain, but when he didn't say anything, I pushed further. "And you were in the building at midnight *because..?*"

"Mmm, sorry darling, I'm not in the habit of sharing intel with strangers."

The city had all but disappeared outside the window, replaced by long stretches of rolling hills and the silhouette of mountains off in the distance.

"Where are we going? Since, apparently, you won't take me to the Wizard."

"Somewhere safe." The long fingers wrapped around my hand tightened. For some reason, it made me feel safer, like for the first time ever, I could drop my defenses and breathe—a little.

"Em sold me as part of some kind of a debt." My voice had a timidity to it that I wasn't used to. Em had preyed on me my entire life, but until today, I never once allowed myself to feel like a victim. Now, I didn't know who the broken girl beneath this bruised skin was. My survival suddenly felt like a gift and not a right. I hated it.

Like a cold draft, the ghost of the panic I felt in that office crept back in. I could feel it in the way each of my wounds seemed to throb with a heartbeat of its own. The fine tremor in my hands hadn't fully gone away since Henry pulled me from the truck. I tugged on the hem of my shirt, tucking my bare knees beneath it, and refusing to make a sound when a sharp pain sliced across my back.

Crowe's hand tightened around mine—a tether to keep me in the moment when it would be so easy to sink into the fear.

42

We drove in silence for several long minutes. The night streamed past the windows in one silhouette after another. I bit down on the thumb of my free hand in a desperate attempt to hold it together. I don't know why being with Crowe made me feel like it was okay to feel all of this emotion. I'd never allowed myself to break before, but on instinct, I knew he'd hold me up if I started to crumble.

When Crowe finally spoke again, he seemed to have resigned himself to something. "The boys are going to kill me, possibly literally, but I'm going to bring you home."

"Home?" That panic clawed its way to the surface, forcing my pitch higher. "Not to The Farm. Aunt Em will kill me. Please, Crowe, you don't understand. Going back is a death sentence."

While I had no idea where I was going, I knew for certain the next time I walked across the dusty grounds of The Farm, it would be while basking in the glow of it burning down.

Or, I'd be hauled in dead. There was no in-between.

"The Farm." Crowe slammed a hand against the steering wheel, swerving the car and hitting the brake. "Ozma be damned! Emily Rosen is your aunt."

It was a statement more than a question. Aunt Em's reputation amongst the criminal networks of Oz was strong enough that nobody dared to mess with any of her shipments, not when she helped ensure all their wallets stayed fat. So it wasn't surprising that Crowe knew her name.

His look of astonishment shifted just as quickly into something far more fierce. "The Cyclone Shipping truck that you arrived on. It came from The Farm. And she...Oz damn, she sold you to Eastin! Her niece. That's a whole new level of fucked up."

I gestured to my general state of distress. "Obviously."

He nodded, tapping against the steering wheel, this time harder than before. Flipping a switch, the car flashed and took over driving itself. I blinked at the steering wheel, watching it gently sway back and forth while keeping us perfectly centered in the lane. This cab was like we'd jumped into the future.

Crowe twisted into the back of the car, pulling out an old zip-up hoodie that was thrown carelessly in the backseat. Then he hit a panel and pulled from it a bottle of water. I hadn't even realized how thirsty and dehydrated I was until that glistening plastic bottle was in front of me.

"Drink this. If you were in the back of that truck all the way from the Dust Bowl, then you probably haven't had anything to drink in nearly a day and, fuck, you're probably starving, too."

I took the bottle, draining it almost completely in one go.

"Easy. You'll make yourself sick like that." He gently pulled the bottle from my lips. I swallowed hard, wiping away the stream of water dribbling down my chin with the back of my hand.

Crowe, using his teeth like some kind of caveman, tore open a protein bar. Not giving me time to process what was in his hand, he shoved it into my mouth.

"Thank you," I said around a mouth of peanut butter and oats. The dense bar stuck to the roof of my mouth, making me start coughing when I tried to swallow the way too-big bite.

Crowe's eyes went wide alarm. "Fuck, you're not allergic to peanuts, are you? Shit. I should have asked first. Can you breathe?" He frantically clambered over the seat, slamming his fist into another panel. "Shit. Shit. Shit. I have adrenaline in here somewhere."

I tugged on the pant leg of the spectacularly defined calf dangling in the air in front of me.

"Hold on. I know it's in here. If I just manage to—"

Crowe's ass was nearly hitting the roof as he tried to get into the seat-back compartment. Seriously, the man must never skip leg day because, damn, those jeans were fitting in all the right places.

I tugged again. "Crowe, I'm fine. You just shoved half a protein bar in my mouth. I'm starving, but that doesn't mean I want to choke on over-processed oats."

He slid back down, a mix of genuine relief and embarrassment pinking his face. "So you're not dying?"

"Not presently, but give me til morning."

"Fearless and a comedian. You really scared me there for a second, funny girl."

"My name is Dorothy...Thea. Call me Thea."

"Thea," Crowe said my name slowly, like he was trying it on for size and deciding if he liked the fit. He held up the discarded hoodie. "This should be soft enough to avoid hurting any of the wounds on your legs." He draped the jacket over my lap, carefully checking that none of the metal parts were touching bare skin. It smelled masculine, like wood and leather. Crowe was right. It was soft and warm, making me feel instantly more secure. I clutched the edges like the bit of cotton and polyester could protect me from what came next. But the adrenaline I was running on had long since faded from my system, and I was exhausted.

I curled as tightly as my poor, lacerated back would allow, feeling where the thin fabric of my shirt had dried to my wounds, sticking and pulling as I shifted.

"Try to get some rest. It's at least another hour before we'll arrive."

"Where?"

"My home. I'll keep you safe." Pushing the hair from my face, he added, "Sleep, beautiful."

Crowe turned on the radio, soft jazz music filling the small space of the cab. He turned the knob, making it only just loud enough to be lulling. There was no use in trying to fight it. The last time I slept was while my arms were suspended above me, and my head kept banging into the metal wall of the container. Hardly what one could call a good night's rest.

I should be terrified about what comes next, fighting sleep and trying to stay alert. I didn't know Crowe and I already learned the hard way that even nice-looking guys liked inflicting pain. My instincts were telling me that I was safe with him. Honestly, I don't know that I've ever actually felt safe before. Certainly not while living on The Farm.

With the last of my strength, not even bothering to open my eyes, I murmured, "Thank you for saving me."

"You saved yourself." Crowe's large hand rested against my knee. Its heavy weight calmed my trembling nerves, bringing me a sense of temporary peace. I knew in that moment my instincts were right; Crowe would protect me.

"Shhh. Sleep, Darling Thea."

-7-
THEA

The shudder of the engine turning off registered dully in the back of my mind. Through the fog of sleep, the metal sounds of a garage door closing filtered in.

"Thea," a smooth voice whispered, along with a feather-light touch that caressed down my temple until reaching the sting of my raw, bruised cheek.

My eyes fluttered open. I wasn't entirely certain what was going on at first. Piercing blue eyes, practically teal in the fluorescent light filling the garage, peered down. A rich, truly masculine smell wrapped around me. I pulled the hoody draped over me closer and willed my brain to catch up.

Crowe rubbed the back of his knuckle over my temple again. "There she is."

Everything came flooding back in a second. The container, Henry, Eastin, our flight from her garage. I sat up, tossing off the hoodie and jolting entirely too quickly for how inflamed the skin of my back was.

"Woah. Woah. It's ok. There's nothing to be afraid of here." Crowe's voice felt soft, like something you would use on a spooked animal. Disgusted by my cowardice, I immediately straightened my spine. I didn't need to be showing any more weakness. I'd already shown more than I should.

"Where is here?" I said, my voice still rough from sleep.

"My home. Come on, I'll introduce you to the guys. Then, maybe we can figure out what the hell comes next."

I nodded and pushed the passenger door open.

The massive garage was well-lit and housed two other matching YBR Cabs, along with two sports cars and a couple of motorcycles. Crowe headed for a door in the corner, elevated slightly above four concrete steps.

"This way."

Ignoring him, I ran my hand down the cherry-red Stingray that we parked next to. It was a gorgeous car. It looked sleek and fast, like something from a movie and nothing like the dusty utility vehicles you'd see around The Farm. Despite logic telling me to pay attention to my surroundings, the only thing I wanted to do in this moment was watch my fingers wrap around the steering wheel. I went to open the driver's door.

"Thea, I wouldn't touch that. Danny can be really possessive."

A much deeper, masculine voice barked out, "What in the FUCK do you think you're doing?"

I spun around, my hands tucked behind me like a child caught stealing sweets from the kitchen. At the top of the stairs looming over Crowe was a tall, broad man with an AR-15 assault rifle tucked into the crook of his shoulder—pointed right at me. His finger was poised over the trigger like he might light up the whole garage at any minute.

AR-15s were the guns of choice by the guards running the perimeter at The Farm, so I was more than familiar with them. I was also familiar with how quickly they could cut someone down when they decided to make a run for it.

Slowly, I raised my hands in the air. Crowe took two steps back, effectively placing himself in the line of fire.

"Crowe, one of your boys?" I said, trying to keep as much strength in my voice as I could. But seriously, he said this place was safe, and not two minutes later, his friend pulled an assault rifle on him.

"Fucking hell, Danny? Overkill much?"

Danny flicked a button on the side, switching the rifle to fully automatic. "No, I don't think so."

"You're just pissy because she was eyeing up your car."

With his free hand, Danny pulled a phone from his pocket, swiped it open, and tossed it down to Crowe. "This came across the wire about five minutes ago." Over his shoulder, I could see a security camera photo of my battered face. "Imagine my surprise when I see *her* climbing out of one of *my* cabs."

"Our cab," Crowe guffawed, but his eyes were still looking at the phone screen.

Danny shifted his weight, squaring off his shoulders towards Crowe. "So how about you tell me why it is that someone with a $50K price tag on her pretty head is standing in our garage? We have protocols, and bringing persons of interest into HQ isn't one of them."

"Thea isn't a threat, you overreacting psycho. Gigi set us up, or *something*. I haven't quite worked it out. Yet. Bringing her here was the only option I could think of."

"Only option you could think of? Fuck, Crowe, we have safe houses for an Oz damned reason."

"Yeah, and Gigi knows all of them. But, she's never been *here*."

"For a good fucking reason. We don't bring anyone here, assets or otherwise."

Crowe tilted his head with a little laugh, about to say something that was quickly cut off by Danny. "I swear, I will break your fucking skull if you crack a joke about her assets."

"I mean–" Crowe sucked in a breath through his teeth "—have you actually looked at her because--"

There was a click and a clear red line painted through the garage aimed straight at me.

"You are such a stubborn ass, Dan. If North is planning something, I'd much rather have a stand-off here than at some shitty apartment on the west end of New Munich."

I could feel my patience begin to fray on both ends. Honestly, these two could make bickering into an Olympic sport.

"I'm standing right here. You could maybe address me directly instead of talking about me like I'm a child. And, Danny, was it?" I added, popping my hip out. It was a mirror of Eastin's stance. I didn't have the shiny silver shoes, but that didn't make it any less confident. There was one undeniable fact, Eastin Witcher had perfected the Boss Bitch pose, and I wasn't so proud as to avoid using it now.

"I don't even have pants on. I doubt you need to worry about me pulling a weapon on you. So how about you stop swinging your big gun energy around."

Danny huffed a long sigh. Flipping the safety on the rifle, he finally lowered it. The red laser centered over my breast disappeared.

"Ok, Princess. Just remember, I don't need this to kill you."

"That's fine, just so long as you remember that I don't need pants to knee you in the balls."

Crowe barked out a laugh and shoved Danny out of the way.

"Careful, Dan, this one is a firecracker. She's bright and fun to play with, but if you choke her, she'll blow your fucking hand off." Crowe disappeared into the darkness of the house, his voice trailing behind him. "Come on, Thea. Don't let this Neanderthal scare you. He's got a big roar, but deep down, he's nothing but a coward."

I quickly caught up to him, smiling with saccharine sweetness as we passed Danny. If scowls could kill, then the way his brows were dipping as Crowe's hand locked around mine were lethal. Maybe that was all the incentive I needed, or maybe I was still pissed he'd pulled a gun big enough to floor a small army. Or, maybe, I just had so much bottled-up rage in me that I needed an outlet, making this the perfect time to prove to him that I don't make idle threats. Whatever it was, it felt damn good to ram my knee straight into his groin.

Danny buckled forward, and rather than letting him fall to his knees where he could whimper in peace, I crowded his space until his gasping breaths were sharing the same air as my controlled ones. With all the sensuality of a lover, I slid my hands along his chest and up to his shoulders until I had pushed him back against the door frame.

My whispering lips brushed his ear, "I'm no one's Princess." I pressed a kiss to his cheek before following Crowe into the building.

Had I pushed the man with the big gun too far? Probably. At this point, I was starting to wonder if it even mattered anymore.

Crowe stood a few feet inside, shaking his head in astonishment.

"What?" I said with an innocent shrug.

"You are just full of surprises, is all. Seeing a man taking a knee to the dick shouldn't have been hot, but fuck if that wasn't the sexiest thing I've seen all night."

"Only all night? Maybe I should be trying harder. Let me know if you need an encore." I pointedly looked down at the swelling line of his zipper.

Crowe coughed a laugh, but his hand moved protectively to guard against any repeat performances. If there was one thing these boys needed to understand clearly, it was that I may be beaten, homeless, and pantless, but I wasn't something to be preyed upon. I had spent too much of my life being pushed around, and now that I was out from under Em's thumb, I wasn't going to let anyone else put me under theirs.

We moved another few feet into the connecting hall before entering a large open-plan room, complete with exposed rafters and ductwork, more like we'd walked into a converted warehouse than a home. A dining table and chairs sat off to one side, with the kitchen island next to it. On the opposite side of the space there was a large sitting area. It was cozy, in a clinical sort of way.

"I say we cash in on the reward and just hand her over to Westin now." A cold, level voice drifted down to us. There was a softness to his letters that hinted at an accent, but I couldn't place where it was from. I craned my neck to look up at a dark figure leaning over the loft railing.

He was almost entirely hidden by the shadows looming around him. They cloaked his identity like they heeled to his command. Beneath his thick hood, I could only make out the sharp edges of his jaw, giving him a distinctly ghoulish appearance. I shivered like it was the grim reaper staring death down at me.

Crowe pulled me tight to his back, but stopped moving when the gleam of a gun muzzle flashed ominously at us.

"Seriously? Another one?" I muttered into Crowe's shoulder. "What happened to there's *nothing to be afraid of here, Thea*? Have you actually met the assholes you live with?"

To prove my point, something hard nudged my back, pushing into the brutalized skin. I hissed at Danny, prompting him to continue prodding me with the tip of his rifle.

"You would be wise to watch the words that come out of your mouth around here, *Princess.*"

I looked him up and down, laying the disgust in my eyes on thick. "I'll start speaking with respect when you start acting like you deserve it."

Danny's face flared red, but whatever he was about to say was cut short by Crowe's reply. "Nobody is going to do anything until we figure out what is actually going on."

The man looming above us yelled down, "I know what's going on. A fifty thousand dollar payout just walked through our doors. This is the easiest score we've ever made. Come on, Crowe, even you aren't that brainless."

"Nobody is handing shit over to Westin," Crowe spat. "That miserable, two-faced witch doesn't deserve anything. I don't care how much she's paying."

I should be pleased that he was defending me, except that it sounded more like if anyone other than Westin was paying for me, then it would be up for discussion.

"I'm worth more than fifty grand," I said, speaking up.

Crowe swiveled around, his face mere inches from mine. At the same time, Danny said, "You think Westin will pay more than $50K?"

"Are you trying to get yourself killed?" he hissed at me. Crowe wasn't wrong. This was a gamble, but if he thought I was folding while I still had cards to play, then he was going to have to get used to surprises.

I patted him on the cheek. "Shh. The adults are speaking."

"Cute." Crowe's hand, still wrapped in mine, tightened in warning.

I pushed as far away as his iron grip would allow, doing my best to address all three men.

"Turns out, I recently became a very wealthy woman."

"How wealthy?" Danny said, gesturing to the row of leather stools lining the kitchen island.

"Damn, now that we're talking money, the hospitality comes out. Well, at least I know your moral compass points to your wallet."

Crowe finally released me, and I walked the long way around the island to the stool at the far end. He didn't let me stray far from him. It would seem he didn't actually trust his friends as much as he originally let on. This newfound protectiveness was actually kind of endearing. I'd never really had anyone try to protect me before.

Swiveling on the stool to face Danny, I answered, "I have the entirety of The Farm and Cyclone Shipping's funds to pull from."

Danny sat up, shock and recognition twisting his features. "Thea, as in Dorothy Rosen?"

"Don't call me Dorothy."

Danny's upper lip curled back and simmering fury glazed his eyes. A slight popping sound drew my attention to where he was clenching his fists tight enough to turn his knuckles white and tiny veins popped in protest. As soon as he realized I'd noted the change in him, he released his grip, and his mask of arrogance fit snugly back in place.

"I must have heard you wrong," said the deep, measured words from above. "Because last I saw of Emily Rosen, she was an old miserable shrew, and you, pretty little flower, are not her." The way his accent curled around the words added an extra layer of malice to every beautiful syllable.

Crowe inclined his head to the loft. "How about instead of acting like a heartless brute, you come down here and join the conversation." The shadowed figure vanished, reappearing in the living area in a matter of moments.

Everything about his presence seemed to fill up the room. I couldn't stop looking at him. His eyes gleamed a striking gray, like fresh tin. They cut through me like an axe, and it would seem that he was getting a good look at me for the first time, too. His assessing gaze faltered as it raked over the red streaks painting my legs and then again at the mark that had blossomed across my cheek.

I could feel the other men's eyes on me, joining the stranger's. If I wanted their attention, I most definitely had it now. "When I turned 21, all of the funds that I inherited from my parents were transferred from my Aunt Em to me. I just need the right person to help me access them and ensure that they can't end up back in the hands of my aunt."

It wasn't lost on me that I was sitting, but none of the men sat. Making their height that much more looming. But then again, Henry looked down on me my whole life, and look where that got him. The image of his shocked, bulging eyes right before he was tossed into the air filled my mind with macabre satisfaction.

"I think maybe we need to start from the beginning," Crowe said. "Gigi requested that one of us be available for the job tonight. When I met her at the rendezvous point, she told me to do a pick up in the basement but wouldn't give me any information beyond that."

"She was infuriatingly vague when I spoke with her on the phone earlier, too," Danny added.

"I secured the loading dock and got a front-row seat in the security booth to watch this little firecracker beat Eastin Witcher's face in with a snow globe."

"Wait, Eastin Witcher is dead?" The third man asked. He leaned with both elbows on the island, and a flash of righteous anger flitted across his stony face. Whatever his story, there was no love lost between him and Eastin.

"She's dead," I replied firmly.

"With that stupid snow globe of the building she keeps on her desk?" Danny asked.

I shrugged. "I didn't have many options."

With that, the third of their party decided he was committed to the conversation and pulled a stool out to face the three of us. "We've all wanted to murder her at one point or another, but how is it *you* managed to kill her? I find it hard to believe that you weren't immediately gunned down. I've been doing this for a very long time, and I've *never* been able to work out a way around her security detail."

I tilted my head to the side and took a moment to study the man. His dark hair was messy, like his idea of grooming was simply running his fingers through it. Equally unbothered was the way a light beard dusted his rectangular jawline. While all of it worked to emphasize his attractiveness, the really astonishing thing was his skin. What was once warm olive toned skin was stained with shades of grey and black. The stream of tattoos peaked out from beneath this tank and spilled down his arms to the tips of each finger. He must have sat for hundreds of hours under a needle. I couldn't help but wonder what might have inspired him to undergo such a transformation. Anyone with that much ink did it for reasons more than aesthetics, even if those aesthetics were magnetic.

"Sure, cupcake." I forced a laugh. It sounded fake, but I didn't care. "You expect me to tell you all my secrets? But what about you? I don't even know your name."

"From where I'm sitting, you don't really have a choice," Danny countered.

I looked over my shoulder to Crowe, hoping that he might speak up.

"I know it's probably hard to talk about, Darling, but we really need the full picture if we're going to keep you safe. Niccolo will play nice. If he doesn't, then I'll shove my fist down his throat so he can't speak."

"You could try."

"Your name is Niccolo?" Well, that explained the accent.

"Just tell us your story," he grumbled.

-8-
DANNY

Dorothy shifted uneasily on her stool. Her fingers kept drifting to the hem of her shirt in a futile attempt to pull it over the curve of her ass, and it was distracting as hell. It was also taking everything in me not to study the angry red stripes curling around the edges of her thighs.

It didn't compute. What kind of treachery had Dorothy done to make Emily Rosen ship her only heir to Eastin Witcher, a butcher and a sadist? She had to know that Eastin would kill her.

Dorothy answered my thoughts, "'When I was a baby, my Aunt Em made a deal with Eastin. In exchange for killing my parents, Em would use the resources available to help secure the Eastern Quadrant. Eastin drove the car my parents were driving into a lake. When they died, all of my family's money went into a trust for my aunt to control until I turned 21."

"Who were your parents that they had enough money to set up two separate criminal empires?" I thought through what I knew of The Farm and every long-standing family in Oz. I couldn't remember any massive criminal names disappearing off the board, but then again, if it was done right, maybe nobody knew. Emily Rosen didn't exist before Cyclone Shipping started providing Oz with everything from imports to people. Records stopped at the formation of the company. She had one living heir, her adopted niece. I had an entire drawer of Farm research in my office upstairs. I felt like a fool for not recognizing the security photo posted with Westin's bid, but I did now.

"They were nobody. I didn't even know I was born into money until Eastin told me."

"Or your aunt was happy leaving you ignorant." Crowe leaned back against the wall, arms folded neatly across his chest. "What were their names? Maybe we'll know something you don't."

Dorothy's eyes narrowed skeptically, but then the ice in her veins warmed. "Ella and Darren Gallant."

My mind came to a screaming halt.

"Holy fuck," whispered Crowe.

Dorothy didn't seem to notice how the three of us all tensed at the name. She kept babbling on. "My aunt changed my last name when she adopted me, but they were—"

"The Premier of Ozmandria, or well, Darren Gallant was until he was assassinated." I leaned into what I was saying, pushing closer to her so she was forced to crane her neck. "Their assassination was what allowed the four quadrants to be established in the first place. When Darren and his cabinet died, Oz became fair game for anyone who could muscle it into their control. I'd say it was a coup, but that doesn't quite cover the way the entire structure of government was wiped out in a single night." I huffed a laugh, "Turns out you actually are a Princess or as good as this fucked up country has for royalty."

The cracked pink lips that up until now had been carefully locked into a tight line went slack. She licked them. "But that's not..."A small disbelieving exhale left her. "I would know if—"

"Would you, though?" Crowe interjected. "You said Em kept you sequestered at the Farm. How would you know anything about Oz, other than what she told you?"

"I wasn't exactly sequestered. We did occasionally travel when Em had business."

"Let me guess, to processing centers in Oz?"

"Mostly, she ignored me. Until she didn't."

"Can we skip ahead to current events?" Nick looked bored, but from the slice of his eyes across the room, I knew better. Dorothy made a tiny annoyed sound, turning away from him and not bothering to acknowledge his comment at all.

"My twenty-first birthday was a month ago, and two days ago, Em decided to let Eastin finish the job she started seventeen years ago. Next thing I knew, I was beaten, ziptied, and headed to East Oz."

Nick circled back to face Dorothy. I knew that comment struck him deep. The tattoos might be covering all of the scars, but it wasn't that long ago we were freeing him from Eastin's basement of horrors. If anyone knew exactly the level of cruelty she could inflict, it was him.

His large hand came up, grabbing her chin and forcing her to look at him. The muscles of her jaw tightened in defiance, her brows pinched together, making those hazel eyes flash with even more ferocity.

His accent was thick, as it always was when he was letting his emotions get the best of him. "What did she do to you? Eastin is...was a sadist, putting it lightly. I doubt she would have waited long to make an *impression*. What did she do that pushed you into bashing her face in?"

Dorothy jerked her face out of his hand, but her eyes lingered on his knuckles. She drifted a finger over the thin white lines pushing up beneath the word, "Again." Her head tilted in confusion, then she looked at the matching letters inked on his other hand. The wheels of her mind turned as she pieced it together, mouthing, "Never Again."

Crowe clapped his hands, breaking the hush that had fallen in the room. "Your fascination with pain aside, Eastin whipped the fuck out of Thea every time she opened that sweet mouth of hers."

Dorothy cringed, fidgeting with the hem of her shirt. For the first time since arriving in my garage, she looked meek.

"Sorry, beautiful, but they would have learned that information regardless when we cleaned up your back. Despite his bedside manner, Nick is best at wound care."

Of course, I'd seen the blood staining her filthy blue shirt. I just hadn't expected it to be hers. Although, now that I was looking, I could see where the fabric had dried to her back.

She gave a wary nod. "What happens next?"

"Gigi's up to something," Nick posited while rubbing the scruff of his jaw.

"That's what I've been saying this whole fucking time. It's nice to know you decided to finally start listening. How could she have known Thea would kill Eastin? She came to us two days ago with this pick-up? I saw it happen. It was lucky Thea got the hit in when she did."

"Unless Gi had her own plan, and Thea beat her to the punch."

"Hmm. Maybe." I ran a hand along the bar. There were too many pieces missing.

"Gigi got me out of the building."

"Actually, I got you out of the building," Crowe retorted.

"No. The emerald got us out of the building, and Gigi gave me the emerald. You just drove the car."

"I did a bit more than that."

I froze. "Emerald, as in a Witcher Emerald?"

"Regardless of Gigi's agenda, I know what I want," Dorothy said, sitting upright and folding her hands neatly on the counter. "I need The Wizard to hack Em's business and transfer it to me or untie whatever she's done to make it look like it's hers. Then I'm going to take my shiny new identity and leave the nightmare of Oz far behind me."

"And you just expect Emily Rosen to take this lying down?"

"No, but when I'm a ghost, and she's penniless, what can she do? Like you said, she's nothing more than an old shrew."

"Nobody sees The Wizard." I waved off her plan.

"No one even knows what they look like. What makes you think they'll help you?" Nick added.

"Gigi seemed to think he would," Dorothy snapped back.

"That's hardly a guarantee," Nick replied with a metallic bite to his tone.

"And you were what? Going to walk your naked, fine ass to the center of Oz?" I added.

"That $50K won't go unnoticed. The moment you walk past these walls, you'll have a dozen hitmen on you," Crowe added.

"True. Which is why we're bringing Dorothy to The Wizard," I said coolly. We would take her right to him, just not the way she was thinking.

"I'm sorry, what?" Nick said, almost laughing out his disbelief. "Danny, I mean, come on. You're going to let an easy payout walk away?"

"We've smuggled harder things into the Emerald City," Crowe said.

"The Wizard is going to give us what is in those accounts, and in exchange, Dorothy doesn't get handed over to Westin."

"That's my money. You don't get to make that decision."

"Nothing is *yours* anymore. Make no mistake, Princess, Eastin might have paid the bill of sale, but we collected the merchandise. You were *ours* the moment you sat your sweet ass in our cab. That air you're breathing might feel like freedom, but it's not. If I wanted to tie you up and mail you off like a pretty little package, I could. You can make all the demands you want, but it doesn't change the fact that you don't have any control here. I do."

Nick cleared his throat. "What makes you think The Wizard will even bother with her."

"Because she has that." I reached out, running an index finger from the base of her neck to where the emerald lay nestled between the valley of her breasts. It glittered in the industrial lights hanging over the island. Green rainbows shot out from it with each rise and fall of her chest, a cadence that sped up the longer my hand lingered.

Thea snatched my finger, twisting it just shy of snapping the joint. "The next time you touch me without my permission, you better be prepared to lose something precious." The fire in her eyes was damn near enchanting, and lethal. No wonder she'd been able to take out Eastin. There was something ruthless living at her core. Any woman raised by Emily Rosen would have to be. I had no doubt she would make good on that promise, or at least try to.

She released me with a vindicated sneer. I shook out my hand, but before she could relax back on her stool, I surged forward. Dorothy might be used to snapping her fingers and watching boys jump, but it was time she realized where her position was.

My hand wrapped around her throat, lifting her into the air. She gave a strangled scream of surprise, but I kept moving forward, toppling her to the ground. Slamming into the tile, Dorothy howled at the impact. I easily pinned her arms above her and braced my legs against the knees she was already trying to ram into me. This girl was scrappy, but even as she fought, her body was betraying her. Dorothy's hips lifted into mine, and her spine arched like she wanted me to throw her around. Fuck me, I wanted to.

"This is how it's going to be. That money you say is waiting for you, is already ours. The Wizard will transfer it to us. In the meantime, we'll keep the Monkeys off your back long enough to claim what's owed." Tightening my grip, I added, "You try anything, and I'll let Nick ship you to Westin in pieces."

The Wizard would want the key to the Witcher Empire. He'd want it enough to finally acquiesce to my demands. I've been waiting years for this kind of leverage, and it fell into my lap from the most unlikely of benefactors.

Crowe snagged the back of my collar, throwing me hard enough I slid into the island. "She's injured, you prick. And that—" He pointed to Dorothy, who was struggling to climb back onto her stool. "—was completely uncalled for."

"She needed to learn—"

"You hurt her again, and it won't be Thea ending up in pieces. I will fucking tear you apart."

Dorothy blinked at Crowe. She looked just as stunned as I was. Crowe had never threatened me like this before. I'd seen other people at the end of that death stare, but it had never been me. What Dorothy didn't know was that Crowe was, in many ways, the worst of us. He seemed like he was supportive, but I'd seen him pull more triggers than anyone, and his hands would never truly be free of the blood that stained them.

"Fine," she muttered. "When do we leave?"

"When I say we do."

"It will probably take a few days to make contact with the Wizard," Crowe added. He reached out and placed a hand over hers. "Not just anyone can gain a meeting with them."

"And what am I supposed to do in the meantime?"

"We'll find you a bed. You can start there."

Dorothy stood up quickly, shoving the stool across the tile floor. It tipped and clattered to the ground with a loud BANG. She winced in pain, then her features locked down in stern determination. With a hard slap against the counter, she said, "Let's get something *VERY* clear. I'm not sleeping with you. Sex is off the table." Then she grimaced and swayed, forcing her to latch onto the island for support. Crowe stiffened, and I knew he'd seen her waver, too. The damage done must have been worse than Dorothy was letting on.

"So dramatic," I intoned, "I meant to sleep. Just because we can see those lacy white panties doesn't mean anyone wants in them."

"I wouldn't say no," Crowe said, raising his hand and laughing.

"Well, I'm not giving her my bed." Nick got up and strode back toward the stairs that led to the loft. "You *cazzos* can deal with it[1]. The entire idea is a bad one. I still say we should just send her to Westin and take the easy payout."

"Oh, but I'm sure you won't have any trouble taking your share of Thea's inheritance," Crowe quipped.

Nick didn't bother turning around or even saying a retort. He held his tattooed middle finger aloft and disappeared into the shadows like he was made of them.

"She can stay with me," Crowe said before turning Dorothy towards him. "But first, we should really assess the damage Eastin and Em's people did." He gave a long scan of her body, lifting up the hem of her shirt to show a dark purple bruise covering her entire side. "You need bandaged up, maybe even stitches. An ice compress for swelling wouldn't be a bad idea either. He won't like it, but I'll make Nick bring the full kit downstairs."

Dorothy wrapped her arms around her middle. "I really don't want *him* touching any part of me."

"Who would," Crowe laughed, his eyes alight with his joke looking to mine for acknowledgement. "It'll be ok. I'll be there. Nothing will happen."

"We can probably find you something for the pain," I suggested. Why was I offering this brat any kindness? She certainly hadn't earned it.

---

1. You dicks can deal with it.

"So I pass out? Thanks, but no thanks. I've seen firsthand what men get up to when women have no choice."

The thought was truly distasteful. I'm sure Emily's boys were less than hospitable to the girls who were processed on The Farm. Why any man would want a limp and unresponsive girl beneath them was beyond me.

My lip sneered up. "Princess, I wouldn't touch you even if you were on your knees begging to choke on my cock."

Lies. All Lies. Her puffy lips wrapped around my dick, tears leaking from her eyes as she begged for air, was just about the sexiest thing to ever cross my mind. "Suffer for all I care, but if you want those wounds to heal, the best thing you can do is sleep."

Crowe punched my shoulder. "You have zero tact. None. Go away. You make literally nothing better sitting around here antagonizing everyone. We'll see you in the morning when you resemble a semi-decent human being." Crowe, the bastard, turned his back on me and brought a soft hand up to cradle her cheek. I can't believe that sweet shit worked for him, but there Dorothy was, lapping it up like a puppy begging for scraps. "Trust me, beautiful, this isn't the first time we've had someone banged up in here. You aren't the worst, and you won't be the last."

Dorothy tilted her cheek into his hand, then realizing what she was doing, slapped it away. "Let's get it over with."

Deep down, a warm feeling of satisfaction bloomed in my stomach. Good girl.

-9-
THEA

Danny pulled a very expensive-looking bottle from an upper shelf, making a shooing motion at me like I was a stray dog who'd taken a shit on his lawn.

Oh, fuck no. I ground my teeth, fighting the impulse to break something he'd miss. I probably shouldn't provoke him further...probably.

"Ignore him, Thea. I'll get you whatever you want downstairs." Crowe started walking down a back hall. Swallowing the bitterness down, I did the smart thing and followed him.

Ice clinked off glass and there was the dull pop of a cork being pulled. The sound grated against my nerves, making a muscle behind my eye twitch.

"Heh, of course you will," Danny scoffed. "Typical spoiled princess. I bet men kiss your feet everywhere you go."

I spun on my heel. Who needed safe? Who needed smart, when this asshole was begging to be put in his place?

With a few quick steps, I snatched the glass from Danny's fingers just as it was raised to his lips. There was a healthy two-finger pour of what smelled like whiskey in the glass, not that it mattered. He could have been drinking battery acid, and I still would have downed the entire amount in one long swallow. It burned going down, warming my stomach and already making my muscles feel more relaxed.

Danny's hand hovered where it had held the glass only a second ago, blinking slowly while trying to process what I'd just done.

"Heh," I said, mocking his dismissive and completely unnecessary exhale, "I've had better." I slid the glass across the counter to him. *Fuck, that felt good.*

"That was a fifty-year-old scotch you just threw back like it was some watered-down rail drink."

Of course he cared more about the manner in which I drank my pilfered liquor, rather than the fact I'd stolen his expensive booze at all.

I picked up the decanter and refilled his glass. The scotch rolled in a slow pour, showing just how smooth it was. How much had that liquid gold cost him? Was that a hundred-dollar swallow? Two hundred?

"That's better." Danny seemed pleased that I'd taken the time to replace what was stolen, but I'd never really been the accommodating type. I lifted the glass and tipped the liquid heat down my throat before he could utter so much as a word in protest.

Bracing both hands on the counter, Danny's long torso easily leaned over the island. Maybe one stolen drink was permissible, but two? The menace in his eyes made them look molten. His hand came forward, and I braced for the slap that surely was coming.

"You aren't scared of anything, are you, Princess?"

Where I steeled myself for violence, there was none. He slowly swiped his thumb over my lip, catching a bead of scotch on his finger. With laser focus, I watched the way the tip of his tongue laved at the surface, teeth raking the side. From the way his lips twisted into a smirk, I knew he was aware of exactly how sensuous that small gesture had been.

"You coming?" Crowe said, dispelling the charge that had filled the air between us. He pulled open a door, triggering an automatic light that filled the hallway with a cool blue glow.

"Run along." Danny looked like he'd just won some unspoken challenge. Fucker.

"Thanks for the drink," I said with a smile, quickly rejoining Crowe.

"Be careful, Princess. This is me playing nice," Danny called to me. "Though something tells me you don't really want it nice."

"I wouldn't know what nice looks like," I replied, not bothering to turn around.

Low enough so that only I could hear him, Crowe whispered, "I'll have to see what I can do about that."

His arm protectively circled around my shoulders, doing little to dispel the unease slithering through me.

"Downstairs?" I said, trying not to let my anxiety make my voice shake. Nothing good ever came of being brought below ground. I definitely didn't like the idea of trapping myself in a place with only one way out.

"Yeah, I've got the downstairs. Nick has the loft. Danny has the suite on the main floor behind the den. You'll like it. It's cozy. The basement has my room, a gym, and... well, it's not important what all is down there." He extended his hand to me, waiting for me to take it. His smile seemed gentle enough.

After meeting the rest of them and seeing a glimpse of what they do, I wondered if this nice guy routine was all a mask he used to lure prey. Whatever it was, it was working. Consider me lured. Despite knowing better, I took his hand. Because, fuck it.

"Color me curious. This place is pretty nice for three guys who *drive cabs.*"

"Sure, it is... *And* I'm sure Em's farm has all those electrified fences and men armed with semi-automatics to keep the cows safe."

"Touché."

"Yellow Brick is just a convenient cover, and the money practically cleans itself." Crowe pushed open a door at the base of the stairs. "Here we are."

Beyond him was a large room. Not a room, but a suite of rooms. There was a small living area with a large fish tank set into one of the walls. It washed the couch, table, and chairs in fluttering light. Beyond that, a large bed sat against a far wall. A forgotten light from an adjoining bathroom leaked into the dark room, illuminating still-rumpled sheets from the night before.

Crowe flicked on a lamp. Like the rest of the house, his room was neat, minimal. It made me wonder if they all lived like at any moment they might never return. "I'll sleep in here on the couch. You can have the bed. It would be better if you could stretch out on your stomach to sleep."

I nodded. The passing time had not made the throbbing at my back go down. My stressing muscles pulled against the wounds every time I tensed up.

Crowe walked over to an intercom set beside the doorway. Pushing a button, he said, "Bring the med kit down here." He didn't wait for a reply before walking to a small kitchenette and pulling two beers from the fridge.

I bent over to look into the fish tank. A large tropical fish with long, colorful spines swam slowly around. It was a massive tank, and yet this fish was the only one in it, along with some plants and a replica shipwreck. Was that because this fish didn't play well with others? Or was she just kept alone to sell off once she'd stopped being useful?

There was the hiss of a cap being lifted, then the cool glass of a bottle slid down my arm to my hand, eliciting a shiver from me.

"The light is better in the bathroom, but you're probably going to need to lay down for this... and maybe drink up. That can't hurt either."

I took a long swig from the bottle. It was a light, malty, pale ale with some serious hop to it. In combination with the scotch, it was strong enough that it made my head swim. I took another swig and smacked my lips at the piney aftertaste.

"Do you like it?"

The label on the bottle was for an indie brewery in Emerald City. I wasn't surprised that Crowe stocked small batch beer. It made sense, in the same way that Danny pouring a fifty-year-old scotch was perfectly logical.

"Sure. Do you have any food in that tiny, tiny kitchen? The booze... it's going straight to my head."

"Yeah," he said with a breathy exhale, reaching up to scratch the back of his neck. "I think I have some crackers in here somewhere. Maybe tomorrow we can try something a bit heavier. If you try to do too much too quickly, you'll make yourself sick."

Crowe tossed me a pack of saltines at the same time the door swung open. A broody, grim-faced Nick waited on the other side. The hood of his sweatshirt was pulled up, casting his face in shadow. I half expected to see a face of bone peaking out.

"You could come in instead of standing there like the angel of death."

Nick moved into the room with near silent steps. He dropped a heavy box onto the floor. Its many drawers and compartments clattered. "I'm here. Came down all these damn steps. So, either we do this now, or I'm leaving, and you can deal with it yourself."

He settled squarely in front of me. I tightened my jaw and strengthened my stance as much as my aching body would allow. Not that it did anything.

"It's cute that you think that baby scowl is intimidating." He reached for the hem of my shirt, the backs of his fingers curling against my upper thighs.

"Hey!" I shouted, slapping at his hands.

"You're going to have to get over it. This is coming off one way or another."

"Not in here, the bedroom," Crowe interjected.

"That's what you object to?" My blood was rising, taking my fury with it. I could feel it burning my cheeks and the back of my eyes. "Not that Nick decided to start stripping me, only that we were doing it in the wrong room? My savior."

Ignoring me, he added, "I saw the beating she took. It's going to take time, and she's going to need to lie down. But first, I'm going to have to clean her up. It'll be a miracle if she isn't already fighting off an infection."

Nick's eyes stayed on Crowe like they were having a long and silent conversation. When he spoke again, the octave and tone of his voice were dramatically different. "Why don't you start by telling me exactly how you were injured." He was unnervingly calm. The steel of his eyes snagged on the bruise along my cheek. The unexpected empathy evaporated the steam of my anger like opening the bathroom door after a hot shower.

I pulled at the wrapper of my beer, tearing off small pieces of the label. I wasn't sure that I liked how easily he had unsettled my defenses.

Nick grabbed my shoulders and started walking me backwards towards the bathroom. "You're going to have to pick. Are you the vulnerable and wounded heiress or the tough-as-nails ballbuster? This flip-flopping of attitude is making me dizzy with indifference."

"Maybe I'm both." My eyes flicked over his shoulder towards Crowe. He put his beer down on a side table and followed along. I did my best to hide my relief. He wasn't going to force me to go through this alone. I'd always licked my wounds on my own before. But nothing had ever been this bad before either, and now that the adrenaline was gone, I was trying very hard not to focus on how completely fucked my situation had become.

The cold tile of the bathroom floor slid under my feet until I bumped into the counter. Nick reached around me, turning on the faucet and pulling the stopper to fill the sink.

"You can be whatever you like, so long as you cooperate. If you don't want me to strip you, then this would be the time when you take this off." He pulled the bottle from my hands, draining the remaining contents. I watched the thick muscles of his throat work as he gulped down the beer, then he effortlessly tossed it over his shoulder to a waiting Crowe like they did this all the time.

I let out a long sigh. It was only skin. I could handle this and whatever else these two decided to throw at me.

Crossing my arms, I attempted to pull the shirt up. It got caught, the fabric clinging to the wounds, pulling at the inflamed flesh, and tugging on the ribs in my side. I barely managed to stop the sound that crept out, strangling it before it left my throat.

A surprisingly gentle hand smoothed down the outside of my arm. "Now, can I help?"

I nodded, not able to lower my pride enough to ask for assistance in something as simple as removing my shirt.

"Turn around." Nick made a twirly motion with his finger. When my back was to him, I felt more than heard him approach. Heat radiated towards me in waves. Shadows fell over me as his broad frame blocked out the light from above. "Can you lift your arms?"

I bit down and lifted them. My teeth pushed against my lips hard enough that the copper tang of blood on my tongue matched the burn along my back. I refused to cry out from such a simple and mundane movement.

Crowe came around in front of me, his sapphire blue gaze steady. A solid lump formed in my throat. He was about to get an eyeful of a whole lot of titty. I linked my fingers together over my head, squinting as Nick started peeling the shirt away.

"Don't tense. Keep your eyes on me, beautiful."

I opened them and forced a slow exhale. The blue of his eyes was so steadying, even more than the soft tone of his voice.

"That's it, breathe."

"*Porca puttana*." [1] The sound that left Nick was akin to a low growl. "That sadistic bitch." Feather-light fingers drifted in diagonals over my back. "Crowe, there must be two dozen lashes here." His fingers traced the lines at the back of my legs, forcing me to jump from the unexpected caress. "Another dozen down here."

"I know. I told you. I saw her take the beating. It was a fucking metal-tipped flail."

"It's probably closer to three dozen," I interjected, lowering my arms to cover my breasts as much as my body would allow. "She struck me three times on the back and once on the legs." I might be mostly naked, but I refused to appear vulnerable.

"This," I said, pointing to my side, "was from Henry's boot." The bruise there was a dark, angry purple, tinged green on the edges from where it was already healing. "I'm fairly certain I have a cracked rib or two."

I framed my face with my palm like I was some kind of sweet model posing for her photo shoot. "And this was from the backhand I took moments before Eastin threw his ugly ass from the top of a high rise." I fluttered my eyelashes for emphasis before my smile dropped into a scowl. "Now, if your eyes have had their fill, can we get on with the sutures and bandages part of the evening. It's cold as fuck in this room, and I'd rather not spend the entire night in only my underwear."

"Before we can do any stitching, you're going to need to clean up as much as you can. I can literally see the filth on you, and I'm going to burn this shirt." He flipped off the sink, steam rising from the basin. Snatching up a washcloth Nick dipped it into the water and a masterfully vivid fantasy popped unbidden into

---

1. Holy shit.

my mind. The brush of fabric and the slide of soap from those strong tattooed hands. Fuck. I mentally slapped my libido in the face.

"I'm not washing myself while you watch, perv."

Nick's eyebrow lifted in challenge, turning my valid concerns into a joke like he'd seen that fantasy play out all over my face. I almost cracked a smile, almost.

"Get out, Nick. I'll take it from here." Nick looked like he was about to protest, but Crowe cut him off. "You've seen what we're working with. Now go get set up in the bedroom. We'll be out in a minute."

The door silently closed behind him, leaving Crowe and I alone. He walked to the tub, turning on the faucet. I crossed my arms over my chest while the room filled with humid air and the mirrors fogged up.

Crowe sat on the edge of the tub, grinning like he'd just scratched a winning lottery ticket. The pure mischief in his eyes made my heart start doing gymnastics. "Come on, beautiful. Come join me. I promise to be gentle."

The draw to him was practically magnetic, making my instincts scream, *"Yes. Yes. Yes."* But I knew better. Yeah, no. This was not happening.

"Cover your eyes. I'm not some stripper on a stage and you look entirely too satisfied by what's going on here."

His hand went to his eyes, fingers splaying to peek through them. "Can you blame me?—"

"Close them." I meant it to be stern, but the laugh at the end of the command belied how good it felt to be the center of his attention. If I wasn't careful, it would be very easy to become addicted to the heat of his gaze.

"—Even in this state, you're gorgeous." Crowe dutifully closed his eyes.

"Right, " I scoffed after ensuring that he was genuinely not looking. I kicked off my underwear and grabbed for a washcloth, soaking it several times before drawing the soapy fabric over my chest and between my legs—definitely not thinking about his long fingers while I did. Or Nick's. Definitely. "Filthy, beaten women do it for you?"

"Strong, impossible to crush spirits do. Beneath those bruises, Thea, yes, *it does it* for me."

I paused.

"Come over here, and I'll show you exactly what *you do to me* and the many, many things I can *do to you.*"

Yes. Yes. Yes. Ignoring the way my body was beginning to chant, I dropped the cloth in his lap and turned my back to him. "How about instead you help me with the hard-to-reach places?"

"Fuck, Thea." His hands settled on my hips, drawing me closer, but it wasn't flirtation coloring his words anymore. "Oz damn, as much as I want to play—" He sucked in air, one hand slipping over my ass cheek. "—and I really fucking do—" I looked over my shoulder, expecting to see hunger in his eyes, but instead found devastating rage. "This is so much worse than I realized. I'm going to beat Danny purple for throwing you to the ground like that."

"I'm fine." I wasn't, but I couldn't handle seeing how my pain was affecting him.

"You really aren't." Crowe tugged me onto his lap. He tenderly kissed my shoulder before dragging the cloth across the few unmarred parts of my skin. Slowly, the dried blood and dirt sloughed off, giving me back a tiny bit of my humanity with each swipe.

When he finished, Crowe tossed the cloth on the counter and cupped the back of my neck. I rotated into him, like a flower turning towards the sun. Brushing his lips over the bruise on my cheek, he said, "How could anyone do this to you—" The fingertips of his free hand ghosted over my throbbing side. "—when all I can think about is dropping to my knees in devotion?"

A loud series of bangs made me jump. Nick yelled through the door, "Flirt later. I'm not about to be doing this all night."

"I wasn't flirting," I yelled back.

"I was," Crowe said with a laugh.

Nick pushed the door open. "Every word out of that brainless head is a flirtation, Crowe. She knows it. I know it. The fucking old ladies that work the community garden down the street know it." He threw a towel at me. "Let's go."

Crowe guided me out the door, helping me to ease onto the bed on my stomach, with the towel loosely draped over my waist and hips.

"We're going to start first by cleaning the open wounds. It's going to burn like a mother-fucker." Nick's heartless indifference shifted like he knew exactly what it was to be draped in pain. "Then, we'll close off the biggest ones, followed by bandages and gauze. After that, I'm going to wrap your torso to try to keep things from shifting." I could almost taste the empathy radiating off of him. "Are you ready?"

I nodded.

"Good. If you can, bring your arms above your head. Don't use a pillow. That will make your back arch too much."

I gently shifted, easing my arms as high as I could manage.

"I know you already turned down Danny's offer for some painkillers, but do you want to reconsider?" Crowe said, lying down on the bed so that he was eye to eye with me. He laced his fingers through the hand closest to him. His other arm stretched over my head to rest against my wrist.

"No. I have a high pain threshold. I can handle it."

"If you say so. I would take it." His eyes flicked up to Nick, and that was the only warning I had before a blistering pain flooded my senses. Crowe's grip tightened, holding my hands in place so I couldn't buck or squirm.

"Shhh," he said gently. The texture of whatever Nick was using to clean the wound raked over my back a second time, and I screamed. I couldn't help it. No amount of self-control could hold it back. A third pass of his hand and my vision turned to white. My teeth clamped down on the inside of my cheek in a miserable attempt to rein in my reaction to the pain. But holy fuck, that hurt. It hurt worse than when Eastin had whipped me in the first place.

"You're doing so good, Darling Thea."

"That's the first two cleaned," Nick said.

"Only two?" I whimpered.

He bent down and swiped up the line of tears that I hadn't realized had fallen from my eyes. "I'm going to put a salve on. That should cool the burning sensation a bit."

The salve smelled heavily of eucalyptus and peppermint and was cold enough that my teeth rattled. The contrast between the hot burn of the antiseptic and the cool relief of the salve was disorienting. I was glad I hadn't had time to eat the crackers because I was sure they would have come back up in that moment.

The night passed in an agonizing crawl. Crowe stayed the entire time. He alternated between holding my hands so I didn't hurt myself and running a cool cloth over my forehead. He only made one joke about the generous side boob I was showing, and by the end of it, I didn't care who saw what anymore. Lying in a bed of only pain, there wasn't room for modesty.

At one point, around my lower back, I blacked out. When I woke, it was to the sound of tape being stretched and torn. My eyes only fluttered for a second before I sank once more into unconsciousness.

A soft brush of fingers against my cheek woke me. "There's my girl."

"Did I pass out again?" I mumbled into the mattress.

"Yeah. You lasted a lot longer than I expected you to. We need you to stand, Darling. So that we can wrap your side and back." Crowe gave a gentle tug on my arm, supporting my weight while Nick wrapped the bandage around and around my torso. With my head still held aloft on Crowe's shoulder, I peeked a glance at the gauze and tape visible on my thighs. I couldn't even remember him touching my legs.

"Done. Lie back down. I'm going to put a cold compress on your back."

I let the soothing chill of the ice pack carry me away. This world was still too painful, too raw, and I didn't want to be here anymore. I wanted to sleep. I wanted to escape into dreams that would hopefully save me from the nightmare that had become my reality.

-10-
THEA

I woke the next morning to the disorienting darkness of Crowe's basement. The only light in the room was the pale green glow of a button on the intercom panel next to the door. There wasn't even a bedstand clock. Putting my hand to my head, I willed my swimming mind to find the surface. Every inch of my body ached. The throbbing heat radiating from my back was intense enough that I was surprised I hadn't scorched the sheets.

Sitting up, the soft bedding slipped from where it'd been draped over my body. Cool air caressed the very naked skin of my chest. With the pebbling of my skin came the flood of memories— Crowe's hands holding me in place and the tender look in his eyes as he kept me steady through the pain. The way Nick's rough palm pressed my shoulders into the mattress when I involuntarily bucked back against him, or how he would soothingly speak in that beautiful language while I fought past the tears.

As my reality came crashing back, I swallowed down the panic. Danny insisted that I was a hostage until he got his payout, but it also meant he needed to keep me safe until then. I just had to keep telling myself it could be a lot worse. I could be trapped in Eastin's clutches, powerless against whatever demented way she'd planned to kill me.

Scanning the darkness, I looked for signs of Crowe. A tinge of disappointment ricocheted unexpectedly through me when I realized I was alone in the dark. I didn't know what to make of that. Did I really want Crowe's blue eyes staring back at me when I awoke? Had that one adrenaline-fueled ride out of town and night of pain really changed me so much? It didn't matter.

He left me to rest for however long I had been down here. Without windows or a clock, it was impossible to determine how long I'd been unconscious.

I fumbled around the side of the bed until I found the nightstand with the lamp. I clicked it on and breathed a long sigh of relief. My anxiety immediately recoiled now that I wasn't suffocating on darkness.

My body was wrecked. There were streaks of something orange around the gauze. The adhesive edge of each itched and pulled at my skin. The bandage at the center of me covered most of my back, but of course, when they bound my ribs, they avoided all the important parts. I tried not to think too hard about what wrapping me had entailed.

On a chair next to the bed was a pair of boxer shorts and a T-shirt. They were huge, but the idea of putting anything form-fitting on made me wince. Not to mention the fact that three bachelor men probably didn't stock much from the women's department. Still, after the past few days, it felt like true kindness.

What I really wanted was a shower. Even with the quick wash-up I'd done the night before, it felt like I was covered in a lifetime's worth of grime. My skin still prickled with Eastin's touch and Henry's abuse. I could smell the desperation leaking from my pores, and I hated it.

I hobbled my way from the bedroom into the ample bathroom. The shower was large enough to house a small city of people, with heads pointing in all directions. The idea of standing beneath that spray was enough to make me moan.

I flinched when I finally met my reflection. The girl in the mirror looked more like a discarded rag doll and less like the woman who would crush Em's empire beneath her heel. Because when the Wizard took Em's money, I would make sure he did more than bankrupt her. I would have him burn every connection, eliminate every ally, and bury her in enough evidence that the authorities would have no choice but to lock her up and throw away the key. I would get justice for all the lives she'd ruined on her path to the top, starting with my parents.

Running my hands over the ends of the bandage, I twisted to try and look in the mirror. There were fasteners holding it together along my spine. I bent my arms behind me as best I could, but my flexibility was shot. Every movement pulled on something it shouldn't, making it nearly impossible to reach the ends. Meaning there would be no way for me to bathe myself without soaking the entire dressing. I didn't know much about triage or wound care, but I was certain you weren't supposed to soak your bandages.

I let out a scream of frustration, throwing the few things on the counter at the far wall. The soap dish and lotion clattered to the floor in an unceremonious cacophony that echoed around the room. It wasn't enough that Em had conspired against my parents, locked me away for my entire life, taken my inheritance, and sold my freedom to a sadist. Now, I couldn't even bathe myself. I felt helpless. The feeling was so potent it made me nauseous.

"Problems?" Crowe's playful voice cut through the silent bathroom, making me jump, while he leaned in the doorway like it was your average Sunday morning.

I grabbed the towel on the rack, pulling it across my chest. Not that it mattered. There wasn't anything in this bathroom he hadn't seen plenty of last night. "No. I'm managing just fine."

Beneath his cavalier smile, Crowe sipped at a mug of coffee. Its rich scent floated to me, making my stomach flip and audibly gurgle. His brows lifted in surprise.

"Do you want some? Nick made it, so it's actually delicious." He held out the mug to me. "Consider it a peace offering."

"Were we at war?" I asked, taking the mug from him. I took a long sip and melted on the spot. A loud groan of pleasure slipped from me. It was rich, the splash of milk making it a shade lighter than chocolate. It wasn't even too sweet. People were always ruining good coffee by making it sweet.

"No, but I'd very much like to be your... ally." Crowe pushed himself onto the counter, sliding down so he was in front of me. Before I knew what he was doing, his hands were on my hips, and I was trapped in the cage of his legs. He was careful not to brush the back of mine as he pinned me in place. There was something warming in that he was still taking care of me, even amidst the guise of being playful and carefree.

"Now what, pretty girl—" He pushed my hair over my shoulder and began tracing the exposed line of my collar with his index finger. "—could the soap dish have done to make you punish it so?"

I narrowed my eyes on him, snatching the wandering hand and biting down on his finger. Hard.

"Ow." He sucked at the raw spot I left behind. "The hell was that for?" He sounded offended, but the mirth hadn't left his eyes.

I shrugged the same shoulder he had just been caressing. "Maybe I don't like—" My hand came up suddenly to my throat. Whatever I was about to say was lost the moment I noticed the absent weight of the emerald. Crowe noticed it too, already raising his hands in defense.

"Stay calm, Thea. The necklace is upstairs. We had to take it off last night, is all. Danny put it in the safe."

"The safe? I suppose that was for my own good, for safekeeping?"

"That is generally what safes are for."

"And it has nothing to do with Danny wanting to leverage the emerald with the Wizard for *my* money. That was the one thing I had to bargain with."

"Well... there is that."

"And now that gives him... *you*, one more way to control me. Ugh." I growled and slapped hard at his chest, trying to push out of the vice-like grip of his thighs. "Let go of me. I can't believe I was stupid enough to trust you. Even after I promised myself I wouldn't."

"Darling Thea, I never pretended you could trust me. I said you were safe with me. Those two aren't the same thing. So long as you had that stone around your neck, you were a walking homing signal. The vault will block the beacon. You wanted me to keep you safe, and that is exactly what I'm doing. You're going to need to wise up to the fact that with safety comes a loss of some of that freedom. Temporarily, at least. Danny won't want to keep you forever."

I pursed my lips because, damn it, he had a point. I hadn't even thought that the coding of the stone could be tracked, but of course it could.

Crowe took the mug from me, sitting it on the counter beside us. Then he grabbed the towel I was clinging to. Slowly, he reeled it in until our lips were only inches apart. "I, on the other hand, could be convinced to keep you." He closed the space between us. The heat of his lips brushing against mine caused the blood in my veins to spike. It moved in a rush that ran all the way down to the soles of my feet and spread out until every part of my body felt hot with it.

As much as that soft contact thrilled me, I didn't kiss him back. The sourness of betrayal was still too fresh to trust myself with the raw vulnerability that came from kissing someone. Perceptive as always, Crowe released my lips.

"Why don't you tell me what had you screaming loud enough I could hear you from the office upstairs."

"I couldn't possibly have screamed that loudly. We're in the basement."

"I guarantee you I can make you scream loud enough to wake the entire Eastern Territory, even from the basement... also, when you throw the soap dish at the button on the intercom, it makes it real easy to be heard upstairs."

"Oh." I looked at the wall where I had aimed my fury. The panel and its green button blinked at me. As if it was mocking me for my stupidity.

"Was it Em? Or Eastin? Fuck, I'd even believe you were screaming at Danny. I know I've woken up plenty of times wanting to cuss Dandy out."

"Dandy?"

"Ohhh." He said with a feral smile, "I guess after the emerald thing, you deserve a win, and what do I care if it pisses Danny off? He pulled a gun on us last night. He deserves a little torment."

"What the hell are you talking about?"

"I can't wait to see his face when he realizes you know. Danny's full name is... wait for it, you're going to love this." Crowe's face was positively alight with wicked joy. "Dandelion."

"Bullshit."

Crowe shook his head, crossing his heart with an index finger. "Honest to Ozma. His mother lived on a homestead outside the Ozmandrian borders. She named all her kids after flowers in tribute to the Goddess of Spring, or some shit like that. Danny's sisters were named Daffodil, Dahlia, and Daisy."

"And Dandelion," I said with a smirk. "He was the only boy?"

"The only boy. After she died, Dandy went to live with his grandmother."

Danny was an orphan, too. I didn't want anything to make me sympathize with the asshole, but there was a unique kind of kinship that came with knowing you shared similar pain with someone.

"The first day at his new school, he took an epic beating from a little punk, bitch. The kid broke his arm and busted his face over something as silly as a name. After that, Dandy dropped the D and became Danny."

"What happened to the bully?"

"Currently?"

I nodded.

"At the moment, he has his legs wrapped around the most beguiling creature he's managed to ensnare in quite a long time." The wrap of his body tightened around mine in emphasis.

"It was you," I said with disbelief. "You beat a poor, innocent child over his name?"

"I wasn't always so nice. Time changes all things."

"And you're not fucking with me?"

"No, although..." The blue of his eyes dipped to the towel. "I could be." He fingered the terrycloth covering my breasts. Crowe's fingers ran beneath the upper edge, brushing lightly against my chest in slow, sweeping strokes that pushed lower with each pass.

He didn't mean it seriously. I knew it was a flirtation, just as everything he'd said since we met was. But it didn't stop my heart from slamming against my ribs, caught somewhere between alarm and excitement.

Without meaning to, I inched towards him. My hips pressed into the curve of his. The carefully crafted space between us all but disappeared. He smelled like warmth. A heady, earthy combination of amber and cedar. Being caught in his gravity felt like lying in a field on a summer day. My skin hummed with a need to be warmed by it.

It took me too long to lift my eyes from what his hand was doing. But when I did, I immediately regretted it. Because the look he was giving me wasn't merely flirtatious anymore. It flamed with desire. The heat of his skin met his eyes and burned away all of my common sense. I wasn't thinking about the pain or the distrust. The only danger I could think about was the kind promised by that look. I wanted his hands on me in a touch that was more than bracing and to know what the weight of his body would feel like pressed against mine.

I swallowed hard, blinking in an attempt to free myself from his lure. It wasn't working. I needed to feel like more than a victim, and beneath his gaze, I felt like anything but.

His hands lifted to my neck, his long fingers cupping the back of my head. I dropped the forgotten towel, instead finding the hard planes of the thighs framing my body.

This time, when his mouth claimed mine, it wasn't chaste or soft. And unlike last time, I kissed him back, allowing his body to surge against me. He tasted like dark coffee. When his tongue moved against mine, I couldn't help but moan. He was delicious. The kiss tasted like everything Em had forbidden, everything I knew I should be cautious of, and everything I wanted to lose myself in.

He savored the kiss, taking his time and learning all the ways our mouths fit together. The calluses on his palm scraped against the soft, exposed skin on the underside of my breast, applying enough pressure to make me gasp.

Crowe's other hand angled my head to expose my neck. The lips breaking away from mine moved down the column of my throat, resting in the sensitive spot just below my ear. "I want so badly to lay you out on this counter and show you how very *nice* I can be."

"Do it," I breathed in a sultry tone I'd never heard before.

"Darling, your body can't handle the things I want to do to it right now." Crowe licked at my neck, biting down so lightly that I gave a whimper of impatience. My fingers curled into his shirt, holding on like it was a lifeline in this sea of desire.

Crowe gave an arrogant laugh into the hollow of my shoulder. "The ways I would bend you..." The hand that still cradled the back of my head tightened, holding me firmly in place. It tugged me backwards until my weight was suspended in his palm. My body arced to offer my chest to him. Golden hair dusted over my chest a second before his mouth did. It was hot against my nipple, but the sensation of his tongue was nothing compared to the teeth that followed it.

"Crowe," I pleaded.

"So sweet." His hand drifted over the bandages. "Are you wet for me, beautiful? Does that pussy ache for my touch?"

When his fingers skated over my lower abdomen, my entire body began to quake. I had to hold onto the planes of his chest to keep from falling the moment my knees gave out.

"All that time locked away on the Farm. Has a man ever explored your body? Has anyone ever held you in their arms until you were trembling beneath their touch? Have you ever been stroked so completely you forgot how to breathe?" His ankle wrapped around my lower leg, forcing my stance wider. "Tell me I'm the first to hear you gasp their name."

"You're the first." It wasn't a lie. I wasn't a virgin. I refused to let that be an asset Em could sell to the highest bidder. It was mine to give, and she didn't have the right to claim it. So, once I was old enough, I bribed one of the guards. He was a tall man that had always looked at me with pity in his eyes. Pity was the closest I'd ever found to kindness at the Farm. He tried to make it good for me. But Crowe, even in these few moments, had heightened my pleasure far more than anything I experienced that night or any night since. I certainly never felt the urge to cry anyone's name before, not the way his name was nearly slipping from my mouth right now.

A low growl of male satisfaction responded to my admission.

All of the blood in my body followed his hand until it, just like he, was centered between my legs. His thumb moved in tight, firm circles against my clit, while his fingers stroked with unrelenting pressure, learning my body in the same way his tongue had learned the shape of my mouth. The combination of sensations wound my nerves into one electrified coil that threatened to consume me if it didn't find release.

I whimpered with need, hanging onto him and pleading with each breath. I pressed against his palm, chasing the climax he denied. It was maddening, to the point that I began riding his hand as he crested me higher and lower, over and over again. Each wave was more intense than the last, but never enough to push me over the edge.

"When I make you come, I want you to scream my name loud enough the boys upstairs hear you. Show Dandy who you really belong to."

Between heavy breaths, I said, "I don't belong to any—"

Crowe stole the words, claiming my mouth at the same time he pressed a third finger into me. The intrusion filled and stretched me until thoughts of ownership drifted away, and there was only the coil of his fingers.

"Say my name, beautiful, and I'll give you what you want."

Still against his lips, I forced the word to take form through my delirium. "Crowe." It wasn't a scream. It was barely a whisper. The best I could manage since I'd forgotten how to breathe.

The heel of his palm rolled against my clit, with a single pump of his hand that twisted within me. I exploded. That wave of heat finally crashed down on me and set my body aflame. My reality blazed around me, breaking apart until the only thing tethering me to this world was the twisted fabric of his shirt between my fingers.

–11–
CROWE

Why the fuck had I decided to wear jeans today? I have an entire drawer of sweatpants and joggers, but I chose today to be the day that I just lounge around home in jeans. And then, of course, I had the bright idea to follow my dick all the way downstairs, drawn by the sound of Thea's raging like a sailor following a siren's song.

I'd left Dorothy just after sunrise. I always rose early, despite how dark my room could be in the mornings. There was too much to be done in the day to waste it sleeping. I did a few circuits in the gym, then headed up for breakfast.

Hours later, the boys and I were going over the details of what we knew about the Wizard and debating the best way to go about ensuring a meeting with them. Nick, no surprise, wanted to force their hand. Danny wanted to go with manipulation and espionage. And I... I couldn't take my eyes off the security feed of my bedroom. I barely heard their bickering over the rush of blood through my ears.

After hours of waiting, the motion alert finally signaled. I'd been checking it all morning like an obsessed addict waiting for his fix. When the notification buzzed against the desk, I practically pulled a muscle trying to slow down my reaction and open the phone in a way that didn't rouse suspicion.

Thea had woken and was walking, perfectly fucking naked, around my room. The feed was in black and white. The night vision made her long, dark tresses glisten like snow. When she finally found the light switch, the colors of the video feed changed, making the bandages stand out in stark contrast against what used to be flawless skin.

Eastin deserved so much more than the two-minute death Thea had delivered. Although, a grim part of me loved the fact that for someone so vain, Eastin no longer had a face.

The map work of lacerations could only have been described as torture. Watching my girl in pain had awoken something in me. Thea quickly forgot her modesty as Nick moved from one long cut to the next, but there was nothing sexual about what had happened in my bed. At least not yet.

Nick might get off on the way a woman's orgasm heightens with carefully applied pain and the rush of endorphins that can only come with fear, but that was never my thing. I wanted to hear a woman scream with pleasure, not agony.

On the security feed, I watched Thea's confusion clear and her resolve harden. She looked just like that girl I'd seen in Eastin's tower, dangerous and fierce, not willing to accept fear when rage was so much more potent. It was that hard edge of her eyes in contrast to the softness of her movements that had hooked me. It was what was hooking me now.

She looked down at the boxers I laid out for her, mine. Just the thought of that sweet cunt rubbing against them had blood rushing straight to my dick. I'd never thought of myself as having a voyeur kink, but as she ran her hands over her breasts I knew the house could be burning and I wouldn't look away. There was no end to the filthy scenarios running through my mind, all to the sound of Danny trying to remind Nick that it was his final call—as if that ever worked.

A furious-looking Thea stormed off-screen, and seconds later, the intercom flared to life with the sounds of her battle cry. Danny looked up, watching with a scowl as the light blinked back off. Nick had a look of indifference that was mildly infuriating. After everything he'd watched her endure last night and his understanding of exactly what she'd gone through to end up in that state, I would have expected a little more softness from him. This morning, it was almost as if tending to Thea made him more bristly.

"Well, looks like the Princess is awake." Danny looked at me with disdain. "She's your new pet. Go deal with it."

I didn't need to be told. I was already slipping my phone into my pocket, grabbing my coffee from the table, and heading towards the stairs.

Now, I was sitting on my bathroom counter, realizing I had a boner hard enough to drill concrete and a girl whose body could most definitely not take the pounding I wanted to give to her. Thea went slack as the flood of her orgasm left her weak. Against my chest, she made tiny mewling sounds of satisfaction. Fuck, I'd give anything to ramp her back up and see how many more sounds I could wring from those sweet lips.

Carefully, I folded Thea into my arms. Her erratic breathing slowed. She peered up at me with glossy eyes, her pupils blown wide and a thin sheen of sweat clinging to her brow. I ran a thumb over it and smirked with pride. "Can you stand?"

There was a moment when her eyes went wide with clarity. Her mouth hung open like she couldn't figure out what to say. She nodded her head, pushing away from me until she was upright. I hopped down from the counter and walked over to the shower.

The water came out of the two frontal spouts in a rush. "Let's get you cleaned up, and then we can put fresh dressings on."

Thea folded her arms over her chest and pressed her thighs together as if she just realized she was naked.

"It's a bit late for that, Darling. I think once I've had your breast in my mouth, you can stop trying to cover them up."

I put my hand into the spray to test the heat, but I couldn't take my eyes off the way her cheeks flushed. Or the way Thea doubled down on her stance. Hands on her hips, she lengthened her spine with a slight lift to her chin.

"Turn around and brace your hands on the counter," I said, not bothering to hide my smile.

"Why? So you can do whatever hypnosis you just did in the hopes that I'll let you touch me again."

"The only thing hypnotic in this bathroom was the sound of your breathing as you came riding my hand."

Dorothy's stance slipped, lips parting in surprise.

"I need you to turn around so I can remove the bandages." I ran a thumb over my bottom lip, remembering the way hers felt against it. The ragged breaths she took as I stole the air from her kiss and the caress of her tongue as she took from me just as much as I demanded from her. "But if you want me to touch you again all you have to do is say, please."

A stuttering breath left her as she tried and failed to answer.

"Speechless. I'm flattered. Now, turn around, beautiful."

This time, she listened, facing the mirror and holding onto the counter. Her expression fell when she saw her reflection. I could see the way her eyes traveled over the mark on her cheek to the hair that was missing its luster. "I don't know how you can call me that. I look like something stuck to the bottom of your shoe, the kind that you can't tell what it is anymore but there are tiny bits of gravel stuck to it."

I moved behind her, pulling her hair back and kissing her neck just above the mark I had left. Our eyes met in the reflection. "You don't get it. The fact that you went through this—" My hand skimmed over the dressings on her back, over the swell of her ass, and down to the bandages taped to her legs. "—and came out on the other side with fists still swinging is what makes you beautiful." I placed a finger to her chin and turned her face to mine. "All of this—" I hovered a soft kiss over the suture tape on her cheekbone. "is temporary. Long after the bruises have faded, your fight will still be what fuels your beauty." I raised my hand back to her ass, squeezing the cheek appreciatively and sucking in a breath through my teeth. "Of course the rest of this doesn't hurt."

She lowered her lashes and pushed back into my hand. "Thank you..." Her voice was so low I wasn't sure if I hadn't imagined it. Thea lifted her head, meeting my eyes once more in the mirror. "... for reminding me that I'm more than what has been done to me." A tear slipped from the corner of her eye and trailed over the bruise. But when she spoke again, it was with conviction. "This morning, when I woke up, I ached everywhere, including my heart. It was hard to feel like I was anything but weak. I hate feeling like everything is out of my control because nothing was in my control for so long, and it nearly got me killed. I don't want to feel that way anymore. I'm done being a pawn in someone else's game." Her lips hardened into a serious line. That ferocity I craved glared back at me so thoroughly that it felt like I was in the presence of something much greater than either of us. It felt like destiny staring back at me through those hazel eyes.

I cleared my throat, trying not to show how deeply this moment was resonating with me. She craved control, but I knew Danny would never give her any. As much as I wanted to give that to her, and sit back to watch what would happen when she was truly unleashed, I knew I couldn't.

"I'm going to start removing the bandages now," I said, trying to change the direction her thoughts were going, "and then we're getting in that shower."

-12-
DANNY

I stared at the black screen, watching a white curser blink at the end of a long line of white text. It had already been thirty minutes since I submitted my query onto the E.C. dark server, but there was no response. The Wizard would have recognized my call sign. They should have known I was reaching out. And yet, nothing.

Yellow Brick was well known in the Cardinal Territories. We've been running jobs across the quadrants for years now. It shouldn't be taking this long; unless we'd been blacklisted. There was only one sin great enough to get blacklisted in Oz—make a move specifically targeting one of the four leaders. Given that, as of sixteen hours ago, Eastin Witcher no longer had a face, that was a very real possibility. Being blacklisted was something *I* couldn't afford, especially not now.

I drummed my fingers over the end of my armrest. If footage from Eastin's tower had leaked and Crowe had been made, then we were fucked. He insisted that he cut the security feed to the garage before Dorothy made her exit, but what if he or the cab had been recognized? YBR cabs were nondescript by design, but still.

For the hundredth time tonight, I rolled the facts over in my head. What the hell had Gigi gotten us into? As much as I hate admitting when Crowe is right, every time that shady bitch pulled strings, we all danced like obedient little puppets. It was something we put up with because, in the end, we usually profited big. I couldn't shake the feeling that this time she was offering us up as a sacrifice to some much larger plan.

And then there was Emily Rosen to consider. She wasn't going to let this turn of events go without consequence. We had her niece. She would be looking for her. No sane person just lets millions walk away. It was one thing when she thought Eastin would kill her, but now Dorothy was in the wind, and that had to rattle the old bird.

" It's been quiet for a while now. Crowe isn't back yet?"

I swiveled the chair towards the doorway. "No."

No, he wasn't. I bit the declaration off like it was a charred piece of grizzle. Crowe's absence was beginning to eat away at me, no matter how many times I tried to remind myself that I didn't care what pussy he slammed his dick into—repeatedly...over the fucking intercom.

"He's been gone for over an hour."

One hour and twenty-three minutes, but who's counting. I kept my expression blank. I didn't care. Dorothy Rosen was not something that I had the luxury of caring about, and I didn't want to anyway.

"It would seem he's taking his ownership duties very seriously."

"*Che deficiente,*"[1] Nick grumbled out, slamming his hand into the door frame. "Gigi played us, and now all of Oz is going to be out looking for that girl." He made a sound of disgust. "And Crowe is what, playing house downstairs? For all we know, he was made, and there are teams of hitmen zeroing in on our location right now. But I'm sure to that missing brain of his, now is the perfect time to get his dick wet."

Now, there was an image, one that I was unfortunately able to add a complete audio track to. Nick was lying to himself. Fuck, I'd been lying to myself since the moment I saw her ogling my car. If Dorothy would give either of us a chance, we'd both drop everything in the middle of a damn gunfight for a taste.

"If there was anyone within a mile of here, we'd know. We didn't pick a place all the way out here by chance."

"Perhaps. Have you heard anything from the Server yet?"

---

1. What a dumbass.

"No…" I shifted in my chair, running a hand along the scruff growing on my jaw. It was longer than I ever let it go. In a week's time, it felt like I had grown a damn mane. Feeling its length didn't help ease any of my anxiety. Normally, I would have shaved in the morning.

Today, all I could do when I woke up was replay every word and glance Dorothy had given me. I laid in my bed, staring at the ceiling, wondering what Eastin had done that made those angry-looking stripes on her legs. It looked like she'd been whipped. Even now, her screams as Nick tended to her were echoing in my head. It had required a surprising amount of restraint to keep myself closed off in my suite, especially when directly below me, Dorothy's voice shredded with pain.

"Danny?" My eyes settled on Nick, bringing me back to the moment. He'd moved to sitting on the arm of a large smoking chair in the corner of the room.

"That's what really has me spooked. My request should have been picked up by now."

A loud buzzing sound broke the silence of the office, making us both jump. My phone vibrated across the table—in a sequence I didn't recognize. Not my burner phone I used for business, my personal one. That wasn't fucking possible. The display showed, "Caller Unknown."

There was a clatter from downstairs, glass breaking, and a clang of something metallic. My instincts reared. This would be a perfect distraction if someone was planning their move on the compound. Nick, already considering the threat, snatched a gun from where it was stashed beneath the side table and disappeared toward the sound. The hallway shadows swallowed him and his tattoos up.

The phone buzzed again.

A second later, Nick reemerged. "Crowe is making food in the kitchen. Would seem I was right about playing house. He's got her dressed up in his clothes and everything."

The phone buzzed a third time.

Reluctantly, I hit the speaker button, accepting the call.

The line was silent for two long seconds before a deep, modulated voice said, *"Put the girl on the phone."*

Nick walked silently to the seat opposite me.

"And why would I do that? I'm the one conducting business, not the stray we picked up along the way. She belongs to YBR, now."

"I'm only going to say this one more time, put the girl on the phone."

I looked to Nick for an opinion. He made a slow shake of his head, reinforcing my concerns. This could be the Wizard. Finding this phone number would require some decent hacking skills. The phone was encrypted and untraceable, and yet an unknown number rang me up like we were old friends. That certainly pointed to the Wizard. Or another player, with a talented hacker on payroll, was entering the game. Either way, putting Dorothy on the phone would mean admitting to the caller she was with us, and that was a liability.

"That isn't going to happen. If you want to do business, you can do it with me or not at all."

"So be it."

The laptop, whose cursor never stopped blinking at me, flickered to full static. The speaker on every device in the house let out an ear-splitting tone. I immediately shielded my ears. Niccolo Chopper, on the other hand, never flinched. I once saw him stare down a raging doberman like it was nothing more than a puppy with a chew toy. In the end, that dog presented its neck and belly in complete submission. So, of course, even in a full auditory assault, he barely moved. His only movement was to swivel his head to check the points of entry for threats.

The lights in the room flashed—and then everything went dark.

The background hum of appliances and air conditioning silenced. No back-up generator clicking on to flood the building with safety lights. Just darkness and stifling silence.

Dorothy screamed, cutting through the tension sharper than any knife.

"What in the fuck?" Crowe yelled from down in the kitchen, followed by a series of popping noises and the sound of an extinguisher firing.

Instinctually, my head swiveled towards the door, following the sound of his alarm. Light flared brightly in the darkness. Deep red and yellow flashes lit up the hall from below. The smell of smoke already reaching the upper floor.

"Right now, Vincent Crowe is pointlessly trying to extinguish the flames in your kitchen. The gas line to the stove is shut, but in thirty seconds, it will switch on and flood the lower level. Which do you think will happen first, ignition or the sound of Dorothea's voice on this line?"

"Go." I snapped towards the door, but Nick was already gone.

I started counting in my head. Something told me the voice on the phone didn't make idle threats. Fifteen seconds later, the sound of Dorothy's whining carried up the stairwell. "Let go of me. Ow, that isn't necessary. Ow, mother-fucker, that hurts."

"If you would just walk like you're told, then I wouldn't have to manhandle your skinny, whipped ass in the first place."

Nick came back into the room, Dorothy slung over his shoulder. Her tiny fists beat against his back until he unceremoniously dropped her into a pile on the ground. She popped up, marching straight for me, until Nick grabbed ahold of her once more.

"What the fuck, Danny? You didn't need to sic your attack dog on me. It's just a power outage." She stomped her feet like a rabid bull, getting ready to charge the moment he released her. Which he wasn't likely to do. Not while there was an unknown threat.

"You hear the brat. You got what you wanted. Now turn the power back on," I said to the phone.

Crowe followed them in. Bracing a gun in his hand, the tactical mounted light illuminating his path. At least he had the brains to realize this was more than just a power outage.

Deep, modulated laughter filled the room. Not from my phone, but from the intercom. *"Now that everyone is here."*

Dorothy's movements stilled, her eyes wide with alarm in the glow from my phone. I stared at the secret camera mounted into the finial of my bookcase. Crowe moved in a slow circle, then moved to the windows to make a scan of the exterior. We had picked this room for our office precisely because it provided a vantage point for three sides of the property. The fourth side was visible over the loft window.

"*Dorothea, recently, you came into ownership of a rare piece of jewelry.*" It wasn't a question. Whoever this was already knew about Eastin's death and Dorothy's escape with Crowe.

"How do you know that?" she said cautiously, but her eyes were like accusing daggers of hatred. She seriously thought I had sold her out. I might be a bastard, but I was a bastard with honor.

Nick gritted his teeth. "Why don't you just tell him the combination to the safe while you're at it?"

"If I knew the combination to the safe, then you wouldn't still have my emerald," she clipped back, struggling once more to free herself from his iron grip.

I pinched at the bridge of my nose, heaving a sigh.

"*I require verification of its authenticity.*"

I leaned forward, silencing Dorothy before she could leak any other vital information. "And who exactly would we be providing this verification to?"

"*You know me as The Wizard.*"

"So you did get my message."

"*Before I can entertain negotiations, I need to verify the stone.*"

"What guarantees do we have that you are who you say you are? How do I know you aren't just a WM merc with hacker skills?"

"*Don't insult me. I could still blow up your kitchen if I wanted. Your safe is on the other side of the compound. I'm sure the emerald would be just fine. You can either bring the stone to me, or I can find it by sifting through ashes and bone. Either works for me.*"

"Where did you want to set up this meeting?"

"*The coordinates will be sent to you on the morning of the ninth. Be in Emerald City by that time.*"

"The ninth is less than a week away."

Nick leaned into me, whispering under his breath, "We have that job in Seebania tomorrow. We'll never make it by Friday."

"*Be there at 9, or you forfeit.*"

"Forfeit what?" Dorothy asked.

"*Everything.*"

There was a bright flash of light, and the house flickered back to life. A swoosh of air pushed my hair out of my face as the vents once more began pumping.

I looked down at the phone. The call had ended.

"Well, that gave new meaning to, 'You don't call him, he calls you,'" Crowe said with an irreverent laugh.

"Do you think that was really the Wizard?" Dorothy asked, looking between me and Crowe, her fingers relaxing from their tight fist, revealing tiny red slashes from where her nails had cut into the bed of her palm.

"Most likely. The security on this house is..." Crowe moved towards her, running a hand down her arm in reassurance. It was surprisingly intimate. "Thea, this place is a fortress. A closed system with an impossible to break encryption. Nobody should be able to hack it, much less control it the way they did. The Wizard is the only person who could pull that off."

"How did he know about the emerald?" Nick asked, looking at Crowe.

"It didn't come from me. I covered our tracks. Security was cut, the cab didn't have anything distinguishable to it, and I eliminated everyone who tailed us."

"Gigi said she was taking care of things in Eastin's building. Maybe something happened to her before she could."

"That *cagna* is just fine."[2] Nick moved into Crowe's space. "Someone out there must be talking about it. Maybe while you were busy staring at her tits, she managed to get a message out."

---

2. That bitch is just fine.

"I've been doing more than just staring at her tits." Crowe ran his tongue over his teeth.

"We heard," I muttered.

"And Thea hasn't had a chance to put her hands anywhere but where I've told her. Westin put the hit on Thea within hours of our escape. Maybe that got the Wizard digging into what happened."

"I don't like counting on maybes," I said, tapping at my laptop. The thing was completely fried. "Bastard." I pushed the useless brick of electronics off the end of the desk. The crash wasn't nearly satisfying enough.

"How long of a trip is it to E.C. from here?" Dorothy asked.

"Days. Two, maybe three." I tapped my phone, pulling up a map of Oz.

Crowe wrapped around Dorothy like he was an octopus. "We've got a job that has to be done before we can leave. You, pretty girl, are going to have to come with us."

Dorothy looked thrilled by the idea of doing a ride-along, giving him a look of such adoration that I made my stomach flip. "Get out of here. You'd seriously let me join in on your little heist, con, hit, thingy you all do."

He kissed the side of her neck. "Sure."

"Like hell she is." Nick's deep timber rattled the glass on the table next to him. "Thea has more stitches than a rag doll right now. She's not doing anything. I'm not putting myself at risk just so you can drag your new plaything along."

"She's not staying here alone, and we need all three of us to do the job," Crowe snapped back.

I ran a hand over my face, already regretting what I was about to say. "Not true. You and Nick could do it without me. You're just going to have to be careful. I'll stay here and babysit the princess."

"Babysit?" Dorothy glared at me.

"Put the claws away, kitten. You're not fooling anyone."

Crowe snickered with mischievous glee. "While we're out, you're going to need to take her shopping. Don't get me wrong, it makes me hard as fuck seeing Thea wear my clothing. But she needs more than my boxers."

Dorothy looked positively rueful at the idea of forcing me into a store. I groaned. Taking women clothing shopping is one of the rings of hell. I was sure of it.

"The Wizard gave us six days. It's going to be tight."

"Then we should start planning this out now."

I slid my phone to Dorothy. "Order something online from OzMart. I'll have it delivered. I'm not spending my day sitting outside a dressing room while you try to decide if the black jeans or the blue ones make your ass look better."

"Jokes on you, my ass looks great in every color of jeans."

"You do have a glorious ass," Crowe added, reaching down and cupping it while moving in for a slow kiss. Dorothy let out a sweet, breathy moan.

"Get the fuck out of here with that shit." My blood began boiling with some kind of primal possessive instinct that had no business rearing its angry head.

"You're just jealous because Thea actually *likes* me. If you two weren't always trying to kill her, maybe she'd like you too."

"In my defense, I haven't tried to kill her in at least a day," Nick said with a wry smile.

-13-
THEA

I slunk from the edge of the toilet onto the tile floor, leaning back against the wall, and immediately regretted the movement when the sore flesh met the unrelenting surface behind me.

Days ago, the need to eat was all I could think about. Being locked in the dark always made it impossible to ignore the way hunger clawed at your stomach. So when Crowe slid his plate of seasoned potatoes at me, he might have been shoving a gourmet four-course meal. It was the most delicious-looking food I'd ever seen. Not that it mattered. Twenty minutes after finishing the last bite, it all came back up again.

"*Che cagna sadistica*!"[1] I lifted my head from the rim to see Nick storming out of the room still ranting in that beautiful language.

"What did that mean?"

Crowe handed me a glass of water and small paper cup of mouthwash. "I think he said something about a woman. He's always grumbling about something. You get used to it. I barely notice anymore."

After swishing my mouth thoroughly, I wiped away the excess with the back of my hand. The walls swayed and the ceiling spun. I gripped the wall and closed my eyes until the spinning in my head stopped. Crowe scooped me up, carrying me from the hallway bathroom to the couch. He slid next to me, lifting my legs to rest on his lap.

Nick reemerged holding two IV bags, one clear and another holding some kind of yellowish liquid.

"You just have IV bags waiting on standby?" What kind of people kept random IV bags in their house? How often did you need to use them before you found it necessary to maintain a stock?

Ignoring me, Nick hung them from a set of hooks beside a large loveseat. A quick scan of the room showed me that there were similar hooks in multiple places.

"And hooks for hanging them?" I added.

"Among other things." He pointed to the chair, commanding, "Come."

"I'm not your dog."

"No, but you *are* a bitch. Now sit that pretty ass down in this chair, so I can get some nutrients in you."

"I'm not letting you put that into me until I know what's in it. Why is it yellow?"

"It's a banana bag. Saline hydration mixed with B vitamins, potassium, and a cocktail of other things your body needs right now. If you can't keep down solid food, then we need to try and replenish you in other ways." He cut a hard look at Crowe. "Which doesn't involve you pressing your *advantage.*"

"What?" Crowe gave a crooked smile, running a thumb over his lower lip. "Increased blood flow is good for recovery." I wasn't sure what he was remembering, but as I watched his finger run along the curves of his mouth, all I could see were those very same fingers slipping over my naked, wet skin in the shower. He had been gentle and careful of my injuries, never pushing things too far. But, fuck if I didn't want him to start pressing more than his advantage into me.

"Go on, Darling. Nicky is right. This will probably do you a lot of good."

"Don't call me Nicky," he snapped, still staring me down and waiting for me to move.

"Aww, what's the matter, Cupcake, don't like being called Nicky?" I said with the most patronizing voice I could muster. Nick's nostrils flared, looking remarkably like a bull ready to charge. So, the immovable mountain doesn't like being called Nicky. I filed that bit of info away for later.

Crowe dropped my feet to the ground and gave me a gentle push towards the empty loveseat. Gingerly, I made my way across the room. Not because they demanded it of me but because my head was already starting to pound from dehydration, and whatever was in that bag seemed like a wise choice.

Settling into the chair so that my back was never fully sitting against the cushion, I presented my arm in offering. "Prick away."

The lines of his face strained against smiling. It was probably my imagination, a facial tick or something in his eye because there was no way this gargoyle was amused. Tapping at my veins, Nick was surprisingly gentle when he inserted the IV.

"How do you know how to do all of this?"

Tenderly securing strips of tape along my arm, he said, "You spend enough time beneath a needle, you learn how to wield it."

"You're not talking about a tattoo needle, are you?"

He turned a knob on the IV, and the yellow liquid snaked through the tubing. A corresponding chill slithered up my arm, forcing me to shiver.

"Wh—" Burning chased away the chill, like he'd replaced the cool saline with liquid fire. "Fuck, Nick. Why does it burn?"

"You can take it." Nick stood up, towering over me. That shouldn't have been so sexy to hear. The man was a supreme level dick, but damn, it wasn't just my veins that felt lit with fire, now. I hated how his voice, and the purring way his accent played with his vowels, made everything sound dirty. "Are you comfortable? It will take at least an hour for that to run."

I swallowed, and fanned my neck with my hand. Was I sweating? "I'm fine. All of this isn't necessary."

"No. It really is. My guess is that you were undernourished long before Emily shipped you away. So stop pretending you aren't hurt before you do something stupid and make your recovery take twice as long. I don't have time to be nursing you all the way to the EC."

"Oh, good. You finally put a leash on your pet." Danny walked into the room, tapping on a tablet.

"Which am I, Danny, a pet or a princess?"

"You're trouble wrapped in pretty packaging. If you weren't worth so much, I wouldn't put up with it." He handed the tablet to Crowe. "Everything is set up. You two need to leave soon if you're going to make it to Crick Link and back by midday tomorrow."

"Wait." I reached out to Crowe's arm. I couldn't bring myself to voice any of my concerns. I felt safe with Crowe. The others made me feel like I had to be on my guard. Not to mention the unease I'd had deep in my gut since I watched Crowe fruitlessly trying to extinguish the flames in the kitchen.

"It'll be fine, beautiful." He kissed my temple. "Danny won't let anything happen to you. Not while there's money riding on the line." Crowe slipped his arms into a shoulder holster, snapping the loops deftly around his belt. I hadn't noticed them hanging beside the door. Where normal houses had a coat rack, these boys had one for their holsters. The same gun he pointed at me in the cab was tucked neatly into the crook of his arm. "Play nicely while I'm gone, and I'll bring you back a present to unwrap." He pointedly looked down, then winked.

"Fucking hell, Crowe." The stylus Danny had been absentmindedly twirling went flying through the air, smacking Crowe in the cheek. "Never refer to your dick as a present again. I won't let you ruin the one remaining good thing about birthdays with images of your cock."

"What about the IV?" I nervously twisted a lock of hair around my finger. I hadn't been able to blow dry it, and my natural wave pattern was kinking into a riot of curls. Whenever that happened, it was nearly impossible to keep my hands out of it.

"I can remove it. They're easier to take out than to put in," Danny said and tossed a set of keys to Nick. "Now get rolling."

Unexpected anxiety crawled up my throat, making it impossible to suck in a full breath. I hadn't acknowledged the sense of safety they'd brought, but three bodyguards made me feel much more at ease than one. Especially when I wasn't sure the one they were leaving me with wouldn't throw me to the Wolves.

Crowe zipped up his leather jacket. "Don't look at me like that."

"Like what?" I uncurled from the ball I had subconsciously bent into. Please tell me I wasn't making *don't leave me* eyes at him.

"I'll see you by lunch tomorrow. I promise."

"Like *what*, Crowe?"

He winked, like that somehow answered my question.

"Don't let her go to bed without changing those dressings," Nick said as he walked out the door. "We'll send word once we're done."

The door closed quickly behind them, neither man taking the time to glance back before it shut.

"Change the dressings?" I said with a reluctant look at Danny. Because that is who he had told, not me. I'd never be able to do it myself, which also meant that Danny would round out the thug hat trick of boys I'd been topless around. Great.

-14-
THEA

"So, what now?" I asked, still staring at the closed door. Perhaps this wouldn't be so bad. I could be overreacting. What did I really know about him? Danny could be the kind of dick that grew on you the more you learned. Maybe, by this time tomorrow, we'd be chilling with a movie, tossing popcorn playfully at one another.

I tucked my legs up as comfortably as I could and waited.

The silence stretching between us became more awkward by the minute. Danny ignored me entirely, pouring himself first one, then two glasses of that expensive scotch. He swirled it, taking his time to savor the smell and taste with each sip. Danny didn't just drink the scotch. He experienced it with all of his senses. All the while, the quiet minutes ticked on.

I looked down at my arm, still tethered to the bag on the wall. The taste of tin had finally faded away and the yellow liquid had nearly emptied. How long had Nick said I had to wait? This self-important prick had made me sit here in silence for an hour. As if I was powerless and had no choice but to watch him make love to a glass of scotch.

"Asshole, I asked you a question." I clipped the words out with as much authority as I could muster.

He set the glass down, the crystal clinking against the marble countertop. Finally, *finally*, he raised those green and amber flecked eyes to address me.

"What happens now is I go to my room and try to pretend I didn't just get saddled with brat-sitting duty. While you try to pretend you're not actually here."

113

"What about this?" I asked, letting the silicone tubing dangle between my fingers.

"Oh, that, Princess, is how I know you won't go wandering around the compound getting into things you have no business being in."

"You can't just leave me chained to the wall."

"You're hardly chained to a wall." His eyes rolled in annoyance until they snagged on exposed areas of my upper thigh.

"I know that. I just spent three days *actually* chained to a wall, you pretentious dick. Have *you* ever been chained to a wall?"

"Yes." He rolled his shoulders back, tightening the seams of his partially unbuttoned dress shirt, exposing the hint of a tattoo along his collar line. Danny noticed me looking, a slow smile spreading with recognition. For some reason acknowledging the fact that I had looked at him with anything other than disdain made me want to start burning things.

"Right, I don't mean whatever kinky shit you're into. I mean, against your will? I doubt you've ever had your hand forced. You've never knelt at the feet of someone you despised and pretended you liked the view." Even though I saw the blood reddening his cheeks with barely restrained anger, some sadistic part of me couldn't stop. So, I added, "Right, *Dandelion?*" The word curled around my tongue in the most salacious kind of way, sparking a deviant thrill within me.

"Crowe, that motherfucker," he hissed under his breath.

The hard angle of his jaw became more pronounced, his lip curling into a sneer. Danny prowled towards me, bracing one arm on either side of the loveseat until he'd caged me in, all of the space being consumed by his broad form. The prick wanted his growly display of aggression to make me shrink. The surrounding air seemed to disappear the longer he waited for me to cower in fear.

My back screamed in protest, but I didn't care. I confidently opened myself to him, freely giving him access to do whatever he seemed to be implying with zero fear. It took a lot more than this to scare me. "Do your worst, *Dandy.* Because when you're done, *I will do mine.*"

Danny hesitated, his sweeping eyes the only movement. I ran my foot up the inside of his supporting leg, hooking it behind his ass and pressing my shin into everything that counted. I gave a tug for emphasis. He jerked forward with a grunt, the displaced weight forcing his hand to brace the wall beside my head. He landed with a hard impact that rattled my entire body. With a quickly recovered smile, his weight pressed firmly against me, refusing to give up an inch of the gained territory.

A low growl came from the back of Danny's throat, and his lips hovered barely an inch from mine. The thick smell of the scotch on his breath mingled with other richer scents, all of them masculine and spicy. It conjured images of dark nights and twisted sheets.

"Princess, you wouldn't be able to withstand my best, much less my worst. You think threatening me will make me want to play with you less? If you're not careful, you might become my new favorite toy." He nudged at my bruised cheek with his nose until his mouth was resting against the tender surface. "I don't scare you. I see it in the stubborn line of those pretty lips, in your smoldering eyes, and the even beat of your pulse. But precious, when it comes to me, chains and whips should be the least of your concerns."

With a smooth movement, he snatched my arm, pinning it to the headrest with his supporting hand and exposing my entire left side. His breath fanned hot over my neck, forcing goosebumps to run everywhere it touched.

Danny's hand swept up the length of my side, dragging the hem of my shirt up with it. Most of my torso was still padded by the bandage, making the patches of exposed skin that much more vulnerable. His hand lingered a fraction longer on the outer swell of my breast, his thumb teasing the edge of my nipple.

Despite the instinct to jolt at the swipe of his hand, I held my breath and refused to give him the satisfaction of my reactions. Even if the soft brush of his fingertips was enough to send my heart fluttering. He slowly rotated my arm so that my palm was facing up. His fingers, once pressing hard at my wrist, began to smooth back and forth over my pulse.

One long stroke of his hand. That was all it had taken to transform my aggression. Now, I was vibrating with desire. As much as I wanted to curse myself for falling so easily into his grasp, Danny's hands on my skin held a kind of danger that a girl could get addicted to. I pulled at my restrained wrists. When they didn't move, a corresponding heat thrummed through me.

Danny knocked my legs open and pressed forward until I was riding the soft linen covering his thigh. On impact, my entire body arched into him. Wounded back be damned.

"How about now?" Danny's voice lowered an octave, the gravelly timber rumbling against my chest. "Do you still want my worst?" The hard, even pressure between my thighs increased.

"I don't know what I want," I said honestly, my brain short-circuiting under the feel of his leg slowly rocking against me.

"Pity." He swallowed hard, lips ghosting over my own. I ached to make contact with them, to lose myself in the viciousness of his kiss. "I can tell you what *I* want."

"Tell me."

Danny's hand smoothed from my wrist towards the crook of my elbow, inch by sensitive inch. I closed my eyes, trying not to whimper as he ground harder against my core.

Hot pain sliced along my arm, my heightened arousal making the pain more acute and morphing my moan into a shriek.

Danny sprang up, pushing off the back of the chair. In his hand hung the IV line, the bloody needle swinging back and forth. He dropped it and the shriveled bag into the trash can, tossing me a gauze pad that Nick had left behind.

I quickly put it to the line of blood trickling down my arm.

"What I want is to pretend your bratty ass isn't here. I don't care what you do, so long it doesn't involve me." His eyes traced down my body, lingering on the visibly soaked fabric of the boxers. He smirked. "That was even easier than I thought it would be. Good to know."

116

My fury reared its head. God damn my libido for overriding my apparently lacking common sense. "You're a real prick."

"I've been told. There's tape for the gauze, if it doesn't stop bleeding on its own. I'll order us pizza in a little bit. Try not to get in trouble."

"I probably can't eat pizza. The grease and my stomach, or something." I knew heavy, greasy foods were out, thanks to my aunt's tender, loving care. My throat still burned from when my potato lunch made its reappearance. I really didn't want a repeat of that experience.

"I don't see how that's my problem. After dinner, we can change your dressings, and then I am done playing babysitter for the night. You can tuck yourself into bed."

-15-
DANDY

Dorothy glared at me over her plate of crumbs. She'd finished the toast she made herself a while ago, but I enjoyed the way her skin flushed when she was angry. Making her wait on me was quickly becoming my new favorite game. Well, besides the one we'd played earlier. *That* had been entirely too much fun and came dangerously close to the edge.

I'd left her raging, and that made it so much harder to get the feel and sound of her out of my head. She'd spread open beneath me in a clear invitation to be wicked. I'd damn near taken that bait.

I couldn't forget who she was or who she *took from me*.

I had three sisters. Had. It was a term I never really accepted, even though I knew it to be true. In my mind, they were still beautiful and young, flower crowns sitting atop their innocent heads while we ran and played in the fields. I closed my eyes before clouds could chase away the warmth of the memory.

The Farm's files were housed on a closed server, making it impossible for even Crowe to hack them. In the months I spent combing public records, I found enough evidence to know that Emily Rosen was never the true owner of Cyclone Shipping. The entire organization, every debauched inch of it, was in Dorothy's name. It didn't matter how pretty those cutting eyes were or how her animosity made them flame brighter.

Princess Rosen wasn't an option. End of story.

So here I sat, enjoying my pizza like it was a three-course gourmet meal to the delightful sound of her teeth grinding.

"Are we going to always sit in silence?"

"I like silence."

"Nobody likes silence." Dorothy got up and began opening all of the cabinets one by one.

"What are you hunting for?"

"Mugs. I was going to make myself a cup of tea. The toast was dry, and all you have in the fridge is beer and an old bottle of soy sauce. I thought mint tea might be good for my stomach. Aha!" she said, triumphantly holding a black ceramic mug aloft.

Dorothy did a small spin on her toes to face the sink. She was uncharacteristically jubilant, smiling genuinely. The transformation was enough to give a man whiplash. Still, her smile was stunning. Until her eyes met mine again, and then her lovely features fell back into a scowl.

"Maybe you only like silence because you're a terrible conversationalist. You don't say more than four-word answers unless you're issuing threats."

"I'm not a terrible *anything*. I just don't need to fill space with mindless chatter."

"Sure. Let's go with that." Dorothy clucked her tongue in disbelief. "Where's the kettle?"

I leaned back in my chair. "You're a capable girl. I'm sure you can figure it out."

She flipped me a middle finger while bending over to check all of the lower cabinets. Damn, her ass looked good in those boxers, and it was only mildly grating that they were Crowe's and not mine.

She popped back up. "What the hell is this?" Holding Nick's imported coffee pot aloft, she lifted the triangular lid. Her nose scrunched, confusion pinning her brows together.

"Nick will skin you alive if you break that."

Slamming it back in the cupboard, she huffed, "Well then, just tell me where the tea kettle is." I *could* tell her we didn't have a tea kettle or that the only box of tea was leftover from the previous owners and probably tasted like drinking moldy bark, but this was so much more fun.

"Fuck it." She filled the mug with water and sat it in the microwave. Yellow light spilled across her face while the mug slowly spun inside. She tapped her fingers against the counter, highlighting her impatience. I could see her trying to hold back, solely to prove my comment about silence wrong.

Dorothy lasted another ten seconds, "Crowe said you met in grade school."

Speaking of mindless chatter, "Apparently, Crowe says a lot of things."

"What happened to make him go from being a bully to whatever *this* is?" She waved around the room. Sniffing the box of tea, she sighed, "Is this stale box of Earl Grey really the only tea you have?"

"I saved his ass," I replied, ignoring her spoiled complaints.

There was a long pause. Dorothy's hazel eyes tightened with annoyance, causing an adorable crease to form at the center of her brow. She waved for me to continue. "And..."

"Fine," I sighed. "That bastard deserves to have a story told about him since he was all too fine with gossiping about me this morning." I took a long sip of my beer. It was one of Crowe's that I'd cracked open on accident, a bitter IPA that tasted like sucking on a Christmas tree.

"Crowe and Nick used to run jobs for Nick's father, Salvatore Ciopriani." I paused, waiting to see any sign of recognition. All she did was blink like big eyed doe. "When they moved over here from Italy, he changed the name to Chopper. He's just the kind of dick to think Chopper sounded cool."

"Aww...I can just imagine a little gangster, Nick. That's adorable." Dorothy settled into the seat next to me, tucking her feet beneath her neatly. She idly dipped the tea bag in her mug. Steam curled around her fingertips. I had never noticed her nails before: short, unadorned by polish. Unlike what I would have expected, they were rough around the edges—like she'd been scraping at the surface of something until they'd gone raw. That made my heart resonate with a compassion I didn't want to feel and tugged at a *long* forgotten memory.

"Nobody has ever described Niccolo Chopper as adorable. Even as a baby, he was intimidating."

She bit down on her lower lip to keep the slight smile from rising. It made something in me flicker.

I pushed it away.

"What kind of jobs?"

"Small time mostly. Picking pockets and delivering packages, that type of thing. Crowe got it in his head that they should try for something bigger to impress Nick's father into giving them more serious work."

Dorothy leaned forward, hanging on my every word like she actually gave a shit. "What did they steal?"

"A car." Her eyes widened, making them shift into a teal color. Oz damn, they were beautiful.

"Did they know how to steal a car?"

"No, but not knowing what he's doing never stopped Crowe before and hasn't stopped him since."

She seemed genuinely interested, which made the ground feel remarkably unsteady. The fact that she kept twisting her hair around her fingers, wasn't helping either. Now that it was clean, the long strands curled into soft romantic waves. I was sure they would feel like silk if I ran my fingers through it. Not that I was imagining brushing it back from her face or wrapping it around my fist.

Swallowing against my dry mouth, I continued, "I would normally never admit this." Like they could tell I couldn't stop staring at them, the long auburn waves slipped over her shoulder, brushing the back of my hand as they fell loosely between us. She was close enough I could smell the rich undertones of Crowe's shampoo mingling with something altogether feminine. Close enough to make me forget myself, my purpose.

"For most of my early years, Crowe tormented me. He was a complete dick. Those movies where the bully always gets his comeuppance? Complete shit. He never got in trouble. Everyone loved him. Everyone *always* loves him." I tried not to make my voice sound as bitter as I felt. Even Dorothy had picked Crowe first—but that asshole wasn't here now, was he? "For years, if he and Nick were coming down one hall, I'd go the opposite way. Then, one day, the two of them approached me while I was at work."

Dorothy didn't need to know any of this, but her attention was focused on me without the flaming animosity, and it was...nice. She wasn't smiling exactly, but her posture had relaxed, and she seemed so much softer. Like something that would be comforting to hold.

Problem was, I didn't do nice. I didn't do comforting.

Downing what was left in the bottle, I moved quickly to the kitchen. I needed to stop this before it became something I actually liked. "We should work on changing your dressings."

Dorothy straightened her back, the ease that had washed over us disappearing as if that girl had never been here. It was better this way. Maybe if I didn't have to watch her hazel eyes soften from brown to green, then it would be easier to hold a conversation without feeling like I was losing myself in it.

I popped open the medkit and gestured at the empty space at the end of the counter. "Lose the shirt."

"You've been waiting all night to say that, haven't you?"

"Don't flatter yourself." I slapped the counter beside where I was prepping what we needed. "Now get that tight ass over here and strip."

"Ugh." She faked a sound of disgust. "It's always, '*strip for me, drop your pants, say my name when I make you come.*' You three are so bossy."

I almost laughed before I caught myself. Crowe always did have a thing for hearing his name, unimaginative fuck. "Princess—" My voice dropped low and gravelly, "—when I make you come, you won't be able to speak, much less remember anyone's name. Now get over here."

The wicked smile she was sporting fell, morphing into a cute '*Oh*' before snapping shut. For once, she actually did as she was told. Sort of. Dorothy walked over to the counter. Facing away from me, she tried to pull the shirt off. The edges snagged on the bandages along her back. I let her struggle for a few minutes longer than necessary just to see what she would do. Dorothy growled in frustration, stomping her feet. It was oddly adorable to watch. When she looked like she might finally explode, I gingerly lifted the garment over her head.

From behind, it was almost amazing how much of her skin was covered in gauze and tape. The lacerations must have run her entire back, or Crowe had been extra generous with its application. Given how soft-hearted he'd been about this girl, it wasn't hard to believe.

Her legs weren't bandaged. Instead, the pale skin peeking out of the boxers was striped with angry red streaks, but it didn't look like they'd broken the skin beyond a few shallow nicks.

"Brace the counter. I don't need you wiggling around, making things harder than they need to be."

She gave an impetuous sigh, then slid her fingers along the edge of the marble. At the same time, she leaned forward, ass popping toward me in invitation. The boxers Crowe had given her barely hung on her hips, dropping low enough to see two of the sweetest dimples at the base of her spine. I ran my thumb over my lower lip contemplatively, imagining how pliant that skin would be beneath my hands.

"Look who decided to let her good girl show. Apparently, you *can* follow orders after all."

Dorothy huffed. "If you don't mind, could you wait until you're in private before you start stroking that ego so vigorously?" She didn't bother hiding the snark in her tone, and I couldn't help but chuckle at it. She never backed down. Even when she was being playful, Dorothy pushed every boundary and button she could find. Why did that make me want her bratty ass more?

The images rolling through my head couldn't be stopped. It would take nothing to lift her onto the counter and spread her wide. Dark hair splayed against the grey marble, and lips parted on a rapturous scream, fighting me and loving it every step of the way. The vision was exquisite. There would be nothing to stop us. The boys were gone until tomorrow. I could take my time, driving her body until Dorothy begged for deliverance.

Fuck. Why had I thought this would be better than talking at a dinner table?

"Problem?" she asked, looking coyly over her shoulder.

I cleared my throat. "No. Just trying to decide where I want to start." A lie. I knew exactly where I wanted to start. By sinking my teeth into her ass right below those two adorable divots.

"Just start at the top and keep telling me your story. It's a good distraction." She flexed her fingers, shifting her weight from one foot to another and making her ass sway with an impatient wave.

"You seriously want to hear this?"

"Yes, now stop being a pussy and start talking."

"Mmm. Keep pushing me, Dorothy." I gave her ass a hard slap. I couldn't help it. She was being a brat. A man could only hold out for so long when faced with this kind of temptation.

She yelped and glanced back at me. Where I expected to see anger, there was only amusement and absolute lust. Fuck, of course she loved it. She probably got off on the fight as much as I did.

"Behave, or there's more where that came from." I made a twirly motion with my finger.

After rolling her storm-cloud eyes, she twisted to face forward again.

"I was fifteen, running the coat check at La Maison Rouge, a fancy French restaurant in town." I didn't particularly like sharing, and I rarely offered up information about my childhood. By rarely, I meant never. I *never* talked about those years with anyone, ever, but it would help distract us both.

I needed that right now, because I was finding it hard to focus...on anything. My mind and my eyes flitted from one part of her body to the next, each more alluring than the last. At the moment, the way her hair pooled around her shoulders was completely mesmerizing. In this light, it was made of so many colors. Brown, black, amber, red. I pushed the errant strands over her shoulders, briefly closing my eyes to the rose-petal softness of her skin. Dorothy sucked in a breath at that first subtle touch. Shit, she was so responsive—if that didn't make me want to start stroking down each exposed inch of flesh.

"Danny?"

I blinked. How long had I been staring at the slope of her neck? I didn't even have a good excuse for why I'd stopped talking. I cleared my throat and continued the story. "The valet station was beside mine. The box where the keys were stored was mounted to a wall in my cubicle." I redirected my hands to the bandages bracing her ribs. Removing the fasteners, I unwound the long fabric from around her waist. Each pass of my hands brushed the underside of her breasts, revealing more and more skin. It was like unwrapping a present, one that was most definitely not mine.

"That's how they planned to steal the car?" she said, her voice broken by an unrestrained breath when my hand finally pulled the bandage free. Dark green bruises blossomed like a spray of flowers along her side. At least they looked like they were healing.

"Exactly. They staked out the cars, and when the one they wanted pulled in, Nick would distract the valet while I handed the key to Crowe." I grabbed gently at the edge of the highest strip of tape. This piece curved along the side of her left shoulder blade. Dorothy jumped from the brush of my fingertips. It was thrilling enough that I let my pinky trail along as I pulled just so I could drink in the way she shivered inch after intensifying inch.

Dorothy's voice was tight, "Did it work? Did you give them the key?"

Gingerly, I removed the first gauze pad. This time, it wasn't Dorothy letting out the broken exhale. The roadmap of cuts was a mess. Some of the marks, while puffy and pink on the edges from healing, were obviously deep. Last night, there had been patches of dried blood that soaked through her shirt, but not enough that it concerned me. Of course, at the time, she had just kneed me in the balls, so I wasn't very inclined to care about the state of her shirt.

Crowe tried to explain the extent of the wounds, but I hadn't expected anything like this. There were four more covered areas to change after this one. *Four MORE.* Fuck. How had she strode so confidently into my home while carrying the weight of this damage? I'd seen strong men broken by half this much pain. There was no way this was caused by a typical whip, even one with many tails.

Staring at those wounds, for the first time, I saw Dorothy for what she was. A fighter. To think I had been calling her Princess all this time. No wonder she hated me. I was a prick. The very fact she'd refused to let us see any sign of weakness while enduring this level of torment was a true statement of her character.

Last night, she screamed loud enough to be heard in the office. I shut the door so I didn't have to listen to her crying. When, an hour later, Nick told me she'd passed out from the pain, I chalked it up to a weak constitution. Now I understood the woman who never flinched and met me blow for blow. She wasn't a princess at all. Dorothy was a fucking queen, looking to reclaim her kingdom in the name of everything she'd had stripped from her.

-16-
DANDY

"Is everything okay? You aren't afraid of a little blood, are you?" She tried and failed to cover up her concern with snark.

"Describe the whip to me."

"What?" Caught off guard by my abrupt change in topic, her voice sounded small.

"Crowe said you were whipped."

The slender fingers gripping the edges of the counter tightened. Her weight shifted back on her heels. It was what she'd done when we first asked her what happened with Eastin. It was a hesitation I hadn't wanted to observe before, but now, felt so obvious. Suddenly, I was seeing so many small ticks that I'd been blind to, a vulnerability in this girl that she kept hidden so effortlessly—like she'd spent her entire life afraid of showing weakness and had formed a natural defense against it.

"It was shorter than a regular whip. Red, braided leather with faceted gemstones running the length of each strand. There were a dozen tails, maybe more."

"That it?"

"No. The end of each tail had something shiny, like a cap."

"Round like a bullet or flat?"

"Flat."

"Fucking hell." I knew exactly what had done this. It was the kind of weapon used to maim. I'd never seen it used to this extent. "It wasn't a cap, Dorothy. It was a blade."

"It was..." Her voice trailed off, the muscles now exposed to the air flexing.

"It's the only way a whipping impact would cut this deep and cleanly with only a single strike. To place something like that at the end of a flail is a creative level of wicked, even for Eastin Witcher. Add in braids and facets; it's amazing there was any skin left to stitch."

Suture tape and stitches were holding several of the large cuts closed. Some of the longer ones looked to be deep too. But nothing looked infected, which was lucky. She'd been given two doses of heavy antibiotics already, but a third dose was probably wise.

"Eastin said she made it just for me. Figures the first gift I've ever been given would be a torture device. Kindness always was the worst kind of betrayal."

That sounded like something Nick would say. I knew what he'd endured to think of kindness as a trick, but Dorothy? I turned her so that I could read the truth in her expressions.

"You've never been given a gift? Ever?"

"Not one that I can remember. In Em's words, I was never 'worth it.'" A stubborn line hit the edge of her jaw, and she shrugged a shoulder. "Who else was going to give me presents, Henry?" She snorted a laugh. "Best present that asshole ever gave me was the face he made when he tipped over Eastin's balcony."

I smiled in sympathy and marveled yet again at the resilience unfolding before me. I reached up to brush the hair from her face so that I could see her clearly. My eyes landed on her bruised cheek. A lot of the purpled swelling had gone down. My heart slingshotted into my ribs as I realized what I was doing—gazing. I was gazing at Dorothy-fucking-Rosen. Not good, Danny.

In the worst recovery ever, I reached past her to grab the washcloth from the basin.

Dorothy gaped at me. "Careful, Danny, if you keep doing things like that, I might start to think you actually like me."

"I don't have to like you to imagine mounting you on this counter."

Dorothy's amusement slipped, replaced by challenge. Probably unwise to challenge a man like me when she was half-naked. A better man would ignore the arousing beauty, but I never pretended to be that man. If anything, she should be reminded of exactly who I was. I let the soapy water drip over her shoulder and tracked the stream as it ran from her collar line to the peak of her breast. With a single finger, I gathered the water beading on the tip.

Dorothy responded beautifully. Her spine involuntarily arched, forcing her breast to smooth against the palm of my hand. When the movement pulled at her no longer braced wounds, she bit down on her cheek, just as she had a moment ago. A tell that she was restraining some much larger emotion.

Because I couldn't help myself, I gave her nipple a playful flick. "Now, turn around." My voice sounded so much more lust-filled than I'd intended it to. There was a gravel to it that made Dorothy tremble. Seeing the tremor snaking down her spine made me want to whisper dark promises to her if only to see how her body responded.

This was a terrible idea. I wanted this too damn badly to be sane. At least it wasn't whatever the hell I had been feeling before.

Her fingers curled along the marble, shifting her ass straight into my groin and fitting far too perfectly to be anything but a fantasy. I should have stepped back. Fooling around with Dorothy wasn't a good idea for anyone involved. It would only confuse things more than they already were. She was a job. A means to a very long end, and I would see it through, even if it meant burning her alive along the way. She was a sacrificial pawn in this game. When she was moving against me, those pink lips curling in triumph, it was hard to see her as anything but that queen.

Despite how badly I wanted to, I resisted the urge to wrap my hand around her throat and pull her flush to my chest. Instead, my hands dropped to her hips, stilling her movements. "Stop playing around," I chided. "Or this will hurt you far more than it needs to."

"Me? I'm only playing a game *you* started."

I dragged the cool cloth along the first several cuts. "I didn't start anything. I was having a perfectly lovely evening, and then you started rubbing your ass against me like a cat in heat."

Dorothy kept her breathing slow and even. She scoffed in disgust but didn't pull away. Instead, she doubled down and rolled her hips so that my hardening dick notched perfectly against her ass. This girl was a damn enigma, a glitch in the fabric of the universe that defied logic and the exception to every rule I'd ever made for myself.

I went back to cleaning the remaining slash marks. Even though I was trying to be careful, more than once, my pressure increased when I became distracted by the flexing muscles beneath my hands or the rock of her ass against my cock.

"So you gave Crowe the key, and then what happened?" she said, between panting breaths. I pulled out the healing salve and eased it over the wounds. Dorothy sighed in relief. The tension immediately left her shoulders, and they sagged into the arms bracing the counter.

"Actually, I told him 'No' and refused to give him the key."

"But I thought—"

"I know what you thought." I moved on to the next strip of tape and eased the gauze away from her tender skin. This patch was even more inflamed than the last. There were areas where one strike must have overlapped with the first. Nick had done a good job, but this would leave scars. When I began cleaning these, she audibly whimpered. A tremor raked her body, and not like the delicious ones she'd done before. I knew this time she was trying to restrain a scream of pain. So, I opted to continue talking.

"The thing you don't get is that you're looking at this logically, and Crowe was a dumb teenager trying to prove himself. That made him reckless and illogical by definition."

"Reckless can be fun."

"Not when it means you steal the wrong person's sports car and then drive it into an emerald mica quarry."

"What?"

"Yeah." I chuckled at the memory. Crowe really is a dumbass sometimes. "When I didn't give him the key, he tried to do a quick snatch and grab. Nick dragged me into the back of the closet and hooked my vest on the coat rack while Crowe pulled the key from the box. Of course, he grabbed the wrong one. So it didn't go to the shiny car that was conveniently parked at the end."

"What car did it go to?" She seemed genuinely hooked on the story now. Dorothy hadn't even reacted when I started on the third gauze patch.

"Have you heard of Mariah Mombi?"

Dorothy sucked in a surprised breath. So she had heard of the former head—or rather headless—leader of the Northern Quadrant. Gigi and her crew got the pleasure of removing it for her.

"I know Mombi," Dorothy said somberly. "She would visit The Farm every year to hand select some of the girls."

Blood rushed in my ears

Hand-select some of the girls.

I tried not to picture my sweet sisters being carted away by Mariah. Fucking. Mombi.

Mombi was the worst of all the people who had seized control in Oz when the Premiership fell. She was notorious for turning those who displeased her into actual ornaments adorning her mansion. That woman had literal skeletons in her closet. Mombi was worse than Eastin and Westin combined. She would relish breaking and destroying everything beautiful that lived in the hearts of the young.

I swallowed hard. I shouldn't ask. I should—not—ask...but I couldn't stop the words from coming. "What kinds of girls?"

"Older ones, mostly. Women in their early twenties. It was always the pretty ones. She'd pick one or two every time. I don't know why or what she did with them."

I clutched the cloth too tightly, making water stream down her tortured back. The palm resting on Dorothy's shoulder tightened. She didn't seem to notice. I reeled back in my emotions before they started spilling out of control.

Twenties would have been too old. Still, a part of me wanted to shake Dorothy senseless, and force the answers to rattle from her, just like I had been wanting to do every second since she'd mentioned Emily Rosen's name. Instead, I resumed placing salve over the wounds and pretended that a lifetime's worth of guilt wasn't crushing me.

"There was a boy she would drag behind her on a leash. Mombi called him Tip, but I don't think that was his real name. I only talked to him once about three years ago. He begged me to help free him. It was Tip who made me realize that I was the only one with the power to do anything about the women being trafficked through The Farm. He was who taught me to push past my fear. Even if it did end up with me sitting right beside the very girls I was trying to save."

"Wait, save? You were going to take down The Farm?" Disbelief tainted my voice, causing that sour feeling to flip in my stomach once more.

"Of course." She nodded. "I never got to tell him my plan because the next time Mombi visited, she came storming through the gates screaming that Em *'sold her a bad slave.'* Tip had escaped, and Mombi blamed Em for it. Then Mombi demanded *me* in repayment."

"But you're her niece."

Dorothy snorted a laugh, "That didn't mean anything to Em. I was nothing but a commodity to her. She threatened to auction me off nearly every day of my life." My hand stilled against her back. "Mombi even went as far as dragging me to her car by my hair. It made Em furious. The two of them fought in the middle of the courtyard. Em pulled a gun on Mombi, declaring that I wasn't available. While she held Mombi at gunpoint, Henry got me out of the car. Back then, I was stupid enough to think she was trying to save me. Now, I realize it was because I was already promised to Eastin." Dorothy's face fell into her hands. "I was so naive. There was so much I didn't know. Just like I don't know why I'm telling you any of this." She glanced over her shoulder at me. "It's not like you care. Let's just finish these bandages. Then you can go back to pretending I don't exist."

I flinched at my own words thrown back at me. Everything was all twisted up. I wasn't sure what to do. Part of me wanted to strangle her for having had anything to do with The Farm to begin with. Another part of me wanted to kiss away the tears I could see forming in the corners of her eyes. I'd never felt so conflicted. Caught in the middle of two warring emotions, I stood rooted to the spot, unmoving like my limbs had been turned to stone—just like the concrete-dipped souls that decorated Mombi's garden.

Dorothy turned away from me with a long exhale. It was enough to break the spell I was under. It felt like time had stopped, sucking me under and spitting me back out like nothing had happened.

"That was the last I saw of Mombi, and I was glad for it. How did Crowe manage to survive stealing her car?"

I blinked, my eyes focusing on what was left of Dorothy's back. The gauze was completely removed now. I ran a finger over the ragged cuts. The small bits of information she'd told me settled together into startling clarity. Dorothy hadn't been double-crossed by Emily Rosen. She'd been victimized by her. Suddenly, Crowe's compassion made so much sense. I prided myself on being able to read people, but I'd gotten Dorothy completely wrong from the beginning. I knew why. I wanted her to be the enemy. I didn't want to hear that she was a victim in all of this. I didn't want to know that she needed retribution as much as I wanted revenge.

"What will you ask for when we meet the Wizard?" I said, my voice still choked off from the emotions rioting in my chest.

"I thought it didn't matter. I thought that I belonged to you now, along with the emerald."

"You do. It does." I rested my hands along her hips, their heavy weight pressing into her soft flesh. "Answer the question. What do you want, Dorothy?"

"A new life outside of Oz." She paused, then twisted to face me. "Actually, more than anything, what I really want is Em gone. I want her to answer for killing my parents, stealing my inheritance, and making my entire life hell. I want her to pay for selling me. I want her to suffer as I have suffered. I want her to feel like she is nothing. When I throw what's left of her away, I want her to know it's because she is nothing more than trash."

I reached up and cupped her cheek. Her brow furrowed at my unexpected tenderness. I didn't care. I was too busy marveling. It was like this girl had been brought to me by fate. I hadn't seen it before, but I was seeing it now.

Dorothy was my mirror. Standing here, with her stormy eyes boring into mine, I knew that this girl had been brought into my life for a reason. In the end, what we wanted was the same thing. I would make her wish come true, and

Ozma willing, she'd help mine come true too, and if not— at least we would make Emily Rosen pay. Together. That was a spectacular thing to imagine.

I leaned forward, brushing my lips to hers.

She pushed off my shoulders, slapping me with unexpected strength. Shock, peppered by desire, ignited along the burn from her hand. I wasn't really thinking, and kissing her in that moment had been instinctual. I wanted to kiss her again, to show her that I understood. To meet the fire in her gaze with the fury that always burned low in my gut.

"What the hell, Danny?"

Before I could answer, something clicked in her expression.

"Fuck it." She grabbed my shirt and pulled me back to her. We collided, her mouth seeking and demanding against mine. Dorothy held my body to her bare chest. My hands sank into her dark auburn waves. Palming the back of her head and holding her mouth to mine as if we were each holding each other hostage, neither one wanting to submit first.

A loud rattling started next to us. I ignored it, focusing instead on the feel of Dorothy's tongue running along my teeth, dueling with my own. I used my free hand to palm her breast, my thumb teasing at her nipple. She arched into me, and I pushed back, pinning her hips to the counter.

It buzzed again, this time longer and louder than the first.

"Fucking hell," I cursed. I had every intention of throwing my phone at the wall. Then I saw the message and released her completely.

"What's 3853?" Dorothy said, looking at the screen.

"Fucked." I quickly typed out a response, "*669.*"

The phone immediately buzzed again, a map pinging their location. They hadn't made it far. They should have been all the way over the border by now, but instead, they were barely an hour from here. Which meant they were intercepted en route, but by who?

I looked back at Dorothy, stealing one more long kiss from her lips. Because Oz damn she tasted sweet. Of course, I wouldn't be able to indulge in it all night like I should. Fate couldn't just hand me the answer to everything and then let me enjoy it. No, instead it had to send me a literal message reminding me just how bad my impulse control was.

"Turn around. We need to get you bandaged back up, then I need to get to the guys."

"Why? Danny, Stop." She grabbed my hand from where it was reaching for the sealed packages of gauze.

"Turn around, Dorothy. I'll explain while I tape."

She did as I asked. Grumbling about being called Dorothy again.

"3853 is code for FUKD. It means the guys are locked down somewhere with no out. They need an exit, and I'm going to give it to them."

"That's what 669 means?"

"Yes. It means I'm on my way. This is because we changed the plan in a rush. If we'd taken the time to adjust properly, this never would have happened. We *never* get pinched."

"I'm coming with you."

"Cute. No, you get to stay here. With the entire alarm and defense system activated."

"No, I'm not staying locked up again."

"Locked up? You're lucky I'm not tying you to my bed until I return." Fuck. We need to put a pin in that idea for another time.

She tried to turn back to face me, but I held her firmly in place.

"Danny, I'm coming with you. I refuse to stay here. If the boys are in trouble, then you can use the extra help."

"And what help would that be? Are you just going to whine and stamp your feet until they put down their weapons?"

Dorothy audibly growled in frustration.

"Not taking me with you was what got us in this mess in the first place."

"First of all, there isn't an us." Another lie, but she didn't need to know that. None of them did. There was so, so much more going on here than I was ready to admit. Instead, I fell back into what I knew—callous indifference.

She scoffed.

"Second of all, you don't have a choice in the matter. I'm not taking you with me. And before you say it, yes, I can make you stay here. And yes, I have no issues in demonstrating it." I slapped the last bit of tape on.

She hissed in pain but spun instantly to face me. Apparently, her outrage outpaced her pain.

I put a finger to her lips, silencing her outburst. "You're too valuable of an asset to take into a high-fire situation. You'll be secure here. Getting out of tight situations is what we do. Waiting here for me to return is what you can do."

"Asset. Are you kidding me right now?" Dorothy fumed. She cocked her arm back to swing at me again, but I caught it in the air. "Fuck you, asshole. I can't believe I let you kiss me."

"Check your facts, Princess. That was *your* wicked tongue waging war against mine."

Dorothy struggled against my grip, raising her other hand, which I caught just as easily. She roared with frustration. Before she could try to knee me, I spun us and pinned her hard against the door of the fridge.

With one hand around her wrists, I pinned them over her head. Her face contorted from the pain. Good. Maybe it would make her wake up and smell the reality.

"You're no better than Em," she hissed through gritted teeth.

I released her like she'd burned me. Crowe was right. Dorothy was exactly like a firecracker, and I was dumb enough to try and hold her.

"When you look at me, all you see is a dollar sign. I'm not a person to you."

My phone buzzed again. A bright yellow alert flashed over the screen. "Fucking hell. One quiet, uneventful night. That was all I wanted."

I slammed my phone down, pushing open a panel on the wall beside Dorothy and pulling a gun from it. I scanned my eyes from her exposed chest to her navel and back up again. It should be illegal to cover such perfect tits, but we were about to have a lot of unwanted company. "You're going to want to put a shirt on. Unless you were planning on letting a third man get a handful tonight."

"Fuck you." She put her hands on her hips, thrusting her chest forward in defiance. "Maybe I will."

I moved in, my hand circling her throat. "Say it again, slower this time."

"Fuck. You. *Dandy*."

I smiled at the challenge in her eyes. Dorothy smiled right back. Yes, she was most definitely my worst and most damaged parts reflected right back at me. Albeit in a much sexier package.

"I love the way your mouth looks when you say fuck." I squeezed tighter and moved my lips over hers. "You *really* need a good lesson on speaking with respect. Especially toward the man that's about to save your ass." I pulled her from the wall and gave her a push toward where her shirt had been discarded on the floor. "Now get dressed."

"I hate you." She snatched the shirt off the ground.

"Get in line, Princess." I pulled out bags from the closet and tossed them at her feet. Dorothy's clothing order had been delivered hours ago, but I hadn't cared to give it to her until now. I thumbed open my security feed. Systems were triggering all over the outer borders and a full breach at the northern fence of the compound. Fucking perfect.

Dorothy crossed her arms, a scathing look on her face sharp enough to cut. She'd thrown on a black pair of jeans with frayed holes strategically torn across her thighs and knees, a light grey t-shirt and tall black boots. I laughed. I couldn't help it. Splayed across her chest in big pink rhinestones it said, "Spoiled", with a tiny heart dotting the I.

She plucked at the edges of the shirt, pouting at the lettering. "This isn't what I picked out."

"Yeah, but it felt appropriate. So, I made a few changes."

"And these?" She reached into the bag and pulled out a pair of underwear that were little more than a series of elastic bands and rhinestones.

"Purely for my entertainment."

"There is literally nothing to cover any part of the body that matters."

"Pretty sure that's the point."

Dorothy threw the garment, and I ducked letting it hit the cabinets behind me.

"You don't have to wear them." I added with pure amusement. Fuck, Dorothy was sexy when she was pissed. "I'm perfectly comfortable with you foregoing under garments all together."

I swiped the display over to the thermal sensors. Four people were working their way towards the eastern wall. In about five minutes they would be trying to smash a window. Ordinarily, it would be impossible to break. The windows were bullet and shatter proof. But whoever this was made it past two previous barriers, in next to no time. They were already prepared to break our security. Which in and of itself was troubling. There was no fire, no explosion, no indication of a cybernetic attack. Meaning they had Crowe or Nick's phone and were disabling one system after another from the inside.

"There's a tunnel in the garage," I said, ignoring the very visible rage pouring from Dorothy. Or maybe that was lust. The flushed cheeks and erect nipples made it hard to tell the difference. Silently thanking myself for deleting the bras from her cart, I palmed her breast through the soft cotton shirt.

Dorothy smacked my hand. "Don't touch me, asshole."

Rather than back away as any respectable man would, I used my position to force her against the wall. She let out a cry that was decidedly moan like, sinking her teeth into her lip the moment she realized that her body had betrayed her. So, the little firecracker liked being thrown around. I'd file that bit of information away for later.

"Why would I do that, when you so obviously love it?" Gripping her leg, I pressed my body against hers until the only thing separating us was that thin bit of sparkly fabric. My thumb slid into the slashed jeans, tearing them until I could stroke the soft flesh of her inner thigh. Another perfect addition to her shopping cart. If we had more time I'd be tearing them from her right now. There's always later.

"Those are my only pants," Dorothy said, panting hard enough to rock our bodies together, the dilation in her eyes increasing with every brush of my finger. The blackening pupils zeroed in on my lips moments before she grabbed a fistful of my hair and dragged my mouth to hers. Kissing her was like eating an entire box of Red Hots at once. The punishing heat battled with the sweetness in a way that left me craving more.

A bright yellow light flashed on my phone. Of all the damn nights to be under siege. On the video feed two more men were scaling the exterior, and headed for the office window on the second floor.

"I hope you're not afraid of motorcycles," I said, stealing one more kiss, then lowering her gently to the ground. I probably shouldn't have been so rough with her, but she wasn't exactly complaining either.

"I thought you said this place was secure," Dorothy said looking over my shoulder at my screen. "Since I've been here you've been hacked and attacked. That doesn't really feel too safe to me." Victory lit up her delicate features. I was tempted to leave her bratty ass here just to teach her a lesson.

I pressed a purple button on my screen. It sent a high voltage electric current to the metal siding on the outer wall. The figures jolted, as a deadly level of electricity funneled through their bodies.

Amateurs.

"It *is* secure. I just don't have time for games. The boys need me, so get your ass moving toward the garage."

"Sorry all I just heard was, 'blah blah blah they need *us*'."

"That smart mouth of yours is going to get you in trouble."

"Nothing I can't handle." She flipped me off, her swollen lips pursing into a blown kiss. She didn't bother waiting for my reply, instead she walked with a clipped step towards my Ducati.

-17-
THEA

Danny threw me a black motorcycle helmet, which I almost missed catching. I was too busy trying to figure exactly where on that death trap he was planning on my ass sitting. As far as I could see, there was only one seat.

"Hit the button on the side to turn the helmet on. That way, I can still talk to you while we're on the road." He hit a similar button on his helmet. The face shield flickered, a visual readout showing on the glass as it connected to his phone.

"*Now* you want to talk?"

He swung a leg over the superbike. It was painted an assaulting shade of red, with a sparkling gold *Superleggera* down one side. It must be worth a fortune. If he had enough money to afford a custom bike like this, what did he need my money for?

The room went dark, yellow safety lights coming to life in the corner of the garage. The power must have been cut to the compound.

"Get on, Firecracker." Danny's voice was serious but unhurried. He truly didn't seem like he was the least bit concerned about the people closing in on us. The low light made fiery streaks reflect off the glossy black surface as he pulled the helmet over his head. He left the visor open so that I could see the devious joy he was getting from my unease. The corners of his eyes creased, and boyish dimples formed along his cheeks. I didn't know Danny was the kind of person that ever genuinely smiled, but here he was.

"Where exactly?"

He thumbed behind him and rocked his hips as far forward as the bike would allow.

I groaned. There was all of five inches of space behind his broad form. The back half of my ass would be hanging over the tail of the bike.

"I won't fit on there. Can't we just take one of those?" I pointed to the sports car.

Danny pulled on a pair of leather gloves. "The tunnel isn't big enough for a car. You're just going to have to hold on."

I slid into the seat, my body having no choice but to mold to his. My arms snaked around his waist. I struggled to find anywhere to hold on as I palmed the solid muscle of his abdomen. Seriously, was he flexing, or was he always this hard?

We rolled toward the corner of the room. The gentle side-to-side movement of the bike already causing my heart rate to spike. Slowly, the walls parted, the headlight illuminating the dark concrete tunnel sloping deep into the ground.

"Don't go too fast."

Danny snorted and dropped the face visor. His fingers flexed against the hand grips. "I don't do slow."

The engine roared, and in a blur, the world around us disappeared. I screamed a gut-wrenching sound as my stomach bottomed out. Squeezing my eyes shut, I plastered my body to his like I could crawl into the safety of his frame. The sound of Danny's laughter carried over the speakers in the helmet. We turned a corner, dipping low and nearly laying completely out before returning upright.

I was going to die. Or vomit. Or vomit, then die.

Within minutes, we were bursting out of the tunnel into the dark night. The compound was nowhere to be seen, just miles of dark woods on either side of a long, straight road. Danny leaned back, more relaxed now that we were away from the threat. My heart was still racing in my throat, but at least now I felt like I could keep my eyes open.

"What's the matter, Dorothy?" He tapped the back of my hand where it was locked in a death grip on the front of his leather jacket. "Did you finally run out of things to say?"

I swallowed my panic, the bile that had risen sinking back down into my gut. After a few minutes, my heart rate slowed, allowing my voice to be steady. "Why don't you care about people breaking into the house? What if they get the emerald?"

"Who says they'll get in?"

He swiped at the screen in the center of his console, pressing a red button that said 'Lockdown.'

"Even without power, nobody is getting into the house without permission. The worst we'll have to do is some body disposal. That's more tedious than anything."

I shivered at his nonchalance. He might as well have been discussing emptying a trash can for how casually he discussed disposing of a person.

"It doesn't matter though. I have the emerald."

"Wait, *you* have *my* emerald?" Boiling outrage quickly overpowered my fear. I pawed at his chest, sliding my fingers along each pocket to find where the gem was hiding. I tried to ignore just how tight the jacket was. Slipping beneath the hem, I smoothed my palms over his shirt. No necklace. Just lots of cut muscle.

"*My* emerald isn't there, but by all means keep searching. Maybe you should check lower, just to be certain."

I'd check lower, alright. I'd check by punching him right in the dick.

"You had no right taking it."

"Technically, *I* didn't take it. Crowe did."

I smacked his back but was afraid to fight back more than that. I was already terrified that we'd crash. "Wait!" I gripped onto his shoulder, pulling back in alarm. The bike swerved, making me scream, and Danny let out a laugh. "There's a tracker in the necklace!"

Danny caressed the thigh pressed against his, still laughing.

"Why are you laughing?" I knocked his hand off of my leg. "Won't Westin be able to find us?"

"I'm counting on it."

"That makes zero sense."

"Sometimes you have to throw a bit of chaos into the mix." Danny tapped the screen again, bringing up a map and zooming in on a construction yard. "Nick pinged me his location. Looks like they're held up near Gorba's. It's no coincidence the guys were intercepted at the same time the compound was attacked. They used Crowe's phone to get past the perimeter defenses."

"Crowe's phone?" A stone flipped over in my stomach as my too-slow mind processed the information. "Then they would have to—"

"Have Crowe? Yeah. Hence, not having time to mess with the amateur attack team."

"But he…" My voice trailed off, choked by a foreign and nervous worry. Did I care about him? When and how did that happen?

"Don't worry, Firecracker. He'll be fine. Crowe's tougher than he looks."

"How far away are we?"

"About forty minutes."

I massaged my already sore thighs. The cuts at my back stretched taut, making them throb too. I rested my head against Danny's back and did my best to relax. His hand dropped to my leg and moved in slow, long strokes. It was almost like he cared.

Almost.

-18-
NICK

I zeroed in my scope on Crowe's limp form. Shit had gone to hell so quickly.
One minute, he was regaling me with all the details I didn't need to know
about Thea, the next, the cab was spinning out of control.

All because that girl was the definition of trouble. The kind that looked
vulnerable and sweet, tricking you into wanting to indulge in it. The kind that
got you ambushed on the I-9 and sent your world spinning out of control.
Trouble was never worth the time, even when it came with spiraling auburn
hair and an attitude to match its fire. Thea was beautiful, no doubt. Then again,
the worst gifts came wrapped in pretty packaging. Case in point: our current
predicament.

None of this would be happening if we had just handed the girl over to
Westin and claimed the reward. Or we could simply send her back to her aunt.
Simple. Trouble gone. Emily Rosen had put out a hit, and all she wanted in
return was proof of death. Easy, except Crowe's history with Westin made him
impossible to reason with. He'd never hand Thea over to a Witcher, especially
now that he was growing *attached,* and there was zero chance of Danny working
with The Farm. So, here we were, knee-deep in shit for a girl who couldn't
possibly be worth all of this trouble.

I looked back through my scope, the night vision illuminating Gorba's construction yard. Dozens of vehicles and equipment were parked in a line to one
side. The rest of the yard was filled with stacks of piping in various sizes. There
were a dozen men running patrol around the perimeter. Not that they did a
very good job of it. It was laughably easy to move into position near Gorba's

portable offices. More than anything, I was annoyed that we would miss the Crick Link job because of this.

What I needed was a distraction and for Crowe to wake the fuck up. Whatever was in the dart had knocked him out instantly. He hadn't even been able to fully swear out his concern, slumping over the steering wheel with a half-muttered "Fuuu—"

In retrospect, it wasn't surprising that he made such a rookie mistake. We'd both been distracted. Crowe was obviously pussy drunk, and I barely heard his prattling because I was too focused on Thea's whimpered cries still rattling around in my brain—triggering memories I didn't need to confront.

I was pushing the image of Thea's silver tears from my mind when Crowe fell into the shifter, knocking us into a lower gear and sending the cab into a full spin. Luckily, the stretch of abandoned highway was empty. By the time the cab slowed, a swarm of lights descended on us, far more than I could handle on my own while trapped in the vehicle. I grabbed my rifle from the back and made the split-second decision to abandon the car.

To them, it would look like I was making a run for it and abandoning my friend, but in reality, I was choosing to pick my battleground. They'd used a tranq dart, so they weren't here to kill. Not yet, anyway. Which meant I had time.

I fired off a quick warning text to Danny. While I was trailing these *cazzos* to this site, my phone flashed a warning notification at me.[1] The compound was under siege. One security feature after another was disabled. So that had been the point of the attack. They'd been after one of our phones so that they could bypass our security and get to Thea.

Trouble. The girl was nothing but the worst kind of trouble.

Once I was in position, I used the time to pull up the compound. I watched Danny and Thea leaving down the escape tunnel on the back of his bike right

---

1. While I was trailing these fuckers to this site, my phone flashed a warning notification at me.

before he set off the lockdown measures. Of course, he was bringing the trouble with him. She could have stayed behind. Even with Crowe's phone, whoever this was would never make it in the building, not once full lockdown was enabled. I thought I could depend on Danny to be smarter, but I saw the way he looked at her when he thought no one was watching, and I definitely didn't miss the way he ran his hands down her legs after she straddled the bike behind him.

With the way that Danny drove, it would barely be another twenty minutes before they were here. Which was a good thing because a man in a suit came walking across the lot. In the silence, the sound of his shiny loafers crunching on the gravel seemed to echo. I zoomed the scope, trying to identify who was dumb enough to ambush us. Not that it mattered. As soon as Danny got here, this moron was getting a bullet straight through his unsubstantial brain.

He loomed over my brother, sticking him in the throat with a long needle. The man tossed it aside and gave Crowe's face a couple light slaps. Crowe's head lolled back, consciousness slowly returning. His eyes lacked focus, and he seemed completely unaware of where he was.

The man in the suit noticed, too. Crowe must not have been waking up fast enough because he clocked him with a hard right hook. The impact forced Crowe's head to slam against the pole, anchoring him to the ground.

That did it. His hands flexed behind him and pulled at their bindings. The well-dressed man snapped to the side, beckoning over the hired muscle that was hanging back. A big man reached down and hauled Crowe upright. His feet scrambled beneath him as his semi-conscious body tried to find footing. The sound of metal on metal echoed off the different surfaces.

Crowe's features twisted from confusion to fury as he finally understood where he was. He said something to the man beside him, earning him a punch to the gut. Crowe, the crazy fucker, laughed. That earned him a second punch.

The haptics on my watch buzzed with an update from Danny. They were still five minutes out.

The man leaned over, gripping Crowe's chin and saying something. Whatever it was made Crowe pull back. Alarm flickered over his golden features, and he yanked frantically against his binds. The man in the suit shifted his weight and pointed at the northern end of the yard. Directly toward where Danny and Thea should be approaching any minute.

Son of a bitch. He knew.

The attack on the compound, our ambush, it was all a ploy to get Thea out of hiding—and Danny was bringing her right here. The man in the suit turned toward me, providing a clear view of his face as *he winked.*

Orin Berret. *Cazzo! Fuck. Fuck. FUCK.*[2]

Five red dots all appeared on my chest. Followed by a flood light illuminating what I was sure had been a perfect place to snipe from.

"Come on out, Niccolo. I wouldn't want your father to hear you died cowering behind a shed," Orin called.

I hated this man, truly hated him.

Slowly, I rose, my hand hovering over my wrist to send an abort code to Danny. If it wasn't already too late. This wasn't an amateur hit team. This was the absolute one group of people we needed to avoid, WM Mercs.

"Ah-ah-aah," he chided. "Hands in the air. Not that it matters. Your message would be falling on *dead ears,* as it were." Orin laughed at his joke.

"Winged. Monkey. Fucker. I swear to Ozma, if you've so much as touched her, I will skin you alive." Crowe pulled harder against the post anchoring him in place. "You're a dead man, Orin. You're already dead!"

The leader of the Winged Monkeys tsked with a disapproving finger wag at Crowe's outrage. "This display is completely unnecessary. That little wisp of a thing barely screamed the first time. Now, Danny..." His voice trailed off with a goading laugh.

I didn't react. I wouldn't believe they were dead until I was holding their cold flesh in my hands. Until then, I refused to play whatever mind-fuck game Orin was trying to force me into. Danny had more lives than a black cat in hell, and if Thea was anything, she was a survivor. That girl would stare down the barrel

---

2. Fuck!

of a gun with a smile that could melt iron. This was a bluff, and I was about to call him on it.

My hands raised high where the Monkeys with the guns could see them, I walked slowly to the center of the lot. The men flanking the perimeter, who I had mislabeled as incompetent, all had rifles trained on me, painting my chest with red laser dots. I had a gun in the holster under my arm and another behind my belt, but I might as well have left them in the car for as much good as they would do me. If I so much as sneezed, it would be the last movement I ever made.

"Isn't this a little below your pay grade, Orin?" I gave Crowe a solid look over. He seemed to be okay and was only held to the rod in one location. Not impossible, but first, we had to get past being fish in the center of a barrel. What I needed was a distraction. "I thought Winged Monkeys didn't fly out of their nests for less than a million."

"Yeah, well, Westin called in a favor. It would seem she's rather attached to a particular family heirloom, one your girl took the liberty of stealing." Orin looked down at his nails, buffing them on his lapel. He let out a low groan of disgust. "Vincent, your face got blood all over my nails."

Crowe spit on Orin's shoes. "Come closer, Berret. I'll paint you in so much blood your vision will turn red. I don't need my hands free to kill a spineless motherfucker like you."

"Cute." The leader of the Monkeys shifted to address me, noting the number of steps left between us. Orin smiled and waved offhandedly towards the northern wall. "As a bonus, I get to deliver one very pretty head to Emily Rosen. Seems that little minx has a talent for making enemies all over Oz. Who knows, maybe other pieces of her will be worth something too."

As if they could hear the threat, there was the pop of gunfire over the hillside.

"Ah, here she comes now. Right on time." Orin's final words were drowned out by the roaring of an engine. A headlight cut through the darkness seconds before Danny's Superleggera flew over the wall—with no rider. I had a millisecond to process this information before the power was cut to the yard, and we were blanketed in total darkness.

Shouting broke out around us, and the lasers that were focused on me shifted toward where the bike had been a moment ago. I pulled the gun from my holster and fired off three bullets in quick succession directly where Orin had just been standing.

I dove for the ground. Heat from a passing bullet buzzed by my cheek, followed by a spray of dirt.

A tracer round streaked through the darkness. It exploded like a firework the moment it pierced the tank of the motorcycle. The bike burst into a giant fireball, the spray of light illuminating the yard.

Orin disappeared, somehow managing to miss each of my bullets. There was no sign of Danny or Thea, so I decided to make a move for Crowe. He was also frantically scanning the yard for a sign of the rest of our team.

"The trailer!" he shouted, but his words were cut off when a booming explosion rocked the ground. Behind me, the trailer roared with flames. Three barrels of fuel rolled toward the row of construction vehicles. I followed their path backwards.

Thea stood draped in shadows. She flicked a lighter, shining just enough light to see the determination in her expression. There was a ferocity to her stance, power behind the way she stared down the scene. For a moment, I could perfectly imagine what Crowe must have seen that day on the video monitor. It was a vision of the woman who bashed in the Queen of the East's face.

Thea dropped the lighter with a smile. The trailing lines of igniting fuel hissed, writhing like snakes over the gravel, illuminating her killer form. Death was never a rider on a pale horse. It was a woman bathed in firelight, her hair glowing a brutal shade of red that reminded me of the poppy fields of my childhood. Not the rainbow flowers of Oz, but the crimson ones of home.

Thea dove behind a stack of pipes. I'd been foolish staring at her and drawing unnecessary attention in her direction. Moments later, the barrels exploded, taking the line of vehicles with them one after another. Bits of metal shrapnel flew in all directions.

I'd wished for a distraction, and Thea delivered. Not wasting a minute of it, I sprinted for Crowe, sliding into the ground beside him with a spray of gravel.

"Took you long enough."

"Took me? You literally were sleeping half this time."

I pulled a pocket knife from my boot and quickly cut his hands free.

"I was drugged," he said with a laugh. A feminine scream from the other side of the yard made my blood ice over.

Crowe pulled the spare gun free of my belt. He fired off two quick shots over my back at where Thea had disappeared.

I spun quickly. His shots went wide, hitting the concrete wall behind Orin. Crowe cursed. "It's the sedatives."

I wanted to make a joke, but I couldn't get past the scene unfolding before me. Orin had a gun to Danny's back, but that wasn't what made my eyes go wide.

Thea had *Danny's* gun pointed at Orin. "How in the hell?"

Mirroring my shock, Crowe added, "Is that Danny's gun...fuck, that's hot."

Orin was too quiet to hear what he said, but it made Thea look like a ghost in the firelight. While the blood may have drained from her beautiful face, none of her ferocity did. Thea shouted a battle cry, "Never! Never Again."

I tightened my fists, feeling the inked letters stretch. We all had our demons, and Thea's were raging. Sirens echoed off the hills, and the lights of many approaching vehicles flickered in the distance.

Thea glanced at the advancing police, and Orin followed her eyes to the horizon. Taking advantage of the distraction, Danny spun, attempting to disarm the gun at his back. A shot echoed around the yard. I held my breath and waited to see my brother fall to the ground. Instead, Orin stumbled back, blood soaking the arm of his fancy sportscoat. He looked as shocked as the rest of us.

Thea had shot him. She'd fired past Danny's shoulder and shot him. Grabbing the wound, Orin ran for the shadows.

Danny took the gun from Thea's trembling hands and quickly fired several more shots into the darkness, but Orin was gone. Crowe and I made it up to them just as Danny took her face between his hands.

"You look unfairly sexy with a gun, Firecracker, but don't ever point one at me again." Then, his face collided with hers in a devastating kiss. Thea's hands snaked into his hair, deepening their embrace. She rolled against him in a way that made the muscles in my body tighten.

"Well, shit," Crowe muttered, eyes locked on the way Thea's hips rocked into Danny's.

Thea tightened her grip on his hair, pulling his head back with a hard yank. His lips dragged through her teeth, leaving them tinged faintly pink from where she had bitten down.

Danny hissed out in pain, or shock, or frustration from being denied. Probably all three. It was so surprising I couldn't help but laugh.

"I think what you meant to say was, '*Thank you for saving my ass, Thea.*'" She gave him a hard shove, forcing him to stumble off balance.

Danny stalked back forward, pent-up anger making the lines in his throat more pronounced. "Orin only got the jump on me because I was too busy defending *you*, Princess. You had one job. Light the gas and stay out of sight. Not flash your tits all over the yard while you bathe in your pyromanic afterglow."

"Don't blame me for that. I did my job. You were so busy crying over your bike you didn't even notice that shiny asshole approaching."

"That bike was one of only 250 made. You don't want to know what I went through to get her."

"*Her?* So I'm only an asset, but the bike is a *her.*"

Thea leapt at him, fist cocked back. She might have even hit him if Crowe hadn't snaked an arm around her waist.

"Simmer down, Darling. I promise I'll let you kick his ass later. See those flashing red and blues. We needed to be gone five minutes ago."

"He's right," Danny added, pulling down on his shirt and brushing the dust from his arms.

"The cab is over there." I pointed toward a darkened area of the yard. "Orin's boys parked it just inside the gates."

"Convenient. Wasn't it nice of them to be so accommodating?"

We ran to the car, and I slipped behind the wheel. Crowe pulled Thea into the backseat while Danny climbed into the passenger side. With a flick of a switch, the screen in the center of the console turned on a night vision camera, allowing me to be able to see without having to turn on any running lights. We rumbled down the dirt road in the opposite direction of the approaching sirens.

"What about Danny's bike?" Thea said, twisting to look out the rear window. "Won't they know it was us?"

I looked in the mirror at Crowe.

"I've got it," he reluctantly looked away from Thea and reached forward for a phone.

"I can't watch," Danny moaned, putting the phone in his hand.

Crowe made a couple of deft movements, and then a final explosion detonated behind us.

"What now?" Thea said, settling into Crowe's side.

"We head to the EC. There's no point in trying for Crick Link now. Especially if we've been blacklisted," Danny said, opening a side panel to start reloading his gun.

"Agreed," I said with a nod and pulled the cab onto the I-9. In just a few short days, we'd be arriving at the glittering heart of Oz.

-19-
THEA

"Your heart's still racing," Crowe murmured into my ear, his feather-light touch lingering over my pulse.

"I suppose all that *would* be a bit terrifying to someone who isn't used to this sort of thing," Danny said dismissively.

Nick's eyes met mine in the rearview mirror, a smirk gracing the corner of his mouth.

I rolled my eyes. Pricks. All of them.

Crowe nuzzled against my neck, running a hand up the inside of the thigh closest to him. "Do you want me to tell him the truth, or do you want to do it?"

"Tell me what?" Danny huffed.

I shrugged. Crowe smiled against my neck, his hand slowly inching higher.

"Her heart isn't racing from fear. It's racing with excitement." With a single finger, he tipped my chin up, forcing me to look up at him. "Isn't it, Beautiful?"

I bit down on my lip and failed miserably at hiding the truth because, of course, he was right. Lighting that fire had made me feel alive, almost as much as the kick from the gun had. Even if it made my back ache like a motherfucker.

With a quick movement, Crowe grabbed my hips. I didn't even know what was happening or how he did it, but all of a sudden, I was straddling him. My shoulders pushed against the front seat, jolting it and forcing me to wince in pain.

Danny shouted, "Fuck off, Crowe. You don't need to be doing that against my seat."

"I'm checking our girl to make sure she's okay." Crowe's hand gently cupped my cheek, the touch gentle despite the mischief in his eyes.

"Dorothy doesn't need to be riding your cock to see she's fine." He punched the back of the seat, making my body jolt unexpectedly against Crowe's. The friction overrode the pain, sending electricity dancing over my skin. Small goosebumps rose along my arms. A fact that didn't go unnoticed by the man trailing his fingers along my jaw to palm the back of my neck.

The slight swelling along his cheek somehow made him more handsome. It contrasted with his usual playful, boy-next-door look, adding an edge of danger that matched the intensity behind his eyes.

"What I want to know is how Thea got your gun in the first place," Nick said.

Crowe tilted my head back and pressed a kiss to the hollow of my throat. Murmuring against my skin, he added, "Mmm, I'd like to know that, too. Nothing gets me harder than a woman with a gun." He pulled on my hips until I was grinding against him. The man definitely wasn't lying. The hard ridge pressed between my thighs proved it. Into my ear, he added, "And, I'd bet anything firing that pistol got you wet."

"Well, I'd like to know how Orin-fucking-Berret got the jump on you. Because saving your asses wasn't on the list of things I planned to do tonight." Danny's voice sounded bitter.

"I bet it wasn't," Crowe said with a laugh, forcing another hard rock of my hips. "I think we all saw who you planned on doing tonight."

I moaned. I couldn't help it. The seam of my jeans was pressed directly against my bare clit, and the adrenaline-laced blood pumping in my veins was making everything more sensitive.

Crowe's eyes glittered in the dark cab interior. They flicked over my shoulder to the front of the cab. "I think Nick likes hearing you moan, sweet girl." From the feral way Crowe grinned, I knew Nick was watching us in the mirror still. "But I think we can do better than that."

Crow lifted the hem of my shirt, pulling it free and tossing it unceremoniously over the seat behind me.

"Fucking hell," Danny cursed, sending the shirt back at Crowe in a blur of pink rhinestones. Crowe ducked, leaning forward and using the opportunity to lick a path up my bare chest.

I wasn't facing them, but I could feel the heat of Nick and Danny's attention on me. I should stop this. Crowe would stop if I said the word. I was certain of it, but the strength he was using to drive me against his impressively hard cock was short-circuiting my brain.

"Crowe...I..."

He silenced my breathy protest with a languorous kiss, robbing me of my ability to think altogether. There was just the rising pressure and the demanding call for release. This night had been triggering on every level, but right now, I existed only in the feel of his body beneath me, the caress of his hands against my skin, and the press of his mouth to mine.

Crowe swallowed my building sighs, and I let myself escape into our increasing pace. Warmth surged along my spine. I felt it from the soles of my feet to the tips of my fingers, just as he slowed our movements to a gentle rock. My orgasm pulled back like the tide from the shore.

"I can feel you trembling against me," he said with a hushed voice. They were words just for me, though I knew the others could still hear him.

"It's the adrenaline."

"Is it? Maybe I need to be trying harder. Fuck, I want to peel these jeans off of you. I know you'd be hot and slick."

His hand tracked over my hip, finding the hole Danny had torn wide earlier in the night. With a single pull, the sound of tearing denim filled the cab, and the fabric fell away, exposing my entire leg.

"Much better." Crowe's long fingers slid beneath the denim. His head dropped to my chest with a satisfied groan when he realized I wasn't wearing any underwear. "Darling Thea, you are full of surprises." He dragged the wetness soaking my pants up, smoothing his thumb over my clit, while two more fingers pushed into me.

I clamped my hand over my mouth, biting my palm to muffle my surprised cry.

Crowe's free hand circled my wrist, pulling it down. "Don't do that. Don't hide. Let them hear all of the wicked things I'm about to do to you." Crowe licked a line up the length of my neck, resting his lips against my ear. "If you were able, I'd be sliding you onto my dick right now. I'd keep each thrust deep as you rode me, ensuring you felt every inch." Raking his teeth over the sensitive spot behind my ear, he added, "I'm not small, Thea. It'd be tight and you'd feel so full."

Danny made a quiet exhale of disbelief. "Are you really buying his delusional bullshit, Firecracker?"

Fuck, I really was. Tingles prickled all over my skin and a devious thrill zinged through me. Danny's comment only amplified the sensation, knowing he was mere inches from me and Nick was close enough that I could have hit him. I ground hard against Crowe's palm, trying to feel even a ghost of what he was promising.

He pushed on my lower abdomen with his free hand at the same time he curled the fingers deep inside me, intensifying the pressure. "The harder we went, the tighter your pussy would grip my cock. Just like you're choking my hand right now. You'd want to go fast, careening over the edge, but I wouldn't let you."

The pressure disappeared long enough for my climax to fade.

I wanted to scream. Those fingers belonged in hell. I ran my nails down his forearm in an attempt to keep him in place. When he decided to continue, it was maddeningly harder and rougher than before, driving me past the brink.

"It would be the best kind of torture." Crowe ran his nose along my collarbone, pressing a kiss in the crook of my neck.

My heavy panting forced my nipples to graze the soft leather of his jacket. My skin was humming, sparking like a live wire, ready to ignite at any moment.

"I'd slowly unravel your senses one nerve ending at a time." He lowered his mouth to my breast, pulling my aching nipple between his teeth. I writhed in his lap, praying in a nonsensical mumble for him to give me what I so badly needed.

"Fucking hell, Crowe, and you call *me* heartless. Just let the girl come already." Nick's voice was tight, like the display that Crowe was putting on was as excruciating for him as it was for me.

"Do you hear that, beautiful? Nick wants to hear you fall apart while you ride my hand." He pushed us forward until I was pressed into Danny's seat. I draped my arm behind me, gripping the headrest to leverage my movements. The soft brush of Danny's hair caressed my wrist. My fingertips grazed the back of his neck. The stripes across my lower shoulders screamed in protest, the pain mixing with the churning pleasure—all of it centered over where Crowe's thumb hovered torturously out of reach.

"What do you think, Danny? Does she deserve it?"

"She did point a gun at me," Danny said with a low tone that rumbled through the cushioning of the seat straight into my chest. The spicy tones of Danny's cologne mixed with Crowe's earthen scent. If I closed my eyes, I could almost imagine I was pinned between them.

"Eyes on me, gorgeous." I opened them, barely seeing his lust-crazed expression drilling into me through the light flashing at the corners of my vision. Crowe slowly pistoned his hand. It wasn't a long motion, but the way his fingertip maintained constant pressure against exactly the right spot was enough to make me whimper a plea to him.

"Please, Crowe." I was so fucking close. "Please."

"Fuck, she begs so prettily," Danny said with longing, his head turning so that the stubble on his cheek brushed my palm and his lips ghosted over my wrist.

"She does, doesn't she?" Crowe said, gripping my breast and driving hard enough to make me cry out but not enough to tip me into bliss. "Thea did shoot that arrogant psychopath. Our girl deserves something as a reward."

There was that word again: *our*.

Before I could process the way he'd laid claim to me, Crowe's thumb finally brushed my clit. Like pulling a trigger, my orgasm ripped through me with all the violence of a bullet tearing flesh. The adrenaline, the pain, the excruciating denial—all of it pushed me to a height I had never been to before.

"Give me your hand."

I lifted my head off the seat, my vision slowly returning to me.

"What?" I was still drunk on my orgasm, so when Crowe slid my fingers between my legs I didn't think anything of it. I jumped at that first sensitive brush. But he increased the pressure of our fingers until they pushed in together. Stretching me wide and making me feel fuller than I'd ever felt before. The foreign sensation of his fingers beside mine made me reflexively pulse around them.

"Oh my god," I rasped out, my voice broken and raw. Had I been screaming? I couldn't remember. "Crowe, I don't think I can—"

Stealing my words, he kissed me. Fuck, he was good at that. When he released my lips, I couldn't remember what I was protesting.

"This isn't for you," he corrected, pulling our hands free.

Gently, he twisted us and extended my arm so that it passed between the front seats. At first, I didn't understand what was happening. Nick exchanged a look with Danny but didn't move.

Danny took my hand from Crowe, then lifted one glistening finger to his mouth.

My mouth hung open, watching in awe as his tongue slowly licked away my arousal in exactly the same way he'd tasted the scotch that first night in the compound.

"You taste exactly like I thought you would, Firecracker."

Nick's hands tightened on the steering wheel. "Fuck me. Like *what*?"

Crowe turned my face to meet his gaze, and licked clean the last of his own fingers. "Sweet, but with a kick."

Nick groaned. "Next time, I'm not driving."

-20-
THEA

Crowe eased me off of his lap, then leaned over me to pull a lever on the side of the seat. "Watch your legs."

A motor whirred, and beneath my feet, the seat began to unfold. Cushions pushed up until the entire back seat was one large, flat bed.

"Your car turns into a *bed?*"

Crowe only laughed as an answer, giving me a knowing smile.

"I don't care how sweet she tastes and how Oz damn sexy she sounds while coming. Do *not* fuck her on the backseat of my car," Danny commanded. His eyes flashed with danger when they finally met mine. That taste hadn't been enough for him.

"*Our* car," Crowe corrected, unraveling the bandage from around my center.

"You sound jealous, *Dandy*," I added with an exhausted yawn. Nevermind that nobody asked me what I wanted. I wasn't planning on sleeping with any of them, but then again, I hadn't planned on anything that had happened in the past week. I certainly hadn't planned to get off in front of an audience. Crowe had a way of dissolving my defenses, and in their place, a reckless abandon was starting to take root.

I think I liked it.

Crowe eased my body down to the soft upholstery. "Turn on to your stomach for me, Gorgeous."

Rolling over with a decided lack of grace, I rested my head on my arms. It was like that orgasm had left me an uncoordinated mess of blissed-out exhaustion.

"Nobody is fucking anyone." Crowe started methodically removing gauze. "You saw her back. That would rip open every one of these stitches."

"What in the name of Ozma? Fuck, Danny, did you do these bandages with your eyes closed." His hands ran over me, checking the tape and making a displeased sound. "I, unlike you, actually care about her well-being and am willing to sacrifice to ensure she heals."

"Yeah, it really sounded like you were sacrificing," Danny grumbled. Nick laughed. I lifted my head to see what a smiling Nick actually looked like, but whatever joy had graced his features was already gone.

"I think it would be best if we let these breathe for a little while," Crowe's hands went from the cuts to prod at my side. "At least it looks like the bruising on your ribs is fading."

Nick grunted his agreement. "Add some of the cream from the kit."

"On it." Crowe flicked open the seatback compartment. Inside were carefully stashed medical supplies for everything from minor cuts to what looked like major surgery.

He rubbed the minty-smelling cream along my battered skin, the coolness of his gliding fingers making me shiver. Once he had cleaned his hands, he brushed the hair from my face and cradled my cheek. "Are you comfortable?"

I nodded, my eyes already drifting shut.

Crowe's hands hooked into my waistband, unbuttoning and he easing my torn jeans down. My eyes flew back open.

"I have to say your choice to omit undergarments is one I approve of."

"I'm so glad I have your approval," I drawled with as much sarcasm as I could muster. "Not a choice, by the way. Danny deleted them from my shopping cart."

"Not true," Danny said, turning to shoot me a wink. Asshole. "I bought her a couple different sets of lingerie. She chose to turn down my generosity."

I propped myself up on my elbows, making sure he didn't mistake my exhaustion for weakness. *Generosity?* Fucking hell, his arrogance was next level. "Those weren't underwear, Danny. They were some kind of bizarre red light district torture device. Assless and crotchless are not functional, and they sure as fuck aren't comfortable."

"Depends on the function," Crowe chuckled. He winked at Nick in the mirror, sharing some inside joke between them that had me all kinds of curious.

"Say fuck again, Princess. You know I love when you talk dirty to me."

Before I could rise to his bait, Crowe threw my discarded jeans at him. Danny tossed them away with a laugh, but it had been enough to dispel the tension rising between us.

Crowe gave my ass an appreciative caress, forcing my heart rate to speed back up. "It should be illegal for a woman to possess both your tits and this ass."

I twisted towards him, ready to protest.

He put a single finger to my lips. "Shh, darling. We're done playing..." He paused that thought and made a slow sweep of my body. "For now." His fingers drifted down my legs and settled behind my knees. "I'm just giving these a once over to be sure Danny didn't tear them up on the bike."

"Oh." I shifted back. My stomach flipped with... disappointment? That was new. Was I actually disappointed that he was caring for me and not trying to recklessly fuck me in the back of a car while his friends watched? My priorities were seriously becoming twisted. Em had starved me of love for so long that I was fawning over the first person to ever show me a bit of kindness. It was pathetic, and my libido was only clouding my judgment. These guys were pretty to look at, but they would sell me out at the first opportunity. I couldn't forget that.

"If I tear anything up, it won't be her legs." Danny's voice dropped an octave, and reflexively, I tensed my thighs together at the image those words created. Goddammit, Thea. We just talked about this.

I pushed onto my knees, refusing to flinch at the ache that radiated everywhere and uncaring that I was naked. "The only thing getting torn up around here is about to be your face."

"Lie back down, Thea," Nick commanded. My mouth dropped open at the unexpected authority in his voice. His grey eyes were hard as he looked at us each directly in turn. "Danny will keep his mouth shut. Crowe is going to keep his hands to himself, and *you* are going to rest."

Crowe pulled a self-inflating pillow from another compartment. This cab really did have everything. He stretched out beside me and gestured for me to snuggle up next to him.

I hesitated because I'd never snuggled with anyone. Ever. It was a new level of vulnerability that I wasn't sure I was comfortable with. "I'm still naked."

"Believe me, I noticed. Come on. Lay down. I promise to behave."

Lowering into the crook of his arm, I awkwardly draped myself over him so that my back was still elevated. "For some reason, I think your definition of behave and mine are very different."

Crowe pressed a smiling kiss to my temple. He didn't argue it, though, confirming everything I needed to know. His fingertips pressed into my hair, rubbing soothing circles along invisible pressure points. I'd thought his fingers were made by the devil when they were tormenting my pussy, but I was re-thinking that now. Because this felt like heaven.

No wonder girls in books were always curling up with their man. The gentle thump of his heart was calming. It took very little for me to slip into the inky darkness of sleep.

-21-
CROWE

Thea's head nuzzled harder into my chest, whimpering at whatever was currently tormenting her dreams. Was it all the violence of the past few days, or did she always sleep so restlessly?

"Shhh," I whispered into her ear. The tension immediately left her sleeping body. Something warm and fuzzy swelled in my chest. I calmed her. *Me*. It was refreshing to be someone's port in the storm instead of the storm itself.

Oz damn it. Was I falling for this girl?

I was. Hard and fast enough I was almost dizzy from it.

Danny turned to look over his shoulder at the two of us. He ran a thoughtful finger over his lower lip, eyes lazily scouring each of Thea's curves. From where he was sitting, he must have had the most amazing view. I almost envied him, except it was my body her naked chest and cunt had been pressed against for the past hour. It was my hand skating down her side, and it was my heartbeat lulling her to sleep.

"Is she waking up?"

"I don't think so," I said in a hushed tone. "She was pretty wrecked."

"Hard to imagine why." Nick laughed quietly. "You edged her during an adrenaline letdown."

"Did you see her complaining?" I grinned. 'Cause yeah, edging was intense, and the orgasm that followed always destroyed you. Which was exactly why I loved doing it. There was nothing sexier than watching a woman truly fall apart. "I would be surprised if she didn't sleep hard for the next couple hours."

The second I saw Thea walk out of the darkness, firelight from the exploding bike illuminating her perfect features, a tidal wave of relief washed over me. It was quickly followed by shock when she dropped the lighter, and the entire damn yard went up in flames. But it was when, smooth as a cat, she drew Danny's gun that I knew she was meant to be mine.

When she slid into that car beside me, I had exactly one driving thought: the need to feel Thea in my arms and see her pleasure, anything to burn away the images the leader of The Winged Monkeys had given me. Because the things Orin had said about her—

"I think now might be a good time—" Danny said, interrupting my thoughts, "—for you to explain how in the fuck Orin Berret got the jump on you?"

"A day early, too. That's what I haven't been able to figure out." Nick tapped his fingers against the steering wheel as he thought. "He had an entire team in place. The yard was set up ahead of time. None of that is done on the fly."

"A team infiltrating the compound, too," Danny added.

Nick continued, "We left only a couple of hours after the call from the Wizard. Nowhere near enough time to prepare anything on that scale."

"And how did the Monkeys know exactly where to intercept us?" I added, thinking about the small sound the dart had made sinking into my skin. We were lucky I hadn't crashed the cab when I was knocked out.

"Maybe he'd always planned on it, and he only had to move the ambush up a day."

Nick shook his head. "No. That doesn't fit. Because it was never about us. He did this to get to Thea. I have no doubt."

I held her tighter to me. It was only a slight increase in pressure to assuage my own feeling of panic. I followed it with a ghost of a kiss to the top of her head. Danny noticed it and cocked his head to the side in curiosity. Fuck it. I didn't care if he saw my emotions. Tonight cut things too close.

Orin had told me, with stone-cold seriousness, that he'd used *my* phone to break into the compound and take her. He detailed to me what she'd felt like as he choked the life from her. The colorful ways he'd abused her body before he'd done it. I didn't want to believe him. Orin was hardly a beacon of truth. I knew he got off on psychologically fucking with his prey, but those few minutes of uncertainty had ruined me.

It had become abundantly clear that in the few days I'd known this girl, she'd gotten under my skin in a way few ever had. One day, I would make good on my promise of death. I would dust off the Scarecrowe and make the sick fucker suffer in a way I hadn't in a long time. Orin would regret ever coming near my girl.

I closed my eyes, taking a deep inhale. She smelled like my shampoo but mingled with the lingering scent of smoke and gunpowder. First chance I got, I was going to wash the violence from her skin. I'd replace it with love and kindness, the adoration she so clearly deserved and never received. Thea's chest subtly rose and fell against mine. I should have removed my shirt before we laid down, a mistake I wouldn't make again. When this was over, Thea and I would sleep naked...every night.

When I opened my eyes again, Danny was still watching me.

"So then, how did he know?"

"Maybe we were hacked."

"Or The Wizard was hacked."

I snorted a laugh. "There is no way The Wizard was hacked."

"Unless the voice on the phone was never the Wizard."

I mulled that idea over. Our system was top of the line. I'd written the programming myself. It wasn't impossible to crack. The Wizard had demonstrated that. But we hadn't just been tapped. We'd been taken over. No, that was the Wizard pulling those strings. "Maybe someone was listening in on your call to Crick Link, and they just moved fast."

"I don't like it. We're being played, and I can't figure out who's playing us."

"Gigi?"

"Oh, she's most definitely playing us, but Monkeys aren't her style. This wasn't her."

"Tell me again why we couldn't just give her back to her aunt?" Nick said. "It would make things a hell of a lot easier."

I was about to snap at him, but Danny got there first. "Because that old bitch sold her own niece. You know my thoughts on peddling people."

"Sold her to a sadist who whipped her in the first five minutes of ownership," I added. Danny flinched.

Nick turned and gave Danny a hard and discerning glare. "I knew that *stronzetto*—" he waved over his shoulder at me. "—was pussy drunk, but you too? Shit, *Leone*, you were alone with her for only a day."[1]

"I'm not pussy drunk. I don't do brats, and Dorothy is as bratty as they come."

"Yes, you do," I said, fighting back a laugh so that it wouldn't wake Thea. He most definitely got off on the fight. He was probably smitten the second she kneed him in the dick.

"We aren't handing her over to anybody. The Wizard is the highest payout. It makes the most sense. We're just going to have to be more careful from here on out. That's all." Danny turned away from us, gazing out the nothingness beyond the window.

"Yeah, it was definitely that *payout* you were thinking of when you licked her fingers clean," I said with total sarcasm.

He'd watched the entire scene from the side mirror, pretending to be annoyed. But I caught glimpses of the lust in his eyes. The memory of the way he'd kissed her in the yard was all too fresh. That wasn't the kiss of someone who wanted a payout. It was the kiss of someone who'd been terrified of losing something precious to him.

I knew and felt that fear running like a current through me. It coursed deeper into my soul with each pump of my heart. It was why I offered a piece of her up to him. I knew Nick would never allow himself to indulge, but Danny needed her just as much as I did. Even if he wasn't willing to admit it.

---

1. I know that shithead was pussy drunk, but you too? Shit, Lion, you were alone with her for only a day.

"So what? We drive straight through to the E.C., and then what?" I caressed a line down Thea's arm with the sole intention of getting her to make that sleepy, mewling sound of contentment again. "Orin is still out there."

"Westin will probably be pissed her sneak attack didn't work. So she'll start trying harder, too."

"What if we made a run for the border?" I said hesitantly. We'd never run from anything before. Maybe I was reading them wrong, but I got the feeling they both didn't want the risk. We had Westin Witcher, Emily Rosen, and Winged Monkeys after us, plus a Wizard to contend with, and only Ozma knew what game Gigi was playing. Whether we wanted it or not, we were tied to Thea's fate now.

I looked down at the auburn waves of her hair, running my hand over where their satin ends splayed against her shoulder. I wouldn't have done it differently, though. Given the option, I still would have stopped my cab. I still would have raced out of the building with her, and I still would have taken her home with me.

"We don't need to stay here with a giant target painted on our backs," I added. There were places we could disappear. Danny and Nick had both spent their childhoods outside of Oz's twisted borders. A job like ours could be done anywhere. There were always people doing shady shit that needed someone shadier to save their ass. Staying wasn't our only option.

"I can't do that," Danny said, still staring out the window at the passing highway. "We're meeting the Wizard, end of discussion."

Nick looked back at me in the mirror. His expression was carefully blank, but we'd spent enough years together that I knew he was questioning Danny's motives just as much as I was.

"Why do I get the feeling there's more riding on this deal than just money?" If Nick wasn't going to call him out on his bullshit, I would.

Danny was quiet for a long time. I didn't think it was possible, but now I was sure—Dandelion was keeping secrets from us. He looked over his shoulder to double-check that Thea was still asleep.

"I need the Wizard to help me with something. I've made requests before, but they've always turned me down. Now that we have the emerald, I have leverage that I've never had before."

"Leverage for what?" Nick asked slowly.

Danny let out a long sigh and looked down at Thea again. "You guys know that I moved in with my grandmother after my mother died."

"Of course. I told Thea that story yesterday morning. About the day we met and what a prat I was." I watched him carefully, trying to discern where he was going with this.

Danny waited another long while before finally saying, "That wasn't my grandmother. She told everyone to call her Granny, but I was placed in her home by social services."

That was news. He was never close with his grandmother, but none of us were close with our families, so I didn't think anything of it. Danny didn't want to talk about it, and I respected that, so I never asked.

"When I was eleven, my entire family was..." Danny groaned. He was rattled. Whatever he was holding onto all these years must be something massive. "Fuck it. I'm just going to say it. The Farm raided the commune that my family lived on. They killed anyone over the age of forty and everyone under ten. The rest carted away in the back of Cyclone trucks."

"*Everyone?*" Nick asked, eyebrows raised in shock.

Danny nodded, then looked back out the window.

My stomach churned with the knowledge, flip-flopping between the revelation about Danny's history with The Farm and the brutality of what he was saying. Children. Fuck. I knew The Farm's practices could be brutal, but killing kids was a whole other level of evil. When I thought of the scared little boy who walked into my classroom all those years ago and the hell I'd put him through just because he was a little different from the rest of us...Fucking hell.

"I've been asking the Wizard to help me with finding information about the people who were taken that day and what happened to my sisters. They always shut me down, but now with the emerald...We can't make a run for it. The Wizard wants Dorothy, and I'm going to deliver her. Just like they asked."

"Fair enough." I ran a hand down the silken arm draped over my chest. Thea murmured a tiny sound that made my heart squeeze. "But if things get bad, I'm taking Thea and making a run for the border."

There it was. I'd drawn a line. He could decide if he wanted to cross it. Conflict twisted Danny's features. When he finally looked at Thea. It flickered between pain, rage, and fear.

"Danny... Thea isn't Emily. You know that, right?"

"I know that now. But it doesn't change anything."

"No, it changes everything," Nick's voice snapped with a harsh whisper. "Eleven years, Danny. We've been in this together for eleven years, and this the first you've mentioned it."

Danny twisted back to face forward. "It's not really something I ever wanted to discuss...and that's all I want to say about it now."

"*Cazzata*! We could have done something. You didn't need to shoulder this on your own. The day you pulled me from Eastin's basement, we swore an oath. We are in this together until the end. You don't get to decide when and how we uphold those vows."[2]

Danny's head leaned against the glass, the strength he'd been holding on to leaving with a long exhale. "Just keep driving. The sooner we pass the Emerald borders, the better."

---

2. Bullshit!

-22-
NICK

"We can't stay in this car forever."

Thea's voice abraded against my overtired nerves, rousing me from the little bit of sleep I was allowing myself.

"We need real food, I need new pants, and Ozma willing, some underwear."

"I dunno, I quite like when you just lounge in the back of the car naked for days," Crowe said, twisting from the front seat to scan over her curves. She wasn't naked anymore, hadn't been since she woke up outside Crystal City on the first day. She was wearing a set of the emergency shorts and shirt we kept in one of the compartments. But they were entirely too large on her, the shorts, in particular, slipping from her hips every time she shifted.

Thea pulled her t-shirt over her knees like that changed anything. Crowe has by far been the kindest to her, but the daggers she was glaring at him right now said she was done playing nice.

I stretched and cracked my spine. It had been an interesting couple of days.

"I'm serious, Danny. If I don't get to have something hot in my stomach, clean water to wash my face, and a pair of pants that don't expose my ass every time I shift, I will start making this drive very, *very* uncomfortable for you."

Danny flashed her a grin in the mirror. "Do tell, *Princess*."

"Please tell me it involves putting on a show." Crowe snickered, nearly climbing into the backseat. "I volunteer to assist. Two for one, you can reward me and punish him."

For someone so small, the frustrated growl that came from her was surprisingly loud.

"I hate you both." She slammed her foot into the back of Crowe's seat. "Ya know what? I'm tempted to fuck Nick right here, just teach you both a lesson."

I choked on the bottle of water I'd just cracked open.

"I'm ok with that," Crowe said, propping an elbow on the window and leaning back for a better view. "I bet big man over there can make you come hard. That's something I'd most definitely love to see."

"As much as I like being a performing monkey for your pleasure, *Vincenzo*—" Crowe winced. He hated that name. It's what my father called him whenever he fucked up, so I only used it when I was trying to make a point. "—we're going to need to refill the tanks soon anyway." The dual tanks in the cab meant we could drive for longer stretches, but we still needed to refill eventually. "A hot meal would do us all some good."

"We're not far from Stone Mountain. There should be a rest area around there we can stop at," Crowe suggested.

I glanced over at Thea. A grin spread slowly over her lips, lighting up her eyes. She rarely looked happy, even if this was the false happiness of victory, and was bound to disappear the second Danny shut her down again.

Like he could hear my thoughts, Danny glowered at me in the mirror.

"You know I'm right." I pressed the button to convert the bed back into a seat. Thea wasn't expecting the sudden change, tumbling into me with a squeak. I grabbed her around the waist to steady her. It'd been a full day since I decided she didn't need to wear the bandage bracing her ribs, so when the motion of the car caused her oversized shirt to ride up, I was graced with the perfect handful of soft skin. She was always soft, a detail I had to ignore every time I swapped out her bandages, but this time, I was unprepared for the silken contact.

On instinct, my thumb smoothed over the surface. Thea's mouth opened in surprise, her pink tongue darting out to wet her lips. Flashes of my mouth on hers cycled through my mind before I snapped my hand back, looking at it like she'd burned me.

She furrowed her brow in confusion, slumping back to her side of the car and wrapping her arms around her bare legs.

"Fine. We'll stop," grumbled Danny. "But when we get back on the road, I'm taking the backseat."

"Well then, I'm sitting up front, and you can snuggle with Crowe." Thea cackled wickedly.

"NO!" They yelled in unison.

I laughed. I couldn't help it. As annoying as Danny and Thea's bickering could be, it was entertaining the way she twisted him into knots. Danny was never rattled in the way she seemed to shake him up. She flicked all his buttons and every switch. I understood it. Being around Thea was like wrestling a live electrical wire. The spark was beautiful enough to power an entire nation but undeniably deadly.

It wasn't worth the risk, or at least that's what I kept telling myself.

My laughter was interrupted when a small hand squeezed my arm.

"You're laughing, like actually laughing." Thea's eyes shifted into tiny crescents as her smile broadened even further. "I didn't think you ever truly laughed."

"I laugh sometimes. You all are just rarely funny."

We passed the last exit for Stone Mountain. "Take the next one. There should be something for the truckers now that we're outside city limits."

A fluorescent sign announced the approaching Pop's Rest Stop. Pop's was a chain of rest areas along the main highways. Large public restrooms you could count on to be clean, a semi-decent restaurant, and a small department store for daily incidentals.

"Perfect, pull in there," Crowe exclaimed, checking that his gun was fully loaded and clicking it back into his shoulder holster. "Pop's always has the best pies."

"I could go for pie," Thea said, tying the laces of her boots.

Danny put the car in park and turned to face Thea. "Stay here with Nick."

"What?!" she shrieked, "I'm not staying in the car."

"Just until we can secure the place, Darling," Crowe added over her pouting.

"You take front, I'll take back," Danny commanded. They slipped out of the car at the same time.

I gave the parking lot a cursory glance out the back window. It was large, featuring a dog park, picnic tables, and two extensive sets of gas pumps. "Actually, I'm going to scan the parking lot. Do NOT get out of this car. Do you understand?" I kept my voice deep and serious. My accent only adding to the severity of what I was saying.

"I don't take orders," she clipped back.

"Yeah, but you're going to follow this one, Trouble." I slammed the door behind me, clicking the arm button just as she tried to wrench her door open. The locks slid into place, preventing anyone—including Thea—from opening any of the doors until it was fully disarmed. There was an emergency release, but she didn't need to know that.

I waved lazily at her. Thea flipped me off. It was adorable, really.

Orin's surprise attack wised us all up to what was at stake here. Yes, this was a random stop, but we'd also randomly moved the Crick Link job up, and look how that turned out.

Danny wanted me to stay with her, but Thea was basically in a mobile vault while in the cab, and I could keep an eye on her while also making sure there wasn't an entire assault team lying in wait for us. We weren't taking any more chances. It was sloppy letting Orin get the jump on us last time, and I wasn't going to risk falling into a similar trap. Thea could just deal with it.

After being sure that it was clear, I returned to the car at the same time Danny came walking out of a side exit.

"Parking area is safe." I nodded toward the building. "No gunfire, so I'm guessing no threats inside."

He shook his head. "Place looks clean. Crowe is getting us a table at the diner. Did you lock her in?" Danny knocked on the glass like a child at the zoo.

Faintly, the sounds of Thea cussing us out filtered through the plated glass.

Crowe came out the front entrance. "Oh, she's pissed. Why is she so fucking cute when she's angry?"

"She really is." Pressing a button on the key fob, the car clicked, and the side door flew open.

Thea tumbled out of the car, swiping at Danny like a loosed cobra. "Fuck you, Dandy!"

He took her by the back of the neck. "Come on, brat, I don't have all day to be waiting on you."

"Waiting on *me*? Assholes, every last one of you." She blew by Crowe and Danny, stopping only to give a childish kick straight at their shins.

"What did I do?" Crowe asked, confused. "Table is ready, by the way."

"I'm not doing anything until I get a clean pair of underwear," Thea snapped. Danny opened his mouth to counter her, but she cut him off. "*Functional* underwear."

"Fine," Danny relented. "Nick, go with her ladyship to get what she needs and meet us inside. I'm gonna take a piss."

I followed Thea around the inside of the store as she picked up a few pairs of leggings, a pack of camisoles, and a hoodie. When she looked at the pack of cotton briefs she let out a groan that was damn near sexual.

I smirked at her.

"Fuck off. You try going a week with no underwear, and then we can talk."

"I never wear underwear."

She blinked at me.

"Like, ever?"

"No."

She pushed her tongue into the side of her cheek, knitting her brows together, and hummed. I had no idea how to interpret that reaction. Snatching a pack of hair ties from beside me, she tapped them against my chest. "Come on, commando. I'm starving."

A quick stop by the bathroom later, and we were approaching a booth where Crowe was already halfway through a plate of nachos. He crunched down on some fresh chips, mouth half full, saying, "We ordered for you. Food should be here any minute."

Thea sighed, "I suppose I'm not surprised. Why should I want to pick my own food, when I haven't had a real meal in over a week? What did you order?"

"Burgers for all of us, and a slice of cherry pie, because it's Pop's. You have to have pie at Pop's."

"You didn't get me cherry, too, did you?" I asked with a groan. Cherry was my least favorite. It was always too tart or too sweet.

"No, you and sour pants over there are having apple. I decided on pecan, but I wasn't sure if Thea would like it, so I went with the safer bet of cherry." With a wink at Danny, he added, "Darling Thea reminds me of cherries and tastes just as sweet."

Danny snorted like they shared some kind of inside joke.

She reached over to his chips, grabbing an extra cheesy one. "Is that supposed to be some kind of a virginity joke?"

"Not exactly," Danny replied, biting back a laugh.

"I'm not a virgin." Thea was visibly annoyed by his mirth, not that I blamed her. He was an ass.

Thea spent her life locked up at the Farm. Emily definitely seemed like the kind of woman who wouldn't have blinked at auctioning off her niece's innocence. The fact she wasn't a virgin was actually surprising. It had me wondering who she'd managed to seduce that wasn't on The Farm's payroll. Or maybe

Emily Rosen had sold it after all. Who knew what kind of damage the little flower was harboring.

Crowe looked confused. "But, you said—"

"I know what I said," Dorothy bit a retort before he could finish his sentence. She punctuated each of her words with the chip in her hands, forcing scallions to go flying and bounce off his nose. "You didn't ask if I was a virgin. You asked if you were the first to make me gasp their name, and you were, but I've had dick before."

This time, it was Danny choking on his drink.

"Just not good dick. Noted."

-23-
NICK

"Can I get you anything else?" the server asked with a sigh after sitting the plates of pie on the table. She looked exhausted. Small hairs sprang loose from her braid, her apron was smeared in sauce and drops of coffee.

"Just the check," Danny said with a curt nod.

She tore off a piece of paper from her pad and sat it on the table. "You pay at the register up front whenever you're ready."

"Thank you—" Crowe hesitated, taking a moment to look down at her name tag. "—Sherri."

She gave him a half-hearted smile, then walked away.

Thea dragged her pie closer, spearing a bit of crust and a big dripping cherry on the end of her fork. "So, how much longer till we're at the city?" She put the cherry in her mouth. All eyes were locked on her lips as she moaned. "Fuck me, this is delicious."

"You don't have to ask me twice," Crowe said, grabbing her hip and closing the few inches separating them on the bench.

She elbowed him in the side. "Back off! That wasn't an invitation, you perv. It wasn't enough that you spent all of yesterday with your hand up my shirt?"

"Where you're concerned, Darling, it will never be enough." Crowe reached up to caress the line of her jaw.

Smooth. You had to give it to the man. He had all the lines. Where I expected her to swoon, Thea only narrowed her eyes in suspicion. That seemed to endear her more to him. I swear, the more ruthless she acted, the more he ate it up.

189

"Gag me. I can't believe you keep falling for his tired horseshit." Danny grumbled, eating a bit of his own pie. "Gross." He pushed his plate away. "I thought you said their pie was good."

Danny was just bitter and letting it taint everything. I thought the apple pie was delicious.

"Give me a bite of yours," Danny said, taking Thea's fork and stealing the bite she was about to eat.

"Hey!" Thea squealed, almost tipping a glass of water over in an attempt to grab the half-eaten slice of pie he'd now also snatched from her. "I was eating that."

Crowe slid his arm around her, pulling Thea back before she did something really stupid, like stabbing Danny in the eye. "Shhh, beautiful. The big baby just doesn't know how to share. Not like me. I have no problem sharing." He scooped up a piece of pecan pie, taking the time to dip it in the small mound of fresh whipped cream. "Wrap your lips around this."

Thea twisted to look at him, the sourness of the moment fading, and she opened her mouth for him to feed her the pie. A soft, appreciative hum came from her, then she snapped her attention back to Danny. "Mine was better."

Danny sank the bite into his mouth before she could protest further, closing his eyes to the taste. "Damn, Crowe, you nailed it. Tastes exactly like cherries." With a final lick, cleaning the last few remaining bits from the fork, he added, "They might be my new favorite fruit."

Crowe choked on an unexpected laugh, small crumbles of pie crust fanning into the air. "Mine, too." Crowe twisted, scanning the restaurant for our server. "Don't worry, I'll find Sherri and get her to bring you another piece. I don't see her anywhere. Where could she have gone? The place isn't that big."

"What the hell do you mean he nailed it? Nailed what?"

Crowe dipped his head to her ear, whispering low enough I couldn't make out what he was saying. But Thea's face, neck, and chest suddenly turned deep scarlet. Her lips formed a little, "Oh."

Danny licked a bit of juice from his finger. There was a menacing sparkle of amusement in his eyes, and suddenly, I knew what the secret joke was.

190

"I do not..." Thea growled, pushing herself out of Crowe's embrace and trying to climb over him to get out of the booth. "Let me out. I don't want to be anywhere near either of you."

He grabbed her hips, flipping her effortlessly so that she was facing him. "Just do something for me." A second later, he was painting her lips with a swipe of pie filling, making them glisten a deep shade of red. Thea seemed too shocked by the sudden change in position to protest, her eyes wide and her breathing quick.

Crowe bent low over her, tracing the path his finger had taken with the tip of his tongue, then claiming her mouth in a deep kiss. I expected her to claw and fight her way out of his grasp, but instead, she melted into the hand bracing the back of her neck, and her hips twisted to curl into his body more. She nearly started purring for him, sounding so purely sexual it made the hair on my arms raise. Damn me to hell, she was something to watch. Even Danny was stunned into silence and staring her down with greedy hunger.

When they broke apart, Crowe remarked, "Now I have a basis of comparison for later."

Brazen fucking bastard, but she was eating it up. The girl looked downright enraptured with him. It did have me curious, though. I reached over and took a small taste. The filling was more tart than your average cherry pie, with just an edge of sweetness. It didn't taste like any woman I'd ever known, but it did remind me of something. A lingering flavor that I couldn't quite put my finger on. It was earthy—almonds or some other nut, maybe? I smacked my lips. What a curious flavor for in a pie.

I threw a few twenties on the table. Sherri could deal with the bill. We'd lingered here too long as it was. "You two just gonna gaze at each other all night? We still have a wizard to appease."

Thea blinked at Crowe, her expression hazy. "Have your eyes always been so blue? They're beautiful. Like tiny pools of starlight." She brought her fingers up to skate them through the blonde strands that were hanging low over his eyes. "And your hair it's so soft."

Was she fawning? It was so out of character that I stopped what I was doing to look back at her. This couldn't be real. There was no way kissing Crowe was that mind-altering, but the wildcat girl, who I'd personally watched blow up an entire construction yard, was admiring his face like it was a masterwork hanging in the Oz damn E.C. Museum of Fine Art.

I snapped my fingers between their faces a millisecond before they started kissing again.

"Right. Right." Crowe shook off the lust, clearing his throat. "Come on, Gorgeous. Let's go." He pulled her out of the booth. The moment her feet hit the ground, she tumbled into him. Crowe barely had the time to catch her before she fell all the way to the ground.

"Whoopsie." The word bubbled out of her on an effervescent giggle. "Damn, you're strong." She stroked Crowe's bicep as he curled his arms around her. "It's all these muscles. I want to lick them."

"Fuck yeah, baby."

"Fuck *no*." I gave them both a push towards the exit.

Crowe ignored me, not that I really blamed him. Why would you want to when Thea's hands were roaming and stroking everywhere they could reach. "You can lick any part of me you want."

"We're leaving."

"Dibs on backseat." Crowe lifted Thea into his arms with a long and completely inappropriate kiss for standing in the middle of a restaurant.

"Not fucking likely," Danny sniped back at him. "There is no way in hell I'm letting whatever the fuck this is happen while I'm in the car. You're sitting up front. I'm taking back. Also, she can walk. There's no reason for the mid-air humping." He pinched the bridge of his nose and squinted. "Why in the hell is it so fucking bright in here? Let's go. These lights are giving me a headache."

-24-
THEA

I traced the stitching along the collar of Crowe's shirt. It was beautiful. I thought he was wearing a plain black T-shirt, but now, in the light of the parking lot, I could see true colors. An entire rainbow lived in each shadow, shimmering as his muscles shifted beneath the fabric. It was plush but not as smooth as the skin peeking out of the collar. I could spend my entire life stroking that skin.

We were still walking across the parking lot. No, that wasn't right. Crowe *was carrying* me across the parking lot. When had he picked me up? The heat of his arms beneath my legs made them feel like they were gloriously on fire. I always felt like I was igniting whenever he touched me.

His lips dipped to mine. Fuck, he tasted good. The lingering taste of the sugary pecan and caramel was too wonderful to ignore. I licked at the edges of his mouth. I don't think I'd ever tasted anything so marvelous.

"Oz damn, Thea. What's gotten into you?" The deep tones of Crowe's voice radiated out in colorful sound waves, rolling over my skin like a warm blanket of electricity.

"Not enough," I said, my voice low and husky. I needed more. I wanted to feel everything everywhere. Brushing my fingers up his neck, I stroked the crow inked against the side of his head.

The bird blinked his beady black eye, ruffling its feathers as he stretched his wings wide.

"Hello, birdie."

The bird swiveled his head, saying, "Did you just call me Birdie?" His voice matched Crowe's perfectly.

195

"You can talk," I gasped.

"Of course I can talk."

I ran my fingers through his downy undercoat. The crow snapped at me, and I recoiled my hand before I lost a finger. One taloned foot at a time, the bird broke free of his tattooed confines. Feathers rained down on us, their velvety surface brushing my skin as the beautiful bird soared over the parking lot.

Nick clicked the security button on the car. The cab lights blinked, momentarily blinding me in a flash of instant sunlight.

"Ahh!" I pushed the heels of my hands into my eyes. The fireworks exploding behind my eyelids refused to fade. Beside me, Danny loosed a string of curses, covering his eyes too.

My vision finally cleared, and I dared to open my eyes once more. The car looked like it was miles away. The parking lot stretched, the long white dividing lines growing infinitely into the distance. With each step Crowe took, our yellow cab sank farther and farther away, until finally the fabric of the ground tore apart, disintegrating like taffy pulled too thin. A black hole opened in the center of the ground. One by one, shipping trucks rolled toward the cracking void.

Why wasn't Crowe stopping? The vibration of his steps was making the crevice gape wider. "Stop!" I cried.

He ignored me.

I screamed and clawed at his arms. "Stop, Crowe, stop! You have to stop! We'll fall in!" I twisted in his grip, trying to get free. His burning arms tightened, holding me closer to his chest. Why wasn't he stopping? Was he going to throw me in, tossing me away like everyone else?

A sound, like the universe cracking open, ricocheted around the parked cars. Gunfire. Danny was shooting his gun at the opposite end of the parking lot.

"Monkeys," he hollered, popping off more gunfire that looked like a stream of golden rings. "We're surrounded. Get her in the car."

The cab was so far away. We'd never make it.

Crowe's arm stretched to a comical length, looking like a long cartoon noodle waving in the air before finally reaching the handle.

I started laughing uncontrollably. It was too funny. Did all of him stretch like that, or just his arms?

Crowe pulled the door open, tossing me over the chasm and into the back seat. I landed against the soft upholstery. Instead of being in the safety of the car, the cushions swallowed me, and I fell into the unending darkness. The last thing I remembered was the way my scream wavered in the air around me before fading into nothingness.

-25-
CROWE

T he doors slammed closed on the car. Locks deadbolted into place, instantly arming us. I'd climbed in the back with Thea, because fuck Danny. Something was wrong with my girl, and I wasn't going to let his selfish ass sit in the back with her. Besides, he was too focused on what was going on outside to care.

"Where are they?" Nick peeled out of the parking lot at a breakneck speed. "No one is in pursuit? Why aren't they following us?"

"They were everywhere. In the air, behind the cars, repelling from the lamps. *Everywhere*. You didn't see them?"

Nick flashed a look at me in the mirror. "No. All I saw was you firing your gun at some scared-as-shit truck drivers."

"I know what I saw. Orin's team was closing in on us. We barely made it out of there."

I ran my hand over Thea's forehead. She was sweating now. Her skin was so hot, her heart racing. "Nick, something is really wrong with Thea." I tapped her cheek. She was murmuring something, staring with unblinking eyes at the roof of the car. Her pupils were blown wide. Her normal blues and greens were gone and replaced with large black discs.

Danny spun around. His gun aimed at me.

"What the fuck are you doing?" I knocked his arm to the side at the same time he clicked the trigger. His gun fired over my shoulder and into the back window.

Nick swerved the car. "*Ma che diavolo*! What the hell, Danny?"[1] He yelled, or I thought he yelled it. I could barely hear anything over the ringing in my ears. The bullet lodged in the glass, a small spider web splintering from where it was embedded.

"Orin Berret, you motherfucker. I'm going to kill you." Danny's face transformed with rage. Baring his teeth in a roar, he climbed over the center console. He dropped the gun, instead deciding to wrap his hands around my throat. "I'll wring the life from your eyes for daring to touch my girl."

We landed on top of Thea. She'd moved on to crying, tears falling in heavy streams from her eyes. For someone threatening death for touching her, he sure didn't care that he'd just driven all of our weight onto her.

"Get. The. Fuck. Off. Me." I slammed my fist into his side with each word. We were going to hurt Thea, wrestling on top of her. I'd made a promise to her, and this tweaked-out asshole was not going to make me break that promise.

Nick grabbed the back of his pants, snaking his arm around Danny's throat and carefully applying pressure. After a minute, Danny's eyes fluttered, and he collapsed into the passenger seat. A sheen of sweat glistened on his brow, and his lips moved with silent words as he stared off at some unseen target.

I fell back, gasping for air. "What in the actual fuck is going on?"

Nick parked the car along the side of the highway and leaned over Danny, opening his eyes. "He was definitely drugged by something. His eyes are blown wide and bloodshot."

"Thea's too...and fuck, Nick, her skin is so hot."

I slammed my hand into the seatback, pulling a thermometer from the med station. It beeped, the read out displaying 105 degrees, and then before my eyes it climbed. "Fuck. Fuck. 106."

"That's really high."

"I know."

---

1. What the hell!

He glanced over the seat at Thea and then back at Danny. "Did she act like she was hallucinating, too?"

I cracked a chemical ice pack open and shook it. "She was flip-flopping between mauling me and screaming." The plastic bag quickly became chilled, and I placed it on her forehead before cracking two more and placing them under her arms.

He leaned over Danny, thumbing back his lips and murmuring a string of soft foreign curses.

"It had to be the pie. It's the only thing I can think of." I tried to remember exactly what it had tasted like when I licked the filling off of Thea's lips. Fuck, that had been so damn hot. All I could remember was how badly I'd wanted to trace my tongue along an entirely different part of her body. Stupid fool that I am, I thought I'd be doing exactly that right now.

"Check the inside of her lips. What color are they?"

"You know what this is?"

"So do you, if you think about it. It was the almond aftertaste, but it wasn't almonds, it was poppy seeds. I knew I recognized something. I just didn't place it. Maybe if the two of you weren't so fucking distracting..."

My stomach churned with what he was saying. Praying that they were their usual perfect pink, I flipped her lower lip down. The skin was a deep shade of purple with velvety blue edges.

I was going to be sick.

Nick groaned, seeing what I saw. "Mother-fucking Morphan." The more lethal, less fun cousin to the designer drug, Morphea. The same drug that Nick's father built his empire on.

"No." I shook my head vehemently. "This isn't happening."

A string of Italian curses spilled colorfully from Nick.

I couldn't look away from the how her lips were slowly turning blue. She was smaller than Danny. The Morphan was probably burning its way through her system faster than it was in him. They maybe had an hour. It all depended on how much poison they'd laced the pie with? From how quickly she'd gone from abusing me to pawing at me, it was a lot.

There was so little time, and we were out here on a random stretch of highway.

"I refuse to let her die. Look at her, Nick! Whatever she's seeing, she's terrified." Thea's eyes shook, tears leaking from their edges. Her mouth twisted into a silent scream, and her fingers tore at the upholstery.

"That's the dream state, it's the last stage before the drug sucks you under."

"That's not a dream state, Nick." Thea looked like she was trying to crawl out of her skin. "It's a fucking nightmare. There has to be something we can do. What about..." My mind was firing out of control, running quickly over everything I knew about the substance. Paralysis followed the dream state. We had to do something before her heart stopped beating.

I shook with the memory of my older sister, Vanessa, twisting in agony on the floor. My vision flickered between Thea and Vee. She was one of the unlucky ones, an unhappy ending to her quick and dirty side affair with Salvatore. She had long legs that opened easily, and he had access to her next fix. It was no surprise the day she made me go to a playdate with Sal's son or when she brought me back day after day after day.

Salvatore brought the last of his Morphea supply with him when they moved to Oz. The tiny pill swept through the quadrants. People were hooked on the way it made your body feel like it was made of cotton candy and made your lucid dreams even sweeter. The demand for it was unreal.

Before long, Nick's father had planted tracts of poppy fields. Unlike back in Italy, here they grew in the wildest, most beautiful array of colors. Nick and I spent hours that first summer playing in the rainbow fields.

Everything seemed like it was going perfectly. For the first time since our parents died, Vee was happy. Sal even went as far as to promise an engagement before the next holiday. We were happy. Harvest came and went. The flowers refined down quickly. The entire process only took a couple of months until there was a pretty new pill in hand. One my sister was all too eager to try.

Vanessa was the first.

It was more than the color of the poppy fields that weren't the same. The soil in Oz held a chemical that mutated the poppies on a genetic level. The Morphea made from the Ozmandrian Poppies came with deadly consequences. Instead of creating euphoric dreams and hallucinations, it elicited terror. Instead of gently falling to sleep, the user fell into a fear-filled paralysis. Their entire body seized, one system shutting down after another until their heart gave out.

"What about what they used on the processing floors for exposure over-doses?" I scrubbed my face, trying to make the memory of my sister vanish. "Maybe that would be enough to hold it off until it burns out of her system." My shaking hand took Thea's. It was clammy and limp. "I can't watch it happen again, Nick."

It took many rounds of experimentation, but eventually, Nick's father and the other chemists managed to make a refined version of the drug. The un-stable original wasn't without its uses, however. Renamed Morphan, it was a powerful poison. The best part being that it took very little to be fatal, and in the autopsy, it would read as heart failure due to a drug overdose. Just another junky who couldn't handle their high. It was the perfect poison. The only visible difference was the slight discoloration of the inside of the lips. If you didn't know what you were looking for, you would miss it. In a country like Oz, where overdoses were as common as the flu, medical examiners rarely gave them a second glance.

Nick tapped his hand nervously on the seat, glanced back down at Thea, then yelled, "Fuck." He spun around, throwing the shifter back in drive. "Hold on."

Quickly, he tore back onto the road. Flooring the gas pedal. "If we can find a pharmacy, then I might be able to do it. Open the med kit and pull two adrenaline syringes out. We might need it... If her heart stops."

I pulled open the drug panel and filled two long syringes with the clear fluid. Then I leaned down to listen to her heartbeat. It was erratic but still beating.

"Hang in there, Beautiful. Just keep fighting."

−26−
NICK

Ten long minutes later, I slammed to a stop in front of a 24-hour pharmacy. I hadn't even cut the engine, and Crowe was already climbing out of the car. I leaned over Danny's still form. His heart was beating, his breathing shallow. My pulse, on the other hand, was rushing in my ears.

Danny looked a bit better than Thea. His skin still had some color to it, whereas her's had turned a sickening shade of gray. If she died tonight, I didn't think Crowe would recover from it. Not after Vanessa died before our eyes all those years ago.

Morphea. Morphan. My father called it our family's legacy. When in reality, it was a curse. Father damned us all the day we left Italy's shores. The only thing I was inheriting was the loss of the few good people in our lives. Even out from under my father's thumb, he was still managing to crush me. If Danny died tonight, I would burn Ciopriani Villa to the ground and ensure the only thing left to inherit were ashes.

I laid my hand over his heart. My father would answer for this in his blood.

"Leave him."

I looked through the window at Crowe, holding Thea's scarily lifeless body in his arms. He couldn't be serious. How could he even suggest such a thing?

"He's too big to carry on your own, and it will take too long to come back for him. Thea doesn't have that kind of time."

"If we don't make it back fast enough..." If we left him here, it was as good as killing him ourselves. As I glanced between Danny and Thea, it felt like all of the blood in my body was draining away.

"He's a stubborn bastard, he'll fight. Her body will give out before his will. If we wait any longer, Thea *will* die. She's already dying. I can't do this without you, Nick."

Not waiting for a response, he took off into the store. He was right. As much as it pained me to leave Danny behind, we'd already wasted too much time.

At this hour, the store was largely empty. A teenager was sitting behind the front register. He was scrolling through his phone, earbuds thumping loud enough that we could hear the bass as we rushed to the back of the store. I doubted he even noticed us. At the back was a small woman in a white lab coat. I loosed a breath of relief. I was so afraid that there wouldn't be a pharmacist on staff this late.

Her mousy brown hair was tied back in a low bun; a long strand had come loose and hung down, covering her small features and large almond eyes.

With a single sweep of my arm, I cleared the counter. Displays of mints, chapsticks, and keychains scattered around us. Crowe laid Thea's body out. Her breaths were so shallow she didn't look like she was moving at all.

I pushed into the back. Making the pharmacist squeak in surprise. I pulled my gun out, pointing it straight between her eyes. "I need two doses of Naloxone in an injectable form. And some activated carbon."

The woman looked from me to the gun, to me, then to Thea, and back to the gun. I glanced at her name tag.

"Look, Sarah, I just need to save her life. Can you help me?"

Her eyes darted over to Crowe, who had one hand on the butt of his gun and his other wrapped around Theas. "You're killing her with every second you hesitate," he said through gritted teeth.

"I... I... I don't have Naloxone as an injectable here, but I have it as a nasal spray."

"That will work. Go get it."

"There's carbon chewables in aisle seven."

"I'm on it," Crowe said, already disappearing down the aisle.

The woman disappeared and returned with two sealed boxes. Tearing at the cellophane, she asked. "What is she overdosing on?"

"She's not OD'ing, she was poisoned with Morphan," I snapped, grabbing the box. She was taking too long. "And so was my brother, who is still out in the car."

"WAIT! Wait." The woman snatched the box back. Her eyes went wide the moment she realized what she'd done. I stood tall, letting my entire 6'4 form tower over her. She shook and held her hands up, eyes trained on my gun. "Please, please. I'm trying to help. I did my dissertation on the study of anti-venom. It's-it's- not the same, but if this is what you say it is, Naloxone won't be enough. It will stop the hallucinations, but it won't stop her body from shutting down. You need to mix an anti-paralytic with it."

The pharmacist turned, not waiting for a response from me. Her shaking hands fumbled through the boxes on the shelf. Until finally settling on an amber bottle.

"What is that?"

I stalked her as she moved further into the back, throwing the supplies down on a workbench.

"Nitrophenyl. It's an anti-paralytic used to treat botulism. It's the best I have here. But it should, hopefully, counteract the effects of the holocyclotoxin. That's what's paralyzing her." She clicked on a light, while simultaneously pulling a pair of tin snips from a side drawer. She made quick work of the nasal spray bottle. Pouring the contents into a test tube while dragging a mixing rocker that looked just a like tiny seesaw closer. "Don't just loom over me. Go to aisle six, find an aerosolizer, and set it up. I'll be there as soon as I'm done mixing it properly."

I studied her for signs of deception.

"Go!"

I holstered my gun and jogged back into the store. Crow had his head to Thea's chest.

When he lifted his panicked eyes to me, I knew. She'd stopped breathing.

"Her heart stopped."

From the back, Sarah shouted, "There's epinephrine in the cage." A small key on a stretchy wristband came flying towards me.

"We brought our own," I said, at the same time Crowe pulled the syringe from his jacket pocket.

"Thigh, not heart. Those movies are bullshit. You need to put it in a muscle, it'll reduce the risk of brain damage, and she won't bleed out," she warned.

Crowe squeezed the needle so a small amount of clear liquid beaded on the tip.

"What do you think we are, amateurs?" He pulled down Thea's leggings and immediately pierced the skin of her upper thigh.

Long seconds ticked by while I waited to see her chest rise. Crowe hovered with his ear to her chest. Finally, his body relaxed, and he placed a trembling kiss to her forehead. "I knew you were a fighter."

With a snap, Sarah commanded, "The nebulizer. Set it up, now. Stop just standing there!"

I slid down aisle six, spotting a green box on the bottom shelf. A small medicinal aerosolizer used to treat bronchial infections. I tore the packaging open and plugged it into the wall beneath the counter at the same time Sarah came back with a generic-looking cartridge.

"I hope this works. Keep the mouthpiece covering her mouth and nose. If she stops breathing, hit her with an extra EpiPen from the cabinet." She slid the cartridge into the top of the nebulizer, then took off at a jog down aisle six.

"Where are going?" I asked.

"You said your brother was in the car." She picked up a portable nebulizer and snatched a pack of batteries from an end cap. "I'm going to dose him. Stay here. I'll be right back."

The whirring of the machine filled the quiet space. My eyes locked on the gentle rise and fall of Thea's chest. Slowly, too fucking slowly, the rhythm became more regular.

Crowe sighed with relief and sank to the ground.

It was his sudden collapse that saved his life.

Following a dull pop, a bullet sank into the wall where his head had been a fraction of a second before. Plaster and drywall burst around us, as three more shots broke apart the wall.

Pulling my gun free, I scanned the store for the shooter. Crowe rolled behind the counter, grabbing Thea and pulling her to the ground with him.

"Looks like whoever spiked the pie wasn't taking any chances."

"Looks like." A flash of brown hair streaked an aisle past us. I trained my gun on the middle of the aisle, firing just as the person would be traveling in that direction. A cry of pain and gurgled exhale told me I had guessed right. "Keep her covered. I'll take care of our *amico*"[1]

Carefully, I prowled towards the fallen attacker. A glock laid halfway down the aisle.

"Don't move," I said seriously, kicking the gun away. It had a hushpuppy silencer affixed to the end. In all honesty, it was a beautiful gun. I'd need to remember to pocket it when this was over. I reached down to her ankle and pulled a pistol from her boot, where I could see the bulge of a small ankle holster.

She rolled towards me and recognition instantly set in.

"Hello, Sherri." Her hands gripped at the wound spilling blood from the side of her neck. "Does the diner always use Morphan in the pie? Sounds like an unsustainable business model to kill off your clientele."

Sherri laughed, blood dripping down the corner of her mouth and staining her teeth. "You're funny."

"I'm really not. Who sent you, Sherri?"

"Fuck you." She spat a blood filled wad at me. I fired a round into her knee. She screamed, and the blood started flowing more freely from the wound at her neck.

"You've only got another minute before you bleed out, Sherri. Better start talking if you want me to do something about it. Who hired you?"

Her jaw tightened in a grimace. She wasn't going to talk. It didn't matter, only one person really wanted Thea dead. "How'd you find us?"

---

1. I'll take care of our friend.

"It wasn't hard. Not with that tracker on your cab. I just had to wait until you stopped. Then, it was just a matter of killing a waitress and slipping something special in the right dish."

Mother-fucking Monkeys. Of course. I should have swept the cab before we left. It was probably bugged too. Which meant he knew where we were going and who we were meeting with. Fuck, that was a rookie mistake. I knew better than that. We all did. This was Thea, blinding us all. Again.

Echoing my thoughts, Sherri said, "That girl has you three so distracted, you never even saw me coming."

I fired the gun twice more. Once into her chest and a second in between the eyes. Patting her down, I found a comms device. I held it to my mouth, shouting nice and loud, "Fuck you, Orin. You come near her again, and I will burn you alive."

I crushed the small receiver under the heel of my boot. It was advanced tech, lending more credibility to Sherri being one of Orin's team. I pulled a picture from her breast pocket. It was of Thea, taken at The Farm. Dusty desert stretched beyond the wire fencing, and her auburn hair billowed in the wind. She looked distantly at the expanse like she was dreaming of a life where she could be free. There was a slight bruise along her jaw, proving that she'd taken a beating not long before the photo was taken. But, she didn't look sad, she looked determined. Beautiful.

I folded the picture and slipped it into my back pocket.

Crowe was whispering something to Thea. She blinked sleepily at him, awake. His eyes met mine for only a second.

"So?" he said, not looking away from her. She was mouthing something, but not vocalizing yet.

"Our waitress decided to follow us. I don't think she appreciated the tip I left her."

"That tracks actually." He nodded, and ran his thumb over Thea's cheek.

"There was someone listening in, she probably has company not far off."

"Good. They can deal with clean up."

-27-
THEA

Everything hurt, even my soul was crying. I could feel it in the deep tremor vibrating my bones. My eyelids felt like they were chained down as I fought the heavy pull of sleep and slowly cracked them open.

I was on my side in a soft bed. Mid-day sun filtered through vinyl blinds onto the bedspread. Facing me were bleary and blinking green eyes. I was momentarily confused by what I saw, like I couldn't recognize the man before me. Danny looked softer like whatever armor he usually blanketed himself with was discarded. In its absence, he looked thoroughly shaken.

What in the ever loving fuck happened last night?

When I tried to force my memory to function, all I could remember were flashes that were more nightmare than reality. It felt like my head was full of cotton candy, leaving my mind sticky and impossible to focus through.

I tried to ask, "what happened?" around my dry and swollen throat, but my vocal chords completely failed me, making only a weak, rasping noise in place of words. I brought my hand to my swollen throat. It took longer to raise my arm than it should have, like my brain was having trouble remembering how to move my limbs.

"Don't speak," he whispered. His voice sounded raw too. "Take it slowly."

Was this the same man who had thrown me against a wall and pulled a gun on me?

What happened? I mouthed with soundless words, trying to sit up. Danny's heavy hand landed on my shoulder, stilling me.

"We were poisoned." His fingers trailed over my cheek. "But you're safe now."

Safe *now*? Like we weren't safe before? Panic clawed at my ribcage. Where was Crowe, or Nick? Were they okay? Was he alive?

Danny's eyes flicked over my shoulder. There was the creak of a wooden chair, then an arm was snaking beneath me to lift my uncooperative body into a semi-sitting position.

"Oz damn, it's good to see you awake, Beautiful."

Dark circles shadowed Crowe's normally bright eyes. The edges rimmed with red. He brought the straw of a children's sippy cup to my lips. The smiling cats and dogs painted around the outside of the cup felt surreal, but I was so grateful for the water that I didn't care where it came from.

After drinking several hard swallows, I tried to ask for some answers. Before I could tell if I had permanently lost my voice, Crowe brought a finger to my lips. "You screamed until you lost your voice, and then kept screaming. That's going to be raw for a day or two, it's better if you don't speak right now."

I was screaming? At what? How could I not remember screaming hard enough to lose my voice? Fuck this fog in my mind. I was made of questions.

Closing my eyes, I mentally berated my inability to remember anything of consequence. There was the diner. We were eating dinner, and then I fell—or I had the distinct memory of the sensation of falling, if not the fall itself.

"Your pie was laced with Morphan. It poisoned you and Danny. You were hallucinating pretty badly, your body entered a full paralysis...and then..." Crowe's voice trailed off, haunted by whatever he was remembering. "We brought you back. That's what matters. The hallucinations ended around midday yesterday. This is the first you've been lucid in four days."

Four days. My body went tense, my fingers finding their way into Danny's hand and squeezing hard. I needed something to ground me from my cresting panic. That would mean. Oh my god—The Wizard.

A sharp pain seized in the center of my chest. We *missed* his deadline. What would he do now? What was I going to do? There was no way I was getting another shot at this. I was never going to get a life of my own. I'd never be free of my chains. I was going to fall back into Em's hands and die in them, probably taking the boys down with me.

No, what was happening was I was going to be sick. Nausea overwhelmed all of my senses. I lurched forward. The room instantly spun, and I barely managed to make the can that was sitting beside the bed. I retched, bringing up bile along with what felt like my entire digestive system.

Crowe pulled back my hair, rubbing my back gently. He moved with practiced efficiency, swiping a wet cloth over my face and handing me the glass of water like he'd done this dozens of times.

"Easy, Darling. Go slowly. Don't move too fast."

I wiped at my mouth with the back of my hand. "Wiz—" I said with the scratchiest damn voice of my life, even more raw after that spectacular display of stomach pyrotechnics. Speaking, even that single syllable, made a fit of coughing start. Crowe brought the rainbow-colored straw back to my cracked lips.

"Drink. I'll tell you if you promise not to jolt like that anymore."

I nodded, sipping slowly on the water, and trying not to wince with each swallow.

"The Wizard made contact and gave instructions. We're meeting him next Friday. There's plenty of time to recover."

I sank back into the pillow. "Thank Ozma."

"Nick has all the details. Until then, you and Danny are confined to this bed... right here." He gave Danny a stern look. "You both need to rest."

"I'm fine," Danny grumbled. "I haven't felt woozy in hours."

"Yeah, well, you tried to shoot me point blank in the back of a car, so forgive me if I don't care about your restlessness."

"I was hallucinating. You'd have shot you too if you looked like Orin Berret."

"Be grateful I'm letting you stay here, and I'm not making you recuperate on the couch. It's taking all of my self-control not to bounce your ass out of this bed."

"Try it."

"Please. You are as strong as a blade of grass right now. A light breeze could knock you over."

"Where are we?" I whispered, then took a long draw from my sippy cup to ward off the cough that tickled the back of my throat. Movement and a reflection caught in my periphery, momentarily distracted as I noticed the IV hanging from my arm. I followed the tube to a bag hanging from a hook beside the bed.

How had I missed that? I glance to my right. Danny, too, was strapped into a slow drip.

"An apartment in Emerald City. It's a small one-bedroom, but it was the closest. Nick is running a perimeter check right now. You don't have anything to worry about. We're safe here."

They kept saying that, *we're safe*, as if neither of them actually believed that we were, and repeating it would somehow make it true.

I nodded, still feeling dizzy and so damn tired. If it wasn't for Danny's hand in mine, I'd have fallen completely out of the bed.

Crowe brushed the hair from my face. "You should try to sleep some more. You'll feel better. I promise."

He was probably right, but I'd already missed so much. His warm hand wrapped around me, helping me back onto my side. It was only then I noticed the subtle burn from my back. It was barely noticeable, nothing like that agony of the previous week. I suppose the benefit of being unconscious for days was that I'd healed some in that time.

I settled into the pillow, meeting Danny's green eyes once more. "Sleep, Firecracker. You can go back to fighting the world in the morning, and when you wake up, I'll be right here to fight it with you."

Damn. That made my heart do some death defying acrobatics. Since when was Danny so sweet and caring? It was disorienting enough to make me dizzy again and I had to close my eyes, just to fight off the spinning.

Crowe's lips gently pressed to my temple, and Danny's fingers tightened in mine. For the first time ever, I felt safe and protected.

For the first time ever, I was exactly where I wanted to be.

-28-
DANNY

There was a small line creased between Dorothy's brows. I'd spent hours staring at it, raising my thumb to smooth it away, only for it to come right back. I hated that even in sleep, she was being tormented by her demons.

I'd awoken from my own drugged-out coma two days before she did and was lucid long enough to earn a front-row seat for the full weight of her hallucinations. The Morphan had done a number on her mind.

Dorothy's tiny body bowed over and over, as though she'd been possessed, and the demon was twisting her spine into knots. It had taken both Nick and Crowe to restrain her as she clawed at whatever invisible foe was attacking her.

I'd thought the cries from when Nick had patched her lacerated back were haunting, but those panicked and fear-driven screams would plague my nightmares for a long, *long* time.

Crowe refused to sleep, choosing instead to drink a straight feed of coffee and spend hours sitting in the uncomfortable dining chair beside the bed. Nick offered to watch over her. Shit, even I tried to talk him into sleeping, but he refused to let me give him the bed, even though I could see how badly he needed to hold her. He was really beating himself up over the entire scenario, assuming full responsibility. But it wasn't his fault.

Orin-Oz damn-Berret, on the other hand, earned himself an excruciatingly drawn-out death. I would make him suffer for every single second of her torment. The long hours watching her sleep were giving me plenty of time to fantasize about all the creative ways to end him. My favorite at the moment was by dosing him with small increments of Morphan. Just enough to make him feel the paralyzing fear but not enough to kill him. Especially now that we knew what to administer to pull him back from death. I'd play into each of his hallucinations, taking my pound of flesh one strip at a time. When he came to, I'd just dose him again. I'd make him holler, and scream, and beg for deliverance—just like she had. When he was good and truly broken, that's when I'd let her have the killing blow because she deserved that much. I would give her that. Some men gave flowers. I would give my girl revenge.

Crowe was slumped on the side of the bed, finally succumbing to exhaustion. Good thing, too. I needed him at one hundred percent. One of his hands was draped protectively over Dorothy's hip. I let out a long, slow breath. He was falling hard, something I had never seen him do before. He never so much as looked at a woman a second time, much less looked after one. The grief in his eyes these past few days had been genuine. I wasn't sure how I felt about that. Because she definitely had her hooks in me, and from the way Nick was hovering in the shadows, I knew he wasn't far behind. Even if that hollow chest of his would never let him admit it.

I didn't know what it was about Dorothy, but she was unraveling my crew one strand at a time. What would happen once we were finally undone?

The crease between her brows returned, and I smoothed it away—again. Oz damn, she was beautiful. I couldn't stop gazing at her. There wasn't a word large enough to explain how thoroughly ensnared I was. I'd laid for hours memorizing the slope of her nose, the long spray of lashes, the tiny freckles dusting the bridge of her nose like stars in the night sky. Everything about her was like she'd been sculpted, right down to the divot of her Cupid's bow. She wasn't just perfect. She was what perfection dreamed about when it closed its eyes. It made my soul ache just to look at her.

I leaned forward, placing a soft kiss to her pouting lips. Just enough to feel the warmth of emotion bleed into my chest. In a moment of honesty I never allowed myself, I acknowledged it for what it was—love.

For the first time since I was a child, I didn't hide. I would never do that again. We'd almost lost her, and she would have gone to the grave thinking I loathed her or, at best, was indifferent. And that...that was unacceptable.

After I fully regained consciousness, Crowe told me the full story of that night. Dorothy died. There was no other way to describe it. This tragically beautiful fallen angel had died. Her wild heart stopped for two full minutes.

That knowledge alone had torn out what little was left of the selfish prick. In the void he left behind, it was filled only with the images and sounds of her. What would I do when she really woke up? When she went back to pushing buttons and starting fires. Would I fight back, or would I kneel before her in submission? I honestly didn't know. No, that was a lie. I knew exactly what I would do.

I kissed her again, this time firmer, drawing the bow of her lips between mine. Her lashes fluttered, and slowly, her mouth responded, moving in time with me. Not wanting to make this more than it needed to be or to cloud the emotion with lust, I pulled back. Her eyes were a deep sea green when they met mine, a color I'd never really seen in them before. Or maybe I'd never taken the time to study them so intently.

She mouthed, "Hi."

"Hi." I laced my hand into hers, settling them between us. Careful not to wake Crowe in the process, I shifted so that my other hand slid beneath her pillow. Her head dropped to rest on my shoulder, peering up at me through her dark lashes.

"Have you been awake this whole time?" She sounded rough but so much better than yesterday when she first awoke.

"For a while. I've found that I quite like watching you sleep. Especially without the nightmares."

That crease returned as she processed what I was saying, and my new habit showed itself. I released her hand, running my thumb over it. She closed her eyes and sighed. The tension in her body ebbed away. I preened. Had I unconsciously trained her body to react to that touch? Why did I like that so much?

When those heavy lids opened again, they landed on the thin red lines circling my wrist. They were still a bit raw. Shortly after I had regained functionality of my limbs, I began throwing punches. So, Nick had hog-tied me in the car. Hearing the full story of how I'd gone straight for Crowe, I wasn't surprised that he didn't take any chances.

"What did you dream of?" she asked quietly.

I'd been wondering the exact same thing. What was it that was making her scream with such abject terror? Did she need to know that she hadn't suffered alone? Was that why she was asking?

"My sisters." I smoothed my palm up and down her arm. It had been such a long time since I'd needed anyone's touch. I needed hers like a shark needed the ocean. "On the last day I ever saw them."

"Tell me."

I swallowed hard, trying to ignore the way my heart hammered against my ribs. I'd never told anyone, not even the guys. But after reliving it so many times this week, I needed to share it with someone and sever the chain that was holding me down. I wanted the weight of this guilt gone. I was tired of drowning in it, of feeling like a coward.

"The Farm killed my mother." Dorothy's eyes widened, then glazed with the icy recognition of what that meant. Of what she must represent to me. I was still having a hard time reconciling the girl who made my heart twist with the villain I'd spent my life loathing. To prove it to myself, I kissed her again. Not with the aggression still looming beneath the surface, but with the tenderness that I'd locked away long ago.

"Emily Rosen's Wolves took my sisters in a raid, all three of them..." Long seconds of pure silence passed before I added, "...and me."

She nodded. In her lifetime, she'd probably seen more doomed souls pass through the Farm's dusty gates than she could count.

"How old were you?"

"Eleven. Before you ask, I never went to The Farm's main compound. I ended up in a Shifting Sands distribution center."

The Farm had perfected their trucks to easily pass over the deserts ringing Oz and had made a literal killing on bringing in *merchandise* from beyond the borders. Even the name, Cyclone Shipping, was a reference to the sandstorms the trucks kicked up during the passing. I knew that those centers were a waypoint on the route to The Farm's main campus, and then again before the unlucky continued on to whoever had bought their lives out from under them.

"There was this one guy. I never knew his real name, but I called him Silver Tooth. He had one shiny tooth that peeked out of the corner of his mouth whenever he smiled, and he only smiled when I cried."

Dorothy stopped the hand that was still stroking her arm and laced her fingers through mine.

"He loved it so much that he chained me to the radiator at the back of his office. He didn't care that it got hot or that it made my chains and manacles burn."

I held up my wrists to her where, beneath the fresh welts, older, nearly invisible scars still lingered. She traced her finger along it before raising the old wound to her lips.

"The day they raided the commune, Silver Tooth never logged me onto the intake form. To the world, I ceased to exist the second he closed those cuffs. I spent..." I let out a long sigh. "I don't even know how long I was there. Weeks, maybe months. He'd throw down scorpions when he found them. The fucking desert is full of them, and they terrified me. Once he figured that out, Dodge The Scorpions became his favorite game. The asshole timed how long it took me to kill them. He'd punch me for every minute I took and caned me for every time the little bastards nipped me."

A silent tear cascaded over her freckle-stained cheek. I caught it with the back of my finger.

"Those were the good days. It was worse when I couldn't kill them. and he had to do it." The scared little boy, who never really left that room, wanted to hide. He didn't want Dorothy to see the weathered pain, but hiding wasn't an option. Not anymore. Not from her.

"One day, he got drunk and fell asleep at his desk, just close enough that I was able to hook my fingers around the keyring. I got out of there and ran like there was no tomorrow because if Silver Tooth caught me, then there wouldn't have been one. When I made it to the highway, a car pulled over. I was afraid it was Silver Tooth come to drag me to my grave. But it wasn't him. It was a school teacher who was alarmed by a lone hitchhiking eleven-year-old. She took me to a police station. I told Child Services about the raid and my captivity. None of it mattered. Emily Rosen was untouchable, and I was labeled as just another orphan. They sent me to the North, and I was put under the supervision of an old woman who insisted I call her Granny. That was the last I spoke of it. The world rewrote my reality, and I let it erase the boy I once was."

The tears were streaming more freely from her eyes now. She choked back a sob, bringing our joined hands before her mouth to stifle the sound.

"Shhh." I cradled her cheek, brushing the tears from her eyes with my thumb. "I've made peace with my time in captivity. It hardened me, taught me the truth of the world we lived in."

"That doesn't make it okay," Dorothy said on a shaky breath.

My eyes distantly focused on the crack in the wall behind Dorothy. "The Morphan didn't bring back those long days and bone-chilling nights. That isn't what still haunts me. It made me see the look on Dahlia's eyes when they grabbed her...the scream that left Daffodil when they tore her dress off... and the way my mother pleaded for *my* life, and not hers, when the gun was put to the back of her head."

Dorothy was beginning to shake. I looked back down at the way her eyes were swimming with grief. How many times had I imagined shoving a gun down her throat while I told her the truth, making her taste the steel of the barrel and teaching her that its bitterness wasn't close to what had taken root in my heart that day? Vengeance. I'd wanted to exact it on that pretty flesh until there was nothing left of her.

I was a coward. I had always been a coward.

"I did nothing, Dorothy."

"You were a child," she whispered, so low I could barely hear her.

"I was old enough. I peered through the slats, paralyzed by fear. I didn't even let Daisy in to hide with me. There was enough room for us both. She was barely a year older than me and practically half my size. I stood there and hid behind my cowardice."

"Danny, I... I'm so sorry. I can't... I.." Dorothy broke. Whatever fragile strength holding her together shattered, and she collapsed onto my chest, sobbing.

In all the times I'd pictured telling her about that day, I never thought her heart would break for me. She'd be sorry, but she'd be sorry for finding herself at my mercy. There would be tears, but not ones borne from her childhood torment mingling with mine. The inky blackness of my guilt lifted from my heart as she shouldered the burden with me. Her slender hands curled into fists, taking the cotton of my shirt with her.

"I hate her so much." Her tortured voice cracked into a growl. I was wrong. Her heart wasn't breaking with sadness, it was exploding with rage. "No, hate isn't strong enough." Her lips moved against my chest. I felt them peel back as she gritted her teeth. "I will burn it down. I will dismantle The Farm brick by brick. I will strip the beams and build a pyre unlike Oz has ever known. Then I will strap her to the fucking center and drop the match. I don't care if I have to take the whole goddamn world with me. *Em. Will. Burn.*"

Fuck, this girl was speaking to the very center of my cold, black heart. I lifted her chin and brushed away the tears from her hot cheeks, kissing the moist skin beneath my fingers. "I will be right there with you for every second of it."

"And I'll bring the marshmallows." Crowe lifted his head, resting his chin on the dip of her stomach.

Dorothy turned. "I didn't know you were awake. You should have said something."

"And miss that fucking glorious declaration?"

Her eyes dipped, embarrassed of how thoroughly she'd dropped the mask. But then, I dropped mine, too. I'd let that thing fall so far I didn't know that I'd ever find it again.

She propped herself up on her elbow, pressing against me for leverage as she swung her legs over the side of the bed. "I'm..." She raked in a long and unrestrained breath. "Does that tub in the bathroom over there work?"

He nodded. "Yeah, gimme a sec, and I'll start it running."

A couple of minutes later, the IV line and bandages were removed, and Crowe was easing her into the warm water. It was intimate watching the way he so thoroughly cared for her. The only bodies I'd ever seen him lower into tubs were the kinds being dipped in hydrochloric acid. This was...loving.

Crowe returned and leaned against the bedpost. "We'll find them."

"So you heard everything?"

"Yeah." His normal, carefree smile was gone, replaced by a grim line—my past destroying even that.

I fell back, pulling a pillow over my face and willing Dorothy's scent to suffocate me. It didn't work. It just reminded me that someone was still fighting, and I'd be proving I was a coward if I didn't fight with her. "I've spent years trying to convince myself that they're gone." I threw the pillow at the wall. A picture of sailboats clattered to the floor with it. "Even if one of them managed to make it through that meat grinder alive, what would be left of the girl I knew? Fucking look at me, and I didn't go through half of what those women experience."

"If you don't face your nightmares, then you'll never banish them."

"Maybe." Steam coiled through the open door, prowling over the ground. "But then what? What do I have left if you strip me of my nightmares?"

"You have her," Crowe insisted. "You have us."

-29-
THEA

I sank deeper into the soapy water, training my ears on the conversation beyond the door. Crowe's voice was low. In muffled tones, he talked Danny out of the emotional spiral he was going down. From the sounds, of it Crowe hadn't known the truth of his childhood. Which meant Danny chose to share that information with me—when he hadn't even trusted it with his boys. It made my chest squeeze with warmth and in equal parts, flip with unease.

I slid below the water and internally sighed as the heat enveloped me. I'd been seeking sanctuary underwater for as long as I could remember. When Em's abuse and her goons were too much, there was always one place I could escape. The silence of being submerged was the only time I could feel truly alone. Closing off my senses quieted my thoughts, giving me peace and the ability to think clearly.

Danny's story rolled around my head. Had I ever met one of his sisters? Seen their matching green eyes peer through chainlink, judging me as I walked by with the illusion of freedom. There was no way to know. Thousands of similarly heart-breaking stories walked over that barren earth. It explained his immediate hostility towards me. If he'd thought that I had anything to do with the inner workings of The Farm, then I would have hated me too.

The night we met, when I told Danny my name, I saw the way his eyes had chilled with blind rage. That version of Danny didn't scare me. I knew how to handle that creature. It was the gentle version that watched me while I slept? The display of vulnerability made me feel like I was flayed open. *That* man terrified me.

229

Two strong hands wrapped under my shoulders and heaved me out of the bath. I jolted in surprise, inhaling a bit of water in the process and flailing my arms and legs in all directions.

"Holy fuck, Dorothy!" I blinked up at Danny. "I did not go through all of the last week just to see you drowning at the bottom of a tub."

"Don't call me Dorothy," I snapped.

"That's hardly the issue here."

"I wasn't drowning." I shot him a furious glare, but it was hard to be angry with him when he looked so concerned. "I like laying under the water. It helps me think, and my mind is still all fuzzy from the drugs."

"I thought you'd passed out again." He pressed my head to his chest, banding his arms around me like he was afraid I might vanish if he slipped even an inch. The fierce pounding of his heart was deafening. My half-sitting, half-laying, naked form soaked through his black shirt and briefs.

"Well, I hadn't." I pried his caveman-like grip from around my waist. Deciding that there was no point in modesty anymore, I stood up...and immediately slipped on the massive puddle of water. I landed hard on my ass and cursed the tile. Not pausing to let Danny come to my rescue, I climbed back into the tub.

"I don't think baths are a good idea right now." He scowled at the water. "What if—"

I cut off his pointless warning, "I'm not wasting a perfectly warm bath when it's right here. If you're so worried, then climb in." It was an impulsive comment. The words left my lips before I'd fully realized what I was suggesting. There was something about Danny that made me feel like I was always arming up for a fight.

Danny's eyebrows sky-rocketed. "You want me to get in the bathtub with you?"

I laughed and flicked a long stream of water at him. Fuck it. I'd come this far already. What did it matter if we went straight into the deep end? "You're already soaked. I don't know what you're afraid of."

Danny turned to the door. Crowe wouldn't be gone for long. Was he worried what the others might think if they found him in a bathtub with me? Did I care? Crowe had made it pretty clear that he had no issues in sharing me, and it was just a bath.

He gave a little nod and, with one hand, peeled his shirt over his head.

I sucked in a tiny breath. Apparently, my ability to breathe was stripped along with his shirt. For all the times that I've been nude around them, the boys had always been infuriatingly clothed. I could sense the power behind each of their frames. Every time I came in contact with one of them, it was like bouncing off of a brick wall. During our long motorcycle trip to Gorba's, I had plenty of time to memorize the feel of Danny's muscles. Sure, I was gripping them out of sheer panic, but I spent enough time clinging to him to know that I'd like this view.

Seeing it was so much better than anything I'd imagined. The man was beautiful, a true work of art. I tracked my eyes along the planes of his chest at the inked masterpiece stretching across the broad expanse of muscle.

A massive roaring lion framed by flowers—daffodils, dahlias, daisies, and dandelions. The jaws of the beast stretched wide, his mane draping over Danny's rolling abdominals all the way down to where it disappeared beneath the the band of his briefs.

"Why the lion?"

"It's a long story. The short version is that Nick's family called me Leone, lion. The name started as a joke, but then I decided to claim it. Or maybe I was trying to fool myself into thinking I was something I wasn't. I mean, who ever heard of a cowardly lion? It sounds like something right off the pages of a children's book."

"Dandy, you *are* a walking contradiction, but you're no coward."

"That almost sounded like a compliment." Danny snared my eye contact, a challenge behind his smirk. "*Almost.*" He slid his shorts down, daring me to drop his gaze. He fucking knew I wanted to. My mouth had been watering ever since I spotted the outline of his erection straining against the cotton of his briefs, the rosy head peeking out from the top of the elastic. It was impossible to miss, but not as impossible as keeping the image of my hand wrapping around— "Don't keep looking at me like that, Firecracker."

They keep telling me that. Were my emotions really so obvious?

"And how is it that I'm looking at you?" I spread my legs, being sure that he saw the way I draped my hand casually between them. He wasn't the only one who knew how to pose a challenge.

He didn't answer, his wicked grin drawing wider with each step he took in my direction. Damn me. I was in trouble. Why did I have to like the fight so damn much? I shouldn't have started poking this particular lion again. He'd been so sweet, and I just had to bring the fight back out in him.

I drew my knees up, making room for him at the base of the tub. The bubbles shifted in the water, covering my chest so that only my knees poked out. Stepping into the tub opposite me, displaced water splashed against the tile. Danny didn't seem bothered by it, and I couldn't take my eyes off of him long enough to care about the mess we were making.

Danny's hands wrapped around my ankles, guiding them up until my legs were draped over him like his own personal Thea blanket. He nestled into his spot, consuming damn near the entirety of the porcelain basin. Broad shoulders draped over the edges, his knees pinning me in on either side.

I swallowed, realizing that I hadn't fully considered just how large he was when I suggested he join me. There was no escaping him. His long arms easily enveloped the length of my bent legs. Whatever power I'd felt by refusing to give up my bath vanished. Every piece of me felt like it was at his mercy.

He released one foot to fall against his shoulder and moved the second so that it lay in the palm of his hand. I squirmed with the first ticklish pass of his fingers against the sole. Danny's eyes sparkled with delight, and his grip on my foot tightened. He'd done that on purpose, just to see me writhe. I was sure of it.

"Stop wiggling and relax," he chided.

"Sure, because torturing the bottoms of my feet is really relaxing."

"Princess, if I wanted to torture you, I would." Just to prove how very wrong I was, Danny gently pressed his thumbs into the arch of my foot. He slowly rolled outward along the tight muscles and tendons. Then, repeated the motion, each time pressing more firmly.

I let out a low moan and sank until my neck rested against the back of the claw foot tub. Danny's legs shifted, wrapping around my body until I was fully cradled by long lines of masculine muscle. His dark chuckle vibrated through everywhere we touched.

Goddamn, he was good at that. If the gangster life failed him, Danny could always find a second calling as a massage therapist. The press of his fingers lingered right on the line between painful and not firm enough.

Distantly, I was aware that the position I had shifted into was probably all kinds of suggestive. I was half draped over him, half straddling his hips. The slowly vanishing bubbles were really only the illusion of cover, but I couldn't bring myself to care. Each stroke of his fingers massaged away the tension that still lingered in my body. A tightness that went deeper than muscle uncoiled within me. For the first time in my life, I felt completely relaxed.

His hands slid higher, moving back and forth along my calf, his thumbs working in tight concentric circles. "Does that still feel like torture?"

I tried to answer but only managed a contented hum.

"When I first woke up, it felt like I'd spent days stretched on the rack. I know how sore you must be."

He wasn't wrong. Even my hair ached.

"Just tell me where it hurts, and I'll soothe your pain." Danny leaned forward working his hands along the back of my legs until they cupped the underswell of my ass.

I cracked one eye open to smirk at him, "Pretty sure I didn't say anything about that hurting."

"No? I just assumed since you're generally a pain in the ass." Before I could react to his jibe, Danny gave a hard tug and pulled my hips fully over his. My neck slipped from the edge of the tub, briefly dunking my head into the water at the same time my thighs spread to wrap around him. Supporting my lower back, Danny helped rotate me upright until I folded neatly in his lap.

The motion deliberately rocked the soft folds of my body against the very hard ridge of his dick. Something he wasn't bothering to hide. A rush of heat flooded my senses, rocketing my relaxation straight into arousal. Streams of water ran over my cheeks, and droplets dripped from my lashes.

I braced the sides of the lion's head tattoo in much the same way as the large hands bracing my waist. I should have expected that. I asked the lion to lay with me; why should I be surprised when he makes me his dinner?

"Woah, that was—" I said, trying to stop the dizzy spin caused by the sudden change of position and rapid acceleration of my heart rate.

"Better," Danny answered for me before drawing me in for a long kiss that did nothing to stop my sense of disorientation. "You were too far away." His lips trailed along my jaw to my neck, sending a hot exhale over my wet skin. A shiver followed his breath, snaking down my spine and ending straight between my legs. "We never got to finish what we started back in the kitchen. The memory of that too-brief moment has been tormenting me. I haven't been able to erase the feeling of you from my lips."

He shifted, one hand ghosting up my spine to cradle the back of my neck. Danny was careful of my injuries, never truly touching anywhere that was raw, but the potential for the contact was making my breaths become shorter. He angled my head back, exposing my throat.

"Or the taste." He dragged his teeth over my neck, sucking and nipping as he descended down to my collar. "It's all I can think about. The way your hand brushed my neck as Crowe made you come, listening to your cries. *That* was torture, Princess, knowing it was his hand you were riding and not mine, wanting to be the one beneath you."

His lips against my skin stretched into a feline smile.

"Maybe you deserved a bit of tort-ure." The last word hitched in the back of my throat, interrupted by Danny firmly palming my breast.

"Maybe..." He rolled my nipple between his fingers with enough pressure to make me wince and tighten my legs around his hips. The hand at my neck grew firmer, immobilizing me. "But then again, you're not stopping me right now. Are you?"

He had a point. Why hadn't I stopped this?

I pushed back against the roaring lion, and to my surprise, he let me put space between us, though his hand didn't leave my neck. "You pulled a gun on me."

"And I fired one for you, too." He dropped his head, kissing the valley of my breasts. Dammit. I hadn't considered how more space just provided access to more skin. "So did you. You shot a man for me, Princess."

"Maybe I shot the wrong man."

"Maybe the wrong man is the man you need."

His hands dropped to my hips. He dragged my body up and down his length, making sure that every considerable inch slid against my exposed flesh. It made my skin feel hot, and blood rushed through my ears. Without thinking, desire took control of my body, rocking my pelvis in time with his movements. Danny let out a low groan. "I've never wanted anything the way I want to possess you and make every inch of you mine."

"I'm more than something to own." I moved to pull myself off of him. His sweet words didn't matter. Danny still saw me as a commodity.

He grabbed my arm, pulling me back down. "You don't understand." He cupped my cheek, forcing me to look at him. His emerald eyes bored into mine. "My thoughts, my desires, my dreams. They are all consumed by images of you, wanting you. The only person who owns anything right now is *you*."

I blinked and tried to remember how to breathe.

Danny kissed me with more emotion than I was prepared for. He moved gently, like he had when I awoke, causing a deep ache to thrum in my chest. He followed that first press of his lips with more to my cheeks and, finally, the center of my brow. It was an act of such sweet devotion, undoing every piece of armor I had guarding my heart.

"I'd give every last bit of me to you freely, for the chance to hold a piece of you."

I ran my hands down his arms to make sure I wasn't imagining this and hadn't slipped back into a hallucinatory coma. But, it would seem Danny really was confessing...whatever this was to me.

Gone was the vindictive prick who calculated my worth in dollar signs. The fire in his eyes was something else entirely, and this caring version of him had me feeling all kinds of vulnerable. Maybe he was ready to confront that side of himself, but I wasn't.

Vulnerable Thea was too similar to weak Dorothy, and that bitch could fuck right off.

That didn't mean I couldn't have a bit of unbridled fun. I bit my lip and let my eyes slide over Danny's body, indulging in the rolling muscles in a way I'd denied myself earlier. When he wasn't being a complete ass, it was hard to ignore how fucking gorgeous he was.

"It would seem you're already holding quite a bit of me," I joked, rocking my hips once more to prove my point.

"Not enough."

I leaned back, running my fingertips along each ridge of abdominal muscle, past the lines of his hips, until I could drag my nails down the length of his cock.

Danny hissed through his teeth, eyebrows rising in surprise at the sudden flip in power.

Because I felt really fucking powerful in this moment. I palmed up and down the length in answer, wrapping my fingers as I went, squeezing harder at the base, and easing as I returned back to the tip. With each swipe, every muscle in his body constricted in answer.

Danny groaned, his fingers digging into my hips.

He felt fucking good in my hand, hard as stone and large enough that I knew I'd be seeing stars with every thrust. He'd come at me with all the savagery of the lion inked on his chest, tearing me in two—and I'd ask for more.

I licked at the seam of his mouth, imagining what it would be like to trace my tongue down the path my thumb was making. "And you want more?"

"Fuck yes, I do."

—30—
THEA

The strength of his body surged up, taking me with him and sloshing water over the sides. I let out a laugh at his enthusiasm. I gave Danny the green light, and he leapt from the tub like a puppy being asked to go for a ride. It only took four long strides and one awkward slide on wet tile, until we were back in the bedroom.

"Wait," I said partly on a laugh. "We're soaking wet. The bed...we can't."

He growled, kissing me again, then reluctantly set me down. "Don't move."

Danny disappeared into the bathroom, returning with a large fluffy grey towel, hastily running it over his hair and body as he walked. The view gave me ample time to drink in each dip and curve of his naked body, and damn...why had I denied myself this the first time?

By the time Danny reached me, he was relatively dry, and the Cheshire grin he was giving me was bright enough to be seen from space.

I reached my hand out to take the towel, but he knocked it away.

"I told you not to move."

I rolled my eyes but couldn't convincingly feign annoyance, not when he was looking at me like I was the beginning and end of the world. Whatever I had left of a defense crumbled with the first press of his lips to my shoulder, chasing the towel with reverent kisses. The longer he lingered, the sharper my senses honed, something that got worse when the soft cloth ran from my neck to my stomach, taking careful attention to dry the curve of each breast.

"Okay," I said on an impatient pant. "I think we're dry enough now."

Danny dropped to one knee, shaking off my hands as I failed to pull him to me. "When I do a job, I do it right. I never do *anything* halfway, Princess."

He lifted my foot to rest on his knee. "Hold on to my shoulders if you need to balance."

At an agonizing pace, Danny circled around my ankle and up my thigh. This was sipping the scotch all over again. He knew my patience was shorter than my fuse, and if he kept savoring *this* experience, I was going to explode long before we ever made it to the damn bed.

"You're going slowly on purpose. After all this build-up, I would have thought you'd *want* to fuck me."

The burn of Danny's green eyes seared straight through me. "You haven't been paying attention if you think all I want is to simply fuck you."

I sucked in a shallow breath, made so much harder by my wild, galloping heart.

Gently, we transferred my weight. Rather than place my foot on his knee, as he had the first, this one he lifted to sit on his shoulder. I bit back a giggle when the stubble on his chin grazed the sensitive underside of my knee.

"Ticklish?"

I tried to scoff, "Like I would admit any of my weaknesses to you."

"Princess, I'm about to learn everything there is to know about you." His hands gripped my ass and pulled me closer, the positioning of my foot on his shoulder forcing my legs to spread wide.

"Firstly—" My words twisted from a snappy comeback into moan the second his mouth closed over my clit. "Fuck, Danny."

Danny rumbled in appreciation, rewarding me by sucking hard enough streaks of light blurred across my vision. His hands braced my ass, forcing my body to stay in exactly the position he wanted. I had to dig my fingers into his shoulders to keep my supporting leg from giving out.

"You were saying?" Danny teased, his voice vibrating through the folds of my pussy. He didn't wait for an answer. Slinging my foot over his shoulder, his tongue delved straight into what might have been my soul.

I cursed, rocking my hips involuntarily towards him, silently begging for him to feast on every bit of flesh he could sink his teeth on.

I'd always wondered what this would be like. I'd given my fair share of blow jobs in exchange for a favor over the years, but the guards at the Farm were never particularly generous when it came to reciprocation. Em's *guests*, even less so. I'd spent countless nights trying to imagine what the flat pad of a tongue would feel like pressed against intimate and sensitive flesh. But this was so much more than that. Danny's tongue moved in a way that made my entire body feel like it had been electrified.

I tried to regain sanity. I really did.

Each time I drew breath to speak, Danny bit down, stealing the air from my lungs. My entire body shook, and just as I was sure I would burst, he paused.

"We'll get there, Princess." He took the time to steady me before rising.

Whimpering at having my climax denied—again—I stepped back until I bumped into the footboard of the bed. What was it with these boys that they were always dragging my pleasure out of me in the most excruciating way possible?

Easily closing the space between us, he kissed me again. I could taste the devilish sweetness of my arousal on his lips. It was sinful and dirty. I definitely didn't taste anything like cherry pie.

Water dripped from my hair down my back, running in streams over the scarred flesh and down to the curve of my ass. Without the distraction of Danny's face between my legs, I shivered with each drop. Coming so close to release primed my skin to react violently to any stimulus.

Danny instantly picked up on it, spinning me and scooping the towel up. He lowered a soft kiss to my shoulder, gently drying my hair and back.

"How's it look?" I said, trying to spy at him over my shoulder.

"Considering how much I've fantasized about this over the past week, pretty fucking fantastic." His palm smoothed over the curve of my behind, squeezing more than a handful of cheek.

"I wasn't talking about my ass," I snapped.

"I was." His hand cracked down, slapping the undercurve of my right buttcheek. The sound cut through the air and echoed through every inch of my body.

"Fuck," I breathed from the unexpected pain and sagged backwards into him. I could feel the outline of his hand continuing to burn, causing my pussy to clench hard on reflex.

"Too much?" he asked with genuine concern, caressing over where my ass seemed to have grown its own heartbeat.

"No. You just surprised me."

"Good, because I imagine spanking this perfect ass every time you open your sassy mouth." He dragged two fingers backwards over my center. "Fuck, you did like that. This pussy is practically weeping for me." Gently, with his other hand, Danny pressed my shoulders forward at the same time he sank those fingers deep inside. "Hold on to the footboard."

I was more prepared for the second slap, but that didn't stop me from bearing down hard on the fingers stroking me. "Damn, Firecracker. We are going to have so much fun. I can't wait to feel you do that around my dick." Danny kissed the barely healed marks at the center of my back. That, more than any other touch, set my entire body trembling. "Tell me if it's too much. I don't want to give you more than you can handle. You've been through a lot lately."

I didn't want to feel the flood of emotion that simple concern brought on. What I wanted was to be fucked hard. I wanted to forget the pain.

"I told you before, Danny, give me your worst." I rocked back against his hand, exactly like I had right before he'd kissed me in the kitchen. Well, not exactly the same. Last time, the distance between us was calculated. Now it felt reckless. "I can handle you just fine."

Danny chuckled darkly, his breath setting off tiny fireworks along my back. "I don't think you can—" I could hear the wicked grin forming, feel the edges of his lips turn up as they brushed the shell of my ear. "—but I'd like to see you try." He pushed a third, greedy finger into me, spreading me wide. Drawing back his hand with a curl, Danny pumped slowly, hitting a new, mind-altering spot.

The wave of my withheld orgasm took me by surprise, building and detonating with blinding speed. One second I was in control, and a heartbeat later, Danny was obliterating my grip on reality. I cried out, buckling over the footboard, my legs completely giving out beneath me.

"I'm going to need you to do that again." Danny scooped an arm around my waist, saving me from crashing to the floor. Throwing me onto the bed, he prowled over me, caging me in long lines of hard muscle. "I want to see the darkness in your eyes when I drive you over the edge."

Hitching my leg over his hip, he thrust into me, hard enough the air in the room vanished. My cry of surprise was swallowed by the press of his mouth.

"Danny." He pulled back and then slammed forward, pushing deeper than the initial thrust. I could taste the passion on his lips, feel the intent behind each measured pump of his hips, sense the undiluted need in the press of his fingers into the back of my thigh. I indulged in every sensation.

"Fucking perfect." Danny leaned back, watching where we were joined. Tightening his grip on my thigh, he pushed harder into me. "You feel so damn good, Dorothy."

"Don't call me Dorothy," I said, threading my fingers into his hair and yanking his head back. I truly hated that, even now, he was still calling me by that name, despite the number of times I'd told him not to. Not that it stopped me from kissing him again.

He laughed, a motion that made his dick flex within me. "Princess, your priorities are all in the wrong place." He gave a long, hard stroke, knocking the bed against the wall. "I'm buried deep enough inside you that I'm sure you can taste me." Drawing all the way out and slamming home, like he could prove his point by power of thrust alone. "But you're worried about a *name* because you do feel amazing. Before this night is out, I'm going to pound your body into the bed, the wall, the floor, and every other damn surface of this room."

Savagery bit deep into his kiss, ensuring that I knew exactly how deeply he was laying claim on my body—Which was not fucking happening. I pushed hard on his shoulder, twisting beneath him and ignoring the ache in my back as I rose to straddle him. If anyone was claiming anything around here, it was going to be me.

Flipping my hair over my shoulder, I rolled my hips and groaned at the new position. Fucking hell, Danny might have been onto something, saying he was deep enough to taste because I had to close my eyes while my body adjusted to the new level of fullness. My back ached, but over the pain, there was only the deep thrum of pleasure—and power.

When I finally opened my eyes, the grin gracing Danny's lips proved everything he'd said earlier about belonging to me. He stroked my breasts, running his hands over my chest before sinking down to rub small circles against my clit.

Biting down on my lip to keep from screaming out, I slowly rocked in time with each stroke of his thumb. As I ground down, a slow heat grew within me, along with my confidence.

I felt powerful, like I owned him. I'd never owned anything before, but right now, this beautiful man was mine. There was no doubt.

Somehow reading my thoughts, Danny said, "Take all of me, every last piece." His hands wrapped around my waist, thrusting up to meet each roll of my hips. Our rhythm increased until I couldn't tell if I was riding him or if he was driving me. Whatever was happening felt out of control.

Danny sat up, one arm pressing down on my shoulders to increase the pressure, while his other sank to my clit. When I was sure that he couldn't hit me any deeper, he thickened within me. "Dorothy, I .."

I kissed Danny harder, cutting off whatever he was about to say and taking back the control I'd let slip. Holding onto his shoulders, I arched my back, offering my chest to him in a demand for the attention I deserved. Danny's mouth closed over the hardened peak of my nipple.

"Looks like you can follow orders after all." I licked my lips. "Good boy."

Danny's eyes flicked up with a growl, "Watch it, Princess." Raking his teeth over my breast, he bit down on the side.

I cried out, not entirely hating the sharp burn left behind by his bite. Against the peachy hue of my breast was a perfectly round mark with the faint impression of teeth.

"Fucking beautiful." Wrapping a hand around my neck, he pulled me down to his level. "But you will definitely be paying for that later."

Pushing against his chest, I rose up. Danny didn't release my throat, which I wasn't entirely opposed to. There was something about the way he manhandled me that made my entire skin feel hot, but there was also a part of me that got off on pushing his buttons.

"What's the matter, Kitten—" I rolled my hips hard enough to make us both groan. "Don't you like being my good boy?"

"You really think I can't top you from down here?" The hand on my throat tightened, pulling down while thrusting up hard enough small fireworks exploded around my vision.

A shadow fell over us, the small amount of light coming from the doorway momentarily blocked out. Crowe leaned in the door frame, casually running this thumb over his lower lip with the same amused look he'd had when he found me screaming naked in the bathroom.

It should have riled me. I shouldn't have wanted the feeling of Crowe's eyes while Danny flexed within me. Alarm bells should be ringing, but recent events had given me a new need to assert control. I had it taken from me in so many different ways that I was beginning to lose count. But right now, I commanded the full attention of two men, and it made my blood hum with excited energy.

Maintaining eye contact with Crowe, I arched to meet each of Danny's bruising thrusts. Crowe licked his lips. A familiar burn climbed up my spine, making my pussy clamp down harder.

If he was aware of his friend's presence in the room, Danny didn't let on, or he didn't care. If anything, he became more determined to obliterate what was left of my senses.

Joining the hand circling my throat, I wove my fingers between Danny's, tightening our grip until the roar of my climax rolled over me. I was a rocket, careening out of my body and demanding that he come with me. With those final thrusts, Danny hit points inside of me that felt like I was slamming into the outer atmosphere.

I slowed my breathing. My throat and mouth were dry, like I'd been panting and moaning, though I couldn't remember doing either. I craned my head back to ensure the wall was still intact but instead snagged on the emerald blaze of Danny's eyes.

"Fuck. That was hot." He drew me to him, kissing me slowly, reverently. "I know I've been calling you Firecracker, but I never thought I'd get a front-row seat to watching you explode."

A too-amused voice floated over from the doorway. "I think my new five-year plan is to see just how many times I can watch Thea orgasm."

-31-
THEA

"I'm more than willing to help in that endeavor," Danny said against my throat.

The sound of our panting breaths filled the small room. My heart was still racing, driving faster with each soft approaching footstep. By the time the heavy, warm presence of Crowe was beside me, I was dizzy with anticipation.

Using a single finger, Crowe angled my head to look up at him. "You are magnificent." Bracing one hand on the headboard, he leaned over us and softly kissed my upturned lips.

I ran my fingers over the crow inked beneath the soft fuzz of hair on the side of his head, holding him to me and welcoming the kiss deeper. My other hand fell to Danny's chest. The solid thump of his heart drummed beneath my palm while Crowe hummed in approval.

My skin tingled in the wake of that kiss. I'd never felt this alive before. Being between these men felt like I'd been living my entire life in black and white, only to realize there was an entire world of color waiting for me.

Crowe's hand brushed along my side, chasing the shivers elicited by our kiss. One finger traced the underswell of my breast to meet where Danny's hand was resting against my sternum. Splaying his hand wide, his thumb smoothed over my nipple.

"The thoughts dancing in my head right now, Gorgeous, they're downright devious."

Danny's eyes traveled from where Crowe's thumb continued stroking my breast possessively to where Crowe was standing bent over us. I tried to read the hardened edges of his expression. It was impossible to tell if the way he stared down his friend was with jealousy or passion, perhaps both.

Crowe scooped my hair back, exposing my neck and shoulder from where the curtain of damp waves had fallen over it. Danny sat up, gently cupping my neck and pressing a kiss to the hollow of the shoulder that Crowe'd exposed.

It was too practiced to have been by accident like they knew what the other would do instinctively. Had they been intimate with a woman like this before, sharing her between them? The image of their lips and burning gazes against another woman's skin made acid flip in my stomach. I swallowed the sour bite of envy before the fluttering emotion could take root.

The boys descended on me in perfect synchronicity. My lion's predator lips moved lower at the same time Crowe's descended to graze the side of my neck. Danny's cock, still buried deep within me, twitched in a heady reminder of the exact position I'd just found myself in. I closed my eyes, caught somewhere between being overwhelmed and perfectly at ease being wedged between them.

Stars fluttered across my vision, making the room momentarily spin, and I swayed. It was only for a second, but that was all it took to bring reality crashing back down on us. The tension in both sets of hands switched instantly from gentle caresses to holding me steady.

"Of course, you've only just regained consciousness, and I..." Crowe's voice trailed off. The blue of his eyes almost seemed to glow in the low light, highlighted even more by the darkness in his blown pupils. The etched lines of concern sent a confused mess of feelings fluttering in my chest. What did he see to make him look at me like that? Or, more to the point, what had he seen?

Crowe gave me a sad smile, pressing a kiss to my temple.

"I'm *fine*."

"You need rest."

He slipped an arm around me, easing me onto my side, while Danny shimmied out from under me and disappeared into the bathroom. Crowe pulled off his shirt and pants, sliding into the bed behind me.

Danny returned with a warm washcloth and a few packs of sterile bandages. I groaned, seeing him set the now too-familiar supplies on the side table. Not waiting to be told, I rolled over. Resting my head against Crowe's stomach, he ran his hand through the damp strands of my hair. I closed my eyes, finally acknowledging the bone-deep exhaustion.

A warm cloth ran over my sex, and I yelped in surprise. I was expecting the cloth at my back like always, but this... I didn't even have words to express it.

"I'm perfectly capable of cleaning myself, you know," I grumbled into the hard muscles of Crowe's abdomen, which rumbled with a low laugh. Honestly, the energy was flooding out of me, and I lacked the will to put up a fight.

The wet cloth snapped playfully against my ass cheek. "Ow," I howled half-heartedly, my laughter betraying any attempts I was making at annoyance.

"Stop being a brat, and just let me take care of you."

Could Danny tell I was rolling my eyes, even with them closed and facing the opposite direction?

"Aftercare is a thing, Princess. You don't have the energy to make it back to the shower... and I sure as hell am not putting you in another tub. So be a *good girl,* and I'll do my best to make it nice for you."

"We can do better than nice." Crowe tipped my head up so that he could kiss me while Danny ran the cloth over each intimate inch with agonizing slowness. By the time he was done, I was a whimpering puddle, having fallen to pieces enough times that I wasn't sure there was anything left of me to be cradled in his lap.

"I can put a call in to our med supplier to get a morning contraceptive dropped off," Danny said casually like he was discussing what we might have for breakfast. It was such an absurd moment I couldn't help but laugh. Of course he had a birth control guy. Inappropriate as it was, a fit of exhausted and endorphin-fueled giggles seized me. The more I tried to stop, the harder they came until tears were streaming from the corners of my eyes, and my stomach ached.

"Why is that so funny?" Crowe asked, tucking back my hair to get a better look at my face. I could feel my cheeks flaming red. "I know we probably should have discussed it days ago, but it's definitely the smart thing to do."

I rolled onto my side so that I could see them both. "Because...because..." The joy vanished as quickly as it came. They waited patiently for an explanation, but nothing really seemed to justify my reaction. How did I explain why there was zero chance of an unwanted pregnancy? I chewed on my lip while I tried to decide how much I wanted to divulge. So many truths had already been shared between us. What was another bombshell on top of it all?

"Em threatened to auction off pieces of me for years. So, it wasn't really surprising when I stumbled on a contract she'd drawn up."

"A contract?"

I nodded. "I was hunting for information that was primed to be leaked, anything that might expose an upcoming shipment. It was sitting in the outgoing business pile. My name was right on top in big letters."

"If you tell me that bitch sold off your virginity," Danny growled low enough I could feel the timber of his voice vibrate the mattress beneath me.

Crowe ran a bent knuckle over my cheek, where I knew there was still the ghost of a bruise.

I shrugged. "She tried to. Was getting ten grand for it, too. Apparently, that's the going rate for a young heiress."

Danny jumped up from where he'd settled at the edge of the bed, shaking his head vigorously. "No," he snapped, as if his denial could somehow alter the past.

"Problem was, I beat her to the punch. By the time Em tried to cash in, there was nothing left to sell. Unlike the other girls, I was supposed to be off-limits to the staff." Danny winced, and I silently cursed myself for not choosing my words more carefully. But fuck it, he knew what that place was, and sugarcoating it wouldn't change the reality of the hell I'd been raised in. "Much to Em's displeasure, I bribed a guard to take the only thing that was truly mine to give." I'd come to terms with how I'd chosen to divest myself of my virginity long ago. It wasn't romantic or sweet or even kind, but it was my choice. I'd never apologize for seizing my freedom where I could find it.

"She'd thrown me in to secure a massive deal with Norman King, and he didn't take kindly to being short-changed. The broken contract cost her big."

"Short-changed?" Danny clenched and unclenched his fists. "Fucking hell. I'm going to break something."

Crowe ignored his fit. "The Norman King who owns every mine in Oz?"

"The same. He buys strong boys to work in them."

"Just add that name to my list of walking dead men, right after Orin fucking Berret," Crowe muttered, leaning down to press a kiss into my hair.

Crowe was keeping a murder list for me? It was sweet in his own macabre way, warming a frozen part of my heart that had been iced over long ago. I've never mattered enough to be worth avenging. The damaged part of my soul liked it.

"The cost of my disobedience was...severe." I wrapped my arms over my stomach, where a small scar was the only proof of what Em had really stolen from me that day. Not meeting their eyes, I hastily added, "While the surgeon was dealing with the internal bleeding, Em had him butcher a few tubes to prevent any future complications my free will might cause."

"Wait." Danny stopped his pacing, spinning in place to face me. "Internal bleeding? You mean to tell me that she beat you hard enough to rupture something just because you decided not to let her sell your virginity to a guy who is more gnome than man?"

"Not exactly. Henry caned me. Em rarely lowered herself enough to touch me."

"She fucking caned you? Because you didn't allow yourself to be raped." Heaving heavy breaths, he picked up a lamp from the side table and chucked it at the wall.

While Danny seethed, Crowe wrapped a possessive arm around my shoulder, pressing a kiss to my forehead like he could somehow heal the horrors of my past. "I get her beating you for blowing the deal. We saw plenty of that bullshit around Ciopriani Villa, but then why the ligation?"

I tilted my chin until I could look at him, if only because I knew that I could find refuge in his steady blue eyes. Crowe's expression was stark, and where his irises were usually bright, now they looked nearly black. It would be terrifying if I didn't know exactly where all that malice was aimed.

"Because once she didn't have to maintain my innocence, there was no point in protecting it. It wasn't often, but —"

Danny gripped the footboard hard enough the sound of splintering wood cracked in the still bedroom. "I swear to fucking Ozma, Dorothy, if you're about to say she gave you to people as a perk, I'm going to—"

I looked away, not able to lie to him. For the first time, they were truly seeing the barbarism of Emily Rosen, my beloved aunt.

Danny's roar was loud enough to shake the room. He knocked over the table holding all of the supplies. Everything crashed to the ground in a loud cacophony.

Quietly, I added, "Don't call me Dorothy."

Crowe glared at him over the top of my head. "You fucking know she wants to be called Thea. You're such a prick that you can fuck her into screaming your name but can't be bothered to call her by the one of her choosing."

Danny paced against the far wall like a caged lion. "Sorry, she just told you that Emily-fucking-Rosen pimped her out to sweeten a few shitty deals, and you're going to focus on the name thing, too. There is seriously something wrong with both of you. Fucking hell, Crowe, why are you not more furious right now?"

"Oh, I am. The idea of anyone ever touching our girl with anything other than adoration makes me want to start stalking the night for heads to roll." Crowe was speaking with such calm, cold fury. It was the complete opposite of the waves of rage that Danny was putting off. Despite that, the hand tracing soothing circles against my arm never slowed. His focus was still on my well-being.

To stop the cold war brewing between them, I explained, "Em called me Dorothy. Her, Henry, the rest of The Farm, Eastin, they *all* called me Dorothy...But *my mom*, she called me Thea." Danny's eyes widened with understanding, his jaw going slack. "I can barely remember her, but I remember that much."

There were very few memories of my life before The Farm. Most of them were hazy and lacking in any real detail. But, I had one vivid and recurring dream. It was of my mother rocking me to sleep.

Her arms held me to her chest, humming a song I've never heard anywhere but with her. The auburn ringlets of her long hair swayed, and the amber hue of her eyes looked like honey. When I was lucky enough to dream of her, I always awoke to her voice softly whispering, *"Sweet dreams, Thea baby."*

My mouth had gone dry, and I swallowed around the building emotion. I pushed away from Crowe, being sure that I could clearly see both him and Danny.

"Em calling me Dorothy was fine. I let her claim that name. In my mind, I was *never* Dorothy. Dorothy was powerless, but Thea is *unbreakable*. When the smoke settles, it will be Thea standing over Em's ashes. I left Dorothy behind the moment I was loaded on that truck."

-32-
CROWE

The full gravity of Thea's confession hung like a volcanic ash cloud in the air. It was the kind of information you couldn't ignore. The kind that ate away at your thoughts and set homicidal plans in motion. My old demons stretched their wings. The man I used to be sharpened his blade and prepared for battle.

Emily Rosen had bad, wicked things coming to her. That was the silent promise I made to my girl as she laid back on the pillow, and I tended to the wounds along her back. All while Danny prowled the length of the room.

"Go get something to eat," I finally snapped at him. "It's been days since you've had a proper meal, and you're making me manic with your pacing. Maybe Nick still has some of the lasagna from earlier left." Danny needed to get a handle on his rage. Behaving like this didn't help Thea. If he really cared, he'd put that strategizing mind of his to work and figure out a plan to take the bitch down.

Danny gave a long glance at where Thea lay on the bed. She lazily yawned and blinked slowly up at me.

"Go, Danny. Thea needs to rest, and she'll never sleep while you're like this." I waved generally at all of him. "Look at her. She can barely keep her eyes open."

With a huff, he trudged out of the room. The door closed behind him with a near-silent click. I pulled the blanket over us and urged Thea to rest against my chest.

"It isn't a big deal," she murmured. "If I had known it would make you both so mad, then I never would have told you."

I kissed the top of her head. "The fact you think it isn't a big deal is exactly why it is. Your aunt abused you so thoroughly you've accepted it as a normal part of life." Her slight frame curled deeper into me. I wrapped my arms around her, hoping that she could sense how I would never let her suffer alone again. "The damage may seem slight, but you've carried that pain for so long you barely feel it anymore. You might have become stronger, but that doesn't make it weigh less."

***

I stared at the claw-like shadows the tree outside the window cast on the ceiling, running my fingers through the tangled mess of auburn waves splayed over my chest. I wanted to fall asleep with her, needed to. I had barely slept more than ten hours combined the past few days. The lulling sound of her breaths, coupled with the sleep deprivation, were as good as any sedative.

Every time I closed my heavy eyes, I couldn't keep the images from coming. Thea's strangled screams cut off by her ragged vocal cords. Was it what Em had subjected her to that haunted those hallucinations or something the men she'd been *given* to had done? Or perhaps it was some other abuse that Thea hadn't even told us about. If Em had allowed her niece to be beaten nearly to death, raped, and sold off to a sadistic butcher, then what else had she rationalized as reasonable?

My dark imagination was getting the better of me, twisting what I already knew with the things I had done in my Scarecrowe days, tangling them together. When I finally gave in, it wasn't into the blissful nothing of deep sleep. No, it was into a new hell of my own creation. I dreamt of torturing Thea. Those screams from her lips fell from the treachery of my own hands.

I wasn't sure how long I was under for when I jolted awake. The room was still blanketed in the thick darkness of night, so it couldn't have been long, but it felt like an eternity.

Thea ran her fingers down my cheek. I could feel them trailing through cold sweat. The welcoming softness in her eyes exorcized the demons still lingering in the eaves of my mind. "Shh. It was only a nightmare."

I sighed a laugh beneath my breath and drew her to me, pressing a kiss to her temple. "I guess you'd know a thing or two about those."

This beautiful creature was so fragile and yet refused to break. She didn't shy from the monsters that stalked the shadows. She stared them down and dared them to do their worst. She waited them out and unflinchingly took the damage they offered. Because, when they were done, that was when she would rise.

I saw it that day in Eastin's office. When she stood over the carnage, a savage goddess painted with the blood of her enemy and dressed in nothing but scars and scraps of lace. Thea should have screamed and run. Instead, she dropped the globe and stared at the ceiling with relief, not terror. Now, she was looking at me with the same expression.

"Do you want to tell me about it?" she whispered.

"The ghosts of my past are best left there, Beautiful. The things I've done...I don't need to burden you with my nightmares when I saw first-hand what yours look like." I tried to smile but couldn't seem to find the energy to fake it. I was still so exhausted, and with Thea, I didn't want to pretend.

"What if we erase them instead." She brushed my sleep-tousled hair from my eyes.

I had to admit, she'd caught my curiosity. "And how do you suggest we do that?"

"I'll tell you one of my nightmares, and then you replace it with a new, better memory." Her hand skimmed over my stomach, resting along the band of my boxers. Suddenly, I was liking this idea a whole lot. "But you have to go first." She bit down on her lower lip, looking unbelievably delicious. "Tell me what you were just dreaming about."

Thea pushed up on her hands and knees, hovering over me. The curtain of her dark hair hung over one shoulder. "Go on." She leaned down, and her lips grazed too damn lightly over the skin just below my navel. Her soft lips brushed the line of hair as she spoke, awakening every impulse in my body. "What scares the scarecrow?"

Alarm bells rang in my ears, drowning out everything but the sound of that one word—Scarecrowe. I ran my hand down her arm, lifting her back up. "Where did you hear that name?"

"Nowhere. I was just being funny. From the look of death on your face, I'm guessing it's anything but. Does it mean something?" She innocently stole a kiss from me, dissolving my shock and replacing it with something entirely more carnal. Her tongue teased at my lips before dropping to my jaw and running down my neck.

I swallowed hard. Thea moved with the flexing muscle, making sure to kiss each swell.

"Tell me," she purred with a seductive voice that was impossible to deny.

"It was me, in my past fucked up life. Before the guys and I started YBR, we worked for Nick's dad." Thea's nails softly raked over the curves of my abdomen. It was distracting enough I stopped talking, forgetting exactly what I was supposed to be telling her, and became laserfocused on the trajectory of her hand. When my story paused, so did those stalking digits. There was more devil in this girl than her angelic features let on.

"I showed a natural proclivity for coercion and intimidation. He'd send me to scare away anyone who might be trying to move in on the Morphea trade and remove the carrion."

"The Scarecrowe."

I nodded. "It was my name."

That sinful hand dipped below the waistband of my boxers, raking her nails slowly up my inner thigh. Her knuckles briefly brushed my painfully stiff erection. It seemed like I was permanently hard around her. The muscles along my spine flexed in an effort to keep myself still. The immediate impulse was to flip Thea off of me and bend her to my mercy. I wanted to demand that she relinquish all control because I've never been truly comfortable being at anyone else's. For Thea, I would try.

"What did you do to them?"

My jaw tensed. I didn't want to share this part of myself with her. I wanted to show her only kindness, not reveal that the man responsible for those fleeting smiles was actually the boogieman.

"I sent messages in broken bones and severed flesh." Her fingers drifted up the length of my cock, gently wrapping around the shaft and sliding in one long stroke. I sucked in a breath. "Devil be damned, your hands are soft."

I reached for her. She smacked my hand away and purposefully pressed it into the soft batting of the mattress. Her message was clear, *"Not your turn."* Yet.

She sat up, hooking the sides of my boxers. "Continue."

"You have a surprisingly wicked side to you. Did you know that?"

Her eyes glittered. "No, I just don't appreciate having the few things I ask for denied."

"Then be careful of what you ask for because Thea, I will never deny you...anything."

She grinned, tapping my hips. I lifted them in invitation allowing her to pull my boxers free. My erection stood proudly between us, more than ready for some attention. She made no small show of gazing down at it. Fuck, the look in her eyes was pure deviance.

"And...keep talking, pretty boy." For emphasis she leaned down and blew a drawn-out breath over the head of my dick.

"Fucking hell. Okay." I was seriously starting to regret the times I'd drawn out her pleasure. Right now, I would give anything to see those pink lips wrap around my cock. I guess that was the point, and to think I'd said I was the one gifted with coercion.

I gritted my teeth, drawing a slow breath through them. Which was nearly impossible with how fast my heart was racing. "I've heard enough of your screams this week to know exactly what you would sound like being tort—"

My words cut off, and my brain short-circuited. Thea sat up, one leg thrown over my hips so that every beautiful, glistening inch of her body was on display.

She took my hand from where I was gripping the sheets and sucked my index finger into her mouth. Her tongue flattened against its length, then swirled expertly around the tip.

I was wrong. *Now* I would do anything. If there was any blood left in my body, it was below my waist. That racing pulse I'd fought against to breathe was now thrumming solidly in my dick, leaving me light headed.

My finger, held hostage between her teeth, she inclined her chin to me. A silent command to continue.

"I dreamt of you beneath my blade, your blood coating my hands and screams of pain on your beautiful lips."

She trailed my wet finger between her breasts, sinking between her spread thighs, parting the flesh so that the slick pad made direct contact with her clit. She shuddered, letting out a low moan that made her entire body roll against mine. "Did it sound like that?"

"No." My voice was rough, less syllable and more groan.

Her hand left mine and returned to my shaft. It was wet and warm from where she'd sank those wicked fingers through the folds of her pussy. She gripped the base firmly, stroking up, running the pad of her thumb over the bead of precum waiting for her. Drawing the moisture with her, the next stroke made my knees bend.

My hand reflexively curved where I still held it between her thighs. I dipped into the wet heat, making her moan louder this time. I ached to grab her hips and slam her down on top of me. It would take next to nothing. She was practically there already.

"Did it feel like this?"

Before I could think, much less answer, her lips closed around the head of my dick. She moved with lightning precision, teasingly licking the crown, then sucking lightly. I could have fucking come right then and there, but at the last burning second she stopped. I groaned. No, I growled.

Frozen in motion, Thea's eyes flicked expectantly up to mine, waiting for an answer.

"Gorgeous, nothing feels like this." Oz help her when I finally got my mouth on her cunt, because the only screams for mercy she'd be giving me were the ones I drove from her with my tongue.

The corners of her mouth lifted in as much of a smile as my cock could allow. Slowly, she sank down until her lips met where her hand gripped me tightly. She drew back up, a whisper of her teeth forcing my heart rate to skyrocket. She sucked and licked, pushing further down with each revolution until the head of my cock pressed against the back of her throat.

"Mother of all that is wicked," I cursed. How had I ever thought she had an ounce of purity in her? Thea's sea-green eyes met mine again, the pupils giant black saucers of dilated lust. The determination behind them sent me spilling down her throat. I pushed against her mouth, gripping the back of her head and being much rougher than I had any right to. In response, she hummed—fucking hummed with pleasure.

My vision vibrated with the tremor pulsing along my dick. The suction she'd started and never truly eased intensified, drawing out my orgasm into an endless stream. I wasn't sure if it would actually end. It redefined my entire notion of what it meant to come. She swallowed, again and again, her tongue pulsing around me. With each surge of pleasure, she obliterated the world.

"Fuuuck, Thea.."

When she was finished, she climbed back up my body, licking her lips. Thea was a goddess, a conqueror, a prowling lioness standing over her kill, ready to tear into my flesh.

"Was that all?"

Was that all? I couldn't fucking remember anything before she'd touched me. She'd woven her spell. My dreams would be of one thing and one thing only, but first...

"No. Your turn, Beautiful."

-33-
CROWE

"On your stomach, Darling." With a smirk, she dutifully followed my directions. The round curve of her ass was gilded in the low light from the cracked bathroom door. I wanted to take a bite out of it. Maybe I would, later.

Using my thigh to force hers apart, I pressed my leg against her core. She was blazing hot and soaked. I hovered my torso over her back, careful not to rub against the still-tender flesh. Danny had already done enough damage for one night. I had to re-tape two of the lacerations after the pounding she'd taken earlier.

I spoke into her ear, my breath shifting the small hairs that hung at her nape. "Was it sucking my cock that made you this wet?"

Thea shivered, clutching the pillow as I pressed harder against her. "Or was it seeing me submit to your will at the mere suggestion of your mouth that did it?"

Her hips rocked in a needy tilt, chasing the friction she was craving. I pinned them with mine, forcing them to still. Thea grunted with frustration.

"No... It's because you know that *you've ruined me*. I felt the wicked depths of hell in that release, bowed at the feet of my dark goddess, and sold my soul for the promise of more."

"I like the sound of that."

"Not as much as I love this one."

I tilted my hips, my already hardening dick rubbing against her ass. She moaned my name. It was so fucking good spilling from her lips that I did it

265

again with enough force to press her entire body into the mattress. The full length of her spine curved, and a delicious cry escaped her.

I reached an arm around her hips, sliding my hand into place so our mutual rocking ground her clit into my palm. The moment I touched her, she rocked faster.

"You like that, don't you, gorgeous." This was her game, and she wasn't going to wait for me. Thea would hunt down her own high and use me to do it. Even pinned beneath me, she refused to relinquish control now that she'd seized it.

If she wanted to set the rules for this game, then I was going to play by them. I eased back from her, anchoring my hand at the base of her neck to keep her in place. She whimpered and wriggled to try and find a way back into my embrace. When she couldn't find it, she growled with contempt.

"Ah, ah, ah. You know how this works." I dragged her hair to the side and kissed the small dip where her neck met her shoulder.

"Fine, *fine*! Ask your question."

"When we left the diner, you were screaming in the back of the car. What did you see?" Of all the screaming she'd done, none of them had unsettled me as much as when I was still holding her. Thea had looked at me with complete and unyielding fear. It was an image I couldn't shake, and I wanted to know what she was seeing.

My beautiful vixen shuddered. Not from cold, or stimulation, but with the memory.

I stilled, her visible distress making my stomach flip. This was wrong. I was a selfish bastard, and what's worse, I fucking knew better. It was her game, but she'd been through a hell of a lot. Offering a token of comfort, I kissed the base of her neck, ready to end this and be content with holding her until morning.

"I was falling and sinking into the ground. You threw me in, and I disappeared beneath the surface."

That wasn't what I was expecting. There was no villain for me to banish, no foe that I could slit the throat of. I lowered beside her, the mattress dipping with my weight. I ran my palm down her arm. "Thea, you don—"

Her face turned against the pillow so that we were looking at each other. "It's okay. I don't want these nightmares anymore than you wanted yours."

My lips barely brushed hers before she drew back, sending a raw ache straight to the center of my chest. I hated how powerless her pain made me feel.

"There was a compartment built into the floorboards for pipe access. The ground had several feet of insulation in it, the kind that always reminded me of pink cotton candy." Her fingers idly twisted into the pillowcase, her eyes growing distant and unfocused. "You instantly sank when you landed on it. You had to find something to hold onto, or the itchy substance swallowed you up. Whenever I misbehaved, Em threw me in the dark and let me fight against gravity—for hours. When I was lucky, I managed to get a grip on a pipe. I could hang so long as my muscles held out, and no one was running the hot water. When I wasn't lucky, I choked on fiberglass."

"Thea..."

She blinked, her vision snapping back to mine. "I don't like the dark or small spaces."

I thought back to her first morning at our compound, to her panic when she woke up in the black of my apartment. I loved sleeping in the dark. Darkness soothed me. Sometimes, it was the only way I could sleep. It hadn't even occurred to me that she might have an issue with it. Fuck me, I was an asshole. I vowed to keep her safe, and instead, I'd immediately thrust her into her worst nightmare.

"Now erase it, Crowe."

I kissed her shoulder. Could I really do this to her? I'd done some fucked up shit to a lot of people, but they'd all deserved it. My sweet girl didn't deserve an ounce of what she'd been given. Thea had that look of grim determination again, the steel in her eyes reminding me that she wasn't made of glass. She'd made up her mind and wouldn't be denied. Tonight, she would destroy her fears, and she'd chosen me as the weapon. "Stay here. I'll be right back."

Climbing from the bed, my mind scrambled to form a plan. The walk-in closet was lined with different styles and types of clothing in all of our sizes. Everything from designer suits to workman jumpsuits, contingencies for whatever type of job we might be doing. I pulled out one of Nick's black but-ton-downs. It was soft and would dwarf her tiny frame.

At the back was a short armoire filled with accessories. I pulled open the top drawer, rifling through the contents until I found what I was looking for.

When I returned to the room, Thea had sat up, hugging her knees. She eyed me with curiosity.

"Come here."

Her eyes locked in on the black silk tie running through my fingers. Thea licked her lips, doing as instructed. She crawled to the end of the bed, her hips swaying with each movement. I let my eyes drop when she stood, taking a moment to commit every curve of her body to memory. "You're so beautiful."

Her cheeks flushed, making the small spattering of freckles more pro-nounced. I laced my fingers through hers and slowly walked us back to the walk-in closet. Her head swiveled taking in the room and noting its compact size. Her heart rate instantly sped up, making her breathing quicker, and the pulse point on her neck fluttered. I don't know how I'd missed it before. She had a solid handle on her fear, probably from years of pretending she had none. Ozma only knew what Emily Rosen did when she discovered weaknesses.

I rotated her so that her back was facing the rack of shirts. Looping the tie around my neck, I held the shirt open for her. Thea's head tilted like she was trying to understand my plan. Somehow, dressing her in a mammoth size clothing wasn't computing for her.

I gave the shirt a shake and smirked. "I've never seen you be shy before."

Thea scowled and thrust her hand into the arm hole.

"Ah...not that one," I said, gesturing that she should put the shirt on back-wards.

"What are you up to, Vincent Crowe?"

"You don't like to be called Dorothy. I don't like to be called Vincent. Or worse, Vinny." I made an overly dramatic shiver, getting a chuckle to rise from her. "Now, Darling Thea, put the shirt on."

The arms of the shirt hung several inches past her fingertips, exactly as I'd hoped.

"This is absurd." She gave a little flap of her arms.

I fastened the shirt down to the small of her back, all the while stealing the small tastes of her neck that our position offered up. The loose shirt hung partially open, giving me perfect view of her peachy ass beneath the dark fabric. I smoothed my hand over it and leaned in to speak against her ear. "If you want me to stop, just say so. I'm not here to terrorize you."

Thea nodded. "I know. I can handle it."

"Okay, then..." My voice trailed off, and I ran my hands down her arms, gripping her wrists and gently easing them behind her. "Still okay?"

She nodded again, a slow breath slipping from her lips. "Don't be a pussy about this, Crowe, or I'll get Danny in here to finish the job. I know my limits, and if you reach them, I'll tell you."

I gave her arms a sharp tug. "It wasn't Danny you saw throwing you into the abyss." I pulled the ends of the sleeves into a tight knot, effectively trapping her hands behind her. It wasn't a true restraint. The arms of the shirt were large enough she could slip out if she really wanted to. I fashioned a similar knot with the bottom of the shirt, wrapping the tails through her arms, locking them against her lower back.

Confident in the work I'd done with the shirt, I slid the tie free. It made a soft sound as it brushed against my neck. Thea shivered. It wasn't strictly part of my plan, but I tossed her hair over one shoulder and undid the top button, loosening it enough so that I could slip my hand into the front of the shirt and palm her breast. Thea arched back against me with a soft moan, the knot of her hands resting hard against my groin.

"Is that incredible pussy throbbing for me yet? I know you secretly love being at my mercy." I nibbled at the exposed part of her throat, rubbing the black silk against her cheek. "Ready to give me more, beautiful girl?"

Instead of answering, she ground her hands against me. I could feel her fingers questing against the confines of the sleeves. When she found no openings, no way to get to me, she swore under her breath.

With a chuckle, I lowered the tie over her eyes. It was already dark in the closet. I'd purposely left the light off, but the blindfold would take away the little bit of ambient light. Phobias weren't conquered overnight, but you had to start somewhere.

I walked with heavier-than-needed steps to the door, making sure she heard as it clicked shut. Silently, I flicked the small light I used whenever I needed to see in the drawers at the back. It was only a dull glow, but enough to allow me to see what I was doing while at the same time fooling Thea into believing she was in the pitch-black and confined space of the closet.

Thea's breathing quickened, her hands pulling at the shirt and the hard edges of her nipples straining against the fabric. I extended my hand, ready to cup her cheek until she calmed, but before I made it to her, she swallowed, and the visible signs of her fear abated. It was impressive how quickly she mastered it. I was going to have to try much harder to force her past this.

I pulled a spare pillow from an upper shelf and dropped it on the floor before her, then, for good measure, added a second one. I kneeled behind Thea, then grabbing her hips, pulled her onto my lap with one leg on either side of my own. At this height, the lower rack of clothing brushed her face. Jacket and shirt sleeves encompassing both sides of her head, no matter which way she turned to escape them. My body stayed braced against hers, keeping Thea in place but also reminding her that, unlike her nightmares, this time, she wasn't alone.

I ran my hands up and down Thea's arms, warming away the goosebumps lining her flesh. Tension built in the muscles beneath my fingertips. Despite how hard I could see her fighting it, her breaths came in quick, tiny pants.

The backs of her legs were soft against my palms. I didn't fail to notice the slight ridges from where she'd taken the first lashing. My fingers caressed the edges, trying to replace their violence with something purer. For the eight hundredth time tonight, I promised Emily Rosen a long and gruesome death.

"Are you afraid?"

Thea's voice was barely audible when she answered, "No."

"No?" I wrapped my hands around her thighs, pulling them apart and using my own widened stance to keep them spread open. "I don't believe you. Your beautiful body is shaking."

"I'm...Yes, this scares me, but I'm not afraid—not when I'm with you."

Even Cupid's bullet couldn't have hit me in the heart the way those words did. They were more powerful than any declaration of love.

I'd spent more than a decade of my life hunting people in the night. I'd seen more fear-stricken faces than I could count, grown men pissing themselves the moment I walked through the door. To hear this devastating woman say that she trusted me implicitly was something I'd longed for my entire life.

Emotion crowded my throat, making it so that all I could manage in response was a short, broken, "Good."

I circled the slick heat of her pussy. Thea's breathing slowed to match mine, the tension in her body shifting from her shoulders to the legs bracing mine. The sweet aroma of her arousal filled the small space. I swallowed a smug laugh, knowing the clothes here would smell of her for weeks.

"Mmm," I purred in her ear, pushing two fingers deep into her drenched core. "So wet for me, beautiful. Your body likes this, even if your mind is rebelling against it."

A tiny cry slipped from her lips. At the same time, my other hand settled into its place beneath the confines of the shirt, ensuring that she stayed pressed against me while also allowing me to tease her nipple.

I was already hard and aching for her again. Something Thea didn't miss. With a long moan, she rocked her bare ass along my shaft in time with each of my lazy strokes. With every tilt, it was becoming harder to keep my focus on her. Her dripping pussy slicked up and down my length. Her bound hands scrambled against my stomach, fruitlessly pulling against the confines of the shirt.

Bound and blindfolded, Thea, literally pinned in my lap, may have been one of the sexiest sights of my life. I pumped my fingers with increasing vigor, addicted to the sound of her breath in my ear. The heel of my hand pushed hard against her clit. The more I moved, the greedier her responding thrusts became. Her pussy clamped down on my fingers, pulsing in time with her mounting climax. Every muscle in her body strained against her bonds, arching her back and fighting the firm grip I kept on her chest. The moment her release crashed down, I pushed her forward.

Thea fell. A panicked scream of fear mixed with unrestrained ecstasy tore from her. Her face passed through the clothing until her chest hit the waiting pillows. My body quickly caged in the space behind her again. The exhilaration of the fall forced her into a second immediate orgasm.

"When you fall, I fall with you," I whispered in her ear.

Her body quaked, a small moan of release coming with every heavy breath.

The pillow angled her hips, aligning our bodies perfectly. My cock slid against her folds. I meant to tease her, but it had been a solid two weeks of denial while I watched Thea fall apart over and over again. I'd never once felt out of control with a girl. Right now, with her throbbing cunt pressed against my cock, I was hanging by my last thread of restraint.

"Do you still fear the fall?"

"Fuck me, Crowe. Now, while my mind is still spinning. I want to feel you inside of me before reality comes back." She pressed that greedy pussy back onto the head of my dick, moving with the full breadth of the little mobility I was allowing her.

"I told you, beautiful, I will never deny you." I thrust forward, my cock sinking deep in one mind-altering hit. Thea screamed, and I cursed. Or, I tried to. I couldn't think, couldn't breathe around the way her cunt was strangling the life from me.

I pulled at the tied sleeves. When I started moving again, I wanted it to be her sweet skin sliding against mine, not Nick's fucking shirt. I needed all of her. The knot slipped loose, and buttons flew in the frenzy of my tearing hands.

Thea's arms came free, immediately falling forward on a sigh. I pulled her back so that she was once more sitting in my lap, this time with my cock seated deep inside her. It felt fucking glorious, the kind of sensation that made the room around us break away. I held her tight against me, angling her face back so that I could steal long, sensuous kisses with each joining thrust. The clothing swayed around us in soft caresses, and Thea never once seemed to notice.

Throwing the blindfold to the ground, I looked at the power vibrating in her eyes. Not a trace of fear was left. Any doubts I'd had about this being the right thing to do were now lost in their depths.

Thea draped one arm around my neck for leverage, while the other dropped between our splayed legs. Her hand circled the base of my cock, feeling my body entering hers. I threaded my fingers between her slender ones, pushing her thumb against her swollen clit and using my index finger to stretch her just a bit more. Sliding along the rigid length of my shaft, her needy pussy took it all.

Our bodies surged as one. The rhythm was hypnotic. My dick slipped through our hands, her pussy clenching hard as I fucked her with slow, deliberately deep thrusts. Finally surrendering her control, Thea erupted. Her entire body flushed bright red, visible even in the low light of the closet. A flood of arousal coated my fingers, slicking down her thighs. Arching her spine and pulling against my legs, her body fought against the pleasure I pulled from it.

She tilted into my hand, forcing my fingers deeper as I increased our pace with every punishing hit. I knew with a few carefully timed strokes, it would only take another minute to shove her over the edge into another orgasm. Tightening my grip on her breast, Thea's nails cut into the back of my neck, where she was hanging onto me like I was the only thing keeping her from drowning.

Sliding my thumb against hers, I caught her clit between us, pinching it hard. The effect was immediate—Thea screamed, the still raw vocal cords shredding apart her cries in wave after wave of ecstasy. Before her body liquified in my lap, I allowed myself the release I'd been denying for days. Closing my mouth over her still quivering lips, I came with such intensity that my vision flared with enough light to make the dark room feel like we were dancing on the surface of the sun.

It took several long minutes to remember what planet we were on. Pulling free, I flexed my hand, already knowing it would be sore for days. Thea blinked up at me in a daze.

Fucking worth it.

-34-

THEA

F alling asleep beneath a rack of designer shirts might be on a list of weirdest places I've ever slept, but it was infinitely less strange than when I awoke, back in bed, wedged between two walls of muscle. It was like waking up in the middle of a very hot, very sexy burrito—but mostly just hot. Crowe at any normal time was a sauna, and Danny, despite acting cold as ice, was warm enough when he slept to melt parts of the sun.

The biggest shock wasn't the surprise relocation, even though it took me more than a minute to realize where in Oz I was. It was the way the boys were laying with me. The bed had been small when it was just me and Danny in it before. With Crowe wedged into the bed too, it was practically impossible to tell what body part belonged to whom. What felt like too many limbs snaked around me. Arms twisted around my neck, shoulders, and hips. Legs wrapped between and beneath my own. There were hands splayed wide over my stomach, breasts, ass and neck.

All of it reminded me of a book I stole from Aunt Em's shelves. I was never allowed to read her books. No one was because, "*Those books aren't for reading.*" What good were all those pretty pages and vellum inserts if you never opened the book to look at them? Those books deserved to be loved and Em telling me not to do something was practically a dare, so it was no surprise when the very next thing I did was steal a book. Reading was the only escape I ever got from The Farm, and there was something especially gratifying in knowing I was doing it with her precious special editions.

I picked that particular book because the woman on the cover looked elegant. She wore a perfectly askew hat, large dress and leaned on a closed parasol like it was a gentleman's cane. Her expression was confident and the dark mansion on the cliff behind her made me think the book was a gothic mystery. The foolish child in me thought I might be getting a novel about a woman detective. To an extent I wasn't wrong. There was murder, and the woman was solving it. She just also happened to be seduced by a man who could manifest tentacles.

The book was undeniably entertaining, and made me question my sanity when I realized that mythical squid shifter porn was actually arousing. Until now it seemed like pure fiction, but here I was, wrapped up in limbs like I was in the middle of my own absurd fantasy.

I blinked my eyes slowly, focusing on where my hand rested against the firm lines of a lion tattoo. From this position he looked more like he was yawning, than roaring. Danny must have found us in the closet, and somehow the two of them moved me back here. Rather than give the other the option of sleeping with me, they'd just decided to stake their claim.

Crowe's deep rhythmic breathing drifted over my shoulder. It was his arm supporting my neck, and reaching around to sleep with a handful of my breast, like it was his very own security boob. Not that Danny's handful of my ass was any better.

Slowly, I burrowed my way out from between them, priding myself on managing to do it without waking either of them up. Even better was that I'd also managed to rearrange them so that they now had new handfuls to fondle in their sleep. I made a quick spin of the room, finally finding where the bag with my clothing was discarded.

My joints and muscles were still sore in a few places, including some delicious new ones that only came from a night of being well fucked. Smiling at the burn between my legs, I stretched. The pull at my back stung a bit more than the previous morning. I probably shouldn't have been quite so zealous with the boys, but then again—I drifted my eyes over the pile of sleeping muscle, remembering the look Crowe had given Danny—I regretted nothing.

Gingerly tugging on some leggings and an oversized sweater that must have belonged to one of the boys, I padded into the kitchen in search of water, and maybe a bagel. Or a dozen bagels, my stomach felt achingly hollow.

Nick was in the kitchen brewing what looked like the world's tiniest pot of coffee, and humming quietly to himself. I didn't recognize the tune, but his pitch was enchanting. It was a deep baritone that wrapped itself around you like heavy velvet. His singing voice was probably something I could listen to for hours. Not that I thought he'd ever sing for me. Unless it was a dirge, or something equally foreboding.

I hovered in the doorway, taking a minute to observe the normally reclusive man. The tattoos that coated almost all of his visible skin were clearly on display. His usual black shirt was discarded, leaving him in only a thin undershirt. Down the length of his arm was what looked like scientific sketches of the bone structure of an arm, the skin flayed and pinned back with tags, muscle removed. Except, these bones were broken in several places. Holding the fractured pieces in place were several vines of blooming nightshade.

Before I could take the time to study how it transitioned over his shoulder into what looked like plate armor, Nick turned. "Were you going to keep staring, or did you actually want something in here?"

I guess I shouldn't be surprised that he was aware of me the entire time.

"You offering?" I asked, coyly leaning against the counter.

His eyes slowly tracked down my body, sending a rush of unexpected heat flooding through my senses. When they snapped back up to mine again they were full of cold indifference, dousing anything I might have been feeling.

"From the sounds of things last night, I'm pretty sure you've already got your hands full."

Heat rose to my cheeks, but I tamped down the urge to be shy. I certainly hadn't cared about being heard last night, so why should I now.

"I was talking about the coffee," I added sweetly, gesturing towards where one of those weird silver coffee pots gurgled on the stove top.

"It's not done yet. You can't instantly have something because you bat those long lashes over your pretty eyes. Some things require time and patience."

"You think my eyes are pretty?"

Ignoring my sass, Nick pulled two clear mugs from a cabinet. Then clicked off the burner and moved the pot to the counter top. "How do you feel?"

The delicate metallic sound of the lid hitting granite rang out. Curling steam filled the air, making me think of magic potions. Nick stirred the contents with a long silver spoon, like some dark cafe wizard. It was mesmerizing to watch.

"Thea? Are you still hallucinating or is watching me make espresso really that hypnotic?" Damn me. His accent was so sexy. I would listen to this man read a grocery list, just so long as he didn't stop talking. Even my name sounded sexier when he said it. Not Thea, but Tay-ah.

"Thea," he repeated, harsher this time. Hearing my name shouldn't make my nipples hard, but here we were. "I asked you a question."

I blinked rapidly, clearing the spell he was casting over me. What had he asked? How I felt? "Better, much better. It feels good to be walking around."

Dark liquid poured smoothly into the cups, making the air instantly aromatic with the rich scent of coffee grounds.

"Did they tell you what happened?"

"I got the highlights."

Nick slid the glass over to me. "I drink my espresso black."

"Shocker."

"If you want to add something to it Danny keeps the sugar and flavored creamers next to the barbaric thing he calls a coffee maker."

"Black is fine. Wait, Danny uses flavored creamer? I just assumed he'd drink coffee as bitter as he is." I moved to the corner where a stainless steel bowl was filled with individual creamer cups, everything from Hottie Biscotti to Marshmallow-Snickerdoodle. I snorted with amusement. "How positively squishy of him."

"Ozmandrians have no idea what a good cup of coffee is supposed to look like, much less taste like." His accent thickened with annoyance. It would be sexy, if it wasn't so damn amusing to see him riled up over something as simple as coffee. "It took me five long, nearly unbearable years before I managed to get these." He tapped the coffee pot with the spoon. "The first time we did a job beyond the borders I bought an entire case of moka pots, and had one put in each of our safe houses. I refuse to ever suffer Danny's swill again. I'd rather drink grey water."

I took a sip. Black fireworks exploded across my taste buds. "What demon did you sell your soul to in order to make coffee this damn good?" I breathed, greedily sipping down more.

Nick laughed. A rough and hearty exhalation shook his chest and made his white teeth shine beneath a wide smile. The sound lingered in the quiet room like a phantom. I didn't dare speak for fear of dispelling the happiness from his features.

He shifted his stance, studying whatever my reaction must have been over a long pull of dark coffee. "The devil took much more than my soul, *fiore mio*—"[1] He lifted his glass to me. "—and I didn't get anything as nice as *this* in return."

I cleared my throat. The now full weight of his attention made my skin prickle. Teasing Nick wasn't like teasing Danny. When I pushed Danny's buttons it made me feel alive. When the fires of his anger rose mine decided to bring along the gasoline. With Nick, everything he did was with the promise of menace. Teasing him felt like I was turning that hot poker on myself, and I wasn't entirely certain that I'd like the bite of pain I felt in return.

---

1. The devil took much more than my soul, my flower-

-35-
THEA

My stomach flipped, rumbling loudly as I started opening cabinets in search of something to eat. The fridge was filled with vegetables, and a large drawer held what looked like half a dozen different cheeses. I settled on taking out a massive hunk of a hard white cheese and a bundle of celery. They didn't go together, but it was as close to ready-to-eat food as I could find. I sat the entire pile on the counter, along with a plate and a knife.

Nick moved closer. The weight of his gravity loomed in my periphery like a giant black hole. I ignored him, unwrapping the cheese. I was about to knock off a hunk from the end when the deep tenor of his voice vibrated behind me, his warmth seeping into my back.

"I was going to wait and see what you managed to do, but I can't in good conscience let you butcher a perfect block of pecorino."

Thick bands of tattooed muscle wrapped around my body. His hands slipped over mine, taking control of the knife and adjusting my grip. Damn, he smelled good, like something spicy with a slightly metallic edge. Whatever it was, it made all of my lady bits sit up and say, "*Yes, sir.*"

"You'll take your thumb off cutting like that." He pushed down on the handle, and a quarter-inch band of cheese fell onto the plate. He picked it up, slipping it between my lips. I tasted the salt of his fingertips before my lips closed around the cheese. I didn't have time to be shocked before my already overwhelmed senses locked onto the flavor of the pecorino. Damn, it was good. Really good. I groaned as the lump dissolved in my mouth.

Nick scooped up the food that I had laid down on the counter, and tossed them back into the fridge.

"Hey! I was going to eat that."

"And now you are not." He motioned to a lower cabinet. "Get the large silver mixing bowl from the lower cabinet. If you're going to eat, then it should be something more balanced than some artisanal cheese and celery."

"I don't really know how to cook anything. Em didn't exactly trust me *near the knives*," I grumbled and sat the bowl between us on the counter.

"Which is why I will teach you how to make something worth eating." He pulled a large bag of flour from an upper cabinet, followed by a blue container of salt and a tall glass bottle. The dark green bottle had a label written in a foreign language. Whatever was in that bottle wasn't from Oz.

"Get me three eggs."

"You could say please," I joked.

He paused mid-scoop of flour, and glowered at me. "And you could go back to eating celery."

I rolled my eyes. "Joking, oh Angel of Death, sir." The corner of his glare cracked just a little. A wave of triumph rolled through me. "Here's your eggs," I added with a bowing flourish.

Within minutes, Nick had turned the mixture into a thick dough. He pulled the bowl from the mixer, laid a cloth over the top, and sat the whole thing in the fridge. The mountain of tattoos and muscles returned to the counter with a container of cherry tomatoes and some herbs.

"Ummm," I said, having no idea of something better to say. "What was the point of all that if we were just going to put it in the fridge?"

He smacked his flour-covered hands in the air, making a small dust cloud spiral around him. "The dough needs to sit. I told you, some things require patience." Nick pulled a frying pan from an overhead rack, where it was dangling. "I'd like to make a cream sauce. Something tells me you'd love that. But I don't know that your stomach could handle it right now. It's probably wiser to make something light."

Nick smacked a clove of garlic with the flat side of a large knife, making me jump, then quickly diced it. "This is olive oil." He twisted open the green bottle.

"It's from the same town I was born in." Golden liquid poured into the base of the pan. "Come here."

I shifted closer to him, feeling the heat from the gas stovetop against my face. He dipped his pinky into the already warm oil, then lightly smeared it over my lips. My heart fluttered in my chest. It was so tender that it was hard to believe that this was Nick standing beside me. He tossed the garlic into the pan, along with some dried peppers. A hiss filled the room, along with the sweet aroma of the cloves. "The oil is great for chapped... or abused lips." His eyes flicked towards the still quiet bedroom.

I ran my finger over my shining lips, then sucked the residue oil from the tip. His eyes tracked my movement, and his breathing hitched slightly. It was barely noticeable, except we were standing so close that I felt the small motion of his stomach against my chest.

Savoring the flavor of the buttery oil, I remarked, "I'll have to remember that."

The next few minutes stretched into awkward silence while Nick sliced the world's tiniest tomatoes in half, then crushed them. By the time he was chopping the herbs into little specks of green confetti, I couldn't stand the quiet any longer.

"So where was that? Where you were born, I mean. I've never met anyone with an accent like yours before."

He didn't look at me. "My accent isn't really that thick. Not like my father's, and my Nonna doesn't even speak English."

"It is when you're upset about something." I walked my fingers along his arm like a tiny bug. Slowly, his eyes slid to the side. My entire expression crinkled with mischievous joy. I was definitely getting to him.

"*Combina guai.* I swear, you are pure, undiluted trouble."[1] Nick playfully swatted at my hand, but when his fingers landed over mine, there was no sting.

---

1. Trouble maker.

Instead, there was a light squeeze, flattening my palm around his forearm. It made something unexpected flutter in my chest.

"You wouldn't know the town. It's in Italy, far outside of Ozmandria's borders. My father thought if we crossed an ocean, then he could set up his very own little Morphea empire. He wasn't wrong, but sometimes I wish we hadn't left home."

"How old were you when you moved?"

"Ten." He bent down and pulled out a silver machine with a huge crank on the side.

"I suppose you ordered a whole case of those, too?"

"In fact, I bought them from the same place as the moka pots. I got a bulk discount." He winked at me. Or was it his eye twitching? I chose to believe that it was a wink.

The more time I spent with Nick, the harder he was to understand. Ninety-nine percent of the time, he was a brick wall, emotionless and immovable. But, that other one percent, he was playful. If I tried hard enough, could I push him as far as goofy? At that moment, I decided that was my next goal. I would make Niccolo Chopper act like a goof if it was the last thing I did.

Nick sprinkled some flour onto the countertop. "Coat your hands with flour so the dough doesn't stick to them."

He separated the lump into smaller sections, handing me one. "Flatten the dough into discs. Watch me."

Oh, I was watching, forgetting entirely about the dough and focusing solely on the way the muscles in his forearms and hands flexed. God, the strength behind such simple movements was making my entire body feel hot. The fact that the ball was exactly the same shape as a breast wasn't helping either.

"Thea." The tattooed lines of his fingers pushed into the dough, the surface swallowing his fingertips up to the second knuckle until he drew them slowly back.

"Yeah?" I remarked dreamily.

"It's your turn, *fiore mio.*"[2]

"My turn," I squeaked, jumping up and nervously palming my throat. Did the air just get thinner? I swear the steel in his eyes cut straight through me.

Nick turned, his massive frame eating up the space between us.

"The dough." He reached over and loosened my grip on the dough ball. Subconsciously, I'd tightened my hand so completely that bits were oozing between my fingers. Ghosting his arm over mine, Nick pushed the ball flat with the heel of my hand. Folding the dough, he repeated the action three times until the mangled lump turned back into something smooth.

"Now flatten it out, just like I did."

"Mmm hmm." I cleared my throat, ignoring the way my pussy seemed to have developed its own pulse. "I can do that."

I did my best to make my dough ball into an even and flat disc. Or as best as I could while flicking my eyes up to his every twenty seconds. Each time, that little crook to the corner of his mouth crept higher.

Nick fed his disc into the top of the machine. It came out the other side in a flat sheet. He did it again and again, the sheet getting longer and thinner until he was satisfied. "Now we cut the pasta."

Threading the sheet through the other side of the machine, the dough split into a dozen long strips. Nick dropped them unceremoniously into a pile before reaching for a new disc.

I plucked a noodle from the pile and laid it over my upper lip. With an exaggerated lift of my eyebrow, I did my best impression of an old-timey gentleman while stroking my ridiculously long mustache.

The restrained corners of Nick's mouth finally broke. It wasn't quite a smile, but it was enough to make me start laughing in triumph.

"Do you want to try...sir." He took a handful of flour and threw it at me.

I spluttered, my noodle-stache falling from my lip. "Cutting the noodles?" It came out as half a laugh and half a shriek from the face of flour I'd just taken.

---

2. It's your turn, my flower

"Pasta, yes."

"You're going to trust me with your fancy *pasta* machine?"

"You don't have to be afraid of it."

I plucked up a pinch of flour and flicked it at him. "I'm not afraid of anything."

He swiped a cloth over his face, without seeming the least bit annoyed. "I think we both know that isn't true."

For a second, the happiness faded from the moment, and a flood of nightmarish memories reeled through my mind.

Nick's deep voice cut through the haze, "Just hold it at the mouth of the machine and turn the crank. The machine does all the work."

The sheet slowly fed out the bottom, and gently, he guided it onto the counter. In tandem, we picked up the sheet, my fingers brushing against his. Nick helped me to feed it back through the machine a second time without letting the dough fold in the process.

"Was it your father who taught you how to do all of this?"

Nick barked a laugh. "Absolutely not. My father never did anything that he could pay or scare someone else into doing for him."

I nodded. "Em was exactly the same. She never went in the kitchen except to yell at the cook for not meeting every one of her unnecessary dietary requirements."

"It was my Nonna Lucia that taught me to cook. She'd beat me raw if she knew I used a dough hook." I glanced back at the mixer, and the weird attachment he'd used to stir the dough. I giggled at the vision of a little old granny chasing a big, brutish Nick around the kitchen with a wooden spoon.

"I loved cooking with her. There was a time when that's what I wanted to do with my life."

I paused, feeding the dough into the machine to look up at him. His expression was distant and lost in a pleasant memory. Like a bubble popping, he blinked and returned his attention to me.

"My father had other plans, and I always knew that it wasn't an option anyway. That's kind of the point of dreams. They're the things you wish for because they aren't truly possible."

I frowned. "That's both sad and wrong. I dreamed of being free from Em and The Farm, and here I am learning to make noodles—"

"Pasta."

"—*pasta* with you. A dream come true." I dropped a handful of pasta on the pile. They weren't as pretty as his, but each lumpy strand was mine. I'd never made anything of value before. I beamed at him with noodly pride. Nick didn't have praise for me, but the full smile he gave me in return was better than any compliment. He handed me another disc, and together, we pushed the last set through the machine.

After dropping the fettuccine into a waiting pot of boiling water, Nick added the tomatoes to the pan of oil. They sizzled. The aroma of the tomatoes mixing with the still lingering garlic made my mouth water, and my stomach rumbled loudly.

Nick looked up from the frying pan, meeting my eyes. Normally, they were so cold and metallic, but right now they felt like anything but. He reached up and brushed at the flour still on my cheek. Then, he looked at his hand, inspecting his fingertips as though they had moved on their own and he could find their malfunction just by looking at them.

"Why don't you go wash off the flour and I'll plate this up for us."

"Okaaay," I said slowly, puzzled at his reaction to touching me. I couldn't tell if he liked the tender action or if he was regretting it entirely.

When I returned to the small table that sat in the corner of the kitchen, two exquisite-looking plates waited on the table, along with a large glass of water.

"You still need to hydrate, otherwise I'd be serving this with Chianti." Nick sprinkled some shaved pieces of the pecorino that I'd tasted earlier on top of the dish.

"Thank you."

Nick smiled again, followed by an immediate frown. Was he not used to being thanked? It wasn't surprising. Danny didn't seem the type to thank anyone for anything, and Crowe seemed like he might always be too distracted to remember anything as mundane as manners. I spun the thick noodles around my fork.

"So, you're a wine guy? Danny has scotch, Crowe beer. I wouldn't have guessed you for wine."

"Of course. I'm not a neanderthal. I enjoy beer too, just not the over-hopped shit Crowe buys. I prefer my beer and my scotch to be malty and a dark wine that has some spice to it."

I shoved the knot of noodles into my mouth. "Makes sense—" I brought my hand to my mouth, covering it to hide the small mouthgasam that was going on. "Fuck me sideways, this is really good." I swallowed hard. "I can't believe we made this."

Nick bowed his head in acceptance. "You're a good student. This was passable."

I gaped at him. "Passable?" Then, realizing my mouth was unforgivably empty, shoved another forkful into it.

"Next time, I'll make Pasta alla Norcina with fresh penne rigate." The way Nick's mouth moved around the rolling Rs, his accent thick with each syllable, mesmerized me.

"I'm listening." Maybe listening to him talk in Italian should be my goal instead. Short term at the very least.

"It's the kind of dish that makes your toes curl. Just the smell of the truffle oil, mixing with the wine and the garlic, is enough to leave you feeling satiated. Especially when the weather is crisp like it's been lately. There are few pleasures in this world as good as a perfectly prepared plate of pasta."

Fucking hell. I rubbed my legs together to ward off the pooling heat. How did he just manage to make pasta sound so arousing?

"You seem very confident of that, Sir." I smirked, taking another bite just to give my mouth something to do other than leaping over the table and devouring him.

We ate in easy silence. I was too busy going to pasta heaven to talk. Nick kept stealing pleased glances at me between bites. He definitely liked seeing someone enjoy his cooking. Which was fine by me, because I more than enjoyed eating it.

When I was half-way through my plate, there was a yell from the back of the apartment, followed by a loud thud and more shouting.

"I don't suppose you'd know anything about that?"

I laughed into my water glass. "What about what?" I'd forgotten how I'd left the boys. I wondered which one had woken first.

Crowe and Danny wobbled in a few moments later.

"Ooo, pasta for breakfast." Crowe scooped up a long noodle and sucked it through his lips.

I snatched my plate away before he could take anything else. "That's not for you."

Crowe leaned over me, stealing a tomato with a wink and popping it between his lips before I could fight him for it, which I would.

"What was that racket back there? Did Danny turn you down?" Nick said with banal amusement. It was impressive how easy it was for him to feign indifference.

"Please, I'm out of his league." Crowe winked at Danny.

"No," Danny said, over the running water filling up the coffee pot. "That asshole was copping a feel of my junk when I woke up."

"And apparently, the civil thing to do when you find a sleeping man touching your dick is to knee him in the balls hard enough that he's knocked out of bed," Crowe said, with more amusement than he should have, after being woken up that way. "Besides, he's leaving out the part where he had his hand holding my ass and was nuzzling his face into my hair. Fair is fair in my book. By my count, I owe you one."

Danny clicked the coffee maker on, then squared off in front of Crowe. "Not a chance, and especially not after I had to listen to you fucking my girl all night."

"Our girl."

"Keep fighting over me, and I won't be anyone's girl," I snapped.

Crowe spun to face me. "And what would you do, Beautiful, deny us both?"

"Maybe, *pretty boy.*" I chewed on my lip. "There's Nick. Who says I need to deny myself anything? Behave, or I'll start climbing him like a tree."

Nick's fork fell from his hand, clattering onto the plate, sending a tomato flying through the air straight into Danny's cheek. If I didn't know better, I'd say he was blushing. Whatever it was made the grey of his eyes brighter and the tan of his skin warmer.

Crowe rested his hand on the back of my chair, forcing my attention away from Nick. He dipped low enough that the heat of his body made the room's temperature spike ten degrees. "Go right ahead, Darling Thea. After last night, I have an entirely new repertoire to fill my fantasies. Fucking my hand will never be the same again."

I couldn't breathe.

"What's that mean?" Danny looked at me like he was entitled to an answer.

Ignoring them both, I twirled the pasta around my fork slowly.

Danny made a pained sound. "I knew when I found the two of you naked in the closet, you'd been doing something kinky."

"Seriously?" Nick reached over the table and punched Crowe in the shoulder. "My clothes are in that closet.

"Trust me, I know." Crowe planted a deep kiss on my lips. "Oz damn, you taste good."

Muttering in Italian, Nick picked up my mostly empty plate. "Now that you two are up, we should discuss our plans for The Wizard with Thea."

Nick returned to his seat, folding his large arms over his chest. He was back to being the statue, his expression frozen into a scowl like he'd rusted in place.

Danny pulled the still brewing pot of coffee from the maker and filled up a waiting cup. Small splashes of quick brew peppered the countertop. He poured in four of the dark red creamer cups, Marshmallow-Snickerdoodle. I had to bite the inside of my cheek to keep from laughing. Nick met my eyes, and I knew he could read my mind.

Danny turned around with his cup of joe, looking perplexed. "You want a mug, Firecracker? I can fix you one."

When I didn't answer, Nick kicked me under the table. I could barely speak, it came out as a squeak. "Nope. I'm good."

"I wouldn't mind a cup," Crowe said, raising his hand like a good little boy in class.

"Fuck off, asshole. Get your own shit."

Danny took the seat beside me, setting his nearly white cup of coffee on the table. "We should probably tell her about the key."

"What key?"

-36-
THEA

A sleek black box sat in the center of the bed, surrounded by a half dozen smaller boxes and bags.

"Danny?" I called, in a long, drawn-out question.

What in the name of Ozma was going on? The boys had been doting but nothing like the pile of boxes currently sitting before me. In my experience, people didn't give you things without expecting something in return. There was no way a pile of boxes could equal anything good. Coupled with our meeting with The Wizard this afternoon, my nerves were shot.

"Danny," I shouted again. If that prick didn't get his muscular ass in here—

"Problem?"

I turned to snap at Danny, but leaning in the doorway was a dick of a different color.

"Oh, Nick..." I said cautiously.

Nick had been extra cold since we'd shared our pasta breakfast like he was purposely avoiding me. I wasn't sure what to make of it. That, too, had left me on edge. Crowe worked dutifully to keep me distracted, but in the quiet moments, my mind would always drift back to the way he'd looked when he brushed the flour from my cheeks. His cool metal exterior melted, revealing that beneath it all there was still the semblance of a beating heart.

"I was calling for Danny."

"I'm aware. All of Oz knows you were calling for Danny. He and Crowe are reviewing the ground plans for the bank. So, Trouble, Is there a problem?"

I gestured to the boxes. "What are these?" I opened the smallest box. Inside was an adorable set of thigh-high stockings with a seam running down the backs of each leg.

"From the designer labels, I'm going to guess it's your wardrobe for this afternoon. You can't pretend to be an heiress in OzMart chic."

Nick turned to leave. I flung the box to the ground, the matching garter belt falling free.

"Wait." I took his arm and dragged him into the room. No longer blocked by the body of a giant, the door swung closed with a soundless click. "You've been avoiding me like if we made eye contact, it might trigger the apocalypse. Did I do something?"

Raising his eyes to purposely meet mine, Nick heaved an impossible-to-decipher breath. *"Tutto, fiore mio. Hai sciolto il filo che teneva insieme tutti i miei pezzi rotti."* He stepped closer, moving into my space until it felt like I was drowning in his shadow. *"E se adesso non vado via, li vedrai cadere uno ad uno."*[1]

"Don't do that..." My thumb smoothed over the broken bone tattooed on his forearm. There was so much more to this man, so much I didn't know. I wanted to uncover each tattered piece. "Don't hide behind that gorgeous language."

Nick's eyes drifted down, staring at his arm as I stroked back and forth. Something warred in the lines of his eyes. His brows tensed together, looking like each swipe of my thumb was somehow hurting him.

"Do you need help dressing?" His voice was extra low, the gravelly accent thicker than usual and rumbling in the still room.

"That's not what you said."

---

1. Everything, my flower, You untied the thread that held all of my broken pieces together. If I don't walk away now, you'll see them falling apart, one by one.

"I know you've healed a lot in the past two weeks, but…" The sentence trailed off as his eyes drifted up to my face and then back to the hand on his arm. "I can help if you need it."

So, we weren't talking about it. Message received.

I released him and began tossing the lids off of random boxes. Fine. If he didn't want to talk about why he'd been icing me out for the past three days, then that was just fine. I didn't need him or his oddly timed moments of kindness.

I flipped open the largest box. A neatly folded brocade pencil skirt and silk blouse sat in a bed of tissue paper, each with a long zipper down the back. Fuck.

Realizing there was no way I'd be able to do this on my own, I finally answered, "I'm still having trouble reaching behind me, but I can just grit my teeth and deal with it like I always do."

"You don't heal by stressing your weak points, Thea."

"That's how I've lived my entire life, *Nick*. All Em ever did was apply pressure to my weak points." I pulled out a lace bra and dropped it on top of the pile. The delicate poppy flowers embroidered along the edges of the cups contrasted brightly against the green brocade, looking almost like tiny drops of blood. Snatching up the thong, I spun the thin garment around my finger. "At least this pair is functional, mostly."

The corner of his mouth twitched. There he was, I knew the softer side of him was hiding somewhere. Dropping the scrap of lace on the bed, I turned around and lifted the hem of my shirt. I made it half-way up before I felt the first pull and hesitated.

Without saying anything, the heat of his presence enveloped me. Even though the brush of his fingers against mine was the only part touching me, I felt him everywhere as Nick took the shirt and lifted.

The collar pulled free, causing my hair to spill down my back. The swaying strands made me acutely aware of how exposed I was. It wasn't like this was the first time he'd seen me without a shirt, but for some reason, his nearness was making my skin feel electrified. The instinct to cover myself pulled hard at my arms, but rather than give into the impulse, I tugged at the tie on my sleep shorts. The satin cord came loose, allowing them to fall to the floor at my feet.

The back of Nick's hand slid against the base of my neck, scooping the stray hair over one shoulder. I closed my eyes, imagining the inked surface of each letter, making contact with my neck and trailing down my spine. Never Again. What nightmare was he running from that he needed to be reminded every time he formed a fist? Right now, I'd give anything to keep those hands on me, trauma and all. This brief softness, in contrast with the strength I knew lay in wait, was a unique kind of torture.

When the heat of his breath drifted over my shoulder, I shuddered, waiting for the second his mouth made contact with my skin. Fuck, I wanted him to. I wanted my body to be ground zero when all that restraint finally detonated.

"Nick." It was barely more than a whisper. "I've never allowed myself to want for anything, but I want you."

He inhaled deep. His nose and cheek pressing into my hair. While his middle fingers on either side of my hips traced the elastic of my panties, pushing them slowly over my hips and down my thighs.

"*Se solo fossi un uomo migliore, saresti già mia.*"[2] The low timber of his voice vibrated against my back, causing the barest hint of a sting with each sinful syllable.

Reaching around me, he picked up the thong and dropped to one knee. The healed scars flamed as his palms skimmed the backs of my legs. When his lips brushed the sensitive crease where my ass met my thighs, the breath I was holding transformed into a silent moan.

"*Il tuo profumo mi fa impazzire. Ogni istante con te rischio di perdere il controllo.*"[3]

He tapped my inner ankle, drawing my attention away from the blood rushing in my ears to the lacy underwear held open for me in wait. When he'd

---

2. If I was a better man, you'd be mine already.

3. You smell delicious. I risk losing control every instant I am with you.

said he'd help me dress, this was not what I was expecting. After stepping into them, the expensive scrap of fabric rose slowly up my legs making my pussy throb with every ascending inch.

"*Amo il modo in cui fremi ad ogni mio tocco.*"[4]

Swallowing my racing heart, I said, "Are you going to tell me what any of this means?"

With a final snap of the elastic, he released me. "No, *fiore mio.*"[5]

Circling his body close, Nick's hands slid in tandem up my stomach before palming my breasts and rolling my nipples between his fingers. My head fell back to his shoulder, at the same time, a low groan rumbled his chest. This. Fuck, his hands on my body felt exactly how I'd imagined, better even. How was he able to walk the pleasure-pain line so precisely?

Nick trailed his nose up my neck, resting just beneath my ear. "I'm not going to tell you what they mean because if I did, there would be no coming back from them."

Having his full attention felt dangerous, like juggling with grenades. Reaching behind me, I looped my hand around his neck, intending to pull his mouth to mine.

Nick stepped back so abruptly that his hands on my shoulders were the only thing that kept me from falling. Snatching up the forgotten bra, he fitted the cups over my chest and slipped the straps over my shoulders.

Securing the elastic band, and resting his hands on my hips, he asked, "Is that too tight? Does it hurt?"

I looked over my shoulder at him, soaking in the heat of his expression as he studied my body. "Nothing I can't handle."

"If I've learned anything in this life—" This time, it was more than a twitch to the corners of his lips, but where normal smiles seemed filled with light, his

---

4. I love the way you tremble at my every touch.

5. No, my flower.

was clouded by shadows. "It's that you'll never know how much you can handle until you've ventured past your limits."

"And what are your limits, Nick?"

"*Tu sei il mio unico limite.*"[6] He circled the garter belt over my hips, then pointed to the bed with a snap. "Sit on the edge, facing me."

If it had been Danny, I would have told him to take that snapping hand and go fuck himself with it. But, with Nick, my body was obeying before I'd even processed the command. As I settled my ass at the edge of the bed, he dropped to his knees, spreading my legs to accommodate the width of his frame.

"Good girl, now lean back."

Forget the lacy underwear. These panties were about to burst into flames. His hands on my thighs were already sensory overload, but when he spoke, accent deeper and thicker than usual, goosebumps broke out over my entire body. Dutifully, I eased back onto my elbows, too aware of how the position tilted my hips up to him in offering. The longer he lingered, the faster my heart seemed to race.

He rested my foot over the center of his sternum. My heart was galloping out of control, but the steady thrum beneath my sole barely even registered as being there. Did nothing unnerve this man?

Nick gathered the stocking in his large hands and slipped it over my toes. His pinky trailed over the center of my foot, triggering my nerve endings one by one. A shiver chased the silken stocking up my legs.

"Nick," I pleaded.

His expression didn't register the way I was squirming beneath his touch or the fine tremor seizing my limbs. Methodically, he repeated the action with the other leg. He drew the satin straps through his fingers, giving the band at my hips a tug before hooking the fasteners to the tops and backs of my thigh highs.

Nick reached up, fingers digging beneath the lace of the garter belt and lifting my hips off the edge of the bed. He dragged his nose straight up the center of my

---

6. You are my only limit.

panties, applying the barest amount of pressure but enough to make me want to scream. Directly over where the lace ground against my clit, he bit down, pulling back so that it snapped on release.

My head fell back with my arching spine. This was going to end one of two ways: with me shamelessly begging to ride his face or the kind of orgasm that left you in tears.

He lifted me further, my entire body seeming to levitate before I was deposited back on my feet. I swayed, gripping his shirt and resting my head in the center of his chest. There was a half second of hesitation before his arms cradled me to him. His heartbeat still low and slow, like none of this was affecting him.

Gripping the hair at the nape of my neck, he angled my head to meet the cold heat of his gaze. The other lifted my ass, grinding my pelvis hard against him. His heart might not be affected, but the cock pressing into my upper stomach definitely was. Had he always been so tall? Fuck, I bet I could swallow this impressively hard dick whole and not even need to bend over to do it.

I raked my nails down his torso before fingering the buckle of his belt. I didn't care how or where he entered my body so long as it happened right now.

With a blur, Nick snatched my hands, spinning me in place so that my back was to his chest. I groaned in frustration, yanking my hands to try and free myself from his manacled grip. Instead of releasing me, he raised my arms high into the air.

"Keep them there."

"What?"

He stepped away, the sudden rush of cold air making my skin tingle.

My arms already felt weak, hooking my fingers over my head to ease the ache of gravity. I could hear him behind me, could feel the lingering presence of his gaze.

"Nick? What are you doing?"

"Dressing you."

The silk of my blouse slid over my arms, the cool fabric extinguishing each tiny flame of arousal as it went. Once it was secure, I stepped into the brocade pencil skirt, the rich emerald color glowing in the dim light of the room.

"Crowe is right about one thing—" Slowly, he dragged the zipper up. His lips pressed against the base of my neck, the static of his kiss making the tiny hairs stand on end. He barely touched me, and yet, I could feel his presence skating over my entire body. "You *are* absolutely gorgeous."

His unusually sweet words of affirmation pushed my heart into my throat. I spun to face him. "Nick—"

The room was empty. Like a ghost, he'd vanished, leaving no trace of having been here other than the butterflies tumbling in my stomach.

The door pushed open. Like flipping a switch, my entire body lit up. I have no idea how to describe what just happened, but I knew there was no way Nick could've walked away from the electricity in this room.

"Good, you're dressed." Danny let the door swing closed behind him. One knuckle ran slowly over his lower lip. "Oz damn, I knew you'd look good in emerald."

I tried not to let the disappointment read too clearly. It was like I'd just dreamed Nick up. If it wasn't for the way my body was still humming, then I'd have started questioning if I really had.

"You shaved." I meant it as a statement, but it came out more like a question. Danny hadn't shaved at all in the weeks we'd been together. "I was just getting used to your mane."

Danny scowled. "It was a completely normal beard."

I stroked his jaw—his perfectly defined jaw. I didn't think it was possible for him to look more stern, but abrasively handsome worked for him. It was probably the endorphin rush Nick had given me because Danny's gangster chic, with a side of fuck you, was doing all kinds of things to me.

The hardened edge of his expression softened, and he tilted into my hand, placing a kiss to my palm. "I have a gift for you, Firecracker."

"A gift?" I looked down at my designer clothing, at the expensive shoes sitting beside the bed. I understood what Nick said that this costume was necessary for what we had to do today, but I don't know that I'll ever be able to accept something without also wondering when the guillotine was going to drop.

Danny pulled a red velvet box from his jacket pocket. He opened it slowly for me, allowing me to peer into the box at the silver chain connected on either end to a curved, slender silver tube. It was a sophisticated-looking necklace and nothing like the glamorous thing I would have expected him to pick. Even the skirt I was wearing was ostentatious in its own way.

This was much more like something I'd have chosen. It didn't stand out, but was still a solid statement.

"May I?" Danny lifted the necklace from the box, gesturing for me to lift my hair. "You said you've never been given a present. I thought it was time we changed that." Gently, he looped the chain around my neck. The metal instantly warmed, resting comfortably beneath my neckline. His fingers lingered around my collar, caressing more than was necessary.

I couldn't help but smile at the small affection. "This really wasn't—"

"I had this made especially for you by a jeweler here in the E.C."

I wanted to say something, but I couldn't find the words. My mouth opened and closed silently.

A gift. A real, no ulterior motive gift. For me.

"It does something special." With a quick yank, he pulled on the ends of the tube. From one end he pulled a thin ruby-colored stiletto knife. The blade was roughly the length of my middle finger, with the chain dangling harmlessly from the end. The highly polished surface glittered in the light.

"This is so you'll never be defenseless again. Do you like it?"

I blinked back the tears welling in my eyes. "It's beautiful."

"The blade's made of titanium. It won't tarnish, and it's quite sharp. So only pull it out if you plan on cutting something."

Danny easily looped the necklace and sheathed the lethal pendant.

"What if I decide it's you that I want to cut?" I leaned up on my tiptoes and kissed him hard enough that he could feel my gratitude, even if I didn't know how to express it.

"Then, make sure you cut deep, Princess, because I don't give second chances."

-37-
THEA

I looked down at my nails and studied the way the jagged edges had grown out in the past couple of weeks. They almost looked feminine again.

"Not long now," Nick said for the third time.

The deep rumble of his voice echoed off of the marble flooring and pillars. From behind leather-covered tables, people spoke in hushed tones that perfectly matched the austere surroundings.

We'd been sitting on a bench in the lobby for what felt like hours. Long enough that I'd studied every small architectural detail multiple times. My favorite part of the lobby was the massive dome we were sitting beneath. The copper was patinated, and light filtered in streams through small panes of glass at the base.

Thin panes of emerald mica enclosed large hanging lights, giving the entire building a cool glow. Heavy vault doors hung open, their giant locking wheels and bolts reminding all who passed of the impenetrability that lay beneath the glitz.

Crowe spent the entire ride spouting facts about the old bank. It was kind of adorable watching him fanboy out over a building. This was the most secure location in all of Ozmandria. Accounts were determined through legacies handed down from generation to generation. Danny grumbled with each new fact. According to Nick, Danny tried and was denied three times to open an account with them.

The Wizard's only instructions for today were given in an envelope. Inside were three things: a time, a random string of numbers, and an old bronze key with a giant emerald in the head.

Currently, said key was sitting in Danny's breast pocket.

Both he and Nick were wearing custom-tailored black suits, looking the part of old money. I was trying very hard not to focus on how good they both looked. Danny's three-piece ensemble highlighted his defined chest, and Nick had the top two buttons of his shirt undone, exposing the upper tattoos that were in direct opposition to the clean lines of his suit. It was enough to make a girl weak.

Not that I hadn't come dressed to kill and accessorized with my own heart-stopping arsenal. I'd chosen to pin my hair up in curls and left my makeup simple, except for a bright red lip, which I'd had to reapply three times already.

I crossed my ankles, the tall stiletto heels clicking against the marble. After waiting for so long in the lobby, I was grateful for the high-cut slit in the back of my pencil skirt. Without it, even that simple motion would have been impossible. Dressed in this costume, I felt nothing like myself but had to admit that I looked like I belonged among the elite snobs strutting in and out of the bank. For all his faults, Danny certainly had an eye for detail.

I fiddled with the necklace he'd given me, twisting the tube idly between my fingers. Knowing its ruby blade was close kept my anxiety at bay, but only barely. For the past ten minutes, I'd been bouncing my knee, nervously scrutinizing every person who walked by. Was The Wizard already here? Why hadn't he shown yet? Was it because this was actually an elaborate set-up?

Danny rested his heavy hand on my thigh, stilling my shaking. I'd thought through my request for the Wizard a dozen times. While things between Danny and I had softened, I still wasn't sure if he'd make a play for The Farm or not. Regardless of anything that had transpired between us or truths we'd bared, I needed the Wizard to make Dorothea Rosen disappear. He was the only person who could do that and it was the only way I would survive Oz's anarchy. Stealing the money out from under Em would be the sugar coating on top.

"*Movement, 3 o'clock.*" The thick walls and iron doors were interfering with the signal, making Crowe's voice crackle over the comms device. He was surveilling from the cab, hardlinked into the security feed, and watching for any signs of a double cross. We could hear each other now, but when we descended into the bowels of the building, where even the granite walls were reinforced with steel, it was unlikely that we'd be able to communicate.

None of them were comfortable with sending me to the basement vault alone. My insistence that I didn't need a chaperone fell on deaf ears, and they wouldn't entertain a single one of the completely logical arguments I'd made.

I still didn't understand why the Wizard was picking a bank to meet in. It added all kinds of complications to the exchange. Only spouses and children were allowed to accompany patrons into the vault. So, Danny was posing as my husband, complete with a matching wedding band that I couldn't stop spinning around my finger. Nobody would ever buy that Nick was our son, so he was standing in as personal security. Bank policy would allow him to come as far as the vault door but not inside. Which was fine by us, since, then he'd be able to stand watch for any unexpected deception.

An elegant woman with silver hair tied in a neat bun greeted us. In the high fashion of Emerald City, the gold-rimmed glasses perched on her nose had a slightly green tint to the lenses. Her expression was tight yet cordial. The designer heels and pantsuit she wore spoke volumes about her position in the bank. This woman wasn't merely a handler. She'd come down from her emerald tower to greet us directly.

"Good afternoon, Mr. and Mrs. Kalidah."

Danny stepped forward to shake her hand. "Please, call me Daniel."

"Of course."

I tried not to stumble over his introduction. The name Daniel Kalidah tugged at the back of my memory, but I wasn't sure where I'd heard it. The woman looked expectantly at me, and I shook her hand in turn.

"My name is Melinda. I'm the manager of the bank and will be your liaison today."

"Is it customary for the manager to meet with clientele?" Danny flashed a glance at the security camera in the corner, where Crowe was undoubtedly watching the exchange.

"*On it.*" There was the quiet clicking of his keyboard.

Melinda shifted the portfolio in her hands. "No, but I wanted to welcome you personally. I understand this is your first visit with us."

I opened my mouth to answer her but was cut off by Danny. "I've had dealings with several other branches, but this is our first occasion here." He brushed a lock of my hair behind my ear tenderly. "My beautiful wife was recently bequeathed a vault key."

I narrowed my eyes at him. *Beautiful wife.* I shouldn't have liked the way he said that so much. Especially since he was using the flattery to steamroll over me. I'd have to remind him of that when we didn't have an audience.

"Focus, Thea. Danny's a professional. Let him do his job," Crowe said in my ear, pulling my thoughts back on point. How did that man always know what I was thinking? *"Melinda checks out. She's been bank manager for the past five years."*

"That happens all the time. Keys are often left in wills." Melinda held out her hand. "I will need to do a quick inspection for authenticity. It's a formality, nothing to worry about."

I swallowed, realizing that if the Wizard wanted to set us up, then this would be the perfect way to do it. If we were found with a fraudulent key, then the only way we'd be leaving this bank was in handcuffs or a body bag. Crowe had been clear that the bank had its own corrupt way of handling business, fraud being at the tippy top of their no-no list.

"Of course," Danny said, pulling the key from his pocket and placing it in her manicured hand.

"Lovely, if you'll follow me, please." Melinda sat the key into a kiosk installed in the wall. "This will only take a moment." The screen flared to life, and a purple light traveled over the surface of the key, reading the key's coding. In my mind, all I could hear was Crowe's stories about what they'd done with past people who'd tried to break into the vault with false keys. A thin beam centered on the stone embedded in the head, glittering beams filled the chamber. It was beautiful.

A number appeared on the screen, which Melinda quickly typed into the tablet in her hands. She hesitated for a second and then looked up at me in surprise. My heart skipped, thinking that it was all over before we'd even left the lobby. Nick moved into position behind me, ready to shield or act as prompted.

"I'm sorry, Ms. Gallant. I didn't realize it was you joining us today. Premier Gallant was a great man. His death was a tragedy."

"Thank you." I flicked hesitant eyes up at Danny, and his jaw tightened. Had the key belonged to my father? How did The Wizard get *my* family key?

"It makes sense that the Gallants would be a legacy family."

The emerald in the key glittered, seeming to give off its own light. It might be the only thing of theirs that I owned. I had nothing from them but broken, sketchy memories—and this mystery key.

"The information I was given wasn't complete. I was only given your married name. If I had known that Dorothea Gallant would be joining us today, then we would have prepared one of the larger rooms. This is unacceptable. I will see to it personally that this never happens again." Melinda's big brown eyes were fixed on me, waiting expectantly for a response.

"That's quite alright." I slipped my arm into Danny's. "We choose to do most business under my husband's name. It helps me avoid the attention of the press. You know how it is." Danny's hand closed over mine, squeezing in approval.

She handed me back the key. "Well, it's working. I don't think I've read anything about the Gallants in years."

"Melinda, we have quite a bit of pressing business for the day. So if you don't mind..." Danny gestured towards my key.

"Of course. I'm sorry." Melinda waved a badge over a panel set into the wall, then placed her hand on the surface. Following the scan, large bronze doors slid silently open to reveal an ornate elevator. "This way, please."

There was only one button on the elevator and a small call box. I hesitated for a second. Danny's hand on my lower back increased in pressure, urging me forward. We'd already discussed this. The safety deposit boxes and vaults were all on the basement level, which would mean getting in an elevator. This wasn't a surprise, but that didn't make the space seem any bigger.

"It's only for a couple of minutes. You've got this, Darling. I'll be right here in your ear the entire time." Except we both knew that was a lie.

"I'm sorry, Ma'am. Is there a problem?" Melinda looked between me and Danny.

I swallowed my fear, and stepped into the room. Beside me Danny, exhaled a slow breath. Part of me wondered if he had expected me to bolt. Scared Dorothy was not allowed to make an appearance, not today. Not ever again.

"Not at all."

The doors slid closed. They were silent, but the thumping of my heart in my ears sounded like a roar. I focused my eyes on the moving arrow that indicated the levels as we passed them. Danny's hand remained on my lower back, his thumb slowly smoothing along my spine. Even Nick pressed closer to me until I could feel his arm brushing mine.

"Breathe, Thea. Another thirty seconds, and you'll be on the gr—," Crowe said, his voice crackling before cutting out completely. I swallowed another wave of fear and fingered the necklace hanging from my neck.

The arrow reached the far left side of the dial, and the doors slid open. I quickly stepped from the metal box of choking death and into the granite hallway. It wasn't until I'd sucked down several large gulps of air that I realized I'd held my breath the entire ride.

Danny wrapped a large arm around me, kissing the side of my neck tenderly. "You okay?"

I blinked up at him in surprise. Crowe was the only one I'd discussed my claustrophobia with, but it wouldn't have surprised me if he'd prepped the other two for what had turned out to be an inevitable freak-out.

I nodded and pushed away from him, reclaiming my independence. We were about to meet the Wizard, the last thing I needed was to appear weak. We followed Melinda past several rooms, each featuring a complicated-looking vault door. I eyed down the half dozen security guards stationed throughout the hallway. My imagination ran wild, thinking of what was held behind the doors to warrant such security precautions. If what Crowe had told me about this bank was true, then every major player in all of Oz used it to hide their secrets.

Halfway down the corridor, Melinda placed her hand to another door. There was a hydraulic hiss and a cranking sound as the barrels and pins spun. With a loud clunk, the locking mechanism unlatched, allowing Melinda to pull the door open.

"Your security detail will have to remain in the hallway," she said, not bothering to acknowledge Nick directly and walking into the waiting room.

Nick nodded at Danny and moved into position beside the door. As I walked by him, he snagged my arm, and drew me close. For a flash, his entire tough facade evaporated, and stark concern shook his features. "Thea, before you go in, I—"

"Sweetheart, you coming?" Danny called from in the room. Behind him, Melinda was watching our every interaction with eagle eyes. Nick released his grip on my arm, smoothing out the fabric of my sleeve.

"Sweetheart?" I mouthed with a silent laugh. Nick's expression morphed back into his usual indifferent self. Whatever it was that had him shook, seemed to have vanished.

"He can wait. What is it?"

"It's nothing." Nick looked over my shoulder at the two people waiting on us. "Good luck, *fiore mio*." He gave me a small push into the room, leaving me more confused than ever.

The interior was spacious, featuring two black velvet couches surrounding a long table. The granite walls were void of decoration, instead, they shone with streaks of green from the overhead crystal lamp. On the far wall, there was another panel like the one we'd seen in the lobby.

Melinda sat the key on the holder. With a flourish, she gestured to the display. "The key should have come with an access code. You'll need to enter it on the display."

Danny handed me the paper with the code. His eyes held mine for a long second, brushing his thumb against the top of my hand in encouragement.

Without taking the time to dwell on the what-ifs, I typed the long set of numbers into the display. The screen flashed green.

Melinda smiled pleasantly. "Your box will arrive shortly. There are no cameras in the viewing rooms to protect client privilege. When you are finished, hit the button beside the door, and I will come to retrieve you." She didn't wait for an answer and disappeared from the room with tight, clipped steps. The vault door closed behind her with a heavy, metal thud.

"So now we wait," I said, circling the room.

Danny's gaze raked over me. He lifted his chin. "Come here."

I stopped. "You can't just command me."

"Fine, then I'm coming to you." It only took three long steps before he dominated the space around me. With one long finger, he traced the collar of my blouse. "I love this look on you."

"You should." I ran my hands over the shimmery emerald skirt. "You spent a small fortune on it."

He grabbed my hips and pushed me backwards, until I was pressed against the cool metal wall.

"Danny, this isn't-" He cut me off with a bruising kiss, one that sucked me down and demanded I submit to it.

"We're alone. Sealed in this room. There are no cameras. No-one's listening in. And you're dressed like that." He slowly began pulling the hem of my skirt upward.

"Danny!" I said more firmly, pushing against his chest. He didn't budge. Instead, he pressed closer and began slowly devouring the skin beneath the exposed neckline. "We probably only have minutes before the box arrives."

"You'd be surprised what I can accomplish in only a couple of minutes. I do my best work under pressure." With my skirt bunched around my hips, his rough palms slid up my thighs and hoisted me into the air. "I'm going to make you come, Firecracker. Stop questioning it. I'll even let you pick. I can fuck you right here, against this wall, and you'll be screaming on my cock within a minute. Or I can lay you out on that table and lick you until your vision turns white."

His hand found my center and rubbed hard against the lacy fabric. I had to bite my lip to stop the whimper that wanted to slip free.

"Tick-tock, Thea."

My heart skipped, hearing him say my name. He hadn't called me Dorothy since my confession, but this was the first time he'd ever used Thea. The easy way he dropped it was like loosing catnip into the air. I grabbed the back of his head and began kissing him savagely.

Danny pulled my underwear to the side and pushed two fingers directly into me. The cry I'd bit back sprang loose. Suddenly, I wasn't caring about any of it. The Wizard, the key, the security team waiting to take us down, none of it. The building could be collapsing around us, and I'd still be thinking of only one thing.

"Your cock, I choose your cock."

Danny laughed. The sound was dark and delicious. "Maybe I shouldn't, we—"

"Shut up and fuck me. Hard. Right now." I tightened my legs around his waist, eager to feel him stretching me wide.

He smiled against my lips and pulled his dick free from the waist of his pants. I felt that first brush of his head press against me, and I couldn't wait any longer. I leveraged my body as much as I could to rock my hips down but barely forced more than an inch forward.

"Tell me something, Princess." He rocked more, sinking another inch before pulling back out.

I whimpered his name in warning, as much as anyone could make any demands while their voice shook.

"Who's larger, me or Crowe?" Danny pushed further, rotating his hips to drag the head of his dick against that one magical point that always drove me wild. Then infuriatingly, he withdrew, rubbing against my clit. The arrogant prick.

"Seriously?" I grabbed his hair and pulled his face away from my neck. "You're looking for an ego boost while half sunk inside me. Like you don't know."

The grin he flashed me was all wicked, power-hungry glee. He already knew the answer. Both boys were gifted in the dick department, but Danny had a solid half-inch on Crowe. He just wanted to torture me into telling him.

"You, Danny, you're larger. Thicker, longer, you've got an all-around beautiful cock. Now, will you please fuck me with it and stop being a clit tease."

"I fucking love when you get demanding."

I lashed out, smacking his chest, but Danny was already thrusting up with unyielding force and claiming my mouth in a bruising kiss. Despite what I'd said, he felt fuller and deeper than I remembered. Our kiss parted on a combined moan of pleasure.

His head dropped to my neck. "You feel— Fuck, the things I would do to you if we had more time."

Like those words had jinxed the entire debauched moment of passion, a buzzer beeped on the far wall. A panel slid aside, revealing a metal-hinged door several feet wide.

"Hold on to me." Before I could protest, an unhinged version of Danny let loose. My entire body slammed into the unyielding stone wall. The impact ripped a scream from my throat, and my vision flared with streaks of white. The pain and pleasure spun together, leaving me senseless. It took an embarrassingly short amount of time before lightning was rocketing up my spine and burning low in my belly.

Before I could come against the wall as he promised, Danny dropped me to the ground and flipped me around. With a hard hand at the back of my neck, he shoved me over the table and thrust back inside. Using the grip on my neck to keep me pinned flat, the cold of the metal table bled through my thin blouse and lace bra, making the ache in my breasts more pronounced.

Each thrust grew longer and harder. His cock strained against my inner walls, our high angle making me take him deeper than when I'd been straddling him. My climax mounted just as I felt it unfurling and making my skin hum with heat, Danny's hand cracked down hard on my ass.

"Fuck." I screamed at the unexpected pain. Danny's hand clamped over my mouth just as I tumbled head-first into my orgasm. I pushed back so that his last few intense pumps hit harder than any other, and I loved it. It was good enough to spiral my first orgasm directly into a second, right along with Danny.

Slowly, he lifted me from the table. Waves of endorphins flooded my system, making my body quiver. A dizzy kind of euphoria swept through me. For a second, I debated throwing him onto one of the couches and riding his cock until he was hard again. The box on the wall beeped in reminder of its arrival. Maybe next time.

Danny's green eyes were bright. "Was I too rough on your back?"

I tucked the hem of my blouse back into the skirt. There were wrinkles pressed into my clothing that I was going to have a very hard time explaining away. Danny ran a hand through his hair, but he was just as rumpled as I was. Nick would take one look at us and know exactly what we'd been doing in here.

I swiped away the smudge of lipstick from around his lips and jaw... and neck. I smirked at him. What could I say, the man was edible. I was going to need to reapply—again.

"Nothing I can't handle. Let's go open this box."

-38-
THEA

I snatched the key from the holder and slipped it into the lock. It turned easily. The door popped open, and I pulled out a long drawer. The only thing inside the box was a laptop.

Grabbing the computer, I sat it on the table between us. The screen turned on. There was no prompt for login information or a home screen with apps to choose from. There was only a floating head. The features of the head shifted, using some kind of a filter that made it impossible to fully identify the person staring back at us.

"Hello, Dorothea," they said with a heavily modulated voice that was neither male nor female.

"Wizard," I replied curtly.

"Show me the emerald." Well, at least he gets right to the point. No small talk for this guy.

Danny pulled a black metal box from his breast pocket. It looked like the kind you would get from a jeweler, except this one was made of a coated heavy metal.

"What about the tracker?" I asked, worried that removing the emerald would alert Westin to our location. The last thing I wanted was to bring more of the Winged Monkeys down on us.

"The walls of these vaults block all outside transmissions. It's why I chose this as our meeting location," the Wizard answered for him.

"Obviously, not all transmission."

"Naturally, I'm the Wizard." Like that somehow explained everything. A small drive popped open from the side of the laptop. "Place the emerald on the panel."

I moved to open the necklace box. Danny snatched my hand away.

"First, I want to discuss payment. There are things we want in exchange for this emerald."

"Once I have verified that the emerald is genuine, then we can discuss what comes next."

I looked up to Danny with a death glare. If he fucked this up for me with his unnecessary displays of machismo, then he would have to deal with much more than my wrath, starting with my fist in his mouth.

"Fine," he said reluctantly and opened the case.

I tried not to grin in victory, but Danny backing down to me was just too sweet not to.

The emerald glittered in its silver setting. Danny lifted it into the air, pausing to admire its glow before sitting the stone in the center of the drive. Something in the computer whirred.

There were several long minutes where the floating head was silent. I shook my foot against my ankle nervously. Danny's hand dropped to my thigh, its heavy-weight doing its best to ground my nerves.

When the Wizard finally spoke again, he said. "What are your demands?"

I looked at Danny. He closed his eyes. A muscle ticked along his jaw. He wasn't going to do it. He was going to let me ask for my freedom and sacrifice his chance for answers. It was taking all of his control to hold back, but he was giving this to me. The realization made my heart begin to race, and warmth bled from the center of my chest down to the tips of my fingers.

Before I could consider what I was doing, I said, "The Farm raided a commune outside of Oz, and they took three girls. I need full details about where they were sold and what has happened to them since, including where to find them now."

Danny's hand slammed on the table. "No. Thea needs to be set up with a new identity, strip The Farm of its assets, and set her up with a comfortable life outside the borders. Somewhere she can be safe and happy."

I kicked Danny beneath the table. He needed closure and answers about his sisters if he was ever going to push past his guilt. Maybe we could even rescue them. There was a chance to save them. I couldn't allow Danny to lose this opportunity, even if he was going to pass it up to give me mine.

"Why exactly do you think that I should do any of this?"

"Because we have Eastin's emerald. It will grant you access to her entire kingdom of sin," Danny answered smoothly.

The modulated voice of the Wizard spoke over the end of Danny's counter. "This emerald is one of a pair. Without its twin, it is useless."

My heart cracked. Useless hope, leaking out of it.

"Yes, this emerald would gain me access to her buildings, but the network is dual encoded. You should have learned by now that the cost of happiness will always be more than the price of suffering."

"How much more?" I asked wearily. Danny's hand on my thigh tightened in warning.

"I called you here to claim the emerald. I had planned to simply take it from you in exchange for the key. I'm sure Vincent can fill you in on its true value. But..." Panic started a slow circle in my gut. I wasn't sure if what followed The Wizard's dramatic pause was going to save or damn me. "Now that I know you plan to dismantle The Farm, I'm intrigued and find myself inclined to help you—"

The breath I was holding wooshed out of me.

"—in exchange for killing Westin Witcher."

"What?" The full gravity of what he was saying settled on me like a blanket of doom. "I can't do that." I wasn't an assassin. I'd killed once to save my own life, but that didn't mean I had the capacity to do it again.

"Absolutely not. That's suicide," Danny snapped. "Westin will have her executed the second she steps foot in the Western Quadrant."

"You had no problem killing Eastin Witcher," The Wizard intoned.

"It's not like I *planned* on killing her!"

"But you killed her all the same." The floating head tilted with impatience.

I shook my head in angry disbelief. "Yeah, I only had to be sold and abused before I was given an opportunity to bash her face in." The lacerations along my back flamed with awareness.

"There were two Witchers ruling half of Oz. With Eastin gone, there is a vacuum forming in the political system. Pieces are already in motion to set up a new chain of command. I don't intend to allow another tyrant to take her place. I intend to turn over the entire house of cards, and to do that, I need Westin gone, and I need the complete keys to their empire."

"But.." I grasped at straws, trying to figure out a way around this. "She'll see us coming."

"Probably."

"We'll never—"

"Bring me the emerald, Dorothea. I'll give you everything you need to dismantle The Farm. You'll be given full access to their files, including those concerning Dandelion's sisters. All of Emily Rosen's assets will be transferred to you, and damning evidence for her trafficking crimes will be provided to every media outlet in and outside of Ozmandria, ensuring Ms. Rosen's incarceration. With both Emily Rosen and Westin Witcher gone from the playing board, there should be no reason for you to assume a new identity."

"How many people have tried to take out Westin Witcher?" I said in a hush to Danny.

"Fucking, hundreds." Danny tapped his finger against the table. "Pretty much everyone in Oz has wanted her dead at one point, present company included."

Everything I've ever wanted *and* Danny's sisters. All it required was killing one, impossible to get to woman. "If by some miracle we manage to kill her, why should I believe that you'll hold up your end of the bargain. You're a head on a screen. How do I even know that you're actually The Wizard and this isn't some elaborate scheme?"

"She has a point," Danny agreed. I made a mental note that at least once, this infuriating man said I was right. "If we're going to do this for you, then the final exchange needs to be in person. I want to watch you transfer those files, and funds."

The head froze. For a second, I thought that maybe we'd pushed him too far and this was the end of everything. Nobody sees the Wizard. We'd leave this bank and spend the rest of our days looking over our shoulders for a bullet that would eventually find its mark.

"That can be arranged. In a show of good faith, I will leave you with this information." There was a ding announcing the arrival of a file. "The moment Westin's head rolls, you'll have your meeting."

The screen went dark, flashing to life once more on a standard desktop wallpaper of the bank's logo and a single folder. I stared down at the emerald still sitting on the drive. It glimmered back at me, powered by its own brilliant light.

"How'd he get this box and my family's key?"

"The Wizard can get anything."

"Except the death of a couple of Witchers, apparently. That he needs a meek little girl to do it for him."

Danny barked a laugh. "There is absolutely nothing meek about you, and it's not just you. You're not alone in any of this. Not anymore."

"You'll put a target on your back if you head West with me."

"Princess, there's been a target on my back since the day I arrived in Oz."

I clicked on the only file in the folder. "What do you think this is?"

A document opened. It looked like a sale file from The Farm. In my investigations, I'd seen several of these before. They held a full detail on the subject. The name was omitted in favor of a number. I suppose the people buying these women had little use for names.

On the top corner was a familiar-looking green-eyed girl with curling brown hair and heavy freckles. My mouth hung open with realization. This was Danny's sister, one of them. She had the same sharp nose, same hard jaw as she stared down the camera with loathing. The girl looked to be in her early teens. The date on the top of the file was from eleven years ago.

Danny grabbed the screen with both hands, gripping the edges like if he shook it hard enough, she might leap from the page. "Didi."

"Didi?"

"Dahlia. We always called her Didi."

Beneath the photo, it listed characteristics: height, weight, ethnicity, and a general description of temperament. It was no surprise that she was labeled as "willful" and "aggressive." There was a caution line saying, "Will bite, runs fast." The final part of the dossier was a lengthy checklist of sexual experience. For Didi, it was blank, labeling her as "virgin."

"What do they put if the girl isn't a virgin?"

I swallowed. "You don't really want to know the answer to that."

Danny leveled a hard glare on me.

"Fine. Older girls and women are given a purity examination. If they're shown not to be a virgin, then one of the evaluators determines skill level and experience."

His face turned green as his eyes scanned the long list of sexual acts.

"It will say the buyer at the bottom," I said, already scrolling down the screen. It was best if he didn't linger on that road for too long.

The bottom line had the sale price listed. My stomach turned. It was abysmally small.

"So that's it. That's what my sister was worth. Fucking hell. I make more than that on a single delivery."

My attention flashed to the right, where a name was listed next to the sale price. I instantly recognized it. Sylvan Deveaux. He was a Farm regular. Sometimes, he bought entire truckloads of people. He returned far too frequently for anything good to ever happen to the ones he purchased.

"So that's the name of the man I'm about to murder, right after I free my sister."

"Danny." I hesitantly put my hand on his shoulder, not entirely certain that he wouldn't snap my wrist on instinct. "Deveaux is a hunter. Certain temperaments attract certain types of buyers. Deveaux always took the fighters. He's a predator. If he had Didi, then..." I couldn't finish the sentence. But, it was unlikely his sister was still alive.

Danny slapped my hand away. "No. Until I see proof, I refuse to believe she's dead. Where do we find this Deveaux?"

"Up North. But Danny—"

"No, Dorothy! She's not dead."

I flinched.

There was another ping from the computer like it was listening to our conversation. A new file opened on the screen. It was a death certificate for a Jane Doe, dated for two years after Didi's sale date. The picture with the certificate was unmistakably Danny's sister, only in this picture, she had several scars scoring her face. In the top corner, it read, "Cause of death: blunt force trauma to the cranium."

I had to physically fight down the bile rising in my throat.

"Fuck you, Wizard," Danny said to the screen, then threw the computer at the wall. It clattered to the floor in a shower of electronic chips, the screen flickering the image of Didi's mutilated face.

"Danny,"

"Fuck you, too." Danny buckled over the table, gripping his hair tight enough small hairs fell to the surface. "Fuck this whole Ozdamn world."

"*Danny,*" I said more firmly when he refused to look at me.

"No, Dorothy. We're not doing this." Still not looking at me, he stalked over to the door.

I knew he was hurting, but hearing that name sliced so much harder than it should have.

"Let's grab the others and leave. I'm done here. I'm done with this." Danny pounded on the button beside the door.

I picked up the emerald and tucked it back into its box. The case, for being so tiny, was surprisingly heavy. Before I could debate my actions, I sat the emerald in the drawer, then sent the box back to wherever it was stored and slipped the key into my clutch.

Danny, finally remembering why we were here in the first place, turned back to me. "Give me the emerald."

"I can't."

"I'm not playing around, Thea. Stop being a brat and give me the emerald."

"Oh, it's Thea again, is it? I put it back in the safe. It's already gone, you great dick waffle."

Danny growled and slammed his hand into the wall beside my head. "The Wizard can access that at any point. He proved that much already."

I stepped close enough that our shoes touched, lengthening my spine to give me as much height as I could. My high heels were finally doing me some good. "It wasn't your decision to make. *I* chose what to do with *my* emerald."

"Don't fucking push me." Any minute flames were going to start shooting from his nostrils like some kind of mythical dragon or raging bull. Either that or tiny bits of brain matter would fly when his rising blood pressure finally made his head explode.

"He already was more than clear that the emerald is useless without the matching necklace. It's safer here than on the road with us."

"Spoiled brat, doing whatever she wants and not bothering to consider the rest of us." Danny reached out, grabbing my throat, and pulling me to him like he was going to try and kiss me. Fucking, typical.

I slapped him in the face. Danny blinked in surprise, a perfect red glow already appearing on his freshly shaved cheek. He didn't release me, only reeled me in further.

"Don't," I snapped through gritted teeth, his lips only a fraction of a space from mine. "Or I won't ever let you touch me again."

"That's fine. Been there, done that. We both know you'll just open your legs for the next man who walks by."

"I know one man they won't be opening for."

The door opened. Danny abruptly cut off any retort he might have made and pushed me away.

Melinda walked into the room, with Nick following closely behind her. One look at Danny's barely leashed fury had her silencing whatever polite greeting she might have said.

As soon as we ascended above ground, Crowe's voice returned. *"From the look on Danny's face, I'm guessing he didn't like the answers he got."*

I shook my head, too busy seething over Danny's callousness to do anything else. I knew he didn't mean it and that his heart was shattering inside. Those harsh words were just the splinters making themselves known, and I was the unlucky one standing in their path when they went flying. It didn't make it hurt less.

"Danny, we'll get them, brother. Every last one. They'll pa—"

The entire elevator shook. The metal cables smacked into the side of the car, ringing the cabin like a bell and making my heart instantly leap into my throat. Panic and true terror for the possibility of being stuck in an elevator flooded me. The lights flickered, switching over to a red emergency light. By the grace of Ozma, the elevator resumed its ascent.

Nick's eyes met mine in the reflection of the elevator door. For a second, I saw what looked like regret. It was a baleful, almost heartbreaking expression. Nick dropped his hand, his fingers brushing mine.

I tilted my head in question to him. The look in his eyes, as his pinky wound around mine, was beginning to scare me. He looked like he'd just murdered someone's granny.

The elevator dinged, the arrow indicating that we were back on the lobby level. I let out a sigh of relief, knowing that we'd soon be free of the confines of the elevator. No falling to our doom, no being trapped in the tiny box of death.

The comms in my ear crackled loudly, before Crowe's broken voice returned. *"Heads up fol—There's maj— heat in the lob--I'm going to try and—"*

Nick mouthed, "I'm sorry."

"Wh—" My question was cut off the same time our reflection in the opening door disappeared—replaced by a waiting pistol.

I felt the hot blood coat my face before I could fully process what had happened. A bullet from the gun tore through Melinda's brow. The green glass at the back of the compartment exploded directly in the center between where Danny and I were standing. I raised my hands in shock, wiping the blood splatter from my cheek.

Nick grabbed Melinda's now very dead body. Shoving me behind him, he used her corpse to shield us as we exited into the lobby.

-39-
THEA

I coughed heavily against the smoke and floating debris in the air. The scene was absolute chaos, like stepping out of a luxury elevator into a war zone. Where there once had been a beautiful dome, now stretches of the sky were visible. Half of the ceiling was blown apart, and a corner of the building was nothing more than rubble. Security guards were slain on the ground, laying awkwardly over patrons and tellers alike.

"Stay close." Danny and Nick took up positions protectively on either side of me, popping off round after round. Gunmen were stationed everywhere, crawling over the wreckage like ants on a garbage pile. Whoever this was wasn't taking any chances.

Crowe's voice had gone eerily quiet, and I tried not to let that one unsettling fact distract me. A masked man in tactical gear lunged at us. Danny pulled a slender knife from his pocket. With a smooth motion, it flicked open. I drove my elbow into the man's throat. Even Kevlar couldn't protect you from a hard hit to the jugular. He stumbled back, and Danny sank the blade between the armored slats of the man's vest.

The attacker fell to the ground, but like a hydra, two more leapt over him. The closest one sank his fingers into my tightly coiled hair, dragging me against his body. I screamed from the sharp pain, cursing myself for having pinned my hair so extensively. Twisting against his grip, I swung my elbows back. The plating in his vest was hard and rigid against my back, probably causing me more harm than him.

Danny lunged at the man. The knife sank into his neck, dousing my beautiful white blouse with crimson blood. The man behind me fell, the hand in my hair pulling the curls free of their pins.

Danny's hand gripped mine. "This way, Firecracker. We're fish in a barrel here. We need to get outside."

As if in answer to his comment, a man on an upper balcony fired down several bullets. They peppered the pillar behind me, sending granite pebbles dusting across my cheeks.

Nick pushed forward, firing with quick, efficient motions and clearing a path. Then I noticed something else—they weren't firing back, not a single gunman was shooting at Nick. I stopped, completely stunned. Nick's mouthed apology from the elevator slapped me in the face.

Danny threw his body into mine just as the wall beside my head blew apart. They weren't firing at the boys, there was only one target. Me.

This was a set-up.

Blood pumped in my ears, drowning out everything but the thump of my heart. I surveyed the carnage like time had slowed. A canister fell at our feet. Nick bent down and tossed it back where it came from, only seconds before light flashed and debris flew in the air. He looked back at me with so much concern, waving us on like he was an avenging angel and he wasn't handing me over to the devil.

Pain sliced through my chest. I looked down expecting to see the blossoming flower of a gunshot wound and rubbed my hand against the burn, but it came away clean. No, this was so much worse than being shot. I was betrayed by the few people I'd ever allowed myself to trust. I'd almost prefer it had been a bullet.

Stupid, dumb, naive Thea. The only people who knew we were meeting here today were The Wizard and us. Which meant one of them must have tipped off whichever hit team had come to claim me.

Well, fuck that. I wasn't going to wait for them to funnel me outside and into the hands of whoever was waiting for us. I pushed myself out of Danny's grip.

He spun, reaching back to renew his hold, but I dodged him. "What are you doing?"

"I always knew you'd sell me out," I kicked him in the groin with every ounce of force I could muster. Hurt, and possibly confusion, flared across his face.

"What the actual fuck, Thea." Danny wheezed, buckling in half and pausing his agony long enough to fire his gun over my shoulder.

I didn't stick around to explain myself, and I sure as shit wasn't going to stay here and let him spin some more lies. Instead, I took off running at a full sprint for the back of the bank. Stray bullets pelted the ground around me, but I didn't slow. There had to be an alley entrance, one they used to load and unload. Or perhaps where the employees entered from. Surely, everyone didn't arrive by trekking up the grand staircase.

Crowe's voice rattled back in my head. I tried not to let relief take root. *"Sorry. I had to deal with some unwanted company. Thea, what in the name of Ozma are you doing?"*

I ripped the comms device from my ear, throwing it to the ground. I didn't need them. My entire life, it had been just me. I ignored the tiny voice that told me I hadn't survived it entirely on my own and pushed through a door in the back wall.

Slamming it shut behind me, I twisted the deadbolt and threw a chair in front of it for good measure. A second later, a body slammed against the wood, rattling it in its frame.

"Thea, don't do this!" Danny said with a muffled yell. "Ozdamn it, woman! Open the fucking door." There was a resounding crack, the wood around the handle splintering apart.

Pushing open the far door, I locked that one behind me as well. I tore the slit in my skirt higher and kicked off my ridiculous heels. Women's fashion was not meant for fleeing your impending doom.

The walls of the bank shook, a second tremor beneath my feet making me seriously worry about the integrity of the building. Insulation fell from the ceiling like snow.

A loud bang made me scream, gunshots just on the other side of the door. Danny must have decided he was done trying to break down doors and chose instead to blow it apart. Or worse, the attack team caught up to me.

I ran down hallway after hallway, taking turns at odd angles in the hopes that it would trip up Danny and Nick. These were considerably less ornate, making me think I'd entered the employee area of the bank. I passed a glass wall, revealing a room with cubicles sectioning off the space and another that looked like a small cafeteria and break room.

Finally, I approached a glass entrance. There was an unmanned security booth, along with a metal detector. When the explosion in the main bank happened, whoever was stationed here must have moved towards the lobby as back-up. Or they took off, not being paid enough to take a bullet for the company.

The metal detector beeped, lighting up red as I slid through it. I knew that Crowe was probably still following my movements on the cameras. I needed to be quick. It wouldn't be long before all the eyes that were looking for me found where I'd disappeared to.

I looked carefully out of the doorway. There was a large parking lot behind the building that afforded little cover, but it didn't look like anyone was there. I'd have to cross that before making it to the road beyond.

Deciding that I didn't have time to debate the validity of what I was doing. I sprinted as fast as I could down the stairs. Staying in the bank was as good as a death sentence. At least outside, I had a fighting chance.

There was no sound of stray bullets hitting cars and pavement, only the slap of my bare feet painfully tearing across the blacktop. I ignored the burn on my soles, definitely not thinking about how Danny's hands had worked the ache from their muscles or the look of pure betrayal in his eyes when I bolted. I didn't need him and his magic backstabbing fingers.

I jumped over a low concrete barrier. My toes had barely brushed the sidewalk when a heavy weight barreled into me. We landed hard on the pavement, my vision swimming from the impact. Pain flared brightly along my entire body, followed by a wet burn where the stone had split open my shoulder.

Groaning, I swung an elbow back, trying to leverage some space between me and the wall of muscle pinning me in place. I expected to see Crowe's satisfied expression I already had my argument on the tip of my tongue. My elbow sank into a fleshy stomach, definitely not the hard planks of Crowe's abs, and panic had me twisting violently.

The man pinning my legs beneath him wasn't any of my boys, but one from my past that I knew all too well.

"Albert. Let me go."

"No can do, honeypot. The price on your pretty head is just too sweet. Em promised me Henry's position when I bring you home."

Ignoring my clawing hands and swinging feet, he twisted my body so that I was on my stomach. Albert was a mid-ranking enforcer at The Farm, sadistic as they come. He was the kind of man who made up for his tiny dick by trying to make everyone around him feel small too.

He spent years being the one to deliver me to whomever I had the pleasure of keeping company for the night. If I fought or tried to run, it was Albert who brought me back, kicking and screaming. Not that it mattered in the middle of the desert, there was nowhere to run to. Eventually, I stopped fighting and channeled my energy into more productive ways of striking back. Albert loved to joke about how sweet I must be and how good I must take it for it to make Em so much money. One time the man leaving me tipped Albert on the way out. I'd never gotten over the smug as fuck way he smiled at me after.

"Get the fuck off of me, you dumb ogre." His entire weight sank onto my lower back. A hard knee pressed between my shoulder blades, forcing me to scream. Despite the flaring pain, I bucked and writhed, doing everything I could to throw him off. It was useless.

"Shh, sweet baby, lay still, and maybe I can make this good for you. I bet you're the kind of girl who likes to be choked."

His hands slid up my sides, getting a rough handful of boob before closing around my throat. I managed to scream one final time before my airway closed off. I mouthed a thousand soundless curses at him.

My arms were pinned beneath me, his weight crushing them into the pavement and restricting my movement. I stretched my fingers, trying to reach for the dagger necklace. My nails were just able to brush the surface. One more inch that was all I needed.

Pressure built behind my eyes, followed by a grey haze around the edges. The harder he squeezed, the more the tension in my limbs went slack. The allure to give up the struggle and give in to the pull of darkness sucked me down.

Albert laughed, spreading my legs and grinding his erection into my ass because apparently choking a woman to death did it for the sick fucker. He yanked back on my neck, forcing me to arch my spine and plastering his disgusting mouth over mine.

He tasted like old tobacco and cabbage, making me want to vomit. I bit down, sinking my teeth as hard as I could into his lower lip. Blood poured from the wound and down my chin. He howled, tightening his grip on my neck but also shifting just enough that my fingers circled the chain.

I yanked hard. The ruby blade slipped free, landing in the palm of my hand. I wrapped my fingers around the tiny handle and jabbed up. The knife slashed across Albert's forearm, but he didn't relent. I did it again and again.

"You fucking bitch!" Albert knocked my hand away, the necklace skittering out of reach, and then he smacked my head against the cement. Tears pricked at my darkening vision. I bucked and squirmed. My torn skirt riding up with each movement, exposing my barely clad ass to the cold air. To my horror, I realized he'd freed his tiny cock, and it was worming its way between my legs.

Just as the world started turning black, Albert's weight fell off of me, landing with a wet sounding thud against the pavement. The entire right side of Albert's head was blown away, torn bits of brain matter hung over the edges of his skull, and one sightless brown eye stared back at me.

I screamed, or I tried to. My vocal cords refused to work, but my entire body cried out in terror. Warm blood seeped beneath my hand, forcing my awareness back. I scrambled to my feet, backing several feet away from his corpse and willing my brain to catch up to the terrifying visage. His pants were still half down, lying in a pool of dirty blood.

Screaming every obscenity I could think of, I kicked him over and over. "Snail dicked! Sleaze bag! Motherfucker!" Even if he was already dead, that waste of oxygen had tried to rape me while killing me. I kicked him again, in the dick, hoping he felt it down in hell. "I hope they shove your tiny dick right up your honeypot."

"Thea!"

My head swiveled madly in the direction of my name, searching the street to see who had shot Albert. It didn't take me long to spot my savior. Crowe was sprinting at full speed down the road.

"Fuck," I cursed. If Crowe managed to make it to me, I didn't know that I would have the strength to resist him. Too much of me wanted to believe that Crowe had nothing to do with this. His shock sounded so genuine. I wanted to believe he cared for me. It was probably that same naive part of my heart that had allowed me to be betrayed to begin with.

None of that changed the fact that maybe Danny, and *definitely* Nick, had set me up. Nick even apologized. I highly doubted that he ever did anything without his brother being aware of it.

No, this stunk of Danny. He would take the coward's way out and make some other hit team do the work for him. Danny was expecting the Wizard to give him exactly what he wanted, and Em would have been the perfect way to dispose of me after my usefulness had run its course. Shit, there was even a paycheck in it for him.

If I was honest with myself, I'd known this was coming all along. Instead of listening to my instincts, I foolishly wanted to believe that there was something more behind Danny's green eyes. I'd passed up my chance for independence and told the Wizard to locate Danny's sisters. Fucking hell, I was a gullible idiot. One sad story, and I rolled over, spread my legs, and let him take everything. I was damn lucky that knife he was swinging hadn't landed in my back.

Well, joke was on him. I had the key, which meant I had the emerald. I'd figure out a way to kill Westin. I'd take down Em, and then I was coming back to deliver exactly what they deserved.

I bent down, cursing at my sore back. Albert's discarded gun was heavier than I expected. I stared at the dagger necklace where it had been tossed aside. The ruby blade was smeared in blood, resembling exactly what the pain in my chest felt like. It made me want to scream, but it would be foolish to abandon a weapon. I snatched it up, sheathing the knife and tying the broken chain around my wrist. Then, I pulled the key out of the clutch and shoved it into my bra.

"Thea." Crowe slowed down, raising his hands and eyeing the gun that I aimed at him.

The ruby stiletto swayed from its chain beneath the pistol, like the pendulum of a clock, reminding me that time was running out. The memory of Danny's voice whispered in my ear, "*Tick-tock, Thea.*"

I shot the ground, blowing apart the sidewalk a foot in front of Crowe.

"There's something poetic about this," I said flatly, doing my best to shove down the raw emotion that was trying to rear its dangerous head. "When we first met, it was you pointing the gun at me."

Crowe took slow steps forward, apparently not caring that I'd just fired a warning shot. "I don't know what the Wizard told you, but you have to come with us."

"Nick set me up. Probably Danny, too." I shook my head. "We're done, Crowe. It's over."

Crowe took another step forward, and I fired into the ground again. He didn't even flinch.

"Please, stop. Please, don't make me shoot you." He had to stop. If Crowe touched me, I wouldn't have the strength to push him away. I knew it, and so did he.

"I've known Nick my whole damn life. He's a cold bastard who's been through more pain than you could ever imagine. The one thing he's not is a sell-out. He would never cross us. Whatever you think you know, it's wrong."

A small red sedan came driving down the road towards us. I moved into the lane directly in the car's path.

"Thea! Stop," Crowe shouted.

I redirected the gun from where it was trained on him, to the driver beyond the glass. The car screeched to a stop between us. I moved around to the driver's side. "Get out! Now."

The woman stumbled from the car. "Please, don't shoot me. I'll give you anything."

I didn't wait. I sank into the seat and pulled the door shut behind me. Crowe slammed against the passenger side, cursing when he realized the auto lock was still engaged. He raised his gun at the glass, then lowered it. There was no guarantee that the bullet wouldn't hit me.

"Fuck!" he shouted, slamming the butt of his gun into the glass until a small splinter formed in the center of the window.

I pulled the shifter into drive.

"Please, Thea. Don't." The desperation in his eyes made me hesitate. "Please, beautiful. Just open the door." He hit the glass again, the crack spreading into a large spider web.

My hands shook where I gripped the shifter. I could feel my heart breaking in two the longer I looked out the window. I almost put the car back into park. Almost.

That hesitation was exactly the reason why I needed to leave. Right now. I stomped on the gas pedal. The tires screeched, sending up a plume of smoke, and the car sped forward. I watched Crowe in the mirror the entire way down the road. He raised his gun, and I braced the wheel, ready for the pull of the tires being shot, but it never came.

Instead, Crowe turned and began firing at people crossing the parking lot after us. Several bullets sank into the side of the car, blowing out the back window. After a few minutes, the sound of gunfire faded. A sign on the corner indicated the on-ramp to the W7 highway was the next left.

I wasn't sure where I was headed, but West felt like a damn good start.

-EPILOGUE-
WESTIN

The sound of a throat clearing annoyingly cut through my haze.

"Madam."

Keeping my eyes closed, I sank further into my reclined position and stretched my arm above me to grab the back of the chaise. This man was truly insufferable, but he was the only person passable for the job. Not to mention the golden idiot owed me.

Taking a hit from the joint dangling between my fingers, I asked, "Is it done?"

"Not exactly."

I cracked open an eye, my vision swimming for a second as I tried to focus on him. "Define, *not exactly*."

"There was another team in place before we arrived." Orin shifted uncomfortably, looking anywhere but at my naked form. Prude, although I'd probably carve his eyes out if they lingered too long. "Perhaps, Madam, you might—"

With a dismissive sound of disgust, I lifted my head to look at him fully. I told Berret to return with either a head or an emerald in hand, and he currently held neither. Rather, he was holding a tablet, and the palor of his skin had paled to a sickly grey, as spineless men always did in my presence.

"There were complications."

"Show me, Orin." I snapped in the air and crooked my finger. If he had to interrupt me, then the least he could do was be quick about it. All this pussyfooting around was giving me a headache and ruining my buzz.

His eyes flicked hesitantly to the foot of the chaise. "Madam, I think this is best discussed in—"

"I don't ask for things twice."

The leader of the Winged Monkeys sidled warily to my side, intently keeping his eyes on his shoes as he approached. Smart boy.

He quickly tapped the screen, pulling up several angles of surveillance footage from the Emerald City Central Bank. Our source had tipped us off to the emerald exchange happening at the historic bank. Orin had one simple job, retrieve my emerald and kill the girl—not necessarily in that order. Twice now he'd failed me.

"I practically gift wrapped this hit for you. How exactly did you manage to fuck it up?"

The footage appeared to be old, by several hours. He should have brought it to me immediately, I'd killed men for less. Zooming in, I watched Dorothy follow the bank manager to the vault elevator, hesitating for several long seconds before entering. Was it being below ground or small spaces that unnerved her? I'd file that under possibly useful information.

"Fast forward an hour," Orin leaned over my arm and tapped the corner of the screen.

A bomb blew apart the front corner of the bank. The heat of the blast turned the copper of the dome bright red. Whole sections broke free of their mountings, spilling in large globs of molten metal and glass onto the screaming bank patrons.

"That's a shame. The bank was a beautiful building."

"Keep watching."

Glowing beams of laser sites cut through the smoke, quickly shooting everything that moved. They didn't bother assessing their targets, perfectly fine with a massacre so long as it got the job done. Ruthless, but efficient. I couldn't say that I disapproved, except that it had apparently fucked up my own plans.

"Those aren't my men." Orin pointed at the masked mercenaries swarming the floor and taking up new attack positions, one of which waited directly in front of the elevator doors.

How in Oz had this other team gotten tipped off about the bank drop?

Orin clucked his tongue. "This team is sloppy. WM hits have more finesse."

"For all the good they've done. Maybe next time you should try the blood-bath approach."

Skipping further in the footage, Dorothy remerged from the vault behind a wall of blazing gunfire and fighting muscle. Say what you will about those boys, they definitely were good at what they did. Precise headshots dropped person after person. Sending a small army to apprehend one girl might have felt like overkill, but this obviously wasn't enough.

"What happened to Eastin's emerald?" I fingered my own, looped on a long chain between my breasts.

"From the readings, it remained in the vault. Thanks to the bug we placed in the YBR cab, we know that they think the emerald is untraceable. It's given us a keen advantage, but all of our information tells us that it's still in the basement of the bank."

Anger and frustration boiled within me. The E.C. Bank vault was the single most secure location in all of Oz. We had fuck all chances of retrieving the emerald now. The only one who'd be able to access that vault would be Dorothy, or someone with her key and code.

With a foot into the neck of the young man kneeling between my spread legs, I kicked him away. He made a pathetic sound as he fell back to the ground, sliding his bare ass across the marble with a squeak.

"You were boring me." I rolled my eyes, not bothering to look at his dejected puppy expression. What was his name? Adam...Alex...It didn't matter.

"Mr. Courtland—" The guard at the door met my gaze. I pointed dismissively at Aaron...or Avery... "This one is to be removed from my vessel, immediately. He wouldn't know how to properly tongue a cunt if it was made of lollipops."

Courtland looked between me and the boy. "Madam, we're currently at sea."

I blinked at the man. Of course we were at sea, we were on a massive fucking yacht. What were we going to do, stay in port and wait for the hit teams to come to us? "I don't see how that is my concern."

The young man, Andy? No, that wasn't it either. Mr. Flacid Tongue made a tiny whimpering noise. He might have been begging, but I stopped caring and didn't really hear him anyway. He crawled back to my feet, clinging to my ankles like a toddler throwing a fit.

I kicked free of his hands. "I've heard enough. Take...Ah—" I snapped at...Anthony? "What's your name again?"

"Roger."

"No, that can't be it. I distinctly remember it beginning with an A. It doesn't matter you're wasting my oxygen with every insignificant breath you take."

I tied my robe around me while Courtland dragged the screaming man from the room. Orin looked like a ghost. Let that be a lesson well learned—I don't tolerate mediocrity.

I swiped through the feeds, flipping across the different areas of the bank to find where Dorothy disappeared. "And the girl?"

Orin reached over me, hesitantly taking the tablet. "I'm sorry. Excuse me, I just need to..." He switched screens to an exterior camera. "There."

Dorothy was pinned to the ground, a massive ogre of a man had his pants down and was working his way beneath her skirt, while the color of her lips were firmly turning blue from the grip he had on her throat. Delicious.

"Is she dead?" I asked hopefully. If nothing else, at least the legacy of the Gallants died today. I wasn't overly concerned about the death of my cousin. Eastin was stupid. I told her ages ago getting involved with Emily Rosen would bite her in the ass. My cousin never had what it took to do anything on her own, she was either leaning on me or someone else. It didn't matter how many heads she stepped on, so long as she had the best view. And look where that arrogance got her—Face bashed in by a meek little girl who can't even fight off the brute raping her in the middle of the street.

I sighed, already bored with the entire encounter. Maybe this time I'd dangle Orin over the sharks after we threw Arthur, or...Austin...whatever his name's body overboard. That would at least be entertaining.

"Is that all?" I started to hand the tablet back, but Orin pushed it away.

"Keep watching."

Boom. I blinked and the man on top of Dorothy was suddenly missing half of his face. She screamed and I frantically zoomed in. Bits of gore dripped from the wound and blood poured onto the concrete like a spilled carton of milk. Unbelievable.

"Who fired that shot?" That girl was luckier than a rabbit's foot in a field of four leaf clovers, though the look of terror on her face was delightful.

"You're not going to like this."

I narrowed my eyes at Orin. Of course I wouldn't, not a damn thing that ever left his mouth was something I liked. He rotated the camera view to look back down the street towards where the shot had been fired.

"Vincent." Ozma's gift to women came sprinting down the street, gun in hand. I zoomed in further, studying the look of determination on his expression. "I should have known. You never were far from Nick and that other idiot."

There was a time when I admired Vincent's ruthless nature, and the boy fucked like he was possessed by an entire legion of demons. I've never found another man who got off on the hunt the same way I did. There's no better aphrodisiac than the spray of warm blood. Then my cousin had to get overly enthusiastic with sweet little Niccolo and Vincent decided to grow a conscience. What a waste.

Dorothy climbed into a shitty mom sedan. Vincent looked like she was cutting his heart out with a broken spoon. Now that was the most interesting thing I'd seen all day. The Scarecrowe was in love. Heh. Place that in the list of things I never thought I'd see. People like us weren't capable of something as mundane as love.

The shitty red car screeched down the road, peeling away in a puff of smoke. The girl has brass ovaries. I'd give her that much. Vincent spun, shooting down the half dozen bikers that tore through the parking lot. Was this a *THIRD* team? Ozma help me. Exactly how many people were after this girl? So much for clandestine meetings with The Wizard. Was nothing sacred anymore?

I paused the footage just as Nick and the other muscle bound idiot joined Vincent in taking out the remaining assailants. That was enough. I'd seen everything there was to see. Dead bikers, a locked emerald, and one very alive girl who just dropped into the wind. Unless...

"Can you pull the plates from that car?"

"Easily. I've already got my team working on activating the satellite tracker for the emergency support system in the car. We should have her location within the hour. A girl like her, I can't imagine it will take much coercion to get her to give up the key."

I scrolled back to the look on Dorothy's face, right after she stood up and kicked a dead man in the dick. I might have liked her, if I didn't hate her so much. Blood coated her hands and freckled her cheeks, but she didn't look scared. Orin was underestimating this girl. Men like him always did.

"You have one more chance. Bring me Dorothy." I pushed the tablet into his chest. "Or I'll feed you to the sharks...slowly. Do a good job, and maybe I'll let you drown first."

"I'll get her, Madam. The key, the emerald, all of it. The guys of YBR are smart, but they're crazy for the girl and that makes them predictable."

They did look infatuated. The way the three of them were tearing into each other proved as much. Dorothy ran and I knew they'd punish themselves into oblivion for letting her drive away. "Love is a sickness—a disease that makes you blind, weak, and reckless. Put a little pressure on the right pretty face, and I'll give you a front row seat to watching them dance."

End of Book 1

Thea and the boys of YBR Taxi Cabs will return in DARK OZ 2: THE WITCH IS DEAD. Coming early 2024.

Click here for a first look at Nick and Thea in Dark Oz 2?

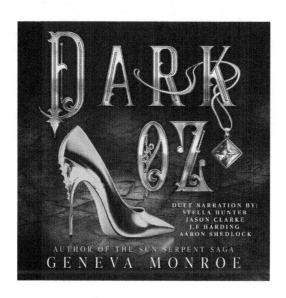

Thea, Crowe, Danny, and Nick will be coming to audio in Spring of 2024, starring Stella Hunter, J.F. Harding, Aaron Shedlock, and Jason Clarke. Make sure to sign up for my newsletter for all audiobook production news and release information.

Join in the conversation at Geneva Monroe's Pretty St@bby Readers on Facebook.

Lions, tigers, and... well, you know how it goes.

Oz damn! Are you reeling? Do you want to punch Nick right in his perfect face? Me too. Did your heart break when Crowe was banging on that glass? Yeah, me too. I adore my boys, even when they make really, really bad choices.

The Wonderful Wizard of Oz has been a favorite of mine since I was a child. There are few stories that captured my imagination in the way this series did. I used to lay in bed and read them over and over again until I'd worn down the bindings and had to invest in a new set.

It wasn't until I'd gone far off the deep end into dark romance that the idea to turn this beloved story into something far grittier occurred to me. I, like so many, adore a good retelling. I love to giggle at easter eggs and insider jokes, and once I started writing Dark Oz, the format came pretty naturally to me–despite being deep in the world of the Sun Serpent Saga.

This book's inception happened on a long drive home from vacation. While listening to the podcast, Cinema Story Origins (side note, I adore this podcast, and you should totally check it out). We joked about how Dorothy's story was primed to be done as a why choose retelling. Over the three-hour drive, I spun through a plot and character backstories. The second we got home, I opened my laptop and dropped the first ten chapters. The next morning, my husband came downstairs, and I was still writing.

Believe it or not, making this story dark really wasn't that hard. If you haven't given these stories a read recently, go back and really look at what's written. There are some truly dark moments in these books. Characters have no issue sacrificing and killing off each other, there are brutal moments of enslavement and torture. I mean, The Witch of the East enchants an axe to cut off poor Niccolo Chopper's limbs just because he dared to love the wrong girl.

There's lots more to come, and something tells me this twisted world, that put its hooks in me, isn't going to be letting go anytime soon. I'm okay with that.

I have this theory: The people you need in your life have a way of arriving at exactly the moment you need them. Every single person listed below is one of those people.

The first person I will always thank will always be my husband. Where usually, I thank him for the never-ending support, this time I need to thank him for something else entirely. Thank you for asking, "How would you do it?" If you had never asked me that question, then I never would have considered this story at all. Every bit of this book hinges on that exact moment in time. Thank you for always pushing me to try new things, and believing in me enough to see them through.

I owe some top-level thanks to Jessica Jordan. Ya know that moment in so many books where the cute, little, and totally innocent FMC knows what she wants, but doesn't have the words to ask for it. Then, the dom heavy MMC pries it out of her?...I'm pretty sure we had our *use your words* moment in this book. Thank you for holding my hand and pushing me to turn Dark Oz into what it had the potential to become.

Alessia Quaranta, meeting you is kismet. I'll never be convinced otherwise. Thank you for lending me your ear, your support, and your infallible knowledge of Italian cooking.

Massive thanks to my editor, Sierra Cassidy. She'll say it was only a manuscript critique–but I'm giving her an edited by line, and she can't stop me. Cue villain laughter.

Andi McClane, at some point something will change color, and you'll know that's for you. Thank you for never telling me, no. Even when I know you don't have the time, you still make some for me.

Reanna Breaux, I'm still working on where those commas go. Thank you for the late nights helping me make this shine and for always being in my corner. You deserve big, beautiful things in life and I hope you get every single one of them.

Chelisse Redman, I hope this book makes you salaciously proud of me.

It's a classic story: Girl writes book, Girl sells book, Another girl reads book and asks to cosplay the FMC, both girls never stop talking and then one day start sending daily pictures of shirtless guys and saucy book bits. Lauren Levandusky, I heart you big time. Writing a book might seem like a weird way to go about finding future best friends, but I'm so glad I wrote a book to find you.

Erica Karwoski, fun fact, when I click on the search bar in Facebook your name is the first one to pop up. When I start typing the @ your name is the first suggested. Thank you for being the first person I always run to when I need... well pretty much anything. I love that I know I can count on you. It turns out that I've come to respect your opinion a whole fucking lot.

Ask any author who they are most grateful for, and do you know who they will all say? The readers. It's not for the reason you think it is. I seriously have the best readers ever. I'm certain of it. I could say that I plan to make my next book a guide to the country's best tire fires, and you guys would have already made a dozen videos and posts saying how you can't wait to read it. Here's the thing, I really want to make you proud. Knowing you're there pushes me to be a better writer. I want to give back just a piece of the awe you've given me. Because of you, I know that something I've created holds value. There's nothing to compare to that.

Thank you for making me feel seen.

Nick might say that his accent isn't thick, but he's Italian through and through. Nothing makes me weak like an Italian accent and a long string of words I don't know the meaning of. If you want to know what all those sweet declarations were that Niccolo was making to Thea, then never fear. I've got every curse and dirty compliment translated for you below.

Enjoy!

Chapter 8

Cazzo - Dicks

Chapter 9

Porca puttana – Holy shit

Chapter 12

Che deficiente – What a dumbass

Cagna – Bitch

Chapter 13

Che cagna sadistica - That sadistic bitch

Chapter 18

Maleducati - Rude people

Cazzo! – Fuck!

Chapter 21

Stronzetto – Little shit

Leone – Lion

Cazzata! – Bullshit

Chapter 25

Ma che diavolo! - What the hell!

Chapter 26

Amico – Friend

Chapter 34

Combina guai – Trouble maker

Fiore Mio – My flower

Chapter 35

(aka get ready to swoon)

Tutto, fiore mio. Hai sciolto il filo che teneva insieme tutti i miei pezzi rotti. E se adesso non vado via, li vedrai cadere uno ad uno.

Everything, my flower. You untied the thread that held all my broken pieces together. If I don't walk away now, you'll see them falling apart, one by one.

Se solo fossi un uomo migliore, saresti già mia.

If I was a better man, you'd be mine already..

Il tuo profumo mi fa impazzire. Ogni istante con te rischio di perdere il controllo.

You smell delicious. I risk losing control every instant I am with you.

Amo il modo in cui fremi ad ogni mio tocco.

I love the way you tremble at my every touch.

Tu sei il mio unico limite.

You are my only limit.

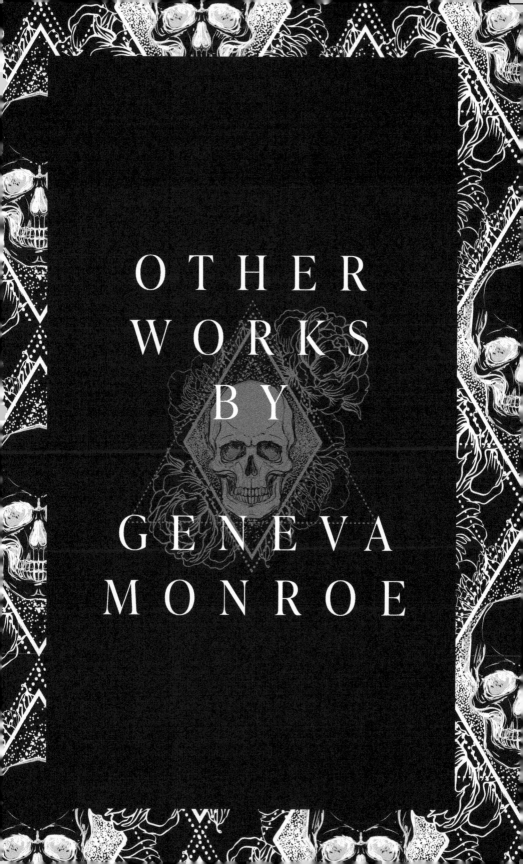

OTHER
WORKS
BY
GENEVA
MONROE

GENEVA MONROE

SUN SERPENT

A cursed kingdom.
A Fire Singer seeking vengeance.
And a prince who is not what he seems...

Under the silks of her circus troupe's tent, Elyria Solaris dances with fire. She disguises her gift as showmanship, but longs for answers about why she has a power no one else possesses.

Somewhere in the city of never-ending night, Prince Cal is looking for the girl who burns the brightest. Only she can stop the horror inflicted on his kingdom by a sadistic lord who controls the minds of his victims.

When Cal spies Elyria, he knows without a doubt that she is the most beautifully dangerous thing he has ever seen. More importantly, she's the Fire Draken he's been waiting his whole life to find.

Moments after Cal serendipitously enters Elyria's life, a loved one's gruesome death sets her on the path of vengeance. Cal will do anything to protect his people, including lying to Elyria about who he really is and promising her the answers that she seeks.

But if Elyria trusts the undeniable spark between them, could it turn out to be the one fire she is unable to tame?

Get SUN SERPENT here. https://books2read.com/u/meqBaE

GENEVA MONROE

STAR SPEAR

SUN SERPENT SAGA VOLUME 2

Betrayed to save a kingdom.
Consumed by wrath.
Which will burn hotter, love or vengeance?

Prince Callen Shadow left Innesvale with one goal: Bring the Fire Singer home, no matter the cost. Seduction and lies were easy for him - until her. Now Cal is realizing the cost of saving his kingdom may be losing the only woman he's ever loved.

Fueled by vengeance and seeking answers about her past, Elyria Solaris leaves the smoldering wreckage of the Great Library and sets sail for Innesvale. But when she arrives, the fearless Fire Singer finds herself facing an unexpected challenge - life at court. As the stakes rise, the lines between love, lust, and betrayal blur.

But the ruthless Lord Malvat will stop at nothing to possess Elyria, and mind control curses were only the beginning. When his pursuit follows them to the palace gates, Elyria must choose between avenging all she's lost, or embracing her incendiary connection to Cal.

Is their magical bond strong enough to vanquish the looming threat before it engulfs them all?

"Star Spear" propels readers on an unforgettable adventure, filled with immersive worlds, intense romance, and breathtaking magic. This thrilling second installment of the Sun Serpent Saga will captivate fans of epic fantasy series like "From Blood and Ash," "Fourth Wing," and "Throne of Glass."

Get STAR SPEAR here. https://books2read.com/u/bwB2kO

Printed in Great Britain
by Amazon

40540496R00209